REMEMBER TOKYO

Other Foreign Affairs Mysteries

Escape to Havana
The Moscow Code

REMEMBER TOKYO

A Foreign Affairs
Mystery

NICK WILKSHIRE

DUNDURN
TORONTO

Cover image: shutterstock.com/TTstudio
Printer: Webcom

Library and Archives Canada Cataloguing in Publication

Wilkshire, Nick, 1968-, author
    Remember Tokyo / Nick Wilkshire.

(A foreign affairs mystery)
Issued in print and electronic formats.
ISBN 978-1-4597-3717-4 (softcover).--ISBN 978-1-4597-3718-1(PDF).--
ISBN 978-1-4597-3719-8 (EPUB)

    I. Title. II. Series: Wilkshire, Nick, 1968- . Foreign affairs mystery.

PS8645.I44R46 2018   C813'.6   C2017-908070-9
                                                C2017-908071-7

1   2   3   4   5   22   21   20   19   18

We acknowledge the support of the **Canada Council for the Arts**, which last year invested $153 million to bring the arts to Canadians throughout the country, and the **Ontario Arts Council** for our publishing program. We also acknowledge the financial support of the **Government of Ontario**, through the **Ontario Book Publishing Tax Credit** and the **Ontario Media Development Corporation**, and the **Government of Canada**.

Nous remercions le **Conseil des arts du Canada** de son soutien. L'an dernier, le Conseil a investi 153 millions de dollars pour mettre de l'art dans la vie des Canadiennes et des Canadiens de tout le pays.

Care has been taken to trace the ownership of copyright material used in this book. The author and the publisher welcome any information enabling them to rectify any references or credits in subsequent editions.

— *J. Kirk Howard, President*

The publisher is not responsible for websites or their content unless they are owned by the publisher.

Printed and bound in Canada.

VISIT US AT

 dundurn.com | @dundurnpress |  dundurnpress | dundurnpress

Dundurn
3 Church Street, Suite 500
Toronto, Ontario, Canada
M5E 1M2

For Tanya, always

CHAPTER 1

Charlie Hillier followed the broad earthen path down its gentle slope, marvelling at the oasis of calm in the heart of a city of twelve million souls. The bustle of people, trains, and traffic that he had left behind just minutes before seemed to belong to another world as he glanced up to the canopy of old-growth trees sheltering the path from the midmorning sun. Whether heightened by the lingering effects of jet lag or not, an almost spiritual sensation gripped him as he followed the path onto a wooden footbridge over a babbling stream.

A few minutes later he was approaching a massive archway that led to the Meiji Shrine beyond, a Shinto temple built in honour of the beloved emperor. Passing through the first gate, he noticed a procession of some kind making its way from the main temple beyond. As he got closer, Charlie realized that it was a wedding party, its participants clad in traditional dress as they made their way to one of the side buildings. He paused with the rest of the crowd gathered in respectful silence to watch as the procession crossed the main courtyard. The bride and groom went first, sheltered from the sunshine that flooded the open space by an ornate umbrella and looking resplendent in their traditional wedding attire. While neither smiled overtly as they made their way past, Charlie envied the serene joy evident in their faces. The whole scene unfolded in orderly peace, and the reverent crowd waited until the wedding party had reached the other side of the courtyard before anyone dared to move or utter so much as a whisper. This was Japan, after all.

Continuing on toward the main temple, Charlie passed stalls selling little strips of paper and good luck charms to place on racks outside the temple. Reaching them, he paused to look at some of the handwritten scrawls in a multitude of languages, recognizing the French word for peace and a number of equally altruistic notions in English, as well as wishes for happiness and love. Not particularly superstitious, he nonetheless briefly considered making a wish before moving on to the temple instead, where some sort of official ceremony was going on inside. He watched it for a while, then toured the rest of the complex of buildings before checking his watch and slowly making his way back toward the main arch, or *torii*, and the path beyond.

Twenty minutes later, he had left the tranquility of the shrine to rejoin the throngs outside Meiji-jingūmae Station. Spotting a familiar coffee sign, he stopped in for a cappuccino and took a seat by the window. Sipping the delicious coffee, he looked out the window at the passing crowds and resisted the temptation to rub his eyes. He had been in Tokyo for almost a week — in many ways it seemed much longer — but he was still waking up at five in the morning, his body clock not yet adjusted to the thirteen-hour time difference from Ottawa. Tomorrow would be better, he told himself. He was to start work at the Canadian embassy, and he was intent on getting himself into a routine as soon as possible. The move into his staff quarters would help with that, he was sure. The hotel where they had placed him temporarily was very nice, and not far from the embassy, but after six days of wandering its cavernous hallways at all hours of the day and night, he was finding himself a bit adrift in its enormity and keen to feather a nest of his own in the city he would call home for the next three to four years.

Charlie was just as keen to start work again, though he was a bit nervous about his looming first day, and wondered how his integration would go, it being months after the usual posting season. But he had already briefly met the ambassador the day after he had flown in, and he had felt somewhat reassured. Charlie's old friend and mentor, Winston Gardiner, had nothing but good things to say about Philip Westwood, not that Charlie could afford to be picky. A few weeks ago, he had been weighing his options for the future in case the Department decided to find a way to let him go. At the very least, his future had seemed bleak, as was any hope of his being posted abroad again, ever. He couldn't really blame his masters for wanting him gone, or at least safely tucked away in an Ottawa cubicle preparing reports that no one would ever read — not after the mess he had left behind in Moscow. And while he wished things had turned out differently in many ways, he had no regrets whatsoever about getting to the bottom of Steve Collins's death. Charlie had been whisked out of Moscow in the middle of the night and, after a short debriefing in London, sent back to Ottawa to await further instructions. Days had turned to weeks, then months before he had been assigned to a desk at headquarters — a position that was an obviously temporary measure while they figured out what to do with him.

Then something unexpected happened. It began with a call from Steve Collins's sister, Sophie Durant, to let him know about an upcoming story in the *Globe and Mail* on her brother's death in Moscow. Reading the article, it was clear Durant had embellished the best parts of Charlie's involvement in the case, and either completely omitted or given a favourable account of the worst. The next call he got was from communications, who wanted to remind him not to speak directly to the media about the Moscow affair, or anything else to do with his work. He didn't, but the article had taken on a life of its own, and its flattering portrayal, not only of Charlie himself but of the whole department, seemed particularly welcome in the wake of a series of front page stories on consular cases that had ended badly in recent months.

In fact, Charlie had suddenly become something of a poster boy. Before the reporter making inquiries around Foreign Affairs discovered that the shining star of consular services had been relegated to toiling at entry-level work in the bowels of the Lester B. Pearson Building, Charlie's months-old and dormant request for a posting had been hastily dusted off and revived. Before long, he found himself on a plane — not to one of the three locations he had put in his posting request, but to Tokyo. The fact that it was about as far as they could possibly send him wasn't lost on Charlie, nor that it was a big enough mission that he could be absorbed without so much as a ripple on the surface. Whatever the reasons, he was grateful for another chance, and eager to show his employer that Charlie Hillier was capable of completing a full posting without causing an international incident. He had every intention of doing just that. Besides, didn't they say the third time's the charm?

CHAPTER 2

Charlie sat at his desk, slurping his coffee and looking out the window at the trees behind the embassy building on Aoyama-dori. The Canadian embassy enjoyed a prime location across the street from the Akasaka Palace in the government district — a part of the city that was almost serene in comparison to the harried bustle of much of Tokyo. The large compound included the embassy building itself, with its unique, sloping glass roof at the front, a complex of staff apartments, and the official residence at the rear of the lot. Charlie's office on the third floor was small but nicely appointed, and offered a view over the green space between the embassy and the official residence. He heard the sound of footsteps and looked up to see an athletic-looking woman in her early thirties standing at his door.

"You must be Charlie. I'm Karen Fraser. I guess we're neighbours."

Charlie stood and stuck out his hand. "Charlie Hillier. Come on in." They shook hands and she took a seat.

"How's the jet lag?"

He grimaced. "It's getting better, but I'm still having a hard time sleeping."

She gave him a knowing smile. "It takes a while. When did you arrive?"

"About a week ago."

"You at the New Otani?"

"Yeah, it's nice enough."

"There's something disorienting about that place, though," she said. "Kind of like the place in *The Shining*, but more —"

"Populated?" He finished her thought.

"Exactly." Her broad smile showed sparkling white teeth that contrasted nicely with her dark hair. "When do you get into your staff quarters?"

"This afternoon, I hope."

"You'll feel a bit more normal when you get into your own place."

They chatted for a few minutes about life in Tokyo and the differences from Ottawa. He learned that she was in her second year of a four-year posting and he tried not to fidget when they went through common acquaintances back in Ottawa — always a tortuous exercise for him. Luckily, Fraser had spent most of her time abroad and was a decade younger than Charlie. If she had heard anything about Charlie's ex-wife, or the reason he had joined the rotational stream in the first place, she wasn't letting on. She seemed more interested in his consular experience, given that they were the only two Canada-based consular officers in the embassy — the rest of the section being made up of locally engaged staff.

"So, where were you before Tokyo?" he asked, knowing where the conversation would inevitably lead, but deciding to get it out of the way early.

"Brussels. And you were in Moscow, huh?"

He nodded and thought he saw the glimmer of a smile in her eyes. "You may have heard I ran into some trouble there."

"Sounds like you did a great job." The smile spread to her mouth, and seemed genuine as she added, "Nice for consular to get some good headlines for a change. Must have been a bit scary for you, though."

"Let's just say I won't be vacationing in Moscow anytime soon," he deadpanned, noticing her wedding ring for the first time. Just his luck. "So, what's consular like here?"

"Not too crazy ... so far," she added, with that twinkle in her eye again. "The usual fare — lost passports and medical cases. We've got about twenty Canadians in jail, mostly on drug charges."

Charlie nodded, reminded immediately of Steve Collins, who had been falsely accused of drug trafficking and tossed in a squalid Moscow jail. "What are the jails like here?"

"Like everything else in Japan," she said, with another shrug. "They're efficient, orderly, and clean. But the focus is definitely punishment, not rehabilitation. You do time here and you know it. The rest of the files are custody disputes — Canadians have a hard time trying to get access to kids from their Japanese ex-spouses, let alone taking them out of the country."

They had moved on to things to see and do and places to eat in the area when a man in his early fifties appeared at the door.

"I think we have a meeting?" he said, looking at his watch. Charlie glanced at the computer clock and saw that it was two minutes after ten. "Sorry, I guess I lost track of time."

"I'll leave you to it," Fraser said, getting up. Something in her expression made it clear she didn't care for the other man, and the tight frown on his face as she brushed by him in the doorway told Charlie the feeling was mutual.

"Louis Denault. I'm the MCO."

"Charlie," he said, gripping the moist hand of his new boss as the two men met at the door. "Sorry again. I'm still getting over the time change."

"It's normal." Denault gave a curt smile before leading him down the hallway to the corner office. "How are you settling in, apart from the jet lag?"

"I'm doing okay." Charlie sat in one of the chairs in front of Denault's large desk.

"Well, we're certainly glad to have you with us." Denault closed the door behind them and took a seat. Charlie noticed that the office was immaculate, with a single file folder the only thing on the main surface of the desk. Denault was similarly well-kept, and he fidgeted with a French cuff as he adjusted himself in his seat. "I'm sure you're looking forward to a change of pace from Moscow. Perhaps a bit of a lower profile," he added, with a little grin that Charlie found instinctively annoying in contrast to Fraser's.

"Just want to help out where I can," he said, taking the high road. He hadn't heard much, either positive or negative, about Denault from anyone in Ottawa in the short time since learning he was to be posted to Tokyo. He was beginning to wonder what he had gotten himself into.

"Well, I think you'll find Tokyo very different from Moscow."

"Were you in Moscow?" He hadn't meant it as a challenge, but Charlie noticed a subtle change in Denault's posture and his mouth puckered as though he had bitten into a particularly tart lemon.

"I just mean things are very organized here. The Japanese run a tight ship, and we try to do the same here at the embassy."

"I'll try to keep that in mind." Charlie was unable to avoid the sarcastic tone that accompanied his words. Denault frowned, appeared to consider a retort, then flipped open the file folder on the desk in front of him.

"I understand you've done some property work. We could use your skills here."

"I thought I was going to focus on consular work," Charlie said, wondering what Denault was talking about. There were no plans to move the embassy, as far as he knew.

"We've had a proposal from a developer to swap some staff apartments out in Toshima-ku," Denault added, seeming to enjoy Charlie's confusion. "They're offering to build us something new just across the street in return." He gestured over his shoulder to the south. "I'd like you to have a look at their proposal, perhaps meet with them, just to see if there's anything there."

"Well, like I said, I was hoping to focus on consular work ..."

"It won't take much of your time, I'm sure." Denault gave a dismissive wave that Charlie found hard to stomach. "They're probably just trying to rip us off, and you'll be able to rule it out quickly."

"Sure, I can have a look." Charlie reluctantly accepted the file and stood. He had spent five minutes with the man he was going to be reporting to for the next four years, and he knew beyond a shadow of a doubt he didn't like him — not one bit.

"Why so glum?"

Charlie looked up to see Karen Fraser standing in his doorway again.

"Oh, nothing. Just a little dragged out." It was partly true, but Fraser saw through it.

"If you're worried about Louis, don't be. He can be a bit difficult sometimes, but he's basically harmless."

Charlie nodded and gestured to the chair. "That's funny. I got the feeling you're not a member of his fan club."

She grinned. "We have an understanding. He stays out of my face and lets me do my job, and we get along just fine."

"Hmm, I might need a few tips on how I can come to the same arrangement."

"You'll get there. Just don't let him push you around."

Charlie tapped the folder on his desk. "He wants me to look at this property swap, but from what I can see, it looks like a load of crap."

"Why are you looking at property?"

Charlie shrugged. "He knows I did some property work on my other postings. Besides, It's not like I can say I'm too busy doing other files, since I don't have any yet."

Fraser gave him the familiar grin. "If you're looking for consular work, I can hook you up no problem."

"Oh yeah?"

"Sure. We've got a Canadian banker in hospital. I was going to do the visit, but if you're interested, have at it."

Charlie flipped the property file shut and gave her an enthusiastic nod. "I'll take it."

CHAPTER 3

Charlie stood at the far end of the subway car, watching the digital display above the door that announced the next stop: first in Japanese, then in English. Satisfied that he had two more stops to go, he relaxed and surveyed the rest of the crowded car, noticing for the first time that he was the only Westerner. Combined with his height, it was enough to make him feel like a bit of an oddball — a recurring feeling since his arrival in Japan. In fact, just about everything seemed different here, from the food to the time change, and from the language to the climate. His first two postings were to places that were hardly similar to Ottawa, yet he hadn't felt as out of place in Havana or Moscow as he did in Tokyo. He glanced down the row of seated passengers and noticed that literally everyone was fiddling with a phone or some other electronic device. This was, after all, the mecca of electronics. Charlie had strolled through Akihabara on his third night in Tokyo, still jet-lagged and even more disoriented by the bright lights and dizzying array of stores, each one ten stories tall or more and packed with the latest consumer electronics.

As they pulled into the next station and a dozen people moved in and out of the car, Charlie's thoughts returned to the job at hand — a Canadian citizen in a Tokyo hospital. Karen Fraser had offered to come along, but Charlie had insisted he could handle it alone. He didn't want to seem like he needed babysitting, and he was eager to dig into his first consular file. Not that there was much information to go on in the file folder she'd handed him when he'd followed her back to her office. It contained some basic information and a contact sheet with Robert Lepage's name and passport number, his date of birth and the address for Tokyo Medical University Hospital in Shinjuku.

As a mechanical voice announced their arrival in Shinjuku-nishiguchi Station, Charlie followed the stream of passengers exiting the car onto the platform, looking for the bright yellow exit signs and the one that would bring him up onto Ome-Kaido Avenue. Back up at street level, he noticed a distinct rise in temperature as the afternoon sun bore down on him. It was late October but the air felt humid and warm. He slipped off his jacket and threw it over his shoulder as he headed northwest, but he was still sweating by the time he reached the entrance to the hospital, wishing he had gotten a cab from the Metro station. He wiped his face with a cotton handkerchief as he stood in a short line behind an information counter, praying that the woman on the other side of the glass spoke English. He was in luck and, within minutes, he was receiving directions for the neuro-logical unit on the fifth floor. As he rode the elevator up, he wondered what had happened to Robert Lepage to land him here. The file was silent on whether Lepage's hospitalization was due to illness, accident, or some other cause. Charlie was no doctor, but neurology didn't sound good.

Stepping off onto the fifth floor, he made his way down to another reception counter and this time his luck ran out. Despite his best attempt at the rudimentary Japanese he had picked up in the last couple of weeks, the nurse at the desk was looking more and more perplexed.

"*Tashkent* Canada," Charlie said, thinking it was close enough to how the Japanese word for embassy was supposed to sound to be understood, but it didn't seem to have any effect. He was running out of ideas when a thin man in his forties came up beside him.

"Are you from the Canadian embassy?"

"Yes," Charlie said, the relief evident in his voice.

"I am Doctor Yamaguchi. I spoke with someone at the embassy earlier today about your Mr. Lepage."

"Charlie Hillier," he said, about to thrust a card at the doctor before remembering the ceremony surrounding business cards in Japan. He paused, turned the card around and face up, and delivered it with two hands and a bow, a gesture Yamaguchi seemed to appreciate as he glanced at the card, smiled, and reciprocated with one of his own.

"I'm the consular officer assigned to Mr. Lepage's case," Charlie said, when they had both pocketed the cards. "Can I ask what his condition is? I have very little information."

"Please," Yamaguchi said, gesturing to a waiting area off to the right. Charlie took a seat, then Yamaguchi followed suit.

"It's a very unfortunate case," Yamaguchi began, and Charlie's heart sank. He didn't relish the prospect of contacting relatives back in Canada to let them know that their son, husband, or father was seriously ill.

"Is he ... going to make it?"

Yamaguchi nodded. "He is in stable condition. He has some broken bones and soft tissue injuries, but they will heal." Charlie nodded, waiting for the *but* that would explain why Lepage was in neurology. He had already interrupted Yamaguchi once and decided to let him get the information out at his own pace. "But he has not resumed consciousness to date."

"You mean he's in a coma?"

The doctor nodded. "It's not uncommon after an incident like this, but the longer it goes on, the worse his prognosis becomes."

"Can I ask what happened to him?"

"He was in a car … accident," Yamaguchi said, the slight pause the first real sign that he was not a native English speaker. "A very high-speed impact, apparently. He is very lucky not to have been killed."

"And when was this?"

"Three days ago. I must apologize, Mr. Hillier, for not contacting the embassy sooner. Mr. Lepage's passport and other identification was … misplaced." Yamaguchi was obviously embarrassed by the oversight, but from what Charlie could tell from the brief research that one of the locally engaged consular officers had conducted, the gap in time made little difference — Lepage appeared to have no immediate living family back in Canada, or anywhere else that they could find. In any event, he had been comatose since he was admitted, and it was starting to look like he might remain so for a while.

"It's a big hospital with a lot of patients," Charlie said. "It's a wonder you can keep track of everyone as well as you do."

Yamaguchi shook his head. "It is inexcusable, and you can be assured that we will take the appropriate measures to ensure this does not happen again."

"So his prognosis," Charlie said, trying to divert the attention away from the poor bastard who would probably lose his job over the error. "Is it … bad?"

"As I mentioned, his physical wounds should heal without event," Yamaguchi said, brightening. "He is young and fit, which should improve his odds of a full recovery. His GCS scores …" he stopped, noting Charlie's incomprehension.

"The Glasgow Coma Scale is the standard measure of consciousness. Mr. Lepage's scores are in the moderate range."

"What does that mean?"

"Combined with the activity found on his brain scans, his GCS scores suggest a significant injury, but one which can still result in full recovery," Yamaguchi said.

"So that's good, then?"

Yamaguchi gave an indulgent smile. "It means Mr. Lepage is capable of normal cognitive function, but … we will have to wait and see how things progress before giving a full prognosis."

Charlie nodded. "Can I see him?"

Yamaguchi frowned, then shrugged. "I suppose there is no harm. Come," he said, getting up and leading him into the hallway and around to the right of the reception area, past a few rooms to the one numbered 5023, and knocking on the closed door. After a moment of silence, he pushed the door open and stepped back. Charlie felt a wave of unease pass over him as he entered the room, intruding as he was into a stranger's private space. A man in his thirties was lying on the bed, one leg in a cast and raised above the bed in some sort of harness. He had other bandages around his left wrist and forearm, as well as an assortment of cuts and bruises on his face. The sound of the respirator dominated the otherwise silent space, as Lepage's chest moved up in down in time with the pump. The expression through the clear mask over his mouth was one of calm, even peace. Charlie had the grim feeling that Lepage might never again open his eyes, and he felt a sudden urge to turn and leave the room.

"These are his effects?" he said, gesturing to a clear plastic bag on a side table.

Yamaguchi nodded. "His passport and wallet are in the hospital safe."

"Right. May I?" Charlie picked up the bag as Yamaguchi nodded. He pulled out a black nylon jacket and a pair of dress shoes.

"We had to cut off the rest of his clothes. They were not … salvageable." Again, Yamaguchi's expression was apologetic.

Charlie nodded and checked the jacket pockets, finding nothing. "I guess his phone and keys are in the safe as well."

"Anything of value, yes."

Charlie put the jacket and shoes back in the bag and looked over at Lepage, still motionless on the bed, apart from the regular rise and fall of his chest in time with the ventilator.

"Has anyone else been to visit him?"

Yamaguchi frowned. "No. That was one of the reasons we contacted the embassy."

"Well, I guess there's not much else for me to do here," Charlie said. "You'll let me know if his condition changes?"

"Of course." Yamaguchi tapped the card.

"Thank you very much for your time, Doctor."

"You're most welcome."

"By the way, I have to say, your English is flawless. Where did you learn it?"

Yamaguchi smiled. "Thank you. I studied for two years in Canada."

"Really, where?"

"Montreal, at the Royal Victoria Hospital."

"Well, it really is a small world, isn't it?"

"Are you from Montreal also?" Yamaguchi asked, as they walked back out into the hall.

"No, I'm from the East Coast."

Yamaguchi nodded but looked puzzled.

It was Charlie's turn for an indulgent smile. "I know they call Toronto and Montreal eastern Canada, but it's really the centre. I'm from the real East Coast — Newfoundland."

Yamaguchi looked intrigued. "Canada is a beautiful country. Such open spaces." Charlie nodded. He could imagine the effect Canada's landscape would have on someone who had grown up in an area as densely populated as Tokyo. "And how long have you been in Tokyo?" Yamaguchi asked, as they walked back down the hall.

"A couple of weeks. I just started work today, and I'm still trying to get my bearings, but I have to say I'm very impressed with Tokyo so far."

Yamaguchi put out his hand as they reached the elevators beyond the fifth floor reception area. "Well, I hope you enjoy it as much as I enjoyed Canada."

"Thank you, and thanks again for your time today."

Yamaguchi bowed as the elevator dinged and the doors slid open. "I will contact you if there is any change in Mr. Lepage's condition."

Charlie arrived late for the reception at the official residence and scanned the room for a familiar face. He waved a polite hello to Louis Denault and kept going to the opposite side of the room and the table of hors d'oeuvres. He slid a couple of the bite-sized snacks onto a plate and was reaching for a glass of white wine when he heard his name.

"Oh, hi, Karen," he said, registering Fraser's friendly smile.

"You survived your first week. I'd say that calls for a drink," she said, tapping her glass with his.

"Yeah, so far, so good."

"Any change in your coma case?"

"Not as of noon today." He had called the hospital for an update before lunch and he had been told that Lepage remained stable but unchanged since Charlie's visit on Tuesday.

"Any luck tracking down next of kin back home?"

"It seems like he was a loner," he said, taking a sip of his wine. "Can't find any contacts either in Canada or here, other than the fact that he worked for a company called Nippon Kasuga."

"Nobody's been to the hospital to visit him?"

Charlie shook his head.

"It's kind of sad, isn't it?" Fraser frowned. "I mean, there he is, laid up in a hospital bed a million miles from home, and he's completely alone. From how you described him though, maybe he'll never wake up."

Charlie recalled Yamaguchi's prognosis, and the comments that the longer the unconsciousness lasted, the worse the prognosis. It had been three more days without a change, and things were certainly looking bleak for Lepage. "It is kind of depressing. He's a young guy."

Fraser's sombre expression lightened at the sight of a dapper man in his fifties heading their way.

"Hi, Cliff. How are you?"

"Better now that you're here," the other man said, greeting her with a double cheek kiss.

"Charlie, let me introduce you to Cliff Redford, my favourite lawyer."

"I'm the only one she knows in Tokyo," he deadpanned as he shook Charlie's hand.

"Charlie Hillier."

"You new in town?"

"Charlie's the new consular officer," Fraser said.

He nodded. "Just finished my first week."

"Well, you'll be almost over the time change by now," Redford said, accepting a glass of wine from a passing server. "What are your first impressions?"

"Good," Charlie said. "I like the city, and the people at the embassy are great."

"Well, he's a natural liar, anyway." Redford tapped Fraser playfully on the arm.

Charlie laughed along. "How about you, how long have you been in Tokyo?"

"Oh God." Redford let out a theatrical sigh. "Moses was still in short pants."

"And what brought you here?"

"Now *that's* a long story. I'll have to take you out on the town some night and tell you," he said. "So, you're doing consular work?"

"Just picked up my first case this week. A Canadian in a coma after a car accident."

"Sounds grim."

Charlie shrugged his shoulders. "I'm afraid so. His prognosis isn't good, and he's got no family that I can find."

"We were just saying how sad that is," Fraser interjected. "There's got to be someone, either here or back home."

Redford slid his hand in his jacket pocket and took out a card. "Well, if you're looking for a good PI here in Tokyo, I can hook you up."

Charlie took the card, which listed Redford as senior partner at Redford & Co.

"Cliff knows *everyone* here," Fraser said. "Plus he's the chair of the Tokyo Canadian Club."

"What's that?"

Redford smiled. "Sounds grand, but it's really just a charitable association for expat Canucks. We spend a lot of our time with guys whose marriages go wrong, to be honest. They find out the hard way that access and custody is a lot different here when the mother's a local."

Charlie nodded, then noticed a good-looking guy in his late thirties approach their little trio.

"Oh, hi." Fraser turned to greet him as Charlie felt a little bubble in his chest deflate. "Charlie, this is my husband, Jeff."

As the two men shook hands, Charlie noticed a strong grip that went along with the athletic frame and the bright smile. "Jeff Fraser."

"Charlie Hillier."

"Karen's told me all about you. Welcome to Tokyo." He turned to Redford. "Hi, Cliff."

"How are the markets?" Redford asked.

"Down again, but that won't stop us from making a killing," Fraser said with a grin.

"Jeff is a securities broker," Karen said.

Rich, too, Charlie thought to himself. *Some guys have it all …*

"Do you speak Japanese?" Charlie asked, guessing the answer but unable to resist.

"Badly, but I get by. I lucked in with a firm that deals mostly with Western companies — thanks to Cliff here."

"You don't know a Robert Lepage by any chance, do you?"

Fraser frowned and shook his head. "Don't think so. Is he in securities?"

"I know he's a banker of some kind. I'm not really sure what area."

"That your coma guy?" Redford asked. "The mystery man?"

Charlie nodded. "He's my first consular case. A Canadian who got into a car accident and now he's in a coma."

"Who was he working for?"

"A company called Nippon … Kasuga, I think."

Fraser shook his head. "Never heard of them, but there are a lot of players here, so that's no surprise." He looked to Redford, who was nodding.

"Their office is in the same building as mine," he said. "I know a few of the senior people, though not that much about their exact line of business. I'll sniff around though, let you know what I find out," he added as the ambassador approached.

"Cliff, how's business?"

"Can't complain. I was just meeting your new consular officer."

Westwood looked at Charlie and smiled. "We're glad to have him. He comes highly recommended."

Charlie smiled awkwardly, wondering what his true status was in the department. Probably somewhere between loose cannon and pariah. But he was here, and Westwood had seemed genuine in their first meeting, when he had told him he liked Charlie's initiative. It had been accompanied by a somewhat veiled warning that staying under the radar might not be a bad idea, at least for a while. He could hardly blame Westwood for that though, given the events in Moscow last year, or in Havana before that. They chatted for a while and then Westwood moved on. Charlie yawned, prompting a smile from Karen.

"Keeping you up?"

I should probably get going." Charlie looked at his watch. "Most of my stuff is still in boxes. I'll see you tomorrow. It was nice to meet you, Jeff. You, too, Cliff."

"Let's do dinner sometime," Redford said. "When you've fully adjusted."

"I'd like that."

Charlie set his half-empty wine glass on a side table and headed for the door. Walking outside, he was greeted by fresh, cool evening air. It was only six thirty but pitch dark outside, as he made his way around the driveway from the official residence toward the apartment complex where many of the Canadian staff members were housed. He had been given the option of living off-site but had opted for the convenience of living literally steps from the office. He knew some people didn't like living near the people they worked with every day, but the complex was big enough that he wasn't too concerned. Besides, he thought, as he shuffled up the stairs to his second floor apartment, his social life was unlikely to attract much attention. He had lied about needing to unpack — the few boxes he had bothered to have shipped from Canada had been unpacked in less than an hour. As he slid the key in the door and stepped into his apartment, it felt sterile, and lonely. He grabbed a beer from the fridge and sank onto the sofa, trying not to feel sorry for himself. He had known Karen Fraser was married, so why was meeting her charming, handsome, and wealthy husband such a kick in the balls? He sipped his beer and tried to ward off the feeling of impending doom, preferring to remind himself that it was only his second week in a new city. He had to give it time.

CHAPTER 4

Charlie scanned the vivid signs adorning the buildings on the crowded pedestrian mall in Akasaka, looking for the restaurant's name. Walking past the front of a noisy Pachinko parlour, with its dizzying lights and electronic sounds, he spotted a familiar logo on the building a few doors up. As he got closer, he made out the word *Shabugen* and stepped into the building, taking the tiny elevator up to the second floor. He followed the smell of food as he stepped from the elevator car and soon found himself in a little restaurant containing what looked like a long bar with stools on one side and pots of boiling water on the other. The room was packed with the Monday lunchtime crowd, but he didn't recognize anyone. He was wondering if it was the right place when a familiar face leaned back out of the row of people and called out.

"Over here, Charlie."

He made his way back to where Cliff Redford was waiting with a Japanese man in his thirties.

"This is Hirohito Kambe, an associate of mine." Redford pointed to the other man, then gestured to Charlie.

"Charlie Hillier." He remembered to bow before sliding onto the stool they had saved for him. They went through the introductions and Charlie learned that Kambe was a lawyer with

Redford's firm. After they had ordered and exchanged a bit of banter about life and work in Tokyo, Redford got to the point.

"I arranged to bump into someone at Nippon Kasuga," he said. Charlie was surprised, thinking Redford was just being polite when he had promised to do some digging the other night at the embassy reception.

"You don't waste any time, do you?"

Redford smiled. "I'm afraid there's not much to tell you. I asked about your man, but they didn't seem all that interested in poor Mr. Lepage, to be honest."

"What do you mean?"

"Nippon Kasuga just sponsored him for his work visa. The guy I talked to didn't seem to know much about him. If anything, once he found out I was involved with a group that looks out for expat Canucks, he seemed to want me to keep *him* posted on Lepage's status."

"That's pretty cold."

Redford shrugged. "They're bankers. They're only interested in one thing. Wouldn't you say, Kambe-san?"

Kambe nodded. "Yes, I suppose that is so."

"I was going to see if I could talk to someone over there," Charlie said. "Try to get more information about Lepage."

"I can give you the coordinates of someone who speaks English, but I wouldn't get my hopes up if I were you," Redford warned. "How is Lepage, anyway?"

"No change, as far as I know. I'm dropping by after work today to check in, see if there's any update on his prognosis," Charlie said as a waitress delivered a selection of bowls filled with vegetables and thinly sliced meat.

Redford smiled at the look of confusion on Charlie's face. "You dip it in the pot for a minute or two. It's easier than it looks. It's called *shabu-shabu.*"

"Sounds simple." Charlie followed their lead and dropped

a few strips of meat and vegetables into the individual pot of boiling liquid in front of him. Redford and Kambe were much nimbler with their chopsticks, but Charlie was just happy he hadn't dropped anything on the floor.

"And still no sign that this poor guy's got any relatives in Canada?" Redford dropped a pile of cabbage into his pot.

Charlie shook his head. "Other than an immigration form indicating he entered the country a couple of months ago, and the sponsorship paperwork filled out by Nippon Kasuga, I've got nothing. Nobody's contacted the embassy, either from here or Canada, and I've checked with the Tokyo Police and no one's reported him missing."

"How long has he been in a coma?" Kambe asked, prodding a chopstick at the water and pulling out a few strips of steaming cabbage that he deposited with ease on his plate.

"Almost a week," Charlie replied, making an unsuccessful attempt at mimicking Kambe's dexterous manoeuvre, before resorting to a clumsy trawl of the bottom of the pot until he came up with something — a strip of meat that he dropped halfway to his plate.

"You'll get better at the chopsticks in no time, trust me," Redford said with a smile. Charlie tried again, a look of grim determination on his face as he managed to retrieve a spear of broccoli with much more finesse. "There you go."

"So, how do you know the ambassador?" Charlie asked, reveling in his small success.

"Phil and I go way back. We both articled at the same firm in Toronto."

"I didn't know he was a lawyer." Charlie bit into a strip of tender beef.

"He only practised for a couple of years before joining the department. He went off to Ottawa and I came out here."

"You just moved here, out of the blue?"

"Not exactly. There was a girl involved," Redford said with a grin. "I came over to visit her, and the rest, as they say, is history. How about you, Charlie? You married?"

Charlie remained focused on extricating a particularly succulent morsel of beef from his pot as the familiar discomfort that always accompanied the question gripped him. He had been divorced for over two years, but he still wasn't really over it in some ways. It wasn't a yearning for his former spouse — that part, he had definitely gotten over. Rather it was the betrayal that gnawed at him, and the sense of failure on his part.

"Divorced," he said, manoeuvring the piece of meat to the edge of the pot before dropping it back in.

"Well there's lots of talent here," Redford said.

Charlie nodded. "Japanese women are certainly very attractive, and they're all so well dressed."

"But?" Redford was grinning.

"Nothing. It's just that they seem sort of … reserved."

Redford nudged Kambe and they both shared a laugh. "Don't believe it, right Kambe-san?"

Redford's associate smiled. "It's very true that Japanese people have a very … rigid exterior, but they are very warm underneath."

"Ain't that the truth," Redford said. "Don't you worry, Charlie. You'll be fighting them off before you know it."

Charlie smiled and dropped some more vegetables into the pot. He wasn't sure about their prediction, but Redford and Kambe's good-natured bravado was infectious and it gave him a positive feeling about what might lay ahead for him in this enigmatic city he now called home.

Charlie got off the elevator on the fifth floor and spotted Dr. Yamaguchi as soon as he turned the corner toward the reception area, engaged in what looked like an animated discussion with a white man in his late thirties. He saw the recognition in Yamaguchi's eyes, and perhaps a hint of relief as well, as Charlie approached.

"Mr. Hillier," he said, "I'm glad you have come today."

"Good afternoon, Doctor," Charlie said, looking at the other man. Though he was smiling, there was something in the way he was eying him that made Charlie nervous.

"This is Mr. Seger, also from Canada," Yamaguchi said, pointing at the other man. "He is a friend of Mr. Lepage."

"Oh, really? That's great." Charlie stuck out his hand. "Charlie Hillier. I'm a consular officer with the Canadian embassy. I've been having a hell of a time trying to find any of Mr. Lepage's family."

"Mike Seger," the other man said. His handshake was firm, but Charlie sensed that it went on just a little too long. "Yeah, that doesn't surprise me," he added, with a shrug. "Robbie's always been a bit of a lone wolf."

"No family at all, huh?" Charlie said, noticing for the first time that Seger had a slight accent, maybe French, or Italian. He had a dark complexion and wavy brown hair. His suit and open necked shirt gave the impression of someone in finance. Charlie guessed he knew Lepage from the banking world.

"Perhaps I can leave you to discuss his case," Yamaguchi said, looking at his watch. "I'm going to be late for my rounds."

"I assume there's no update on his condition," Charlie asked, eliciting a shake of the head from Yamaguchi.

"I'm afraid not. His condition remains the same."

"Thanks, Doctor."

"Rob's tough," Seger said as Yamaguchi moved off. "He'll pull through, I know it."

"How do you know Mr. Le … Rob?"

"Come on, I'll buy you a coffee," Seger said, heading off toward the elevators, as though the decision was a foregone conclusion. They took one down to the ground floor and found the visitors' cafeteria.

"So, you're with the embassy, huh?" Seger said as they settled in a corner booth with their coffees.

"Yeah, I've only been in Tokyo for a couple of weeks."

Seger smiled. "A newbie, huh?"

"To Tokyo, yes. It's not my first posting," he felt the need to add.

"Right. So your job is to get in touch with relatives back home, for people like Rob?" He gestured upstairs with a thumb.

Charlie nodded. "It's usually more along the lines of lost passports, but we have medical cases like Rob, as well as Canadians who've gotten themselves in trouble here."

"You mean, like, jail?"

Charlie took a sip of his coffee. "Sometimes, yes."

"Well it's good to know you're looking out for Rob's interests, and I want to offer my help in any way I can. You asked how I know him. Well, we go way back, me and Rob. We grew up in the same part of Toronto." Charlie nodded, though he was puzzled, since the more he heard Seger speak, the more he detected a distinctively French-Canadian accent. As though reading his mind, Seger added, "When my family moved there from Quebec City — when I was twelve — I thought my life was over. Maybe it would have been, if it wasn't for Rob. His parents, too, God rest their souls."

"I understand they died when Rob was in his teens," Charlie said, recalling the mental calculation he had made on discovering their death certificates. "And he's got no siblings, or other immediate family that I could find," he added, hoping for confirmation from Seger, who obliged with a nod.

"His parents were killed in a car crash when we were seventeen. No other family. There might have been an uncle who wasn't really an uncle for a little while, but Rob was pretty much on his own. He took off when he was eighteen — headed out west — and we kinda lost touch for a couple of years. Then he came back with a university degree — he was always a smart guy, so it wasn't a surprise."

"So, he was back in Toronto?"

Seger nodded. "Yeah, and we ended up hanging out again, so it was just like old times."

"And what brought you to Tokyo?"

"I had some business in Hong Kong; had a few extra days and thought I'd drop in on Rob — check out Tokyo. We set it up by email a couple of weeks ago. Then I get here and he's not responding to emails, so I know something's wrong." Charlie encouraged him with a nod. "Then I find out he's been in an accident and he's in here." Seger shook his head.

"Do you know much about his employer, Nippon Kasuga?"

Seger shrugged. "No idea. I tried talking to someone over there and they gave me the cold shoulder, you know? They don't seem too concerned that one of their employees is in a coma. Heartless pricks," he muttered, taking a sip of coffee.

"Yeah, I kind of got the same impression."

"I think I'm all Rob's got," Seger said with a grim smile. "Apart from you, of course. So if there's anything — I mean anything — I can do.... If you hear of any change in his condition, or if there are any costs he needs covered, promise me you'll let me know as soon as possible."

Charlie accepted the business card Seger took out of his jacket pocket and slid across the table.

"My cell's on there, so you can call me anytime, day or night."

"I'll do that," Charlie said, noticing the name of Seger's company — Paragon Properties. "You're in real estate?"

Seger nodded. "Asia's an emerging market for us. We've had some interests in Hong Kong for a while, but we're looking at Japan, as well, especially with the Olympics just around the corner."

"So, how long are you here for?"

"Well, like I said, I'm not really here on business this time, so I'll be here as long as it takes — until Rob's back on his feet."

Charlie smiled, thinking most people couldn't afford the luxury of an indefinite stay in a city like Tokyo. Seger was either well off or a very good friend — perhaps both. "Well, there's not much we can do until Rob's condition changes," he said. "But I'll certainly let you know as soon as I hear anything. As for costs, I understand from Dr. Yamaguchi that Rob's hospital costs are being covered by Nippon Kasuga's insurance, so that's not an issue."

"Still, if there are any extras — like if he needs a private room when he comes out of intensive care — I'll cover it."

Charlie gave a nod of acknowledgment and glanced at his watch. "Thanks for the coffee. I'd better get going."

"Good to meet you, Charlie. It's nice to know there are people like you looking out for Rob."

They shook hands and went their separate ways. Charlie made his way back to the nearest Metro station and joined the evening rush hour crowd, immersed in a sea of dark suits and white shirts. He glanced at his fellow passengers, noticing that none of them seemed to be looking at him, despite the incongruity of his blond hair and relatively lofty height. This was another aspect of Japanese society that he had come to recognize in his brief time here — it was rude to make direct eye contact with strangers, especially foreigners. As the train moved east, Charlie began to consider his options for dinner.

He hadn't bothered to really stock his refrigerator yet, and the prospect of making dinner seemed a chore. On the other hand, finding a quiet corner in a restaurant seemed an impossibility in Tokyo. The sheer volume of people usually meant he found himself in close proximity to his fellow diners, all of whom seemed to be enjoying each other's company while he ate alone, in awkward silence as he tried to occupy himself either with his BlackBerry or his Japanese phrase book. Maybe he would stop off at the grocery store after all.

Charlie got off at Akasaka-mitsuke Station and walked into a twenty-four hour convenience store at street level, looking for something quick. Finding nothing particularly appetizing among the array of plastic-wrapped single servings of God knew what, he continued on up the street, pausing at the door of a couple of restaurants to survey the plastic samples of the food on offer, before remembering the British-style pub that lay a little farther up the street. As he walked on, Charlie saw a fleeting image of Rob Lepage in his hospital bed and felt profound guilt. Here he was feeling sorry for himself over another lonely dinner, when Lepage was unconscious and alone in a hospital bed, thousands of miles from home, his only nutrition being pumped into him by way of a tube. What the hell did Charlie have to complain about? As for being alone, he had been in town for less than two weeks. He had to give himself time to settle in. Perhaps he should focus on what he could do to help Rob Lepage, assuming he ever came out of his coma, rather than worrying about his dinner plans. Arriving at the pub and finding it relatively quiet, he settled into a seat at a corner table and resolved to give Lepage's file another read first thing in the morning. There had to be something more he could do.

CHAPTER 5

Charlie was sitting at his desk, reviewing the results of an internet search on Paragon Properties that he had conducted after a fresh look at Rob Lepage's file proved completely fruitless. Paragon's head office appeared to be in Montreal, though it was not entirely clear from the website, which was either badly designed or deliberately short on information. He yawned, tried to sip from the empty coffee cup on his desk, and briefly considered a second. He had gotten home from dinner early and spent an hour or so flipping through the channels, finally settling on one of the few English options — an episode of a comedy show he had seen before — before turning it off in favour of a book. He had gone to bed relatively early but had awoken at five, with no hope of resuming sleep. It wasn't even ten yet and he was tired already.

"Keeping you up?"

He glanced up to see Karen Fraser standing in his doorway and realized his mouth was stretched wide in a yawn.

"Sorry." He clapped a hand over his mouth. "I just can't seem to get a decent night's sleep. It's driving me crazy."

She smiled. "It'll pass, don't worry."

"I sure hope so."

"How's your coma guy?" Fraser took a seat opposite his desk.

"No change. It's not looking good."

"That really sucks. Say, did you see the email this morning?"

"The lost passport?" Charlie nodded. "I told Louis I'd take it on. It's not like I can do much for Lepage, as long as he's still lying in a hospital bed. I did meet one of his friends from Canada yesterday, though."

"Oh yeah?"

"He was supposed to connect with Lepage last week and when he didn't get an answer to his emails, this guy tracked him down at the hospital. Says they grew up together."

Fraser nodded. "Well, at least your guy's not totally alone now … apart from you, I mean."

They chatted for a while about another consular file Fraser was working on, then they moved on to a departmental announcement about changes to consular services, speculating on what impact, if any, it would have on their jobs. As the conversation wound down, Fraser got up to leave, but paused at the door.

"Listen, if you're not doing anything this weekend, we're going out with a bunch of people on Friday. Dinner, some drinks … maybe even some karaoke. Why don't you join us?" Charlie's smile faded a bit as he imagined himself as the only single guy in a group of happy couples. He had been there before and it was no fun being an awkward third, fifth, or seventh wheel. Fraser seemed to read his reservations. "It's a really fun crowd. Different ages, some couples, some singles. You should really come out."

"Thanks," he said, wondering if he was giving off a desperate vibe, to the point that she was trying to set him up out of pity. Considering the types of evenings he had spent so far — last night being a prime example — he didn't have much to lose. "Sounds great," he added, glancing at his watch and noticing it was a couple of minutes past ten. "Oh, I'm late for a meeting with Louis."

"Better run," she said with a knowing grin.

It was five after by the time he made it to Denault's office. He could hear him on the phone, so he hovered outside the open door until he heard him hang up, then rapped on the door jamb.

"Oh, there you are," Denault said, waving him in and making a show of looking at his watch. Charlie decided to ignore it and took a seat.

"I need you to meet with that property developer this week, to hear them on this development next door," Denault began, reaching for a file folder on his side table and sliding it across the desk. "This is their latest proposal."

"Sure," Charlie said. "I've got that passport file from this morning to work on, plus the Lepage case, but I'll get to it."

Denault gave a thin smile and shook his head. "This takes priority, and as I understand it, your medical case is in a coma, so there's not much to do there."

"Actually, I've been in touch with a family friend ..."

"Anyway," Denault continued, cutting him off. "Please meet with the Miton people as soon as possible. As I mentioned, if it's not a realistic proposal, then it won't take much of your time. The HOM would like an update by the end of the week," he added, using the acronym for head of mission, or ambassador.

Charlie glanced down at the file and bit his tongue. When he looked up, Denault was staring at him with a puzzled expression on his face. "That's all."

"All right then," Charlie said, getting up and heading out of the office. By the time he had reached the other end of the hall, he was steaming. He thumped into his chair and tossed the file on his desk, then spent a few minutes stewing. He was wondering how to go about cancelling his own posting when he recognized Dr. Yamaguchi's name on an incoming email message and clicked it open. He had an update on Lepage's condition. Charlie snatched up the phone and dialed Yamaguchi's number. After a few rings, he was directed to voicemail. Rather than leaving a message, he hung up the phone, slid on his jacket, and headed out the door, careful to avoid Denault's corner as he made his way to the elevator.

"Ah, Mr. Hillier," Yamaguchi said as Charlie arrived at the fifth-floor reception area. "I see you got my message."

"Has there been a change in his condition?"

Yamaguchi nodded, though there was nothing in his inscrutable expression to indicate whether Charlie was about to hear good news or bad. For the first time, the unsettling possibility that Lepage had taken a turn for the worse entered his mind.

"Mr. Lepage recovered consciousness briefly this morning."

"Well, that's great," Charlie said, feeling a wave of relief, until Yamaguchi's frown stopped him short. "You said … briefly?"

"He's been in and out of consciousness ever since, but I was able to perform some initial tests while he was awake."

"And?" Charlie was wondering what it would take to get this guy to spill the beans.

"The results are generally positive, and I am optimistic that this transitional period will pass."

"You mean he'll be out of the coma for good?"

"That is my hope." Yamaguchi nodded. "But I do have some questions for you."

Charlie shrugged. "Of course."

"You mentioned that Mr. Lepage was from an English-speaking part of Canada, is this correct?"

"He's from Toronto, yes. Why do you ask?"

"Because his initial communications were in French. I spent some time in Montreal, as you know, and while I am not at all fluent, I recognize the language."

Charlie was taken aback. "He was speaking French?"

Yamaguchi nodded.

"As far as I know, he's an English speaker," Charlie said, trying to recall if there was anything in Lepage's file to suggest he was francophone and thinking not. "I suppose it's possible he had some French in his family background. Lepage is actually a French name, now that I think of it."

"Hmm." Yamaguchi crossed his arms.

"Were you able to understand what he was saying?"

"Not really. I thought he mentioned his employer, Nippon Kasuga, and I'm sure he said Montreal, but it was all very ... disjointed. Also, as I mentioned, I have to confess that my understanding of French is limited."

"I guess that's not unusual — his words being disjointed?" It was a question and not a statement, Charlie being in no position to be suggesting what was or wasn't normal behaviour for someone coming out of a coma, much less to an experienced neurologist. "As for the French, I just assumed he was an anglophone, but it's just as likely that- French is his first language. Canada's a bilingual country, after all." Charlie suddenly thought back to Mike Seger's explanation of his own accent. It seemed odd that he hadn't mentioned Lepage speaking French as well, if that were the case. He looked at Yamaguchi, who seemed to be turning over the information and possibilities in his own mind, preoccupied by something.

"His … girlfriend seemed confused," the neurologist said. "She had never heard him speak French before."

"His girlfriend?" Charlie's eyebrows shot up. "What girlfriend?"

"You didn't get my voicemail?"

Charlie's growing confusion must have been obvious.

"I left it after I sent my email," Yamaguchi said, his expression turning apologetic. "You must had already left your office … a woman arrived this morning who said she and Mr. Lepage were … *are* in a relationship."

"Did she leave her name?"

"She's with the nurse." Yamaguchi gestured down the hall. "Come with me."

Charlie followed him around the corner and immediately noticed a striking Japanese woman in the hallway outside Lepage's room, in a heated discussion with a nurse. Charlie put her in her late twenties, with a tall, athletic figure. He had noticed Japanese women were big fans of leather boots, but the stilettos this woman was wearing were distinctive, and seemed at odds with the rest of her outfit, which was more conservative. As she turned at Charlie and Yamaguchi's approach, he saw her face and noted that she was very attractive, but there was something in her eyes that suggested a hardness beyond the conventional Japanese reserve. Yamaguchi exchanged a few words with the woman and the nurse, who headed off toward the reception area, then he switched to English.

"Ms. Kimura, meet Mr. Charlie Hillier, from the Canadian embassy."

Charlie felt a frisson as she gave him a once over with those eyes before switching to a demure smile and bow. "Aiko Kimura."

"A pleasure to meet you, Ms. Kimura," he said, reciprocating with his own bow. "I understand from Dr. Yamaguchi that you're … friends with Mr. Lepage?"

She looked to Yamaguchi and back, a thin smile briefly appearing on her face. "We are more than friends, Mr. Hillier."

"Well, that's great." Charlie avoided her gaze. "I've been looking into Mr. … into Rob's case for the past few days, and I'd really like to ask you some questions, if you wouldn't mind."

Kimura looked at Yamaguchi again and gestured to the closed door behind her. "You'll let me know as soon as he wakes up again?"

"Of course."

"In that case, Mr. Hill—"

"Call me Charlie."

"Charlie," she repeated. For the first time, he saw what he thought was her real smile, and detected something sly about it. "I'd be happy to talk to you."

"Can I buy you a coffee downstairs?"

She nodded, and after further assurances from Yamaguchi that he would let them know of any change in Lepage's condition, they headed for the cafeteria.

CHAPTER 6

"So, you work at the embassy?" Kimura asked as they took a seat at a table in a quiet corner of the cafeteria.

"That's right. I'm the consular officer for Rob's case." Charlie flipped the plastic tab open on his coffee cup. "That means I look out for his interests as much as I can. Usually, a lot of that is getting in touch with relatives back in Canada. In Rob's case though, I haven't had any luck, which why I'm glad I bumped into you."

Kimura paused with her coffee hallway to her mouth, a puzzled frown on her face. "I don't know if he has any family in Canada. We didn't talk about that."

"Well, let's start with you two — how did you meet?" Charlie continued, sensing an odd, underlying resistance.

She shrugged and slid off her jacket, revealing a skin-tight long-sleeve denim shirt that outlined a taut physique. He noticed the edge of a tattoo — flames or the outline of an animal? — peeking out from under the collar of her shirt, extending to the base of her neck. "A mutual friend introduced us at a party. We exchanged numbers and then got together a little while later."

Charlie nodded, though he was finding getting information from Kimura a bit like drawing blood from a stone.

"You know the company he works for, Nippon Kasuga?"

She shook her head and grimaced, as though the thought were outlandish. "I don't know it. I know he's a trader, that's all."

"You're not in … securities then?"

The thin smile returned as she turned her attention to the lid of her coffee cup. "No."

"Your English is very good, by the way."

"Thank you. I learned it in school, and from television," she added. "All those American movies."

"Really? That's pretty impressive." Charlie kept smiling, thinking she sounded like a native speaker to him, not someone who got the gist of a language from watching TV. "What line of work are you in?"

"Sales. Online sales," she said. This time, instead of looking down at her cup she kept eye contact with him, as though inviting a challenge with those cold, dark eyes.

"So, how long have you and Rob been seeing each other?"

Another shrug. "Six weeks, maybe a little less."

"Did you meet any of his co-workers or friends here in Japan or from Canada?"

"Rob and I spent a lot of time together," she said. "But he never mentioned friends or family from Canada, and I didn't meet any of his co-workers."

"Do you know how long he was planning to stay in Tokyo?"

"Indefinitely, I think. You say you haven't found any of his family in Canada?" she asked, in between sips of her coffee.

"No, not yet."

"But you'll keep looking, of course," she added.

"Yes, but at this point there's not much to go on." He thought of the company listed as Lepage's previous employer, which Charlie had discovered was out of business. Not much of a lead. "I take it you weren't with him on the night of the accident?"

She shook her head. "I had to work, and he was supposed to go to Osaka on business for a couple of days, so I wasn't worried when he didn't respond to my texts."

"But you eventually got worried and tracked him down here?"

"That's right," she said as Charlie spotted Mike Seger walking past the entrance to the cafeteria, headed for the elevators. Just before he was past the cafeteria doors, he saw Charlie and smiled, changing course and heading to their table.

"Did you hear?" he said as he approached the table. "He came out of it this morning."

"Yes, I know. I just found out myself," Charlie said, realizing he had promised to let Seger know as soon as heard any news. Seger was looking at Kimura, who continued to sip her coffee in the same leisurely fashion. "And I bumped into Ms. Kimura, here. She's Rob's girlfriend."

Seger showed no outward reaction to the news, but Charlie detected a slight pause as he processed it. "I didn't know Rob had a girlfriend," he said, sliding onto the seat next to Charlie and extending his hand over the table. "I'm Mike."

"Aiko Kimura," she said, accepting his hand and shaking it. An awkward silence descended as she and Seger appeared to go through a silent mutual appraisal.

"So what's the good doc saying?" Seger finally asked, breaking off the staring match.

"He's cautiously optimistic," Charlie said. "Rob's been in and out of it today, and I don't think he's out of the woods yet, but Dr. Yamaguchi seems to think his chances for a full recovery are good."

"Is Yamaguchi here?" Seger gestured upstairs.

"We left him ten minutes ago, so he should still be around if you want to get an update."

"I think I'll do that, in a minute," he said, turning his attention to Kimura, who sat with the same indifferent expression on her delicate features. "So, you're Rob's girlfriend, huh? Must be a recent thing."

"We've been together for a couple of months."

"Funny, he never mentioned you," Seger said. He and Kimura locked stares again for a moment too long before he smiled. "That's just like Rob, though. He's always played his cards close to his chest, and I can see why he wanted to keep you all to himself."

Kimura gave a cold smile before firing off her own retort. "It is unusual that he didn't mention his friendship with you, either."

"We go back a lot longer than you think, hon," Seger said with a chuckle, crossing the index and second fingers of his right hand and holding it up to illustrate their bond. Charlie was about to mention the fact that Lepage had been speaking French when he had awoken from his coma when Seger's phone went off.

"Shit, I gotta take this, and then I should probably head upstairs. Listen, it was nice to meet you … Aiko." He slid off the chair and looked to Charlie. "I'll be in touch, okay?"

Charlie and Kimura watched him leave, then she looked at her watch. "I should really be going. I have to check in at work, then I'll come back to see how Rob's doing."

"Can I get your contact information?" Charlie asked, as she stood to go.

"Give me your card and I'll send you an email."

"I know there's one in here somewhere." He rummaged in his pocket, coming up with a slightly bent business card. Thinking it unworthy of a formal presentation and sensing that Kimura couldn't care less anyway, he handed it over.

"Goodbye, Mr. Hillier."

He watched her go and finished his coffee, wondering if he should go back upstairs, but he decided he should really go back to the office and try to set up the property meeting if he wanted to avoid a run-in with Denault. As he made his way back out to the hospital entrance, he considered the odd exchange between Seger and Kimura. Maybe it was nothing more than cultural differences.

Charlie had just finished a workout in the staff recreation centre and was heading back to his apartment when his phone went off. Recognizing the number, he took the call and heard Seger's gravelly voice on the other end of the line.

"You hear?"

"Hear what?"

"Rob's in the clear. He's out of the coma, for good. Yamaguchi thinks it'll take some time for him to be a hundred percent, but he's gonna be fine."

"That's great news. Really great. Have you talked to him … Rob, I mean?"

"Yeah, I went back in this afternoon and he was wide awake. We had a long talk."

"And how did he seem?"

"It was weird," Seger said. "One minute he seemed totally normal, and then he was kind of … out of it."

"Have you talked to Dr. Yamaguchi?"

"I just spoke to him a little while ago. He said it's normal for Rob to be a bit disoriented. He thought he might be a little better tomorrow, after some rest."

Charlie tried to remember when Denault's biweekly administrative meeting was scheduled for tomorrow, and decided meeting with Lepage was more important — surely even Denault would acknowledge that. "I'm going to try to go over there tomorrow and talk to him. Thanks for letting me know."

"I was hoping I could meet with you tomorrow," Seger said. "To talk about Rob's arrangements at the hospital — getting him moved to a private room, stuff like that. I figure you can probably help run interference with the bean-counters at the hospital. I want to pay for everything, I'm just not that good with filling in forms, and I got the impression that they like their rules and regulations here, you know what I mean?"

"I could meet you at the hospital if you like."

"I'm going to be around the corner from the embassy for another meeting around eight thirty," Seger said. "What if I dropped in on you there? We could head over to the hospital together afterward."

Charlie could think of no obvious conflict in his morning schedule. "Um, I don't see why not. I'll expect you around nine, then?"

"Perfect, see you tomorrow."

Charlie slid his phone back in his pocket and climbed the stairs to his apartment, wondering what Seger thought Charlie could really do for him. He supposed a meeting couldn't hurt. He entered his apartment, got a glass of cold water from the fridge, and sat on the couch. It was good news about Lepage. He had never actually seen the man conscious, much less spoken to him, but he felt like he knew him already, and Seger's description of Yamaguchi's prognosis sounded positive. Perhaps things were looking up.

CHAPTER 7

Charlie finished typing an email and glanced at the clock on his computer. It was almost nine thirty and there was no sign of Mike Seger. He had already tried his cell number and gotten no answer or voicemail option, and he had called down to reception ten minutes ago to confirm Seger wasn't waiting there. Thinking that maybe Seger's prior meeting had run late and anxious to get over to the hospital to talk to Rob Lepage for the first time, Charlie decided that Seger would have to catch up with him there. He headed downstairs and saw one of the embassy's locally engaged drivers waiting by the side of a Toyota minivan, on time as always.

"How long will it take us to get to Tokyo Medical University Hospital?" he asked, as the driver pulled out onto Aoyama-dori and joined a light stream of traffic.

"Fifteen minutes," the driver replied, glancing in the mirror. Charlie pulled out his phone and tried Seger's number again, getting the same ten rings before the call disconnected. As they made their way west out of the government district of Akasaka and into Shinjuku, it occurred to him that Seger might have decided to go directly to the hospital. Charlie glanced out the window, noticing that although the districts were quite different, the crowds on the sidewalks and at the intersections all looked the same — the men in white shirts and dark suits, the women in designer dresses and leather boots. He had noticed the forecast on the television while he ate breakfast, unusually warm for late October, and the sun was indeed shining. A few minutes later, they pulled up to the main entrance of the hospital and Charlie got out, thanking the driver and telling him not to wait. He hurried inside, took the elevator up to the fifth floor, and rounded the corner to the reception area, where a nurse he hadn't seen before was sitting behind the counter. After his best attempt at a natural-sounding greeting in Japanese, he reverted to English and hoped she could follow.

"Dr. Yamaguchi is with another patient right now, but I will tell him you are waiting," she said, pointing to the waiting area. He took a seat and was checking his BlackBerry for messages when he looked up and saw Aiko Kimura coming down the hall.

"Good morning, Ms. Kimura." He got up and met her in the hallway. Her reaction was her trademark cold smile, but there was something new in her expression today — concern, Charlie thought. "How's he doing?"

"His memory is affected," she said, and Charlie suddenly felt bad about judging her. Perhaps she really did care about Lepage and just expressed her feelings differently than he would have expected. He had to remind himself that he was a visitor to another culture.

"Is it bad? I mean, can he remember … you?"

She shook her head. "He can't remember anything at all. Not me, not what month it is, not what he's doing in Tokyo."

"Dr. Yamaguchi said it might take some time for him to regain his memory after he came out of the coma," he offered.

"It's probably temporary," he added, suddenly realizing that Mike Seger had described Lepage as displaying at least intermittent lucidity the night before.

"I have to make a phone call before the doctor comes back" she said as Charlie stepped aside to let her pass. Before she had reached the elevators, he called out after her, "You haven't seen Mike Seger here this morning, have you?" Noticing her puzzled look, he added, "The man we met in the cafeteria yesterday."

She shook her head and pressed the call button for the elevator.

Charlie went back to the uncomfortable chair in the waiting area and wondered what it would be like to discover that someone you had been intimate with for a couple of months suddenly didn't know who you were. Off-putting at the very least. He was wondering how fruitful his interview with Lepage was going to be if the man didn't even know his own name when Yamaguchi appeared at the door to the waiting area.

"Mr. Hillier. I'm glad you are here. Please come." He gestured toward Lepage's room.

"How is he?" Charlie asked, as they made their way down the hall.

"His long- and short-term memory have both been affected … significantly."

"That doesn't sound good."

"I'm still optimistic that he will make a full recovery, but it may take more time than I originally thought."

"I guess we should be glad he's come out of the coma for good," Charlie said. "When I heard the news from Mr. Seger last night, I was really relieved. By the way, you haven't seen him here this morning have you? I was supposed to meet him at the embassy and he didn't show."

Yamaguchi paused a few doors down from Lepage's room. "No." There was hesitation in his tone, and he was clearly struggling with whether to voice whatever else was on his mind.

"Is there something wrong?"

"I wanted to talk to you about Mr. Seger's request."

"What request?"

"He wanted me to release Mr. Lepage to his care. I assume from your reaction that he didn't mention this to you?"

"No, but surely he's not yet ready to be discharged, anyway."

"Certainly not. But Mr. Seger was most insistent that he be discharged at the earliest possible opportunity. He offered to pay for all costs to date, and I believe he was trying to offer me more than that," Yamaguchi continued, his expression conveying his embarrassment at the distasteful topic he was forced to discuss.

"Are you saying he tried to bribe you? Maybe you misunderstood?" Charlie instantly regretted the choice of words. "I mean, I think maybe Mr. Seger's intentions were honourable."

Yamaguchi's expression told Charlie he was having none of it, though he didn't oppose the statement. "He seemed quite eager that Mr. Lepage not stay in the hospital any longer than absolutely necessary."

"Did he say why?" It was sounding more and more bizarre to Charlie.

Yamaguchi shook his head. "He seemed to think that Mr. Lepage would be better off, almost as though he was in some sort of danger here."

"Look, I know he can be a bit pushy, but I'll straighten it out with him when I see him, and explain that Rob's not going anywhere until you say so."

Yamaguchi seemed appeased by the assurance, and gave a slight bow to show his gratitude. "Would you like to talk to him now?"

Charlie nodded, but as they approached the closed door, he felt a building tension for some unknown reason. Yamaguchi opened the door and led the way into the room. It had two beds, the first empty with the curtain surrounding it pulled back. On the far side of the room lay Lepage, his head to one side as he looked out the window at the bright sunshine. He turned as they arrived at the foot of his bed. His clear blue eyes gave him an intelligent air, but they seemed vacant as they scanned Charlie.

"Good morning, Mr. Lepage. I'm Charlie Hillier, with the Canadian embassy here in Tokyo."

"Hi." Lepage looked to Yamaguchi, as though for confirmation, before returning his attention to Charlie.

"I'm really glad to see you out of the coma. How do you feel?"

"Pretty good, I guess. I'd be a lot better if I could be out there, though," he said, pointing to the window. "Unfortunately, it looks like I'll be here for a while," he added, looking down the bed at his cast.

"I understand that'll heal just fine." Charlie gave him a reassuring smile. "I was hoping to ask you a couple of questions. I don't know if Dr. Yamaguchi mentioned it, but I've been assigned to your case by the embassy. It's standard procedure whenever a Canadian is hospitalized."

"Yeah, he mentioned that," Lepage replied, nodding at Yamaguchi, then glancing back at the window.

"Apart from making sure you're getting the treatment you need," Charlie continued, "which Doctor Yamaguchi here is taking care of, I need to get in touch with your family and friends back home, so I can keep them informed of your condition."

Lepage nodded, but offered nothing more.

"I haven't been able to locate any direct family from the information I have, but you have had some friends here in Tokyo who have come and visited. Aiko Kimura, for example."

Lepage nodded again. "Yeah, I met her this morn— I mean, she came to see me."

"There's another friend — Mike Seger, from Toronto," Charlie continued, watching for any recognition in Lepage's eyes at the name, but seeing none. "I think you spoke yesterday," he added, pausing until it became clear that Lepage was unsure of whether the conversation had taken place. "He'll be back later today." Charlie looked to Yamaguchi and back to Lepage. "Do you remember the night of the accident at all, Mr. Le ... can I call you Rob?"

"Sure, yeah, Rob's fine."

"Do you recall anything about the accident, Rob?"

He shook his head. "Just what they've told me here. I was in a car crash, and I guess I'm kind of lucky to be alive."

Charlie nodded. "I think that's probably true. Sounds like it was quite an accident. Do you know how long you've been in Tokyo?" Lepage seemed about to say something, then just shook his head. Charlie gave him an encouraging smile and tried again. "I understand from immigration records that you've been here for just under four months. What about your employer, do you know —"

"Look, Mr. ... Hillier. I can't remember *anything*, okay?" Charlie noticed Lepage's expression had changed, and his bright eyes look darker. He glanced out the window, before adding: "I can't even remember my own fucking name."

"Perhaps we should let Mr. Lepage rest," Yamaguchi suggested gently.

"I'm sorry," Lepage said, banging the side of the bed with his hand. "It's just so goddamn frustrating."

Charlie got up out of his chair. "You've got nothing to apologize for, and the doctor's probably right — we should leave

you to rest." He reached into his pocket and pulled out a business card, scribbling a number across the bottom. "This is my
card, and that's my cell number. If you remember something,
or if you need anything, please don't hesitate to get in touch,
day or night. Even if you just want to talk to someone."

Lepage nodded and accepted the card, looking at the red
and white of the little flag in the top corner. "So I guess I
really am Canadian, huh?"

Charlie smiled. "You bet."

"Thanks, I appreciate you coming by, and again, I'm sor—"

Charlie held up his hand. "You're in good hands here,
Rob. You just need some time, and some rest, and I'm sure
it'll all come back to you."

They were back at the reception area before Charlie spoke.
"I can't imagine what he must be going through — a real
nightmare. Do you really think it will come back to him?"

Yamaguchi nodded. "Did you notice he remembered
your name?"

"Is that good?"

"It means his short-term memory is already repairing itself."

"But he didn't seem to remember Mike Seger at all, let
alone talking to him yesterday."

"His memories may come and go," Yamaguchi said calmly.
"He may have difficulty recalling things that he had no
trouble describing just hours earlier. Though it may seem
unusual, this is … expected. I am confident he will regain
most of his memory, though there may be some gaps."

"How long do you think he'll be here?"

Yamaguchi shrugged. "His physical injuries, combined
with the after effects of the coma, will keep him in bed for
another week. After that, it will depend on how he responds
emotionally. Amnesia can be a very traumatic experience in
itself, and you can see that he's not unaffected."

"Can't say I blame him."

Yamaguchi smiled. "But he's young and physically strong, so I remain optimistic. He will have to be discharged into someone's care, though," he said.

Charlie considered the only two possibilities — Seger, who hadn't bothered to show up this morning at all, and the cagey Kimura. Neither seemed a great candidate, but maybe he was being too harsh. Besides, from what he could see, there was no one else.

"I should get back to the embassy. Please let me know if anything changes. And I'll have a talk with Seger, don't worry. If you see him first, just tell him to get in touch with me."

Charlie made his way out into the warm midmorning sun and considered emailing the driver, but decided to take the subway. He was getting more and more familiar with the efficient system, and it would probably end up being quicker, anyway. As he descended the escalator to the platform level, he thought of Lepage. It was great news that he was out of the coma and apparently on his way to a full recovery, but he just couldn't imagine how lost he must feel, knowing nothing of the past. As for Seger, he wondered what was behind his apparent insistence to have Lepage released into his custody when it was clearly premature.

Charlie had been back at the office for about an hour, and was on hold with an administrative assistant at Miton trying to work out a mutually acceptable time for a meeting to go over the proposal for the new staff quarters development, when Karen Fraser appeared at his door. Her usually playful expression had given way to something much more sombre. He put his hand over the receiver and mouthed "You okay?"

She nodded, but it was unconvincing. "Come see me when you're done," she whispered. A few interminable minutes later, with the property meeting tentatively set, he hung up the phone and headed two doors down, where he found Fraser in her chair, her eyes trained on her computer monitor.

"What's up?"

"What's the name of the Canadian guy — the friend who was in town to meet Lepage?"

"Mike Seger, why?"

"I got a call from the Tokyo Metropolitan Police. They've got a guy with a Canadian passport in that name."

"They're holding him? Why?"

"They're not holding him … he's in the morgue." Charlie stood frozen in place at the door as he processed the information, barely hearing Fraser confirm the obvious. "He's dead, Charlie."

CHAPTER 8

Charlie got off the train at Kasumigaseki Station and walked up the stairs to street level. He emerged onto a wide boulevard, bordered by tall, grey monolithic structures that suited their government tenants well, Charlie thought, as he noticed the usual assortment of dark suits and white shirts on the busy sidewalk. Unlike some other parts of the city though, virtually all of the men here wore ties. As he walked north toward the large green expanse that surrounded the Imperial Palace in the distance, he noticed one building that stood out from all the rest. Unlike its towering geometric neighbours, it was only a few stories tall, in red and yellowy brick and of an ornate Victorian design, in stark contrast to the sea of grey all around him. He checked his map and realized he was looking at the Justice building, which meant that the building opposite, on his side of the street, was the headquarters of the Tokyo Metropolitan Police. He approached the entrance, where a white-gloved guard in an immaculate blue uniform eyed him suspiciously. Charlie glanced at the gun at the man's waist and bowed in greeting.

"I'm here to meet with Inspector Kobayashi," he said, then presented the guard with his business card. The guard seemed a bit put off, but accepted the card after a moment's hesitation, then said something in Japanese accompanied by the universal hand gesture for *wait*. He returned from the little hut a few seconds later with an older man wearing a dark suit and tie, who gave a curt bow before speaking in a clipped and formal tone.

"Please, come this way."

Charlie followed him through the gate and into a reception area, where he was asked for his passport and given a visitor's pass. Then they were in an elevator on their way to the twenty-second floor. He followed his guide through a maze of doors and whitewashed hallways until they came to another reception area.

"Please," the man said, gesturing to one of the two chairs before disappearing through a secure door. He had just settled in the uncomfortable molded plastic chair when the door clicked open again and a woman in a dark pantsuit appeared, her black hair tied back in a severe bun. Her inquisitive eyes met his, and he couldn't help thinking he saw a glimmer of delight at the obvious surprise on Charlie's face.

"Charlie Hillier," he said, standing and bowing at the same time, still wondering if she was here for him. He had not been expecting a female inspector, and it occurred to him that she was the first woman he had seen since entering the building.

"Inspector Chikako Kobayashi," she replied. Whereas his greeting had been hurried and awkward, Kobayashi had managed an elegant bow while also offering her card in the standard, two-handed presentation, name facing out. Charlie accepted it, fumbled in his pocket for his card holder, and came up empty, realizing he had left it in his desk drawer. He fished a dog-eared card from his inside jacket pocket and tried to compensate for it with his most formal presentation. She gave him a friendly smile as she accepted the card.

"Thank you for coming on short notice," she said, in lightly accented English. "Please come with me."

She led the way back through the secure door, past a warren of hectic cubicles where phones rang and printers whirred. On the far side, she led him into a small meeting room with a table and four chairs. She gestured to one side of the table and sat opposite, in front of a single file folder. Its bottom edge was perfectly parallel with the edge of the table. Kobayashi was all business as she opened the file and carefully pulled out a document with Japanese text on one side and English on the other. Charlie made out the English title before she had begun to speak: *Police Report — Foreign National.*

"I regret to inform you that we believe a Canadian national was found dead early this morning in the Roppongi Hills prefecture." She paused, then pulled out some more papers from the folder and slid them across the table for Charlie to see. They were photocopies of Mike Seger's passport. "I also understand that you knew the man we consider to be the deceased," she continued. "Again, I am very sorry."

Charlie looked at the photocopied passport picture, which showed a much more serious version of the man he had briefly known. It occurred to him that he had just spoken with Seger yesterday, and now he was dead. "I didn't know him well," he said. "We met a few days ago, in connection with a consular case I've been working on."

Kobayashi nodded. "I understand that you are prepared to make a formal identification of the body?"

Charlie nodded. He hadn't been anywhere near a dead body up until a few years ago — a definitely unexpected and unwelcome part of his job with Foreign Affairs — but he was far from used to the idea and, whatever his recent experience, it didn't make the prospect of viewing Seger's corpse any more palatable. "Can I ask what happened? I mean, how did he die?"

"We were waiting to contact you before conducting any examinations, but we suspect ... a possible non-accidental death."

"Can you be more specific?" Charlie asked, wondering what the hell a possible non-accidental death looked like.

"He was found in an alley in a part of Roppongi where assaults and other crimes are not uncommon. He had no wallet, phone or ... jewellery."

"What did he die of?"

"Again, without the results of any examin ..." She paused, seeing his plaintive expression and abandoning the stock response. "He had a wound to his head — it might have been fatal."

She let him digest the information, then pulled out another set of papers and set them in front of him. "If you can please sign these, I can take you to do the identification."

He glanced at the forms and then looked back at her. She had the same, stoic expression on her face, but her eyes were softer — more empathetic, somehow. He picked up the pen and signed the forms in triplicate. "Where is he?"

"Downstairs. I can try to answer some of your questions when we're done. Please, follow me."

Charlie sat at the table in the cafeteria, the disturbing image of Mike Seger's lifeless body still fresh in his mind. The bruising on his face was consistent with Inspector Kobayashi's theory that he had been mugged, though whether his attackers had intended to kill him was less than clear. Charlie had only known Seger for a couple of days, but his death was no less unsettling. He looked up to see Kobayashi standing by the table. She had set a cup of coffee down in front of him and seemed to be waiting for his permission to sit.

"Thank you." He gestured to the chair opposite him.

"It is always an unpleasant task," she said as he sipped at the aromatic coffee. "But we are grateful for your co-operation."

He nodded, wondering how the Japanese bureaucracy would respond if no one had been available to identify Seger's body. Not well, he thought, considering the number of forms he had filled out after the identification was done. "So, do you normally handle liaison on consular files?"

Kobayashi nodded. "In some cases. I will be happy to assist you with the medical examiner's office if you decide to request an autopsy, and with the release of the body, once you have been in touch with the family."

Charlie considered the prospect of finding and contacting Seger's family back in Canada. It was bad enough in Lepage's case, having to deliver news that a loved one was in hospital. Suddenly, that sounded like good news. "How long do I have?"

"We will hold the body for as long as is necessary, Mr. Hillier."

"Call me Charlie, please." He noticed her awkward smile. "And what about the results of the blood tests, and any other preliminary medical findings?"

Kobayashi's face returned to its default setting of pure business. "I will let you know as soon as possible, of course. Tomorrow, we may have some preliminary results, I think."

Charlie nodded and sipped at his coffee. "Your English is very good."

"Thank you," she said, with another demure smile and a slight bow of her head. "I studied English literature at university, and also spent a year in Australia."

"Well, it was obviously time well spent. I have a feeling my Japanese won't be anywhere near as good as your English after a year here."

"I'm sure you are being modest."

He laughed, and noticed a slight grin on her otherwise impassive face that made him wonder if she was pulling his leg. The truth was, he spoke mostly English at the embassy and the best he could realistically hope for was to stumble through those occasions when he had no choice but to speak Japanese.

"Tell me something," he said, taking advantage of the moment of levity. "Do you think Seger was murdered?"

She frowned and spoke after a short pause. "I think it is too early to tell. Perhaps when the preliminary medical results are back, we will have a better idea."

"But you have a hunch." It was a statement, not a question, and it was based not on the bruises on Seger's face or any of the other information he had learned. There was something in Kobayashi's hesitation that told him she knew.

She seemed to weigh her response.

"How well did you know Mr. Seger?" she finally asked.

"Like I said, I just met him a few days ago, and I barely scratched the surface, if you know what I mean. Why do you ask?"

"He was found in an area where there is a great deal of prostitution."

Charlie considered the information and, somehow, was not surprised. It certainly didn't seem beyond the realm of possibility to imagine Seger in a strip club or a brothel.

"Murders are not common, but assaults are," Kobayashi continued.

"You mean it might have been an assault that accidentally went too far?"

"Let's talk again tomorrow, when the results are in," she said. "We shouldn't jump to conclusions."

"Good advice," he said, draining his coffee. "In the meantime, I'll make some calls and see if I can locate his next of kin."

"Until tomorrow then?"

Charlie stood and bowed. "Thank you, Inspector, you've been very helpful."

"Thank you, Mr. Hill—"

"Charlie, please," he said, with a smile.

"Very well, Charlie."

CHAPTER 9

Charlie got out of the embassy car in the underground drop-off point under Mori Tower, a sleek fifty-five-storey office building in Roppongi. He took the escalator up to the main level, noticing that the lineup was just as long at a Japanese Starbucks as anywhere else in the world as he inhaled the smell of freshly ground coffee beans. He promised himself a pit stop on the way out. Making his way over to the reception counter, he pulled out his passport.

"I have a meeting with Nippon Kasuga," he said, pulling up the meeting notice on his BlackBerry and searching for the name of the person he was to meet. "Mr. Etsuro Mashida."

"Passport, please." The young woman behind the counter tapped some efficient keystrokes before glancing at his passport and ultimately producing a visitor's badge. "Floor thirty-seven," she said, handing him the badge and pointing to the bank of elevators beyond the security gates.

"Thanks." He clipped the badge onto his jacket and walked through the guarded entrance and into a crowded elevator. He glanced at his watch and realized he was a few minutes early. Stepping out onto thirty-seven, he was greeted by another receptionist and offered a seat in one of the many soft leather chairs in the large reception area, the decor suggesting that Nippon Kasuga was doing just fine. Two men in the ubiquitous dark suit and white shirt ensemble sat on the other side of the room, the younger one immersed in his phone, while the other, who looked to be in his sixties and wore a pale-blue tie, read a newspaper.

Charlie turned his attention to the table in front of him, glancing at the firm's brochure. He had done some online research on Nippon Kasuga, and from what he could tell they were an established securities firm that had been around for about fifteen years before being gobbled up five years ago by a larger competitor. They had retained the smaller company's name in the merger though, which was listed on the Nikkei. It was also a member of a number of Japanese, Asia-Pacific, and International financial associations. Cliff Redford had said something about Japanese business culture being all about the facade, and the fact that a firm hadn't been caught at something didn't mean they were squeaky clean. Not that Charlie had any reason to believe something was amiss with Nippon Kasuga, though he did find it odd that they seemed to be completely disinterested in the fate of one of their employees, or contractors — or whatever it was that Rob Lepage was to them. He looked up as a man in his early forties came around the corner and made his way to where Charlie was sitting.

"Mr. Hillier?"

Charlie smiled and got up. "Mr. Mashida?"

"Yes. Welcome." Mashida bowed and produced a business card. Charlie accepted, and this time he was ready with his own to exchange after a quick bow. All in all, his delivery was pretty good, and he silently congratulated himself for his improving form.

"Please," Mashida said, leading the way back past reception, along a rounded hallway, and past a series of occupied meeting rooms. At the fourth door, Mashida opened it and led him into a small meeting room with a spectacular view of Roppongi and the northwestern sprawl of Tokyo beyond.

"Great view," Charlie commented, as Mashida followed his gaze. He wasn't sure about his geography, but he thought the mountain in the distance looked familiar.

"Mount Fuji," Mashida said, confirming Charlie's suspicion. "We can only see it on a clear day. Today, you are in luck." He pointed out some landmarks and then they made their way over to the table, exchanging pleasantries for a few minutes before Charlie decided to get to the subject of the meeting. He always felt that his transition from banter to business was awkward and wondered whether he came across as blunt to his Japanese host. If he did, Mashida gave no indication.

"I wanted to talk to you about Rob Lepage."

Mashida nodded. "Of course. It was a tragic accident, but I am very glad to hear that Mr. Lepage will make a full recovery."

"Well that's certainly what we're hoping for," Charlie said, wondering if Mashida knew something he didn't. Dr. Yamaguchi had certainly been optimistic about Lepage's recovery, but the fact remained that the young banker didn't even know his own name. "I understand you sponsored him, for immigration purposes, so I assume he was working for your company?"

Mashida smiled, but there was something in his expression that betrayed a discomfort with the topic. "Mr. Lepage is what we call a foreign consultant. He was brought in because of his specialized expertise."

"And I understand he'd been working with Nippon Kasuga since coming to Tokyo about four months ago?"

"Yes, that's correct."

"Do you mind me asking what his specific expertise is?" Charlie watched for a reaction, but this time, Mashida gave nothing away.

"North American markets, and financial systems, mostly."

It sounded a bit vague to Charlie. Then again, he knew next to nothing about global finance. "And how long is he expected to stay in Tokyo, assuming he makes a full recovery?"

Mashida shifted slightly in his chair. "He was to be here for a year, initially. After that, it would depend on finding a mutually agreeable arrangement."

Charlie went through some more questions about Lepage's work, some of which Mashida clearly didn't want to get into, citing client confidentiality. As for the rest, Charlie got similarly vague answers, but whether it was his own lack of understanding of securities practice or an attempt by Mashida to be deliberately obtuse, he wasn't sure.

"Do you know what he was doing on the evening of the accident?"

Mashida shook his head. "I understand he was on his own time. We don't interest ourselves with our employees' activities outside the workplace."

"I just wondered if you knew any of the details about the accident, or the events leading up to it. Have the police spoken to you?"

Mashida seemed to recoil at the thought. "Why would they?"

Charlie shrugged. "Just to try to get a sense of what happened. It seems as though no one has much information about the accident."

"Not unusual in the case of accidents, Mr. Hillier."

Charlie smiled. "No, I suppose not." He noticed Mashida glancing at his watch and figured he was running out of time. "Do you know another Canadian named Michael Seger?"

Mashida shook his head. "I don't know this name — Seger. In what way is this person connected to Mr. Lepage?"

"He's a friend of Mr. Lepage's." Charlie decided to omit the fact that he was lying on a slab in the morgue, most likely as a result of foul play. He pulled out a photocopy of Seger's passport picture and put it on the table. "He visited him in the hospital."

Mashida barely glanced at the picture before shaking his head. "I have never seen this man before."

"Just a long shot," Charlie said with a smile, tucking the picture back into his pocket.

Mashida gave a little shrug and Charlie proceeded to ask a few more questions about Nippon Kasuga's work and Lepage's prospects when his recovery was complete.

"We hope he will return very soon," Mashida said. "Until then, we will continue to cover all costs related to his medical care," he made a point of adding.

"That's good of you," Charlie said, though he wasn't sure if it represented anything above and beyond standard practice for any Japanese employer. "I want to thank you for your time today."

Mashida stood and led him back out to reception, where they parted ways with a formal bow. As he rode the elevator back down, Charlie reflected on the meeting. He hadn't learned much, other than getting confirmation that Lepage worked in a world that was very foreign to Charlie, and the fact that Mashida didn't know Seger, which was no surprise. All in all, it had been a necessary but largely fruitless exchange. Maybe Kobayashi would get back to him soon about the results of the preliminary medical examination on Seger's body. He was back at lobby level, on his way down the escalator to fulfill his promise to himself to pick up an aromatic coffee, when his phone went off. He saw a local number and hit accept call.

"I'm very sorry to disturb you, Mr. Hillier."

Charlie recognized the voice at once. "Inspector Kobayashi? You're not disturbing me at all. What can I do for you?"

"I have some results that may be of interest to you, regarding Mr. Seger."

Charlie considered his schedule and quickly dismissed the administrative meeting at eleven. This was far more important. "I'm just leaving Roppongi now. Do you want me to meet you at your headquarters?"

"If it is convenient for you, then yes."

"I'll be there as soon as I can."

"I will leave your name at the entrance."

Charlie hung up the phone and kept walking past the Starbucks. He had detected a difference in Kobayashi's tone since yesterday. Excitement was too strong a word, but the reserve in her voice had failed to conceal a heightened interest.

Charlie hustled up the steps of Kasumigaseki Station and set off north toward the police headquarters building, wondering what news Kobabyashi had to deliver. He didn't have to wait long, as she was waiting for him as he came through the general reception area.

"Thank you for coming," she said with the usual bow. Charlie reciprocated and followed her through the secure doors. This time, though, instead of taking the elevators up to the homicide department, she led him to a little meeting room on the main floor, just down the hall from general reception. She had the same thin file folder under her arm as she shut the door behind them.

"So you got some results from the medical examination?"

She nodded and took out a sheet of paper that looked like a lab report, or would except for the Japanese text that was illegible to Charlie. "There was a considerable amount of alcohol in Mr. Seger's system," she began, which didn't sound surprising to Charlie. From what he had heard of nightlife in Roppongi, it was almost expected. And Seger's weathered features and gravelly voice, tinged by years of cigarette smoke, had given the impression of someone who enjoyed life and all of its vices. He was a big guy, though, and didn't seem the type not to be able to hold his liquor.

"How considerable?"

Kobayashi glanced at the lab results. "Point one three percent blood alcohol."

"Hmm," Charlie said. It was almost twice the legal limit in Canada for driving, but for a practiced drinker like Seger, not so much as to be disabling. Something in Kobayashi's expression told him there was more, though. He looked at her and waited for her to continue.

"There was something else in his blood, traces of fluni-trazepam."

Charlie frowned. "What's that?"

"It is also known as Rohypnol," she said.

"You mean … roofies?" he asked, eliciting a puzzled look from Kobayashi. "That's what we call it in Canada — or the date rape drug. It has the effect of incapacitating someone, so they wake up unaware of what's happened to them."

Kobayashi nodded. "Yes, that is the effect. It is unfortunate, but incidents involving this drug are not uncommon, especially in the part of Roppongi where Mr. Seger was found. Certain criminal elements take advantage of the victim, but violence of this nature is not usually part of the pattern."

Charlie had been warned about these types of incidents in his personal security briefing. The description was similar to Kobayashi's in that violence was not the primary concern. Rather, the victim's plastic was usually lifted and a number of items charged on it before it was tucked back in the victim's wallet and he was sent on his way in a cab, barely conscious. In Seger's case, either something had gone wrong, or this wasn't just the usual fleecing. He could imagine Seger putting up a fight, but it was hard to tell how he might have reacted under the influence of the drug.

"What about cause of death?"

Again, Kobayashi glanced at the report, but it was clear she knew the answer. "Trauma to the back of the head, possibly by a rounded object."

"Why would they drug him and then beat him to death?" Charlie wondered aloud. "It doesn't really make sense."

"Perhaps he resisted, or fell," she said, obviously considering the same possibilities that Charlie had a few seconds earlier. But as they looked at each other in silence in the seconds that followed, it was clear that neither of them was buying it. "Were you able to contact any of Mr. Seger's family members?"

Charlie shook his head. "I'm afraid I'm O for two." He noticed her reaction and added: "I mean, I'm not having much luck locating family members, either for Mr. Lepage or Mr. Seger. I was hoping maybe Rob Lepage's employer might have known Seger, but I was just there and ... no luck."

"Who is Mr. Lepage's employer?"

"Nippon Kasuga — a securities trading firm," he said, seeing from her reaction that she hadn't heard of them. "I'm waiting for some callbacks from Canada though," he added, "so I may have something to go on soon, with any luck. I'd like to get someone to request an autopsy, under the circumstances."

"Well, we will await instructions, and Mr. Seger's body will be held here until then — you need not worry."

"Thank you." He glanced at the paper on the table between them. "Nothing else out of the ordinary in there?"

She shook her head. "Mr. Seger's cardiovascular health was not optimal, but he was otherwise generally fit."

"So he didn't just drop dead from a heart attack or something?"

"No. I understand your wanting an autopsy, but I must warn you, it may not reveal anything more about how he died."

"I know." Charlie frowned. "I just have a feeling something's not quite right."

"You seem as though you have experience with these matters."

"You could say that," he said, deciding not to get into the other suspicious deaths he had come across in recent years. He had no objective reason to suspect anything other than the most likely explanation of Seger's death — a random scam gone wrong — but he couldn't shake the feeling that there was something more just below the surface. "Well, I won't keep you. Thank you again for this information, and for your time."

"I have been asked to provide whatever assistance I can to your embassy in this matter," Kobayashi said as they reached the secure doors again.

"I appreciate it." As they bowed by the door, he noticed that although she was wearing her hair in the same severe bun as the day before, there was something different about her overall look. Was she wearing makeup? And he detected a light floral scent that he hadn't noticed the day before.

"Goodbye, Mr. Hillier."

"Charlie," he said with a smile.

CHAPTER 10

Charlie held the phone receiver to his ear as he listened to the ringing at the other end for the eighth time. He was mentally double-checking the time difference between Tokyo and Vancouver when he heard an abrupt click followed by a female voice at the other end.

"Hello?" The voice seemed breathless.

"Is this Maria Taylor?"

"Yes." The speaker was still catching her breath, but he could tell from her guarded tone that he had better get to the point fast.

"I'm calling about your brother, Michael Seger."

There was a pause at the other end, and Charlie was on the verge of asking whether she was still there when the woman spoke again. "What about him?"

Charlie detected a distinct shift in her tone, from guarded to downright hostile, at the mention of Seger's name. He knew the Surrey RCMP had already been in touch with Seger's only living next of kin a few hours earlier, so he wasn't sure what to expect when he called, but the detached, almost indifferent air was a surprise.

"I'm very sorry for your loss."

"And you are?"

"I'm sorry. My name's Charlie Hillier. I'm a consular officer at the Canadian embassy in Tokyo. Were you aware that your brother was in Tokyo?"

"Like I told the cops, I haven't seen my brother in years."

The conversation was not following the course that Charlie had predicted. "Well, I want to assure you that I'm here to assist you in making the necessary arrange—"

"I don't think you understand. I'm not interested in any arrangements for my brother. He's been dead to me for almost a decade."

Charlie tried again. "Well, I'm sure you'll want to be involved in —"

"Look, Mr. … what was your name again?"

"Hillier. Charlie Hillier"

"Right. I know this is gonna sound cold, Mr. Hillier, but my brother and I were not close. Not in the least, and I am not interested in any arrangements to get him back to Canada. For all I care you can let the Japanese cremate him or whatever they do over there. I really don't care."

"Mrs. Taylor, I'm sure this is upsetting news. Maybe I should call back tomorrow."

"You can call back tomorrow, next week, or next year if you want, but it's not going to change anything."

Charlie tried a different tack. "Are you aware of the circumstances of your brother's death?"

"Sounds like he went on a bender and got mugged. A real shocker for my little brother, Mike."

"Did the police mention the possibility of an autopsy to you?"

"I told them not to bother. I figure Mike probably got what he deserved. Look, I've got to go pick up my kid in a couple of minutes …"

"Maybe I could call back later, or tomorrow?"

There was an audible sigh at the other end of the phone. "You sound like a nice guy, Mr. Hillier, and I'm sure you're just doing your job. If there are forms I need to sign as his sister, then I guess I'll sign them, but you can go through my lawyer for that. Please don't call here again."

"Mrs. Taylor ..." he began, then stopped, realizing he was listening to a dial tone. "Shit." He put down the phone and looked up to see Karen Fraser at his door.

"Everything all right?"

Charlie shrugged. "That was Mike Seger's sister."

"The guy they found in Roppongi?"

He nodded. "She doesn't want anything to do with him — her own brother. Said he was dead to her. She basically told me to tell the Japanese to toss him in an incinerator."

Fraser whistled. "That's pretty cold. Must be a hell of a family story there."

"Uh-huh. But whatever it is won't help my consular case." Charlie leaned back in his chair and sighed. "I was hoping to get her to request an autopsy."

Fraser came in and sat in one of the chairs on the other side of his desk. "You think that's necessary? I mean, we pretty much know what happened, don't we?"

"Maybe. The blood test showed there was Rohypnol and booze in Seger's system, which certainly seems consistent with him having wandered into the wrong bar in Roppongi. What's strange is that he ended up dead."

Fraser was frowning. "I suppose it *is* pretty rare for a foreigner to actually end up dead, as opposed to ripped off. You have another theory?"

He shook his head. "I've got nothing, which is why I was hoping an autopsy might give me some clues. He seems to have died as a result of a blow to the head by a rounded object."

"You talk to the RCMP?"

He nodded. "Sure. I've got a follow-up call with someone in Ottawa tonight at nine."

"The time difference is a killer when you have to deal with HQ," she said, getting back up. "Well, good luck. Oh," she added, pausing by the door, "the reason I dropped by.... Have you got your costume for Friday?"

"Costume?"

"I didn't tell you it was a Halloween party?"

Charlie's face said it all. "Do they even celebrate Halloween here?"

"Are you kidding? They go crazy, but don't worry, you don't have to do anything elaborate. Just paint your face if you want."

"Right," he said as she smiled and disappeared into the hall. He had forgotten about the weekend get-together and, come to think of it, he couldn't recall Fraser mentioning that it was a costume party. The idea of scouring costume shops for something suitable didn't really appeal to him, but he couldn't very well go without a costume. Apart from sticking out like a sore thumb, he'd come off as a spoilsport. A vampire costume was pretty easy to put together, and he could always fall back on something he'd tried in a pinch many years before — taping fake court documents to a suit and going as a lawsuit. His mental inventory of what he would need for a pirate costume was interrupted by a little ding on his computer, announcing a new incoming message. Recognizing Dr. Yamaguchi's email address, he leaned forward and scanned the message, asking Charlie to drop by the hospital this afternoon, at Rob Lepage's request. He wondered what Lepage wanted to see him for, then double-checked that he didn't have any meetings after lunch, before sending back a reply confirming that he would come over around two.

He decided a cup of coffee was in order and was halfway to the machine at the end of the hall when he heard his name and turned to see the RCMP liaison officer walking toward him.

"Oh, hi, Steve." Charlie wondered whether Steve Fortier's presence had something to do with the call to Ottawa that they were supposed to make together at nine. It crossed his mind that it might also have to do with his recent conversation with Seger's sister, but he had only been off the phone with her for ten minutes. "I was just getting a coffee. You want one?"

"I'm good, thanks. Listen, I was just going over this Seger guy's file and something isn't adding up."

"Really? What is it?"

"You said he told you he made a side trip to Japan to visit Lepage from Hong Kong, right?"

"Yeah." Charlie nodded, growing more curious by the minute.

"Well, I ran his passport, and he came direct to Narita from Montreal."

"He wasn't in Hong Kong?"

Fortier shook his head. "Not in the last few months. He spent a week there about two months ago, and hasn't been back since."

Charlie frowned. "That's weird. I'm sure he told me he came via Hong Kong. Why would he lie about that?"

"I don't know. And there's something else — this company," he added, looking at a photocopy of Seger's business card that Charlie had given him. "Paragon Properties. It has an address in Montreal, but I can't find any record of incorporation anywhere. It *was* registered in Hong Kong, but it was discontinued two years ago." He produced a photocopy of a corporate registry search.

"Can I see that?"

Fortier handed it over. "You can keep that. I have the PDF."

Charlie scanned the document, confirming the name was identical to the one on Seger's business card, which listed the company as having a head office in Montreal and another office in Hong Kong. "What do you think this means?"

"Could mean a few things," Fortier said, with a shrug. "Maybe he ran out of cards and was using his old ones, but that wouldn't explain why he told you he was in Hong Kong before coming to Tokyo."

"Or?"

"Or maybe Seger was lying, both about the company and his travel plans."

"Why would he do that?"

Fortier shrugged. "That I don't know."

Charlie stepped off the elevator onto the fifth floor of the Tokyo Medical University Hospital at precisely two o'clock, according to his watch. He was proud of the fact that he had timed the trip so well, considering he had opted for the subway rather than bothering a driver. He knew it probably had more to do with the efficiency of the Tokyo Metro than his own skill, but he had to acknowledge that he was getting more and more comfortable with getting around in his new home. He asked for Yamaguchi at the reception desk and was told he was on rounds, but that he had left instructions for Charlie to be brought in to see Lepage. After signing a visitor's log, he was led by a nurse he had seen before down the hall to Lepage's door. Entering the room, Lepage turned to greet him. The vacant look that Charlie had noticed the last time he had visited was gone, replaced by an intensity in the banker's eyes that Charlie quickly realized was intense concentration.

"Charlie," he said, after a slight hesitation. "Right?"

He nodded and smiled. "So you remember. That's got to be a good sign."

Lepage's expression conveyed a mixture of satisfaction and relief. "Yeah, the doctor says my short term memory's fine, but I still don't trust it myself."

"All I can say is that from what I've seen of Dr. Yamaguchi, he seems to know what he's talking about," Charlie said. "If he says it's fine, I'd tend to think he's right."

Lepage smiled. "I guess you're right. I am pretty lucky."

"He said you wanted to talk to me about something?"

Lepage seemed to hesitate for a split second, then plucked something off the side table and handed it to Charlie."

"What's this?"

"It's the key to my apartment."

Charlie looked at the key card, then back at Lepage.

"I was wondering if you could check it out for me. Just make sure everything's in order." He seemed embarrassed at having to make the request.

"Um, sure. I can do that."

"Dr. Yamaguchi said visual cues can be really good for memory, and since I can't really go anywhere right now," Lepage continued, pointing to the cast on his leg, "I was hoping while you were there, you might find something to bring back — like a picture or something — that might help me to remember."

Charlie nodded. He was thinking the idea was sound, except for his own involvement, considering they hardly knew each other. He would have thought Lepage would have asked Kimura first.

"I don't want to impose," Lepage said, as though reading his mind.

"No, it's no problem, really."

"I'd ask Mike," he said, picking up a business card from the bedside table and tapping it with his finger. "But I'm having a hard time tracking him down."

Charlie froze at the sight of the card and its familiar logo. He assumed — although he didn't really know why, now — that someone had broken the news that his friend had turned up dead.

"What?" Lepage asked, in response to the look on Charlie's face.

"I ... it's just that ... well, I'm afraid I have some bad news."

"About what?"

"About Mike," he said, wondering whether he should hold off breaking the news until he spoke to Yamaguchi. Lepage had already been through a lot, and he didn't want to make things worse. Then again, he supposed Lepage would find out sooner or later.

"What about him?"

"You, uh ... so, I guess you remember talking to him, a few days ago?"

Lepage looked puzzled. "Yeah, why do you ask?"

Charlie hesitated, deciding there was nothing to gain by asking Lepage why he didn't seem to remember the meeting with Seger just twenty-four hours after it had occurred. He obviously remembered it now. "Mike, uh ... he died the other night. The police are still looking into it. He might have been mugged."

The look on Lepage's face was a mix of shock and confusion. "I ... I can't believe it."

"I really am sorry," Charlie offered. "I know you two were friends, and I'm sorry to spring it on you like this. I thought you knew."

They sat in silence for a while, then Lepage shook his head. "I can't ..."

Charlie waited for more, but Lepage was silent again. "Can't what, Rob?" he prompted gently.

"I can't even remember him … before the accident, I mean. I think we were pretty good friends, and I've got … nothing." He shook his head, glanced at the business card, and then looked out the window. "No recollection at all. How can I feel grief for someone I can't even remember?"

Charlie shifted from one foot to the other. "I'm sure it must be awful, but like we were saying, you have to have faith that your memory will come back — and the medical signs are all good. Maybe I can find something in your apartment that will bring it all back for you," he added.

Lepage slowly nodded. "I sure hope so."

"Do you want me to get in touch with Aiko, maybe bring her —"

"No."

The speed and tone of the response was as clear an indication that Lepage could give that he had avoided assigning the task to Kimura for a reason. Charlie decided not to delve.

"No problem. I can go tonight." He stopped himself from asking Lepage for the address just in time, realizing he had the information on file already. He had just put the key in his pocket when he heard the hinges on the door creak and Aiko Kimura appeared behind him. She glanced from Lepage to Charlie and back, her hard glare softening slightly as she approached Lepage and took him by the hand, before leaning over and kissing him on the cheek.

"How do you feel?"

"I'm good. Charlie and I were just talking about the latest news back in Canada. You know, trying to shake something loose," he said, tapping his forehead.

"Of course," Kimura said. She shed her colourful scarf and grey three-quarter-length coat and draped them over a chair, taking a seat on the edge of the bed. Her form-fitting white blouse and the black leather pants she wore tucked into the same stiletto boots she had worn the other day left no doubt that she had the figure of a swimsuit model underneath. Charlie was intrigued by Lepage's little charade, but decided there were any number of reasons why someone might not want a girlfriend rummaging through their apartment, especially if he couldn't remember her beyond the past few days.

"Well, I was just leaving." Charlie moved away from the foot of the bed.

"You don't have to go," Kimura said, her tone and body language suggesting the opposite.

"I should really get back to the office. I'll check in on you again soon though," he said to Lepage, making his way to the door.

"Thanks for dropping by, Charlie," he heard Lepage say as he reached the hallway and headed quickly for the elevators, feeling his pocket to make sure the apartment key was in there.

CHAPTER II

"You're sure this is it?" Charlie looked out the window at the large, glass-clad building in Harajuku. Addresses in Tokyo, especially residential ones, were difficult for Westerners to follow, so he had given Rob Lepage's address to one of the embassy drivers rather than run the risk of going to the wrong place.

"Yes, this is Omote-sando Hills Residences."

"Thanks. I can make my own way back," Charlie said, getting out of the van and instantly feeling foolish as he caught sight of the name emblazoned on the side of the building, next to the entrance. He took the key card out of his pocket and went up to the front door, steppi SACCADE ng inside the ultra-modern lobby and heading over to an electronic directory. There were only ten floors, which was a small building for Tokyo, so it didn't take him long to find Rob Lepage's name next to apartment 903. He took the elevator up to the ninth floor and followed the numbers until he found himself in front of Lepage's door. He felt like a bit of an intruder as he slid the key in the lock and turned the handle.

On the other side of the door, he found himself in a foyer that was spacious by Tokyo standards. The foyer and the hall beyond were lit by a soft light; as he walked forward he found a wall switch that, when touched, flooded the room with bright light. He hadn't known what to expect of the state of the apartment, given that Lepage had not been here in over a week, but the air seemed fresh and everything was immaculate. He walked into a living room furnished with a couple of bright, modular sofas and centred by a glass table. As he made his way through the room, he had the sense of being in a boutique hotel. There wasn't a speck of dust, and everything was arranged perfectly. The other thing he noticed was the lack of anything personal on the table, or on the shelf by the window. There were no plants, pictures, or other knick-knacks on the single bookcase. The kitchen was similarly spotless, and Charlie realized that Lepage must have a housekeeper who had been making regular visits despite the occupant's absence and who may not even know Lepage was in hospital. There were no dishes in the sink, no water glasses on the counter, and no magnets or papers on the stainless steel fridge. Nothing to disturb the perfect sterility of the place.

Charlie continued on into another little hallway that led to the bedrooms, the first done up as a guest room. The second had been converted to a study, with a large corner desk topped with a desktop computer, printer, and three monitors arranged in a row. Even here — where he assumed Lepage must spend most of his time given the nature of his work and the fact that he apparently didn't spend much time at Nippon Kasuga's offices — there was little evidence of a human presence. There was no clutter, no loose papers or pens, much less photos or posters on the wall. Apart from the desk, there was a small bookcase with neatly ordered boxes on every shelf. He decided to come back to the room later, and continued on to the master bedroom at the rear of the apartment. It was centred by a large bed, the sheets tucked with military precision. There were matching side tables — adorned only by a pair of lamps and some sort of docking station that included a digital clock on the left table — and a leather club chair in the corner. Again, there were no pictures or other personal effects anywhere that he could see, and he was beginning to think his task of finding something to jog Lepage's memory was an impossible one. What was Charlie supposed to tell him if he returned to the hospital empty-handed? And what did the place say about Lepage — that he was obsessive-compulsive, or that he had an overzealous housekeeper?

Charlie flicked on the light in the ensuite and found a corner whirlpool tub and shower enclosure next to a toilet with so many buttons and features that it seemed capable of launching a satellite. (There had been a similar model in his hotel room and he had learned that they were standard fare here in Japan.) He surveyed the gleaming fixtures and popped open the mirrored cabinet above the sink to reveal a spare toothbrush, some aftershave lotion and hair gel, a couple of antiperspirant sticks, and a bottle of Tylenol. No prescriptions or anything else of a personal or peculiar nature. This was getting ridiculous, he thought, as he made his way back into the bedroom and over to the walk-in closet. Here he found a half-dozen neatly arranged suits, some sport coats and pants of different shades of grey and blue, arranged over a selection of dress shoes that gleamed like mirrors. A quick search through the drawers was as fruitless as the same exercise everywhere else in this apartment — absolutely nothing to distinguish it as the home of Rob Lepage as opposed to anyone else, either in Tokyo or on the planet. Was Lepage some kind of cyborg?

Returning to the room converted into a home office, Charlie pulled one of the storage boxes off the shelf and glanced at the neatly-arranged file folders inside. He plucked one out and skimmed its contents — correspondence from the Tokyo Stock Exchange regarding the listing of a high-tech company, some approval letters and other correspondence from brokers and banks. He flipped through the contents for a while and, finding nothing of particular interest, he moved on to the other folders, which contained the same sort of materials. He went through the other boxes and after five minutes, he had come up with precisely nothing of interest. He took out a letter addressed to Lepage at Nippon Kasuga, not because of its content, but because he thought it might jog something in Lepage's memory. Besides, it was the only thing he had seen in the whole apartment that had his name on it.

Turning to the desk, Charlie saw that the computer's power light was on, so when he clicked the mouse, the screen came to life. Unfortunately, it was the standard password page. He considered calling the hospital to get it from Lepage, but decided that might be beyond the scope of what Lepage had asked Charlie to do, even if he did remember the password. He looked at the letter in his hand, thinking it would be pretty pathetic if that was the only thing he could bring back, and decided to take another look around the office. He pulled out the top drawer and riffled through an assortment of Post-it Notes, paper clips, and pens. The pens were different colours but otherwise the same, except for one. He pulled the oversize blue, red, and white pen from the back of the drawer and found himself looking at the familiar logo of the Montreal Canadiens hockey team. So Lepage was a Habs fan. Charlie was excited by the possibility that the pen might be just the kind of thing that might actually stir a memory. It seemed a little odd for a Toronto native to be a Montreal fan — the two teams being the ultimate arch-enemies. That reminded him that he had meant to ask

Lepage about whether he spoke French, given Yamaguchi's observation of his first words when he had emerged from the coma. But he had been preoccupied with delivering the news of Seger's death, and then Kimura had arrived…. He would have to remember to ask Lepage about it when he went back to the hospital.

After completing his search of the other drawers and finding nothing of interest, Charlie returned to the bedroom and went through the dresser drawers again. He selected a couple pairs of cufflinks, as well as two ties, thinking they, too, might be cues for something. On his way back to the entrance, he spotted a thin pile of mail on the hall table, neatly arranged next to a lamp. There were four pieces of mail in all: two of the envelopes looked like junk mail, with indecipherable Japanese characters, a flyer for an Omote-sando sushi restaurant, and a postcard with a picture of a snow-capped mountain on the front. He picked it up and examined the photo, recognizing it as Mount Fuji, and flipped it over. Other than Lepage's handwritten address, it was blank, which struck him as odd. He put it back on the little pile, then changed his mind and took it back, thinking it might have some meaning for Lepage.

He found a plastic bag in one of the kitchen drawers for the items he had selected and left the apartment, heading for the Omote-sando Metro Station. He didn't have much time to make it home for a quick shower before changing into his impromptu costume and meeting up with Fraser's gang in Shinjuku. He would drop by the hospital tomorrow and see if his slim pickings from Lepage's apartment would be of any use. Yamaguchi had thought it was worth a shot, and though he had been disappointed not to find some photos, Charlie hoped maybe the pen might evoke something. You never knew.

If he usually felt a little self-conscious as the only Westerner on the subway, being the only person dressed as a vampire wasn't making Charlie feel any better. He had felt downright ridiculous getting on the train in the very proper bureaucratic district of Akasaka and, taking a seat between two men in suits who did their very best not to make eye contact, he had begun to seriously question his decision to accept Fraser's invitation. But he had relaxed a bit as they headed west and a sprinkling of other people in costume appeared on the platforms and joined his car. There were all sorts of outfits, but there was definitely a theme in the women's costumes — short, frilled skirts and striped tights, like some of the cartoon characters he had seen in front of the stores in Akihabara.

By the time he came up out of the subway station in Shinjuku, he felt much better. He found the landmark Fraser had given him easily, at the eastern entrance, and was relieved when she appeared with her husband and four other people a few minutes later. Charlie breathed a sigh of relief that he hadn't opted for a pirate costume, as Jeff Fraser was a dead ringer for Johnny Depp. The other four were dressed as a nurse, a nun, a cartoon character of some kind, and a cowboy — he soon realized the nun was male and the cowboy female. After the introductions, they made their way to the restaurant where the rest of their group awaited. Charlie chatted nervously with the nurse as they made their way along the brightly-lit but narrow streets, deeper and deeper into the entertainment district. Charlie's nerves had nothing to do with his costume — the majority of the people on the street here were in costume — but the realization that the average age of Fraser's friends seemed to be a decade or more younger than him. He tried to be positive, but he wondered how the evening was going to turn out. Along the way, Charlie learned that the cowboy and the nun were American, and the nurse was Australian. By the time they got to the restaurant, they were all chatting easily.

After a few drinks and a good meal of meat that they cooked themselves on a grill in the middle of their table — which he learned was called *yakiniku* — they set out on a bar-hop that took them through some of the tiniest bars in Tokyo, a few seating only a half dozen people at a time. By the time they made it to a batting cage they were all pretty buzzed, but everyone was game to try hitting a hundred-kilometre-an-hour fastball. Charlie surprised himself by making decent contact a few times and got some cheers, but Fraser's husband stole the show with a handful of homers. After that, it was on to a little karaoke bar, where Charlie found himself belting out a couple of Bryan Adams songs.

He was so caught up in his own alcohol-emboldened performance that he didn't notice one of the two Americans they had met at the bar sidle up to the nurse. By the time his number was done and he returned to their table at the far end of the bar, the two were ensconced in the far corner, and Charlie was left to half perch on the end of the bench seat, feeling like the loser in a game of musical chairs.

As the evening wound down, he watched as the newly formed couple slid into the back seat with the nun and the cowboy, while Charlie was hustled into the back of another cab, next to the Frasers. They went their separate ways back at the staff compound, and Charlie could hear giggling as Fraser and her husband negotiated the external stairs to their apartment, while he slid the key in and opened his door, entered the darkened living room, and slumped onto the couch. He told himself he didn't need the potential fallout of a loosely work-related hook-up that had the real possibility of going wrong; and the other guy had to be at least ten years younger than him. Besides, other than some friendly banter throughout the evening, he hadn't given her any indication that he was interested in her romantically. But none of that made the image of her sitting next to her American companion in the back of the cab any less haunting.

He gazed around his empty apartment and realized that, like Rob Lepage's, it lacked any sense of home or expression of his own personality. The only difference was that his place was filled with government-supplied furniture, as opposed to the high-end stuff in Lepage's apartment. In fact, the only difference between him and Lepage was that Lepage was apparently rich. Both were equally alone, although in Lepage's case it was due to likely temporary amnesia, whereas Charlie had no such excuse. In any event, Lepage had the sexy, if somewhat enigmatic, Aiko Kimura waiting patiently on the edge of his bed for him to remember her name. Charlie should be so lucky.

He debated getting a beer from the fridge but decided against it — he had had enough. He had the first inkling of the amount of alcohol he had consumed when he went to brush his teeth and the bathroom started spinning. Then he remembered drinking sake at the end of the meal at the restaurant and felt the first hint of alarm about what his morning would be like, given the highballs at the karaoke bar and the beers he'd had along the way.

He was about to flop into bed when he decided to check his email one last time. He clicked his BlackBerry to life and found himself staring at a message from his brother in St. John's. On its surface, it was the usual greeting, just checking in. But Charlie knew the subtext: *What the hell are you doing in Tokyo?* It occurred to him that the last time he saw his brother, Brian Hillier had tried to persuade him not to go to Moscow, but to come work for him instead. His brother's building supplies company was booming, and he didn't seem too concerned that Charlie lacked any relevant experience whatsoever. Charlie had wondered at the time whether Brian was making the offer for their parents' sake, who couldn't fathom why Charlie would suddenly decide in middle age to traipse off to the four corners of the Earth. Given the way things had turned out in Moscow, Charlie thought with a grim chuckle as he stared at the email, he might have been better off accepting the offer. But whatever his brother's motives, he had known then — just as he knew now — that he could never accept. To do so would be to admit defeat, to be permanently compared — unfavourably — with his successful older brother and his perfect family. Charlie wasn't sure what Tokyo had to offer, but he wasn't prepared to throw in the towel just yet. He turned off the BlackBerry and set it on his night table, deciding he would wait until he was a little more clear-headed before sending off a response.

Collapsing on his pillow, he closed his eyes and fought the urge to feel sorry for himself as the image of his ex-wife's face appeared. He forced his mind to replace it, and for a moment his mind went blank before another face emerged, her delicate Japanese features calming him as he drifted off to sleep with the memory of that distinctive floral scent lingering in his nostrils.

CHAPTER 12

Despite the overcast sky, Charlie was squinting behind his sunglasses as he made his way along Aoyama-dori mid-morning on Saturday. He had started off the day by suffering through a breakfast of coffee and orange juice before emptying the contents of his stomach into his toilet bowl. Things could only get better after that, but he still felt fragile. He popped another mint in his mouth as he reached the Metro station, descended to platform level, and bought a ticket. Arriving at the same station where he had met Fraser and the rest of the gang the night before, he hurried past the meeting point toward the hospital, clutching the plastic bag with the pathetic assortment of quasi-personal effects from Lepage's apartment and wondering if it was even worth giving to him. He tried to ignore these doubts as he took the elevator up to the fifth floor and spotted Dr. Yamaguchi behind the reception counter, chatting with a nurse.

"Mr. Hillier. I'm sorry I missed you yesterday."

"You were on rounds," Charlie said, with a wave of the hand, hoping he looked better than he felt. The smell of disinfectant was causing his stomach to gurgle and roll in a most unsettling fashion. "How's our patient?" he said, with a cheer he didn't feel.

"No change." As usual, Yamaguchi's even tone left Charlie to wonder whether this was good news or bad. "Were you successful in finding some personal effects?" He looked at the plastic bag in Charlie's hand.

"There wasn't really a lot to choose from, but I brought a couple of things. Are you going to come with me when I give them to him, to observe his reaction?"

"If you wish." Yamaguchi came out from behind the counter and accompanied him down the hall. After a knock on the door, they entered the room and found Lepage sitting up, looking alert. His face broke into a smile.

"Hey, Charlie." His eyes went straight to the plastic bag. "Any luck at the apartment?"

"I brought you a few things," Charlie said, walking around to the side of the bed, as Yamaguchi took up his position at the foot. "I don't want to get your hopes up, though."

"What do you mean?"

"Just that there wasn't a lot there, in terms of personal stuff." He watched Lepage's face fall a little and backpedaled. "You know, because you've only been here a short time, and the company probably provided you with a furnished place, so it's understandable that you haven't really had the chance to personalize it … yet."

Lepage shrugged. "Yeah, I guess. So, what did you bring?"

Charlie rummaged in the bag and brought out a bright red silk tie. Its weight, combined with the label on the back told Charlie it was out of his own price range. He set it on top of the comforter and watched as Lepage eyed it, then picked it up.

"It's kind of … bright," he said, after a while. Charlie glanced at Yamaguchi, but whether it was just the doctor's usual inscrutability or because of Lepage's lack of reaction, Charlie saw no evidence to suggest any sort of breakthrough.

He pulled the second tie out of the bag. This one was of the same quality silk, but the pattern was a more conservative black, with small white dots. He handed it to Lepage.

"How about this one?"

Lepage took it, ran it through his hands and turned it over, looking at the label, then putting it next to the red one. "It's not really giving me anything. What else have you got in there?"

Charlie pulled out the two pairs of cuff links and set them on the edge of the bed.

"These are nice," Lepage said, selecting the silver acorns first, then the gold squares, centered by black stones. "But they don't really mean anything to me either. You didn't find any pictures, huh?" he asked, staring at the cuff links.

"Maybe they're still in storage," Charlie offered, though he hadn't seen any unpacked boxes anywhere. He handed Lepage the letter he had taken from the home office. "How about this?"

Lepage scanned the text, but again showed no spark of recognition, so Charlie pulled out the postcard of Mount Fuji. "I found this on the hall table — looks like it was just delivered."

Lepage looked at the front of the postcard for a moment, then flipped it over, his eyebrows creasing as he frowned. "It's blank."

"Yeah, I wasn't sure if it was an inside joke or something …" He paused, seeing the confusion on Lepage's face and thinking maybe the postcard was a poor choice if he was trying to jog a memory. Clearly, he had just added to Lepage's disorientation. He kept digging at the bottom of the bag and brought out the pen. His best hope. As Lepage reached out and took it from him, Charlie thought he saw something — a spark in Lepage's eyes — but it was gone as quickly as it appeared, replaced by a shrug and a sigh.

"You a Habs fan, Rob?"

Lepage looked up at him, then back at the pen. "A what?"

"It's a Montreal Canadiens pen. I figured you for a Leafs fan." Charlie smiled, tapping him gently on the arm. Lepage just looked at him with a bemused expression on his face, then it brightened.

"The hockey team … of course."

"You remember, then?"

"I remember hockey … I remember the Leafs and the Canadiens, yes." Lepage was nodding, as though something were falling into place.

"Well, that's good, isn't it?" Charlie looked to Yamaguchi, who was smiling.

"Yes, that is a good sign."

Charlie saw the positive news as an opportunity and didn't hesitate. "Doctor Yamaguchi mentioned that you might have been speaking some French when you first came out of the coma," he said, watching as Lepage's face took on a puzzled look. "Do you speak French?"

"Do I speak French?" Lepage's puzzlement turned to sheer confusion. "What are you talking about? I don't … at least I don't think I speak French." He paused, as if struggling with the concept. "Like, I know how to say a few words, from school, but I don't actually *speak* French."

"I may have misunderstood. You were talking quite rapidly," Yamaguchi said, though Charlie thought he had sounded pretty convinced when he had first mentioned it. "What about the pen, Mr. Lepage. Do you remember it?" Yamaguchi changed the subject.

Lepage turned the pen around in his fingers and stared at it, as though willing it to conjure up some memory, before shaking his head. "Not really."

"But you remember the team. This alone is positive."

Lepage shook his head and his features darkened as he looked at Yamaguchi. "No it's *not*. It's so … frustrating, my God — when am I going to remember?"

"You are making good progress, Mr. Lepage," Yamaguchi's tone was soothing, but not enough to overcome Lepage's obvious agitation.

"Bullshit. I still can't remember a fucking thing!" He tossed the pen at the wall. In the silence that followed, Charlie picked it up off the floor and offered it to Lepage.

"You should keep it. Maybe it will jog —"

"I don't want the fucking pen! You keep it, if it's so goddamned important to you. All of this shit," he said, sweeping the items from the comforter. Charlie stooped to collect them from the floor and put them back in the bag. Looking up, he saw that Yamaguchi was gesturing subtly toward the door.

"I should get go—"

"What is happening here?" Aiko Kimura was suddenly standing in the doorway, hands on her hips, her dark eyes aglow in a way Charlie hadn't seen before. "I heard shouting out in the hall."

"We were just trying to help jog Rob's memory with some personal items, that's all," Charlie said, straightening up.

Kimura brushed past him and sat on the edge of the bed, running her hand down Lepage's arm.

"Well, it doesn't look like you're helping him. He looks upset." Lepage began to protest but she cut him off with a wave of her hand. "I think you should let him rest," she said, looking first at Yamaguchi and then at Charlie. The two exchanged a glance in the awkward silence that followed, and then Charlie headed toward the door.

"I was on my way out, anyway."

Lepage seemed to want to say something but remained silent. Out in the hallway, Charlie paused and waited for Yamaguchi to catch up.

"What do you make of that?"

Yamaguchi shrugged. "As expected, I suppose."

"Really? I was kind of hoping for more of a reaction, to the pen at least."

"It's a slow process. But he remembers the hockey team, which means his long-term memory is coming back."

"I guess so." Charlie nodded. "Is she here every day?" he added, gesturing back toward Lepage's room.

"Ms. Kimura? Usually, yes."

"I get kind of a strange vibe from her, don't you?"

"She can be difficult, if that's what you mean."

Charlie's ears perked up. "In what way?"

"She has been … unhappy with the speed of Mr. Lepage's recovery. She wants him released to her care as soon as possible."

Charlie frowned. First Seger, now Kimura, both had seemed to want Lepage out of the hospital ASAP. "I still have a hard time seeing them as a couple."

"People can surprise you," Yamaguchi said, looking at his watch. "I have another appointment, so I have to leave you. I appreciate your efforts today, and don't be discouraged. I'm still optimistic that his memory will be fully restored in time."

They shook hands and Charlie returned to the elevator. On the ride down, he couldn't stop thinking about Lepage's expression when he saw the pen. There had been something there — a flash of recognition — Charlie was sure of it. It was as though Lepage had wanted to conceal it, but why? After all, it had been Lepage's idea for Charlie to go look for items that might jog his memory in the first place. It didn't make any sense.

Charlie headed back to Shinjuku Station, his mind replaying Lepage's reaction at seeing the pen, and the look in Kimura's eyes when she found Charlie and Yamaguchi in Lepage's room, as though they were intruders. After getting on the subway car he stood in the corner and put his hand in his pocket, realizing that he still had Lepage's apartment key. It wasn't worth going back now — he would return it the next time he went to the hospital. He plucked his phone out of his jacket pocket and saw an email from Karen Fraser, asking him whether he had enjoyed last night's outing. He was about to respond when he saw another unread message from a Japanese account that he didn't recognize. Clicking it open, he realized it was from Chikako Kobayashi, asking him if he would be available to meet her today. It seemed odd that she would want to meet on a Saturday, but he realized that as an inspector, she probably worked more than her share of weekends. Coming up out of the Metro at Akasaka, he sent her a reply, suggesting they meet for a coffee. He got a response a few minutes later, with the address of a coffee shop on Aoyama-dori, just down the street from the embassy.

Charlie was sitting at the window when he saw Kobayashi approaching the coffee shop. She was dressed in a carbon copy of the outfit she had worn the other day, but for the fact that this one was navy blue instead of charcoal, over a light-blue shirt instead of a white one. Her hair was tied back in the same way she always wore it, but she seemed more relaxed today. She smiled as she recognized him at the window and made her way through the shop to meet him.

"Thank you for meeting me," she said, after the usual bow.

"I was just going to order. What can I get you?"

"Oh no." She began to wave her hands, and it was only after Charlie's insistence that it was his treat that she finally allowed him to order her a small cappuccino. When he returned a few moments later with the coffees, Kobayashi got down to business.

"I wanted to give you an update on the Seger case," she began, stirring the foam on the top of her drink, then delicately setting the spoon on the saucer. "First, the Japanese authorities have decided to proceed with an autopsy, provided your embassy has no objection, of course."

Charlie shook his head quickly, thinking that was great news. "There's only one family member that I was able to contact, and I'm pretty sure she's not going to mind. I'll confirm as soon as possible." He took a sip of the delicious coffee, then set the cup down. "What made you change your mind?"

"It wasn't my decision, of course," she said. "But there are indications of foul play that we think warrant further investigation."

"Something new?" They had known from the start that Seger had died from a blunt force trauma to the head, and Kobayashi had also mentioned that while people being drugged for their credit cards was not uncommon in Roppongi, murders related to those scams were.

Kobayashi sipped at her coffee, then nodded slowly. "You mentioned that you met with a Mr. Mashida at Nippon Kasuga, yes?"

Charlie nodded. He had told her about his visit to Nippon Kasuga's office in Mori Tower, and the fact that Mashida had never heard of Mike Seger. "That's right."

"I checked with reception at Mori Tower, and there is a record of Mr. Seger visiting Nippon Kasuga two days before he was killed."

"What?" Charlie remembered the detailed process he had gone through himself to get a visitor's pass to enter the building, but it hadn't occurred to him to check if Seger's name was also in the system. "Why would Mashida lie about that?"

"I intend to ask him, but I would like to speak with Mr. Lepage first, with your permission."

Charlie shrugged, thinking she probably didn't need his permission to interview someone, Canadian or not, who might have information useful to a Japanese homicide investigation. He wondered how Lepage would react though, to find himself being questioned by the police in relation to his friend's possible murder — a friend he couldn't remember. As if he wasn't disoriented enough.

"You have reservations?"

He shook his head. "No, I think it's a good idea for you to talk to him. I'm just concerned that he may feel a little overwhelmed. He's just gradually getting his memory back and he's a little … fragile."

"Perhaps he would feel more comfortable with you there?"

"Yes, I guess I could arrange it, and sit in. When would you want to interview him?"

"It's not a formal interview. Just a few questions, but the sooner the better."

"Did you want to do it tomorrow … or this evening?" He looked at his watch. "I just came from the hospital and he was a bit upset. He's having a hard time with the memory loss."

"Tomorrow would be fine. In the morning, perhaps?"

"I think I can probably arrange that. It's not like he's going anywhere. Do you normally work on Sundays?"

She smiled. "Sometimes. Not often."

They chatted about the case for a while and as they finished their coffees, they slipped into a more relaxed exchange about life in Tokyo. He learned that she lived in the Asakusa area, and had been an investigator for five years.

"You must have been very young when you were first appointed," he said. She seemed embarrassed and he wondered if he had offended her. "I just mean that investigators are usually a bit older … in Canada. Maybe it's different here."

If she was indeed offended, it didn't last, and she asked him about Canada. He was surprised to discover that she knew where Newfoundland was.

"Tokyo must seem very different to you." Her smile, though demure, lit her face and the corners of her soft but inquisitive eyes.

"It is very different," Charlie said, nodding. "But I'm starting to get used to it. I think the time difference really messed me up for a long time. I feel like I'm over that now, and I'm ready to start exploring the city a bit more."

They chatted for a few more minutes, their coffees long finished, and eventually headed to the exit.

"I'll confirm there's no objection to the autopsy," Charlie said as they stood on the sidewalk outside the coffee shop. "And I'll set up a meeting for tomorrow with Rob Lepage at the hospital,"

"Thank you, and thank you again for the coffee."

As he began walking up Aoyama-dori, he realized they were headed in the same direction.

"I have some business at the local precinct," she said as they approached a building he hadn't noticed before, despite walking by numerous times on his way to the embassy from the New Otani Hotel.

"I'll be in touch," he said as they parted ways at the precinct entrance. As he walked on up the hill toward the embassy compound, he felt an excitement that added a little spring to his step. Whether it was the prospect of getting a lead from Seger's autopsy or something else, he wasn't sure. But it made him feel good, so he decided not to question it too much.

CHAPTER 13

Charlie shut down his computer and looked at his watch. He had dropped by the office — deserted on a sunny Saturday afternoon — to call Mike Seger's sister and to make arrangements with Dr. Yamaguchi for a possible interview tomorrow. Seger's sister had seemed more concerned about having to foot the bill for the autopsy, but once she accepted Charlie's assurances that it wouldn't cost her anything she agreed readily. He sensed she would have agreed to anything just to get off the phone. As for Yamaguchi, he had no objection to the interview and didn't think Lepage would either, though he agreed to run it by him and get back to Charlie with a confirmation email. He was debating where to go for lunch when he heard footsteps in the hall. A few seconds later, Louis Denault appeared at his doorway, dressed in jeans and a sweater. It was odd to see him in anything other than his usual uniform of a dark suit, white shirt, and muted tie.

"Working weekends your first month here, Charlie?"

Charlie smiled, though he knew Denault's statement carried a serious undertone, having made the point at Charlie's first staff meeting that there was no money in the embassy budget for overtime for consular staff. "Don't worry. I don't plan to put in a claim," he said. "Just figured it was easier to drop by the office to make a couple of calls than do it from home."

"That's the problem with living so close to your place of work." Denault gave a thin smile. "This to do with your consular case?"

Charlie nodded, before he realized that Denault might not be asking out of general interest or making casual conversation. He realized his misstep and tried to correct it, but it was too late. "I just figured it was easier to make a long distance call from here, that's all."

"I'm sure you mean well, Charlie, but we have to remember our role in the system."

"What do you mean?" Charlie felt his face growing hotter by the second.

"I just mean there's a process to follow, and sometimes going outside of that process isn't helpful."

"I'm really not sure what you're getting at ..."

"Did you meet with Nippon Kasuga this week?"

Charlie was taken aback. "As a matter of fact, I did."

"Why?"

Charlie had to restrain himself from saying something he might regret, considering that whatever else Denault was, he was Charlie's immediate superior. "They're Rob Lepage's employer. I thought they might have something in their files that would put me in touch with Lepage's family. Why are you asking, anyway? Did they complain or something?"

"Not to me." Denault's face bore a smug look. "The HOM did get a call though, wondering what his staff thought they were doing."

Charlie was about to ask for more, then made a snap assessment that Denault was bluffing. The little Charlie knew of ambassador Westwood he liked, and he didn't see him getting bent out of shape because one of his consular staff was trying to do his job. "Well, he never mentioned it to me."

"*I'm* mentioning it to you … now." Denault's smug grin was back. "And how's the property file moving along, by the way?"

"I've got a meeting this week," he replied, which was only partially true. He owed Miton a confirmation email, which he now realized he should have sent on Friday.

"I'm just saying don't get too caught up in one file." Denault's features morphed into fake concern. "We don't want you burning out in the first six months, and the property file's a priority."

And one murdered Canadian and another laid up in a hospital bed with amnesia is not….

Charlie decided to keep the thought to himself. "Got it," he said instead.

"Well, enjoy your weekend."

Charlie nodded and watched as Denault left, wondering what he would say if he knew about Charlie's plans for tomorrow.

Charlie arrived at the hospital ten minutes ahead of time for the interview on Sunday morning and found Inspector Kobayashi sitting in the little reception area on the fifth floor. After they exchanged a quick greeting, he set off in search of Dr. Yamaguchi, who was just coming down the hall.

"How is he this morning?" Charlie asked.

"He is in good form." Yamaguchi looked past him to the reception area, where Kobayashi still sat. "Is that the inspector?"

Charlie noted the surprise in the question, assuming it was related to her gender, and perhaps her relative youth — possibly both. His own instinctive response when he first met her, apart from finding her strikingly attractive, had been similar, based on what he had heard about Japanese society. "Yes, so we're ready when you are."

"We should wait for Ms. Kimura," Yamaguchi said. "She wanted to be here."

Charlie frowned. "I didn't know she was coming."

Yamaguchi looked sheepish. "She came in when I was discussing the possibility with Mr. Lepage. She was quite insistent. I hope the inspector won't mind."

Charlie shrugged. He was pretty sure Kobayashi wouldn't mind. She might even have a few questions for Kimura and he thought it might be interesting to see how she responded. "We'll wait, then."

"I have a quick matter to attend to, then I will join you."

Charlie made his way back to the reception area and took a seat on the sofa opposite Kobayashi's. She looked different today for some reason, but he couldn't place it. Her hair was in the same conservative style, and she wore a white blouse under a navy blazer. Then he realized what it was — she was wearing jeans, though the denim was dark enough to pass for slacks.

"Mr. Lepage's girlfriend wanted to attend, so we'll wait until she arrives. If that's all right," he added.

"Of course."

They sat in silence for long enough that it was starting to become awkward.

"Thank you again for the coffee yesterday," she said, although she had thanked him three times the day before.

"My pleasure. It's a beautiful day out there," Charlie felt the need to add, though the reception area was windowless.

"Yes, I love this time of year. Spring also, but especially fall."

"I hear the cherry blossoms in spring are spectacular."

The conversation moved into the features of the various Japanese seasons, and Charlie was surprised to look up at the clock and see that it was now fifteen minutes past ten o'clock. As if on cue, Yamaguchi appeared in the doorway and Kobayashi stood. Charlie followed suit and made the introductions.

"No sign of Ms. Kimura?" he asked, after Kobayashi and the neurologist had had a brief exchange in Japanese that Charlie half understood as polite banter. Yamaguchi shook his head and looked at his watch, then at Kobayashi. "I must apologize."

"Maybe we should start without her," Charlie suggested, not wanting to get into a prolonged exchange of apologies. Part of him was reconsidering the wisdom of allowing Kimura to participate anyway — she seemed to have an unsettling effect on Lepage. Yamaguchi and Kobayashi exchanged a quick look, then she nodded. "That would be fine."

Yamaguchi nodded his own approval and they set off for Lepage's room, finding him sitting up. He was clean-shaven and looked well-rested. His face lit up with a smile as they entered and Charlie introduced Kobayashi.

"I am very grateful to you for agreeing to talk to me today," Kobayashi began. "And may I say I am very sorry that your accident has left you injured."

Lepage shrugged and gave her a boyish grin. "It gives me something to do, since I won't be going anywhere for a while," he said, pointing to his casted leg. Yamaguchi directed the inspector to a seat by the window alongside Lepage's bed, while Charlie stayed standing, leaning up against the wall.

"How long will you be here in the hospital?" she asked.

Lepage smiled again. "You should ask him." He pointed to Yamaguchi.

"He will have a walking cast within the next week. Whether he can be released will also depend on how the other injuries are healing."

"He means this." Lepage tapped his head.

Kobayashi nodded. "I understand you have some memory loss?"

"I seem to be okay for remembering things after I came out of the coma. As for before, let's just say it's hit and miss."

"But you're making progress," Charlie said. He was trying to be encouraging, and he got an understanding smile from Kobayashi, but he decided he should probably keep his mouth shut and let her get on with her interview.

"I am remembering some things from before," Lepage said. "A little more each day, but it's patchy."

"Do you remember the night of the accident at all?" Kobayashi pulled out a little notebook and an elegant pen adorned with flowers and some Japanese characters.

Lepage shook his head. "I'm told I was in a car accident but I don't remember a thing."

"Do you remember the type of car you were driving?"

"One of your colleagues from the Tokyo Police showed me some pictures from the scene, so I know the car was black, but that's about it, I'm afraid. I don't know what road I was on or what time of the night it was."

Charlie knew from the police report that Lepage had been pulled from the wreck of a late model Nissan 370Z on a stretch of elevated highway in the Yokahama district. He glanced at Yamaguchi to see if he had any reaction to Lepage being unable to remember any of the details of the accident, but saw nothing. Kobayashi went through a series of questions related to the accident, then moved on to Lepage's work and how long he had been in Japan.

"I know I was working for Nippon Kasuga, but that's only because they've been in touch with me."

"And you were working in the banking field?"

Lepage nodded. "Apparently since the summer. I have a vague recollection of arriving in Tokyo in the summer — I remember it being very humid."

"And the nature of your work — can you be more specific?" Kobayashi looked up from her notes.

Lepage shrugged, then looked out the window and sighed. "No, which means I'm probably not going to be much use to them if I ever do get out of here. I guess I'll be heading back to Canada." He looked at Charlie, who couldn't help thinking Lepage's prospects sounded pretty bleak — going home to a place he could barely remember, where he had no family.

Kobayashi flipped the page of her notebook and wrote something at the top of a clean sheet. "You're aware of the death of your fellow Canadian, Mr. Seger?"

Lepage nodded. "Charlie told me. It's … awful."

"I understand he was a friend?"

"So he told me, but I have to say, I really don't remember him. I know that sounds bad, especially since he's dead because of me."

"Why do you say that?" Kobayashi looked up from her notes.

"Well, because he was only in Tokyo to see me."

"He told you that?"

Lepage nodded again. "He said he was in Hong Kong on business, and he decided to get in touch with me by email when he found out I was in Tokyo." Lepage looked to Charlie, then back to Kobayashi. "Apparently I told him to come and we'd get together, then when he did, I didn't respond to his emails … until he tracked me down here."

"Have you been able to review these emails?" Kobayashi asked him, then turned to Charlie.

"My phone was destroyed in the crash. As for my home computer, I'd be happy to have Charlie have a look, but I can't …"

Lepage paused and looked sheepish. "I can't remember my own password."

Kobayashi gave another understanding smile. "I could get the emails from the service provider, with your consent, of course."

Lepage shrugged. "I don't see why not." He looked to Charlie, as though for approval.

"That's up to you," he said, thinking it was really none of his business. "But it might help jog your memory."

Kobayashi scribbled a note then resumed her questions. "Mr. Seger came to visit you in the hospital, yes?"

Lepage nodded. "He was here the day I came out of the coma. He was here a couple of times before that, when I was unconscious, I think."

"And you recall your meeting?"

"Yes."

"What did you talk about, when he visited?"

Lepage shrugged. "The usual stuff, I guess. He asked about the accident, how I was feeling. He tried to get me to remember growing up in Toronto — mutual friends and that kind of thing. But it was sort of pointless. I still can't remember."

"That must be very difficult for you," Kobayashi said. "Did he ask about your work here in Tokyo?"

"Not really. I mean, he asked a couple of questions about Nippon Kasuga, I think, but that's all."

"What kind of questions?" Kobayashi's tone was even, though she had looked up from her notes again at the mention of Lepage's employer.

"I don't know. How they were treating me … were they covering the hospital costs and that kind of thing."

"Nothing about the kind of work you were doing?"

"A little bit, I guess. But like I said, I can't even remember

what I was doing there. I know I was in securities, but ..."
He trailed off, apparently embarrassed at his inability to
remember.

"Did Mr. Seger mention that he planned to meet with
someone at Nippon Kasuga?"

Lepage frowned and shook his head. "I don't think so."
Then he seemed to recall something, adding: "He did say he
wanted to talk to the hospital about getting me released to
his care and that he might need to talk to Nippon Kasuga —
he might need their support. Something like that."

"Mr. Seger wanted to have the hospital release you to his
care?" Kobayashi looked to Yamaguchi, who had been standing statue-like against the wall.

"We had some preliminary discussions to that effect," the
neurologist said, prompting Kobayashi to start scribbling.
"But I did make it clear that there was no question of releasing Mr. Lepage until he was medically cleared."

Kobayashi nodded, and seemed satisfied with the
response. "If I understand correctly, Mr. Seger visited
you on the afternoon of the twenty-ninth of October.
Depending on the exact time of his death, that would have
been the day of, or the day before, he died." She paused
for a second as Lepage awaited her next question with
the same alert look in his eyes. "Did he mention anything
about where he was going that night, or whether he was
meeting anyone in particular?"

"No," Lepage said. "Charlie asked me the same question
and I wish there was something I could say that would help,
but there isn't. They told me he was found in Roppongi."

"You think there's some significance in the location where
he was found?" Kobayashi asked.

"Just that it seemed like Mike knew how to have a good
time." Lepage smiled, as if remembering something. "He

told me some stories about when we were younger, and I got the impression he still liked to let loose from time to time."

"These stories ..." Kobayashi began.

"It was harmless stuff," Lepage said, with a wave of his hand. "Just teenage boys sneaking beers under our coats — that kind of thing."

Kobayashi smiled. "I understand." She continued the line of questions for a while, until she had covered the necessary ground and began to wrap up the interview.

"I feel really bad about Mike," Lepage said as Kobayashi flipped her notebook shut and slid it into her purse. "I mean, I know I can't remember, but it seems like we were pretty good friends when we were younger, and to think he died here, and the only reason he was here was to visit me.... Will you let me know if you find out anything?"

Kobayashi nodded and stood up. "Of course. And thank you again for your time today. If there is anything that you would like to add to what we discussed today, please do not hesitate to contact me."

Charlie chatted with Lepage for a moment, while Kobayashi and Yamaguchi did the same in Japanese, then he and Kobayashi took the elevator down to the lobby. Charlie's stomach made a grumble that was loud enough to be heard over the mechanical whirr of the elevator.

"I guess it must be lunchtime," he said, to cover his embarrassment. "I don't suppose you know anywhere good around here?"

Kobayashi smiled. "I was going back to Asakusa. There are many good places to eat," she said, hesitating for a split second before adding: "I would be very happy to show you."

Charlie shrugged. He had no plans, certainly none as good as lunch with Kobayashi. "That would be great, if you don't mind."

She led the way along the same route back to Shinjuku Station that Charlie had become familiar with, and they chatted as they joined a steady stream of pedestrians headed in the same direction. It wasn't as crowded as a weekday, but it wasn't exactly quiet, either. They rode the subway northeast for about twenty minutes, continuing their relaxed banter. It had been a gradual process but the car had become quite full for the last leg to Ueno Station. They had been standing comfortably at the back of the car, holding the overhead handles and maintaining a professional distance. Now the crowd had pressed them together so that their arms were touching. As the car jolted forward, her hip pressed against his thigh for a very pleasant moment, until she regained her balance and gave him an embarrassed smile.

"I apologize."

"No problem. I guess Asakusa's a popular place on Sunday," he remarked. Standing next to her, he was forced to look down, and he could smell the flowery scent of her perfume as they rode the last minute in silence. The squeal of brakes was soon followed by another swing in momentum that pressed them together again for a few seconds before the car came to a stop and the doors opened. About half of the passengers got off in a thick stream that flooded the platform and swarmed toward the escalator that led up to street level.

"Many people come to the Sensō-ji Temple," Kobayashi said as they stood on the escalator and Charlie marveled at the crowd.

"I was just at a big temple last week, on the other side of town."

Kobayashi smiled. "There are many temples and shrines in Tokyo. One of the biggest is Meiji, which is not far from the hospital."

"That's it," Charlie said. "It's beautiful." He remembered the almost eerie peace of the walk through the park, just a few hundred feet from a busy Metro station.

"Meiji is a Shinto temple. Sensō-ji is Buddhist, and much smaller, but very popular, especially with tourists," she added, as the escalator disgorged them onto the street. "There are many stalls leading up to the temple. Over there," she said as they followed the crowd to a large arch with a massive red lantern below it. Beyond the arch, Charlie made out a broad pedestrian street lined on both sides with stalls. There were a dozen people taking pictures of friends under the arch.

"Hey, you mind taking a picture on my wife's phone?" a burly man asked Charlie in a southern accent. His wife was standing five feet away, the arch in the background behind her and an American flag in the shape of the state of Texas emblazoned on the front of her hooded sweatshirt.

"Uh, sure."

"You American?" the man asked.

"Canadian." Charlie accepted the phone and lined up the shot as the guy stood next to his wife and they both smiled for the camera. "There you go," he said, returning the phone.

"You want one, too?" he said, looking first at Charlie, then at Kobayashi.

"You make such a nice couple," his wife said taking her camera from her husband.

"Ah, we're good, thanks," Charlie said as he and Kobayashi exchanged awkward smiles and then set off down the pedestrian street.

"I can show you the temple if you like." Kobayashi gestured down the crowded strip. "The restaurants are just a little farther on."

"Sure."

Charlie followed her as they passed what looked like a wide range of restaurants, but he realized these were probably tourist traps — somewhere no self-respecting local would eat. They strolled through the crowd, past a series of stalls selling the same sort of kitsch — from lanterns to kimonos and inflatable samurai swords. Halfway down, Charlie saw a cloud of smoke rising up in front of the steps leading up to the temple. A few seconds later, he could smell the incense in the cool, autumn air. As they got closer, he could see a lineup of people with incense sticks, waiting their turn to put them in what looked like an enclosed fire pit and then wave the smoke over themselves as they prayed with hands clasped.

"Some people light them for prayer, or for good luck," Kobayashi said. "Others put coins in the box at the top of the stairs." As they approached the temple and made the slow climb up to the top of the steps, Charlie saw that people were indeed tossing coins into a large box and then performing a series of bows and claps before either moving on into the temple or turning around and descending the stairs again. He fished in his pocket and pulled out some coins, tossed them in, and bowed quickly.

"There's a ceremony going on inside." She looked past the entrance to where a line of monks were taking part in a ceremony that involved a series of bows and chants. One of them was waving a long stick that seemed to be covered in long strips of cloth or paper.

"It's a beautiful temple." Charlie was drawn to the intricate woodwork in the walls and ceiling, and on the massive pillars framing the front doors. They looked around for a bit and then walked back down the main steps.

"This way." Kobayashi led them to a side street that was remarkably quiet in comparison to the crowded path leading up to the temple. He followed her down an even smaller one, stopping in front of a red door with a little wooden sign overhead, adorned with some Japanese characters.

"Very authentic Japanese food," she said.

Charlie nodded. "I'm sure it is."

They went inside and, after a brief exchange between Kobayashi and an elderly woman who might have been the proprietor and who seemed to know her well, they were seated at a table on the far side of the room. Despite the lack of obvious signage outside, the room was full, mostly with families.

"Do you like Japanese food?" Kobayashi asked, after they were seated and a pot of tea was delivered to their table.

"I haven't had anything I didn't like yet."

"They have a standard lunch menu, if you'd like to try?"

Charlie shrugged. "Why not." He poured tea for her and then himself, and they began to chat about the Sensō-ji Temple and the Asakusa area, which he learned was where Kobayashi had grown up.

"My parents moved to a smaller apartment north of here, when my two brothers went out on their own."

"What do your brothers do?"

"My older brother is a teacher, and my younger one works in a laboratory."

"He's a scientist?"

Her face broke into a grin. "No, more of a personnel manager," she said recovering her composure. "I'm sorry to laugh, it's just that my younger brother was always a bit of a … clown."

Charlie grinned. "So not your typical scientist."

"Not exactly."

"Do you still live in Asakusa?"

"I live with my parents. It's about twenty minutes away."

Charlie nodded. He figured Kobayashi to be in her midthirties, and couldn't really imagine her still at home, but he had to remember this was a different culture.

"It's not so unusual in Japan, for daughters to stay with their parents ... until they get married," she said, apparently reading his thoughts.

"I don't think it's unusual at all," he lied.

"In Canada it is probably more normal to leave home much earlier, yes?"

"I guess so, but kids are staying home longer these days, or even returning home after they've left," he said, remembering an online article he had recently read about the phenomenon of empty nesters suddenly finding themselves with a kid or two in the basement after several years away. He had thought of his two nephews at the time, since his own prospects for children seemed slim now. His ex-wife had always refused to even discuss the possibility, and he hadn't really thought much about whether he wanted kids himself.

"What do your parents think of your job?" he asked, picking up on the slight hint of surprise in her eyes and wondering whether he had wandered into a social no-go zone. "They must be very proud," he added, trying to minimize the damage.

The look on her face confirmed his fear that he had strayed from light conversation into something a little more personal than he had intended. "They thought my choice of career was ... unexpected," she said, as if that explained everything. She seemed to recognize that Charlie wasn't following, so she gave him an indulgent smile and continued. "We have a saying in Japan: *Deru kui wa utareru*. It means ..." She paused for a moment, searching for the words. "'The nail that sticks out gets hammered down.'"

"I think I understand."

"My father had different plans for me." She gave a little shrug. "He is a retired academic and he felt I should follow him. He thinks my talents are wasted with the police."

"Well, the Tokyo Police obviously don't agree," Charlie said with a smile. "Since they made you an inspector at such a young age."

She seemed embarrassed by the praise. "He doesn't have a very high opinion of the police generally, and thinks maybe it is not a place for a woman." Charlie's surprise must have been obvious, as Kobayashi added, "It is not such an unusual attitude here."

Charlie nodded, recalling an article he had read as part of his pre-posting briefing on Japanese culture, to the effect that despite being highly progressive in some areas, the country still clung to some traditional beliefs and practices. *Omiai*, for example — the practice of formal meetings arranged by parents to determine a couple's suitability for marriage — wasn't routine by any means, but it wasn't unheard of either. He could see how Kobayashi's career choice might have made some waves, which only made it more admirable. "And how does your mother feel?"

Kobayashi's expression lightened and she let out a little laugh. "She can't understand why I am not married, but I think she is proud of me, deep down. Also a little afraid."

"I guess it can be a dangerous job," Charlie said as a server arrived with several plates of rice, noodles, and some sort of deep-fried finger foods.

"I think she worries more about how my colleagues treat me," Kobayashi said, after the waitress had left. "She imagines they are much worse than they are in reality."

"Do they give you a hard time because you're a woman?"

She looked thoughtful as she gestured to the rice, then watched as Charlie spooned some onto his plate. "At first, yes, but I have found my place now. It is not such a big problem anymore."

"You mean they've realized you're there to stay."

"Exactly." She smiled as Charlie looked at the plate of noodles in front of him, and the thin strands of something that sat on top as a garnish. They looked like ultra-thin versions of the same noodles, but they appeared to be … *moving*.

"They move with the steam." She made a half-hearted effort to stifle a laugh. "They are not alive, Charlie."

"Right." It was his turn to look embarrassed, but Kobayashi was quick to throw him a face-saving line.

"It's a common reaction," she said as he tentatively scooped some of the noodles onto his plate.

"So, what did you think of Lepage?" Charlie asked.

She looked thoughtful for a moment, then gave a little nod. "I don't think there's much he can tell us about Seger's death."

Charlie considered the statement, and her expression, as he bit into a forkful of the still moving noodles. "But there's something else?"

"I don't know yet, but I'm not sure he's telling us everything."

"You think he's lying?"

She shook her head at the word, as though it were abhorrent. "Do you find it strange that his memory is so … segmented?"

"I thought that was how amnesia works," Charlie said. "Remembering things after the traumatic event means the long-term functioning of the brain is intact, but memories from before the accident are temporarily lost."

"But he remembers some things from before, yes?"

Charlie chewed his noodles and remembered Lepage's reaction at seeing the pen with the Montreal Canadiens' logo. He could have sworn that what he saw in Lepage's eyes was recognition, yet he had said it had stirred no recollection at all. Had he been lying?

"I apologize if I have offended you," Kobayashi said, making Charlie abandon his internal debate and look at her. Her face looked almost pained.

"Offended me, how?"

"I sense that you believe Mr. Lepage ..." She stopped and seemed to search for the right word. "Believe *in* Mr. Lepage, and you may be right. But in my experience, I'm afraid many of the people I interview do not tell me the truth."

"You're doing your job," he said, after a brief pause. "And I'm not offended at all. If there's something Lepage's holding back that could help solve Seger's murder, then I'm just as eager to find out what it is as you are. My only question is, why would he lie?"

"A good question. Maybe his email account will give us some answers."

"How soon do you think you'll be able to get access?"

She poured them both some more tea. "Tomorrow, I think."

"Thank you," he said, taking a sip of the tea. "And we might have the autopsy results tomorrow, too. Maybe between the two we'll catch a break?"

"I hope so," she said, a slight frown appearing on her brow.

"You're not so sure?" he said, misinterpreting her expression.

"It's just that I will be under pressure to move on to other cases if something doesn't come up soon on the Seger file."

He nodded. "I'm sure you have other files, and I guess your superiors don't want you making a mountain out of a molehill," he said, taking a spoonful of rice. When he looked up, he saw puzzlement on Kobayashi's face. "I'm sorry — it's an expression. It means to make too much of something minor. In other words, they'll want you to close the case unless there's a very good reason to keep it open. If they're anything like Canadian police, I mean," he added.

She smiled. "That's true."

The proprietor came by to check on their meals and Kobayashi introduced Charlie, translating the old woman's rapid-fire Japanese. He thought he heard the Japanese words for Canadian embassy in Kobayashi's description and wondered if he was being introduced as a friend or some sort of work-related acquaintance. He was going to have to make a more concerted effort to improve his Japanese.

"You mentioned Lepage's girlfriend was supposed to be at the interview today," she said, after the old woman had moved on to another table.

He nodded. "She made a point of saying she wanted to attend, so I thought she would be there."

Kobayashi chewed her food in silence, looking at him. Her face was friendly but those eyes were quite intense, and he could sense the activity behind them as she appraised him. He could only imagine their effect in an interrogation. "But you weren't surprised?"

"I'm sorry?"

"You weren't surprised that she didn't show up today," Kobayashi continued.

"Not really, I guess."

"Why not?"

He smiled. "I don't know why exactly. Just a feeling."

"Feelings should never be ignored," Kobayashi said, sipping her tea in silence, while Charlie wondered what or how much to say next. He decided to come at it logically, from his first impression.

"I just have a hard time seeing the two of them together. They seem so … different."

"How so?"

"She seems a bit rough around the edges for him, that's all." He realized he had confused her again when he saw her expression and quickly explained. "She seems a bit … harsh — her manner and the way she dresses, whereas Rob seems more clean-cut and friendlier." He played with his teacup in the silence that followed, and felt her appraising eyes on him. It occurred to him that his comments might say more about him than Kimura — his judging her for the clothes she wore. And who was to say that her gruff exterior wasn't just her way of being protective of Lepage?

"She has made an impression on you, that much is obvious," Kobayashi finally said.

"It's just that though — an impression. I could be completely wrong."

"I doubt that," she replied, with a little smile. "Do you have contact information for Ms. Kimura?"

Charlie shook his head, realizing that while he had given Kimura his card, she had never sent him the email she had promised with her own coordinates. "I know she works at a call centre, and has odd hours. But she's at the hospital all the time. I can tell Rob you'd like to get in touch with her if you like."

She shook her head. "That won't be necessary."

Charlie glanced at his watch and realized they had been there for almost ninety minutes. "Well, I should probably let you enjoy the rest of your Sunday. Thank you for the wonderful lunch," he said, which led to a five minute negotiation during which he was finally allowed to pay the bill, but only after promising to let Kobayashi reciprocate some other time.

They went their separate ways outside the restaurant, and as he made his way back to the main pedestrian street leading up to the Sensō-ji Temple, Charlie found himself contemplating several elements of the lunch. The first was Kobayashi's obvious doubts about whether Lepage was telling them everything. Whether it was her instincts as an inspector or something more, Charlie didn't know, but she had got him thinking, too. He couldn't shake the odd sensation he had felt on watching Lepage's reaction to the pen. If he had recognized it, why would Lepage conceal the fact, especially if it was evidence that his medical condition improving? But the lunch hadn't just shown him that Kobayashi was a perceptive investigator, it has also given him a glimpse of her more personal side. He imagined her returning to her parents' apartment. Would she mention the lunch meeting? Probably not, and even if she did, she was sure to describe it as a purely work-related function, just as she had seemed to introduce him to the restaurant's proprietor in his official capacity.

Too bad, he thought, as made his way to the end of the crowded street and caught sight of the sign for the Metro. He felt a flush of pleasure when he recalled smelling her floral scent as they stood in close quarters on the Metro, and the look in her eyes when she smiled.

CHAPTER 14

Charlie sat at his dining room table, scraping the bottom of the takeout box with a spoon — he had abandoned the chopsticks, but not before taking some satisfaction from having made it through 90 percent of the meal. He scooped the last of the rice out and popped it in his mouth, savouring it as he scrolled through the results of some internet research with his other hand. Kobayashi had definitely got him thinking about what Lepage should and should not be able to remember, and while he had come across plenty of online materials on amnesia, there was nothing so far to suggest that Lepage's description of how his own memory was returning was at odds with medical reality. There was also the fact that Dr. Yamaguchi didn't seem suspicious, but Charlie couldn't help feeling naive when Kobayashi had raised the possibility. She was right — he wanted to believe Lepage — and while there was still nothing concrete to suggest he shouldn't, Charlie felt he owed it to himself to at least do his homework.

He spent another fifteen minutes online, the result of which was that virtually anything seemed possible when it came to the way a person's memories came back after a traumatic event. The exercise was not only frustrating, but a good reminder of why you shouldn't try to play doctor on the

internet: if you looked hard enough, you could find something
that supported any number of completely opposing diagnoses.
Charlie tried to sip from the empty beer bottle and glanced
over toward the fridge, considering another, when his line
of sight was interrupted by the wooden bowl on the counter
where he kept his keys. He got up and walked over to the
counter, ignoring his keys and focusing instead on the white
key card at the bottom of the bowl that he had intended to
return to Lepage at this morning's interview. He glanced at his
watch and made up his mind, then plucked the card from the
bowl, grabbed his jacket, and was out the door.

Charlie arrived at Lepage's apartment building in Omote-
sando Hills fifteen minutes later. Despite the chill in the
evening air, he could feel a sheen of sweat on his forehead as
he stood outside the building entrance, feeling the outline of
the key in the pocket of his jeans and considering whether
he should turn back. Then he made up his mind and trotted
up the front steps two at a time, with a friendly nod to the
young couple passing by on their way out of the building.
Charlie made his way quickly to the elevators and stepped
inside a waiting car. He pressed the button for Lepage's floor,
then the one to close the doors, keen to be underway before
another resident showed up. The doors were almost all the
way shut when a slender arm clad in black slid between
them, jolting them open again.

"*Moushiwake arimasen*," he said, surprised to see that the
arm belonged to a tall, red-headed woman in running gear.

"No worries," she said with a British lilt. Her attempt to
conceal a smirk was less than successful as she removed a
pair of high-end ear buds and rolled up the cord. "American?"

Charlie turned to look at her full on. She was maybe a couple of inches shorter than him, with her hair tied back in a ponytail, her cheeks rosy from exertion and the cold night air. He tried not to linger on the clinging black pants and long-sleeved top, both adorned with familiar athletic logos.

"Why do I get the feeling that I just asked you where the Metro station is?" he said, which made her laugh out loud.

"No, not at all." She shook her head, her face lighting up with her smile. "It was just a very formal apology, that's all."

"Oh really? I thought that's what I was supposed to say."

"I usually go with *gomen*, or *gomenasai*, but I'm quite informal."

The elevator chimed and the doors opened onto the ninth floor. She looked at the panel with the single floor button lit up, then back at him.

"After you," he said, realizing they were going to the same floor.

"You live here?" There was a trace of something in her eyes that might have been fear. He wanted to put her at ease as quickly as possible.

"No, I'm a friend of someone who lives here."

"You're not a friend of Rob's, are you?" she asked as they stood in the hallway.

"Rob Lepage? Actually, I am. Do you know him?"

"Sort of … I haven't seen him around much lately, though." Again, Charlie detected something in her body language. Suspicion, anxiety, or general awkwardness? He wasn't sure.

"Look, Ms.… My name's Charlie Hillier by the way. I'm with the Canadian embassy," he added, plucking a card from his pocket and giving it to her. She seemed satisfied that he posed no danger to her, but she still looked puzzled.

"Elizabeth Farnsworth. You said you're with the embassy.… Is everything okay with Rob?"

"I'm afraid Rob's been in an accident."

"Oh my God." She put a hand over her mouth. "Is he …"

"He's in hospital, but he'll make a full recovery, according to the doctors." Charlie could see the relief in her eyes and in her body language as she processed the information. "Can I ask how well you know Rob? I've been trying to reach his family back in Canada and haven't been having much luck."

She looked at the card he had handed her and then back at Charlie. "If Rob's in hospital, then what are you doing here?"

"He asked me to drop by his place and pick up some things," he said, taking the key from his pocket and showing her, thinking he was telling the truth, sort of. She seemed to make a decision and then pointed down the hall toward Lepage's apartment.

"I'm just down the hall from Rob's. Why don't you come in, instead of us discussing this out in the hall?"

"Sure, thank you." He followed her past Lepage's door, noting that she was across the hall and a few doors down, at the far end. She opened the door and the lights in the entrance came on automatically, revealing that Farnsworth was somewhat less of a neat freak than Lepage.

"I'm afraid it's a bit of a mess. I had some friends over last night and the cleaning lady hasn't been round yet." She kicked aside a jumble of mismatched footwear and plucked a few empty glasses from various surfaces as she made her way through to the living room. By the looks of things, she had hosted quite a party. "Maybe we'd better go in the kitchen."

"You should see my place," Charlie said, trying to put her at ease. He noticed the apartment was quite a bit smaller than Lepage's and any view was largely obscured by a residential tower that dwarfed the building they were in.

"Cup of tea?"

"Sure." Charlie smiled. He hated English tea, but refusing would be rude, and he knew how seriously the Brits took their tea. "I appreciate you taking the time to talk to me like this."

"It's no trouble." She filled the kettle and pointed to the little table for him to take a seat. A moment later, she set a tray down in front of him and sat opposite as she waited for the kettle to boil. "So, what happened to Rob? What kind of accident was it?"

"A car crash."

"When?"

"About ten days ago."

She winced. "And he's been in hospital since?"

"Yes." He sensed she was preoccupied with something, but he wasn't sure what. He decided to try to find out. "Do you know him well?" he asked.

"Maybe not as well as I thought, if he's been in hospital for ten days and it hasn't occurred to him to get in touch. I could have brought him some —"

"I should tell you, Ms. Farns—" he began.

"It's Elizabeth, please."

"Elizabeth, right. Rob has a head injury and his memory has been impacted, so if he hasn't been in touch, he's got a good reason."

Her hand went to her mouth again. "Listen to me, thinking of myself. How bad is it?"

"He's got some amnesia, but the doctors are optimistic that he'll make a full recovery." He let her digest that information for a moment, while he tried to think of another way to phrase the same question he had already asked twice, the answer to which was key to knowing whether he was dealing with a casual acquaintance or someone who might shed real light on Lepage's life, maybe even a family contact. "Can I ask what your relationship with Rob is?"

"We're friends," she said, pulling her hair out of the elastic that held it in place and fluffing it out as it fell to her shoulders. "We were more than that for a while, a couple of months back, but we're just friends now."

"I assume you met because of your proximity?" He gestured to the hall, in the direction of Lepage's apartment.

"The only two Westerners in the building, as far as I can tell," she said, with a shrug and a smile. "It was only a matter of time before we got to know each other. I wouldn't want you to think badly of me," she added. "But I suppose we had a little fling. We're both unattached and Rob's a good-looking guy and a lot of fun." Her smile faded just a little. "Anyway, we stayed friends … afterward."

"Did you socialize with any of his work colleagues, or other friends in Tokyo?"

"He didn't talk much about his work — I know he was in banking, as am I, but our paths didn't cross professionally. I think he was making a lot more money than me," she added, with another smile. "I never met any of his colleagues, though."

She got up in response to the whistle of the kettle.

"Did he ever mention his family? Or his hometown? Anything like that?" he asked, as she rummaged in one of the cupboards, causing an avalanche of little cardboard boxes and metal tins containing a wide assortment of teas.

"Honestly, you must think I'm such a slob," she said, picking through the boxes on the counter while Charlie got up and collected the tins from the floor.

"Not at all."

She smiled and pulled her hair out of her face as she leaned on the counter. "Not like Rob — have you been in his place?"

He nodded. "Not much out of place over there, that's for sure."

"Always seemed a bit … I don't know, *sterile* to me. Which I always found odd because Rob's not like that himself; he's really quite a warm person when you get to know him. Herbal okay?"

"Sure." Charlie regained his seat. He waited for her to bring the pot over before trying again.

"I've really struck out in terms of trying to connect with Rob's family back in Canada …"

"Sorry, I didn't answer your question. No, he didn't talk about Canada much and never mentioned his family. I don't know if he had any siblings or anything like that, I'm afraid." She poured her tea into a mug. "Listen to me prattling on.… How *is* Rob? You said he's expected to make a full recovery?"

"That's what his neurologist says, and he has been making steady improvement since coming out of the coma."

"A coma! That's more serious than I thought." She frowned. "I have to go see him. Where is he?"

"I'm sure he'd like to see you," he said, wondering if Lepage would even remember her. He had to believe, though, that intimacy with the Lycra-clad beauty sitting across from him would be something that would be difficult to forget, all things considered. "He's at Tokyo Medical University Hospital in Shinjuku." He fished out his BlackBerry and pulled up the contact number for the fifth floor reception desk. "They seem to be pretty flexible with visiting hours, but you should probably call ahead."

Farnsworth sipped her tea. "I'll try to go tomorrow. I'll have to double-check, but I think I can get away from work a little early." She put the mug down on the table and ran a hand through her hair. Charlie could tell something was up.

"Everything okay?"

She hesitated for a moment. "I'm just thinking how odd it would be if he doesn't recognize me."

"It's something you need to be prepared for," he said. "But he's making progress every day. You being there could actually help him ... maybe trigger a memory."

"Of course." She let out a sigh. "I should be thinking about how I can help with his recovery ... I'll be there."

They sipped their tea in silence, Charlie doing his best to pretend to enjoy what seemed to be a liquid cocktail of weeds that he found vaguely nauseating.

"Did Rob ever mention a Canadian friend who was coming to visit him here in Tokyo?" he asked, putting the mug back on the table.

She shook her head and frowned. "Doesn't ring a bell, but I haven't really seen much of Rob lately ... I mean, before the accident, obviously."

"When was the last time you saw him?"

She shrugged and ran a finger around the rim of her mug. "Three weeks ago? I had coffee at his place. We bumped into each other in the elevator on a Sunday morning."

"How did he seem?"

"He seemed fine. He was a bit hungover ... too much sake the night before," she added, with a grin. "Not that I know how that feels, of course."

Charlie smiled. "And he didn't mention this friend, Mike Seger, who might be in town?"

"No. Like I said, he didn't talk much about his life in Canada, and I never really met anyone from his work."

Charlie debated whether to refrain from asking his next question, but decided to go ahead. "You'll forgive me for asking, but you're not aware if Rob was seeing ... anyone else?"

If she was taken aback, Farnsworth didn't show it. "I don't know, but it wouldn't surprise me at all. Rob's a good-looking chap, after all. But as I said, it's been a few weeks since I've really talked to him."

"Well." Charlie pushed the mug of tea to the side as though it were empty. "I should be on my way. Thank you very much for the hospitality." He made his way to the door, navigating the cluster of shoes.

"Can you text me that phone number?" she asked, opening the door for him.

"Of course." She gave him her number, and he added it to his contacts.

"I'm glad I bumped into you," she said, leaning on the door frame as he stepped out into the hall. "Rob's very fortunate to have someone like you on his case," she added with a kind smile before closing the door.

CHAPTER 15

Charlie was sitting in his weekly administrative meeting, pretending to listen to Denault as he droned on about reducing paper filing and other new and boring cost-cutting initiatives. He had spent the whole day thinking about the Lepage file, and waiting for a call from Chikako Kobayashi that had never come. He assumed the autopsy report on Mike Seger and the results of the requests for Rob Lepage's email accounts had been delayed, but he was disappointed that Kobayashi hadn't been in touch anyway. He had enjoyed walking around Asakusa with her, and having lunch together, even if it was just a working lunch.

"Right, Charlie?"

He was jolted back to reality by Denault's voice, and when Charlie looked down the table at his boss's expectant features, he had no idea how to respond.

"Sorry, I was just thinking of how to reduce my paper filing," he said, clinging to the most recent thing he had registered.

"Well, we've moved on to performance appraisals but please, share your ideas with the team."

Charlie stole a glance at Karen Fraser, who was concealing a grin on the other side of the table as the rest of the group waited for his response. "It's nothing.... It needs more thought before it can be of practical use."

"Well this is the place to air it, get some feedback from your colleagues," Denault persisted, though it was obvious he knew Charlie had been day-dreaming his way through the meeting.

"Just, I was thinking of using the scanner more, to create electronic documents," he said feebly, thinking it sounded good.

Denault smiled. "You mean, like item five on the agenda, that some of us were discussing five minutes ago?"

Charlie shrugged and Denault looked ready to continue his badgering when they were interrupted by a knock on the conference room door. It opened and Denault's assistant poked her head in.

"Head of mission's looking for you."

"We're pretty much done here, anyway." Denault shuffled his papers into a leather folder and left the room.

"But we still have two agenda items." Fraser tapped her printed agenda in mock indignation, after he had gone. "Not to mention Charlie's great idea for reducing our environmental footprint."

"Hilarious." Charlie rolled his eyes.

"Preoccupied with the Lepage file?" Fraser said as they made their way out into the hallway.

"It's that obvious?"

"Pretty much, though no one could blame you for drifting off in there." She gestured to the meeting room they had just left.

"Do we really have those meetings *every* week?"

"I'm afraid so. He's a bit of a stickler when it comes to the admin stuff. That one was a bit more boring than usual though, in fairness. Tell me about your consular file — that's sure to be more interesting."

They arrived at Charlie's office, and he took a seat behind his desk while Fraser deposited herself in one of his client chairs.

"There isn't much news to tell," he began. "I was hoping to hear from the police inspector with the results of Seger's autopsy." He scanned his inbox for the hundredth time and saw nothing from Kobayashi.

"How about Lepage? Is his memory coming back?"

"Sort of."

She frowned. "What about relatives in Canada — you have any luck?"

He shook his head, then brightened. "I did bump into a neighbour he was friendly with." He was about to add where he had met Farnsworth on Sunday but stopped short of divulging that particular bit of information. He was pretty sure Fraser wouldn't care one way or the other, but his being at Lepage's apartment building on a Sunday might raise questions he would have difficulty answering. He had gone there with the intention of entering Lepage's apartment with less than clear permission to do so, after all.

"I find that so … depressing," Fraser said. "Him being laid up in a hospital bed on the other side of the world from home, and no family at his side."

"I wouldn't feel too bad for him," Charlie said, thinking of Kimura and Farnsworth. "He seems to have a lot of friends."

Fraser seemed poised to ask what he meant when his landline rang. He glanced at the display and noticed it was from the police. "You mind?" he said, getting a nod from Fraser. He grabbed the phone and heard Chikako Kobayashi's familiar voice.

"I'm very sorry not to have called you earlier," she began, in her usual conciliatory tone. "But I have some news that might interest you regarding your consular file."

"Do you want me to come by the station?"

"Actually, I have some business to attend to at the Akasaka prefecture, but I should be finished around five o'clock."

Charlie looked at his watch and saw that it was almost four. "I could meet you there at five."

"Very well," Kobayashi replied.

"Was that your police investigator?" Fraser said, after he had hung up the phone.

He nodded. "Apparently, there's an update."

"Well, I'll leave you to it," she said, getting up.

Charlie laughed and watched her go. He had a few things to wrap up before leaving for the five o'clock meeting. The prospect of an update intrigued him, especially when it meant seeing Kobayashi again.

"Thank you for meeting with me on such short notice," Kobayashi said, after she had gotten Charlie through the reception area and into a meeting room at the rear of the Akasaka precinct building, halfway down Aoyama-dori from the embassy. It was tiny compared to the main building in Kasumigaseki, but much easier to get into.

"Please," Charlie said. "I appreciate you getting in touch."

Kobayashi spent another few seconds on formalities before she got into the actual subject of the meeting. "The first matter concerns the results of the autopsy on Mr. Seger. I thought they would interest you."

"Any surprises?"

She gave a subtle shrug. "Generally, no. Mr. Seger died as a result of blunt force trauma to the head. Specifically, a blow to the rear right quadrant of the skull. He would have died almost instantly."

Charlie nodded. "That's pretty much what we understood to have happened."

"Yes, and the detailed analysis confirmed the level of alcohol in his blood at 0.13 percent. As we discussed, not insignificant, but not incapacitating for a man of his size."

Charlie sat through a slight pause, sensing that there was a "but" coming.

"But there was no Rohypnol in his system."

"What? But the earlier test indicated there was."

Kobayashi's expression was a mixture of agreement and embarrassment. "It seems the first sample was improperly … processed. When I discovered the result of the second test, I asked them to repeat the test, just to be sure."

"And?"

She shook her head. "No Rohypnol."

"That certainly changes our working theory — that Seger was the victim of a routine scam gone wrong."

Kobayashi said nothing, but Charlie could tell that she was thinking the same thing.

"And the autopsy didn't give us any clues as to what kind of weapon was used to kill him?" he asked.

She shook her head. "The fatal wound made a round depression in the skull, so it was something very hard and rounded — not sharp. And we have already established that he was not killed where he was found," she added. "Any physical evidence the weapon might have left would be at the scene of the … killing."

"Which could be anywhere," Charlie said, noting her careful choice of words, adding: "Are you treating it as a homicide?"

"Not officially." She paused, and her expression suggested she might be leaving something out. "It is still characterized as *suspicious.*"

Charlie nodded, thinking it sounded like a way for the police to avoid launching an expensive investigation into the death of a foreign national whose family didn't seem to give a shit about what had happened to him. Apparently bureaucracy was as alive and well in Japan as it was in Canada. Kobayashi conveyed the rest of the substance of the autopsy, none of which seemed out of the ordinary or offered any further clue as to what had actually happened to Mike Seger that night, or where he had been killed before being dumped in a grubby Roppongi alley.

"You mentioned you had some other information to pass along," he said, when she had finished with the details of the autopsy.

"It's about Ms. Kimura."

Charlie was suddenly curious. "What about her?"

"You mentioned she worked for a call centre."

Charlie nodded.

"I did some research but was unable to find anyone of that name and of her approximate age working at any of the registered call centres. I assume you haven't heard from her since yesterday?"

Charlie shook his head. "I did speak to Dr. Yamaguchi earlier and asked whether she had been in to visit Rob today, but he hadn't seen her."

Kobayashi said nothing as he considered the coincidence that Kimura, who up until two days ago had been an almost constant fixture at Lepage's bedside, had apparently fallen off the face of the earth around the time she learned that Lepage was to receive a visit from a Tokyo Police inspector. "There are, of course, many unregistered call centres in Tokyo — they are illegal and don't keep employment records," she added.

"Right. Well, I've already asked the doctor to let me know if she shows up at the hospital, and I'll do the same with Rob when I go see him after work today. That reminds me," he said, remembering Elizabeth Farnsworth. "I bumped into a neighbour of Rob's last night. A British woman who lives in his building."

"You were at Mr. Lepage's apartment?" Kobayashi's tone was even, but Charlie could tell she was fishing for an explanation.

"No, no … I was in the neighbourhood and I just swung by his building. I met her in the lobby," he said, a bit unsure as to why he was lying, or whether Kobayashi was buying it. He sensed she was not, but he carried on anyway. "She wasn't aware that Rob was dating a Japanese woman."

"What was this woman's relationship to Mr. Lepage?"

"I gather they were intimate a few months ago, and had remained friends, apart from being neighbours. She did say they hadn't seen much of each other for the past few weeks though, so it may not mean anything."

"Did she know Mr. Seger?"

He shook his head. "No, I did ask her about Seger, but she'd never heard of him. Rob didn't talk much about his work colleagues or friends, apparently. She also didn't know anything about his family back in Canada."

Kobayashi frowned. "Unfortunate."

"I agree."

"I got access to Mr. Lepage's email account," she said, prompting an optimistic look from Charlie.

"I meant to ask about that."

"I'm afraid there was no correspondence with Mr. Seger." Kobayashi's tone was apologetic now. "Or from anyone in Canada, either," she added. "In fact, Mr. Lepage seems to have made very little use of his personal email account."

"Really? Nothing at all?"

She shook her head. "A few routine emails to accounts at Nippon Kasuga, as well as some … garbage?"

"You mean junk mail?"

She smiled. "Yes, junk mail."

"I'm sure we'll find out a lot more through his work email," Charlie said, sipping the remnants of cappuccino foam at the bottom of his cup. When he looked back up, Kobayashi had an odd look on her face.

"It seems that Nippon Kasuga has refused to consent to the release of Mr. Lepage's email account information," she said.

"Can they do that?" He remembered a recent news story about the lengths to which a well-known internet service provider had gone to resist attempts by the authorities to access their clients' account information.

"I'm afraid so, for now." Kobayashi seemed embarrassed. "We would have to obtain a court order to force them to divulge the account information."

"Like a warrant?"

She nodded.

"Would that be difficult to get? I mean, it is a homicide investigation."

Her expression seemed pained, and he remembered that officially it was still just a suspicious death as opposed to a formal homicide investigation. "I'm afraid the connection between Mr. Lepage's email account and the deceased may not be obvious to a judge in this context."

Charlie nodded, understanding her predicament. "I suppose not. But what does it say about Nippon Kasuga that they won't release it voluntarily?"

She shrugged. "They say it's standard policy, to protect the privacy of their customers' financial information."

"I guess that sounds pretty reasonable," he said, watching her reaction. She was clearly not buying the corporate line. "But you don't agree?"

"It may be so, but maybe not."

"I guess it's not worth going to the trouble of getting a judge to sign off," he said, more a statement than a question. She didn't respond, but she looked stung and he realized she had interpreted his remark as a direct attack. Apart from not being what he intended, it was the equivalent of a slap in the face in Japanese culture, where direct challenges were a definite no-no. He cursed his ham-handedness. "I'm sorry. I didn't mean to suggest that you're not doing everything you can."

She smiled. "It is I who should apologize. You must find the Japanese approach very ... frustrating."

"Not at all." He shook his head, though he was intrigued by Nippon Kasuga's response, corporate policy or no corporate policy. It just didn't sit right with him, and he sensed that Kobayashi felt the same way.

"I should go." She looked at her watch. "I have a meeting with my superior to discuss the progress on this case."

"I'll let you know if I make contact with Ms. Kimura," Charlie said as they got up and headed toward the door of the coffee shop.

"Thank you," Kobayashi said. "But please be careful." He wondered what she meant as they shared a moment of silence, before she added: "Whether it is officially a homicide investigation or not, a man is dead."

CHAPTER 16

Seeing the darkening sky outside his office window, Charlie checked the time and decided to save a draft of the email he had been working on for the past hour rather than try to finish it now. He was eager to get over to the hospital and talk to Rob Lepage. He was just as curious to see if Aiko Kimura would be there this evening, and how she would react if he asked her to meet with Kobayashi. He was in the process of shutting down his computer when he heard footsteps outside in the hall. Expecting Fraser to appear and assume her characteristic lean against his door jamb, he was disappointed to look up and see Denault there instead.

"Oh, hi, Louis."

"I thought I heard you in here. Glad I caught you."

"Actually, I was just on my way out," Charlie said. If he had hoped to discourage Denault with the statement, it didn't seem to work. He took a seat in one of Charlie's chairs.

"I won't take much of your time, but I do have a request."

Charlie bit back his irritation. He had put in more than a full day and he was in no mood to waste time filling in one of Denault's administrative forms, but he decided to hear him out.

"What's up?"

"How's the property file going?"

Charlie suppressed a sigh, but obviously wasn't completely successful in concealing his irritation.

"There's no need to be defensive, Charlie." Denault played with a cufflink. "I just would hate to see you get off on the wrong foot here, especially with the HOM so interested in keeping the momentum going."

Charlie chose his words carefully. It was true that he hadn't put much effort into the property file in the past few days. On the other hand, from what he could tell, the broad strokes of what was on the table was a non-starter from Canada's perspective, though he was sure Denault hadn't characterized it that way in his briefings with the head of mission.

"I'm still working on the logistics of the meeting," he said, knowing he was on thin ice, given that he hadn't called back to confirm his availability for a meeting.

"The HOM would like an update."

"No problem. I'll call them again first thing tomorrow and firm up a date, then I can give him a briefing."

"I was thinking now — I was on my way for our regular bilateral and I know he'll be asking, so I thought it would be good if you can bring him up to speed yourself. I wouldn't want to misstate your progress," he added, crossing his legs and making himself comfortable in the chair.

"Except that there's not much to tell him right now," Charlie said evenly.

"It won't take long." Denault stood and smoothed his pants. "Besides, he's expecting you."

"Why is he expecting me?"

"I said I'd swing by and see if you were still here."

"Well, in that case," Charlie said, not bothering to hide the sarcasm in his voice. "I guess I'll come along, though I'm not sure what I'm supposed to tell him."

"Relax, Charlie," Denault said, slapping him on the shoulder in an overly familiar manner that Charlie didn't appreciate. "It's all very informal," Denault added, adjusting his tie in the reflection offered by the glass-encased map of Tokyo that had come with Charlie's office.

It was almost seven by the time Charlie stepped onto the crammed westbound subway car, aided by a not-so-gentle push from one of the pair of uniformed, white-gloved plat-form attendants keeping people clear of the doors. He cursed Louis Denault as he let the crush of people gently push him toward the rear of the car, where he eventually stopped and grabbed hold of an overhead handle as the doors slid shut and the car moved off. The briefing with Philip Westwood had been a complete waste of time, though Charlie had known that going in. The only reason he could think of for Denault to insist on holding it was to try to make him look bad in front of the ambassador. But Westwood had seemed more interested in Charlie's consular files, offering a few words of encouragement and a request to be kept apprised of important developments on both the consular and property files — the latter reference seemingly added for Denault's benefit. For his part, Denault had seemed disappointed — even a little bitter — as they left the meeting, cut short by the head of mission himself, who had realized he was due at an impromptu cock-tail party at the French ambassador's residence.

Charlie tried to put it out of his mind, the frustration of the experience serving only to ramp up his blood pressure as he stood on the crowded train. Turning his mind to Rob Lepage, it occurred to him that he hadn't had a chance to contact him to let him know that he would be able to come over for a visit this evening after all. Then again, since visiting hours were until at least nine, he supposed it didn't really matter, as Lepage would be laid up for another week. He made a mental note to ask Yamaguchi when he thought Lepage might be released.

As the car began to slow and the intercom voice announced their arrival at Yoyogi Station, the crowd shifted as people made their way toward the doors, only to be replaced by new-comers arriving from the platform. One of them, a woman with a hairstyle similar to Kobayashi's, reminded him of their trip together on the Metro, the smell of her perfume in his nose as they stood close. As they moved off again, he thought of Kobayashi's comments about Aiko Kimura, wondering whether there was any significance to Kobayashi not being able to locate her on a list of registered call centre personnel. Maybe she was being paid off the books, but it could be something more. He decided to ask Lepage about her again — maybe he had remembered something about how they had met.

Charlie followed the swell of people exiting onto the plat-form at Shinjuku Station and up the escalator, marvelling, as he still did regularly, at the orderly conduct of such vast congrega-tions of people in such confined spaces. He was approaching the entrance to the hospital when he spotted a familiar profile heading down the steps onto the street, heading his way. On instinct, he ducked into a convenience store and pretended to look at the magazines as he kept a peripheral view of the street, watching as she walked by in a distressed leather jacket, tight jeans, and high-heeled leather boots — there was no mistaking Aiko Kimura. She wore a black and white checked scarf and her usual expression of distaste as she looked down at her phone. A pair of teenage boys on their way into the store almost tripped over each other's feet as they took in her shapely figure.

Charlie waited for a few seconds, then stepped out onto the sidewalk and looked east, immediately picking out the checkered scarf amongst the crowd headed back toward the Metro station he had just come from. He made a snap decision to follow, conscious that if he was going to try to do so unobserved, he would have to remember that he didn't exactly blend in with the rest of the crowd.

He stayed well back and was not surprised to see that she was making her way into Shinjuku Station, which meant that he would have to close the gap to make sure he could get on the same train. He had worked his way to within fifty feet of her by the time they hit the escalator, then watched as she boarded the crowded subway car before entering by the door at the far end, keeping an eye on her as she stood with her back to him by the other entrance. He was taking a big chance if she turned around, since he was the only Westerner in the crowd. But she was facing the other way, with her head down, focused on her phone. Charlie did his best to conceal himself among the bodies pressed around him as the car moved off, just in case. He needn't have worried, since she kept her head down for three straight stops.

Charlie glanced up at the subway map and sensed where they were headed, despite Kimura's claim that she worked night shifts in Ueno, which lay in the opposite direction. Sure enough, just as the brakes came on to announce their fourth stop, Kimura looked up from her phone momentarily and then stepped out onto the platform at Roppongi Station, joining the thick flow of commuters headed up to street level. Charlie kept his distance as he followed her out of the station and onto a crowded street, managing to take a discreet photo of her in profile with his phone as she reached the top of the stairs. She continued walking with her head down, her attention divided between her phone and navigating the crowd in front of her.

They proceeded away from the station, down a main street first, before taking a couple of turns and progressing onto less and less travelled streets. Luckily for Charlie, even these were still crowded enough that he didn't feel exposed, as long as Kimura didn't turn around. He watched as she made her way into a six-storey building that was crammed between a convenience store and a much taller apartment block. He stopped on the opposite side of the street, but he could see her through the glass of the entrance door standing in front of the only elevator. The outside of the building had a number of colourful signs depicting the various businesses in the building, with Japanese text beside a floor number.

The elevator door slid open, and as she stepped inside and turned to face outward, he slipped behind a concrete pole, though he needn't have bothered — she was still engrossed in her phone. As soon as the elevator door slid shut, he hurried across the street and into the building, keeping his eye on the display above the elevator as it went from two to three, then hit four and stayed there. He stood watching it until it went back to three, and then walked back outside and down the street, wondering what to do next. Taking the elevator up to the fourth floor was too risky, as the small building probably only had one business suite per floor, meaning he could find himself face to face with Kimura as he stepped off the elevator. On the other hand, he was curious as to what was on the fourth, and he was pretty sure it wasn't a call centre.

He was considering his next move when a young man in biker leather walked up to him and thrust a colourful flyer in his hand.

"You like sexy girls?"

He scanned the flyer, which depicted an array of scantily clad women in sultry poses below some Japanese text. His eye was drawn to the one line of English: *Tokyo Dreams*, next to the same logo he had seen on the fourth floor directory of the building Kimura had just entered.

"Hottest ladies in Tokyo, just waiting for you, and the first drink's free," the man continued. He was in his early twenties, with sharp features and a number of facial piercings.

"It's a strip club?"

"If that's what you want it to be," the other man said with a lopsided smile. "Come check it out," he said, taking Charlie by the arm.

Charlie resisted the tug and stood his ground. "No thanks."

"Come on, man. I know you'll love it. You like topless?" He was following Charlie now, as he turned and began heading back toward the Metro station. "How about naked? We've got it all."

"I'm not interested." Charlie continued on his path, made a mental note of the little street's location and tucked the flyer into his pocket. He was pursued for fifty feet before the man finally gave up and turned his attention to a couple of young men who looked like they'd had a few too many.

Back outside Roppongi Station, Charlie stepped out of the stream of charcoal suits and white shirts to think. The odd sensation he had felt from the moment he laid eyes on Aiko Kimura had just turned into distinct unease. He tried to be objective, reminding himself that there was no proof that she actually worked at the strip club, brothel, or whatever it was that occupied the fourth floor of the building she had just entered. So why wasn't he surprised by the colourful brochure that he took out of his pocket and examined again? Kimura wasn't featured on the pamphlet, but he had no trouble imagining her there. Then there was her mysterious disappearance ever since Kobayashi's arrival on the scene at the hospital. And what about her non-existent job at a call centre that required her to keep such odd hours?

He tucked the pamphlet back into his pocket and glanced at his watch, then hurried toward the entrance to the Metro.

"Charlie? How's it going?" Lepage seemed genuinely pleased to see him, Charlie thought, as he stepped into the room around quarter to eight. He had been mistaken about visiting hours, and had mustered all of the charm and goodwill he could manage to get past the nurse at the fifth floor reception, with a promise not to stay for more than a few minutes.

"I'm good, Rob. I meant to get here earlier, but I got sidetracked."

"No worries. I was just watching soccer." He gestured to the little flat screen on a table in the corner. "It's the only thing I could find that doesn't require me to understand Japanese."

"I thought maybe Aiko was here."

"Not tonight," Lepage said, keeping his eyes on the television for a moment, before locating the remote and switching it off. Charlie considered challenging him, but realized that it was possible Kimura had not visited him, despite his having followed her from outside the hospital. "I had a visit from Elizabeth earlier today. She said you'd bumped into her and told her I was here."

"She mentioned you two had been close at one point," Charlie said. "So I thought she should know. I hope you don't mind."

"Why would I mind?" Lepage said, but Charlie sensed he did, somehow. Lepage looked at him for a moment, before asking, "Any news on Mike?"

Charlie hesitated, wondering whether Lepage still thought his friend was alive. Then he remembered that his post-accident memory should be intact. "You said you were expecting results of the autopsy," Lepage added, aware of the pregnant pause.

"Right." Charlie nodded. "Well, the results are in, but there isn't much in terms of determining what actually happened to him."

"That doesn't sound very helpful."

"It's not."

"Aiko said maybe he said the wrong thing to the wrong guy."

Charlie perked up at her name, and the fact that she had theories about Seger's death. "Speaking of Aiko," he said, trying to assess what was going on beyond those bright eyes as Lepage held his gaze again. "I was wondering if I could get her contact information, for Inspector Kobayashi."

"The cop? Sure. She's probably the prettiest cop I've ever seen, by the way," Lepage added, with a smile that quickly faded as another thought seemed to occur to him. "I, uh … I don't remember her number. She always calls me, not the other way around."

"I can check with reception," Charlie said, gesturing out toward the hall but knowing somehow that the exercise would be fruitless. He was more interested in examining Lepage's features as he spoke. He seemed embarrassed by his inability to recall his girlfriend's number, which was perfectly normal, Charlie supposed. Unless the expression was not embarrassment at all. "Do you know when she'll be back?"

Lepage shook his head and avoided Charlie's eyes for a split second, glancing over toward the television again. "She doesn't seem too happy with me."

"What do you mean?"

"Think of it from her perspective. I'm supposed to be her lover, and I can't even remember her phone number. How many women *aren't* going to be pissed off at that?"

"There is the fact that you have amnesia."

"Which doesn't seem to be cutting it anymore," he said, shaking his head. "For all I know, she's not coming back."

They sat in silence for a few moments, before Charlie spoke. "Do you really not remember *anything*?" Lepage seemed surprised by the question, his gaze dropping to his hands. "About Aiko, I mean," Charlie added.

"I really can't. I wish I could … but it's just not coming back."

Charlie had the sudden need to get out of the room. "I'm sure it will," he said, getting up.

"You're going, already?"

Charlie shrugged. "Visiting hours are over."

"I'm getting the cast off tomorrow morning," Lepage said, pointing at his leg. Charlie paused at the door.

"Already?"

"They'll give me a walking cast."

Charlie smiled. "That's great. Are they going to release you?"

"I'm supposed to talk to Dr. Yamaguchi about that tomorrow. He's going to want some assurances that I can make it on my own." Lepage hesitated, and looked a little sheepish. "I was wondering if you might be able to help. Maybe agree to check on me from time to time — by phone, I mean. You wouldn't have to babysit me, or anything."

"Of course." Charlie returned to Lepage's bedside and patted him on the arm. "I'll do whatever I can to help."

"Thanks, man." Lepage smiled. "Somehow I knew you would."

Charlie turned and left the room. As he made his way back to reception to inquire about Kimura's phone number, the image of Lepage's smile filled his mind and he was overcome by an unsettling feeling — like he was being played.

CHAPTER 17

Charlie was reviewing the materials that Miton had provided in support of their proposed property development in preparation for the meeting at eleven when his phone rang. He looked at the display and saw Cliff Redford's number. He checked the time and confirmed he still had a good thirty minutes before the Miton people arrived, then picked up the phone.

"Good morning, Cliff."

"Charlie. How are things?"

"Good. Just reviewing our property needs."

Redford chuckled. "Well, I have some swampland in Toyama to sell you if you're interested, but that's not why I'm calling. Have you talked to Lepage lately?"

"I was at the hospital last night," Charlie said, remembering that in addition to representing the embassy on numerous legal files, Redford was also the head of a not-for-profit organization that helped out expat Canadians. He knew Redford had visited Lepage in hospital, and was sure to have left him his card and an offer to help out in any way he could. "Rob said they were thinking about releasing him soon."

"I just got off the phone with Yamaguchi," Redford said. "He's concerned that the lack of any family members to discharge him to will make Lepage's release difficult."

"Yeah, Rob asked whether I'd be willing to look in on him now and then if he gets released. I said that wasn't a problem."

"That's good," Redford said. "But I think there's an insurance issue as well. These hospital administrators give new meaning to the word *bureaucracy*, and they're tighter than a nun's arse. Not Yamaguchi, but the people he reports to."

Charlie laughed. "Surely they're not going to keep him indefinitely if he's medically cleared."

"No, but they can drag things out if we don't give them a little shove in the right direction. I'm going to make a few calls and then head over to meet with Yamaguchi around six. I was calling to see if you wanted to join me."

Charlie hesitated as he noticed an incoming email from Kobayashi. He scanned it quickly and saw she was writing to tell him that there was no new information on the Seger case and that she was in Nagawa for the day on another case, but would be in touch tomorrow.

"Sure. I'll meet you there."

He had barely hung up the phone when it rang again, this time from reception to let him know that the Miton party was here early. He gathered his papers into a folder, adjusted his tie and double-checked that he had a stack of pristine business cards in his pocket before heading for the elevator.

Charlie was on his way up the steps to the main entrance of the hospital when he heard his name, turned, and saw Cliff Redford heading toward him.

"Hi, Cliff."

"Good timing. Ready to see if we can spring our jailbird?"

Charlie laughed. "Hopefully he's ready."

"Are you kidding? How would you like to be cooped up in this place for weeks on end."

"I just meant, if his memory's not completely restored …"

"I guess it isn't," Redford continued. "Though it's a wonder he hasn't lost his mind completely in here," he said, looking around as he hit the call button for the elevator. "Best thing for him is to get back out onto his feet again — breathe some fresh air, go back to his apartment, and reconnect." Charlie nodded, thinking it sounded like a reasonable prescription, despite the fact that Redford was a lawyer, not a doctor. "From what Yamaguchi said on the phone," Redford continued, "it doesn't seem like Rob's a danger to himself — his memory after the accident seems to be working just fine. It's not like he's going to forget where he lives once he's been there, you know what I mean?"

"That's my understanding, too." Charlie nodded.

"I think Yamaguchi just needs some assurance that someone will check in on Rob from time to time. Make sure he's reintegrating, managing his finances, and all that, you know?"

"Right," Charlie said, though Yamaguchi had mentioned no such requirement to him. He wondered what else the doctor had discussed with Redford.

"There he is now," Redford said as the elevator doors opened onto the fifth floor and they caught sight of Yamaguchi talking to a nurse in front of the reception desk. The doctor smiled as he saw them approach.

"Mr. Hill … Charlie, and Redford-san."

"Doctor," Redford said, bowing quickly. He was as informal as they came, but he had been in Japan long enough to know that there was no skipping the traditional greeting, however abbreviated.

"Come." Yamaguchi led them down the hall with an enthusiasm that suggested a surprise awaited them in Lepage's room. They weren't disappointed when they stepped inside and saw Lepage dressed in a polo shirt and a pair of khakis, sitting in the corner chair instead of laid up in bed in a hospital gown. His right foot was enveloped in a walking cast, but he looked fit as a fiddle otherwise. He stood up, as if to demonstrate his ability to do so.

"Ta da!"

"You got the cast off," Charlie said. "Congratulations! It must be nice to be out of that bed."

"You have no idea."

"Well, that's phase one," Redford said, slapping Lepage on the shoulder. "Phase two is to get you out of here altogether."

"Yes, I wanted to discuss the possibilities for Mr. Lepage's release," Yamaguchi said, his features resuming their normal, businesslike appearance. "Given that he has no family here in Tokyo, and his employer is unwilling to assume responsibility."

Charlie's eyebrows shot up.

"Don't look so shocked," Redford said. "Most employers won't go near a foreigner when there's a risk of being stuck with the medical bills."

"I thought they had insurance."

"For his hospitalization and treatment here, yes," Redford said. "But discharge is different, right, Doc?"

Yamaguchi nodded. "It is true that Nippon Kasuga's position is expected, and in the absence of a family member to sign off on Mr. Lepage's release, I must ask whether there are other possibilities."

Charlie looked at Lepage, then Yamaguchi. "What do you need us to do?"

"I think what he needs," Redford cut in, "if you'll allow me, Doc, is the assurance he was talking about. That we'll look in on Rob here on a regular basis."

"That's all?" Charlie had been expecting to be asked to formally sign off on Lepage's discharge. While he was prepared to do so in his personal capacity, there were limits to what he could undertake in his capacity as a consular officer, and he was pretty sure Denault wouldn't be on board with him assuming the care of a consular case. "I've been coming here on an almost daily basis for the past week anyway, and Rob's apartment is closer to mine than the hospital, so it'll actually be easier for me to check up on him there."

"And Nippon Kasuga's offices are in the same building as mine, so there we go," Redford added, as though to seal the deal. Yamaguchi still seemed to have reservations.

"I'll have to discuss it with the hospital's administration. It is a bit ... unusual."

"And if they're concerned about insurance, I can have a word with the hospital's carrier," Redford continued. "Come on, Doc. You know he's better off back out in the world." Redford gestured to Lepage, who looked on hopefully.

"I didn't mean to suggest that I don't support the idea," Yamaguchi said. "I do, but I will have to make the case to the board in the morning."

"Not until then?" Lepage's disappointment was obvious.

"I'm afraid not."

"And what do you think of your chances?" Charlie asked.

Yamaguchi paused, taking in Lepage's forlorn expression before allowing a smile to bloom on his face. "I think they're good."

"You want me to attend the meeting?" Redford asked, but Yamaguchi waved him off.

"I appreciate the offer, but I think it would be better if I handled it."

"Whatever you say, Doc."

"Thanks, guys," Lepage said after Yamaguchi had left. "I don't know what I'll do if they tell me I have to stay here after tomorrow."

"Don't worry about it," Redford said. "We're gonna see to it that tonight's your last night in here, right, Charlie?"

Charlie nodded. "You bet."

They chatted for a while and then agreed to touch base midmorning. Riding the elevator back down to the ground floor, Redford patted his stomach.

"I don't know about you, Charlie, but I could eat."

Charlie looked at his watch and noticed it was almost seven. He hadn't eaten since the small bowl of noodles at the embassy cafeteria at lunchtime. "Me, too."

"I know a good *yakiniku* place near here. We could walk."

"Lead the way."

Fifteen minutes later, they were being seated in the far corner of a bustling restaurant on the edge of the entertainment district. Redford waved off the waitress's attempt to give them menus and chattered something in Japanese to her, prompting her to nod and smile. The only word Charlie thought he recognized was "beer."

"I ordered the set menu."

"Not your first rodeo, then?"

Redford laughed. "I haven't been here in a little while but it hasn't changed much. It's a really good mixed grill, you'll see."

They chatted for a bit, then the waitress returned with two frosted glasses of Asahi beer. "Cheers." Redford tapped his glass off Charlie's.

"Here's to getting Rob out tomorrow."

They each drank, then Redford wiped foam from his top lip and grinned. "They say no good deed goes unpunished."

"What do you think his odds are of getting out tomorrow?"

Redford shrugged. "Probably fifty-fifty, maybe a little less. The Japanese are sticklers for adhering to policy, and I can't think of anyone worse than hospital administrators."

Charlie was surprised, given Redford's apparent enthusiasm back at the hospital.

"I don't mean we won't spring him eventually," Redford said quickly, noting Charlie's dejection. "It might take a little persuasion, but we'll get there. It'd be a lot easier if there was a family member."

Charlie shook his head. "I've tried everything I can think of to track down someone back in Canada, believe me."

"I'm sure you have. What about the girlfriend?" Redford said suddenly. "I hadn't thought of her."

"I don't know …"

"What do you mean?"

"There's something about her," he said, realizing that Redford had never actually met her. He pulled out his phone and selected the photo he had taken of her coming out of the Metro, enlarging it so that most of her face was visible in profile. Redford took the phone and examined the image.

"Pretty easy on the eyes."

Charlie frowned. "I have a hard time seeing the two of them together. And she hasn't been around lately."

"Really? I wonder why."

Charlie sipped his beer in silence.

"There's obviously something you're not telling me, Charlie," Redford said with a smile. "But I'm a patient man, so I'll just sit here until you decide to spill the beans."

"Maybe it's nothing," Charlie began. "But she's kind of made herself scarce ever since she found out Inspector Kobayashi was asking questions about Seger."

"Oh yeah? Maybe she doesn't like cops. I'm curious to

meet this Kobayashi, though," Redford said. "A female detective in this city? She must be tough as nails."

"And I think Kimura lied about what she does for a living," Charlie added, ignoring the reference to Kobayashi.

Redford shrugged. "What did she say she did?"

"Call centre worker."

"And you don't believe her?"

"Kobayashi checked her name against some list of registered call centre people, but it's more than that." He paused as Redford watched him dig in his pocket for the brochure. He set it on the table between them and Redford picked it up and examined it.

"She works *here*?"

"What kind of place is it?" Charlie asked, feeling foolish as he heard Redford's reaction.

"Well it ain't the Girl Guides, that's for sure."

"Strip joint?"

"Something like that. They call themselves companions."

Charlie frowned. "You mean she's a hooker?"

"Not necessarily. The service offered depends on the place, but I'm guessing from this there's more than stimulating conversation on the menu." Redford tapped the picture of an almost topless woman. "And I guess that would explain Ms. Kimura's reluctance to fraternize with the police."

"Are these places illegal?"

"Not officially, but prostitution is, if that's what's going on. This is in Roppongi," he added, looking at the address. "We could go check it out after dinner if you like. Maybe our friend's working tonight."

"Hmm," Charlie said as Redford stood.

"I'm going to hit the head. Be right back."

Charlie sat there, thinking about Kimura and wondering what Rob Lepage was doing dating a sex worker. She was pretty hot, but Lepage was young, handsome, and rich — it just didn't add up. He plucked his BlackBerry out of his pocket and scanned his emails, surprised to see a message from Elizabeth Farnsworth, asking him to meet her for coffee or lunch tomorrow. He checked his schedule and sent a reply suggesting lunch at a little bistro down the street from the embassy, in the direction of Omote-sando. Now *there* was someone Charlie could see Lepage with, he thought, recalling the image of Farnsworth as he had encountered her in the elevator of Lepage's building. Smart, sexy, and athletic. She and Aiko Kimura appeared to inhabit very different worlds, yet Lepage had apparently been involved with both. He wondered what Farnsworth wanted to talk to him about and, seeing no immediate response from her, he tucked the phone back in his pocket.

He sipped his beer and scanned the room around him, noticing two men at a nearby table, one of whom was lighting a cigarette. Charlie watched as he clicked the lighter and drew on the filter, attracting the flame to the tip and igniting it, and exhaling a cloud of blue smoke a second later, before removing the cigarette from his lips with his left hand. Something about the process, or perhaps the smell of the tobacco, reminded him of his smoking days, and he felt a strong urge to light up. He kept watching the cigarette, but his eye was drawn to the man's little finger, the end of which was missing. He found himself staring and when the man's eyes met his, Charlie quickly looked away.

"They haven't brought the meat yet?" Redford said, resuming his seat and following Charlie's gaze over to the next table for a moment, as Charlie shook his head and took a sip of his beer.

"Careful who you're staring at in here," Redford added quietly.

"What do you mean?"

"I think your friend's a member of the society for a better Japan, if you know what I mean."

"I'm not sure I do ..." Charlie stopped speaking as the waitress arrived and deposited a large plate with a selection of thinly sliced meats and an assortment of bowls containing chopped vegetables. He waited until she had left before he continued his thought. "What do you mean — a society for a better Japan?" he asked, keeping an eye on the two men at the other table, now occupied with grilling their food.

"That's what they like to call themselves.... Everyone else calls them yakuza. You didn't notice the left pinky?"

"Is that for real? Cutting off their little fingers?"

Redford nodded and took a sip of his beer. "Sure, though there's less of it with the younger generation." He gestured to the grill in the centre of the table. "Here, let's get this thing started." He pointed to four cuts of meat that had a slightly different texture than the others. "Put a couple of slices of that on the grill."

"What is it?" Charlie asked, arranging two of the larger pieces on the grill while Redford put some broccoli and mushrooms on the other side.

"Best you don't know," Redford said, eliciting a look of alarm from Charlie. "I'm kidding! It's just different cuts of beef. How the hell do I know which is which?"

Charlie laughed and took another pull on his cold beer, which was going down very well. "So, are they common?" he said, lowering his voice.

"What, our fingerless friends?" Redford chuckled. "Sure, they're around. Not like they used to be, of course. They pretty much ran things back before the real estate bubble, and even had the tacit support of the cops. But then the bottom fell out and a lot of people blamed them. So much bad debt in the marketplace, plus they were getting out of hand, executing people in broad daylight. It was pretty crazy." Redford shook his head, as though remembering the times.

"And now?"

"They've had to diversify, get creative, even blend in. They're like any organized crime group anywhere, I suppose. Some of their business is the usual stuff — prostitution, drugs, gambling, and such, but they're into international finance as well. There was even a story that a Yakuza-backed outfit had conned $350 million from Lehman Brothers before it went under." Redford paused to flag down the waitress and point to their nearly-empty beer glasses before continuing. "But they pretty much keep to themselves. I've been working here for thirty years and I've never crossed paths with them."

"Would they be involved in the Rohypnol stuff that goes on in Roppongi?"

"You mean, what they think might have happened to this Seger fellow? Naw," Redford gave a dismissive wave. "Too lowbrow for them, and attracts too much attention from the boys in blue. Speaking of which, there's no break in that case, is there?"

Charlie shook his head. "The best guess still seems to be a fleecing gone wrong," he said, unsure whether to reveal the autopsy results that showed that there was no Rohypnol in Seger's system after all.

Redford drained his beer and stared at Charlie. "You don't seem convinced."

He shrugged. "I don't know what to think. I hardly knew Seger, but he struck me as the kind of guy who might have seen a few sticky situations in his time. Maybe his luck just ran out."

"That's done," Redford said, pointing to the lightly charred meat on the grill, plucking a piece off with his chopsticks, and depositing it on his plate. Charlie followed suit, though less adroitly.

"Mmm," Charlie said as they both chewed the succulent meat.

"Good, isn't it? Tongue's my favourite."

"Tongue? I thought you didn't know which cut was which."

"Some people get turned off by the idea of eating tongue." He paused and smiled as Charlie resumed chewing.

"Well, whatever it is, it sure tastes good."

They debated Lepage's prospects for release for a while, then chatted about life in Tokyo as they gradually made their way through the meat and vegetables before them.

"So, you're a single guy in Tokyo. How've you been making out with the ladies?" Redford asked, with a wolfish grin. Charlie laughed. He knew Redford enough to know that he liked to play the part of the scoundrel, though he was apparently very happily married to a Japanese woman.

"I haven't really had much of a chance to wade into the dating pool, what with work, and getting sett—"

"We both know that's a crock of shit," Redford cut in. "There's only one priority for a single man, and it sounds like you've been ignoring it. We've got to do something about that right away," he added, as the waitress arrived at the table. They waved off her offer of dessert and Redford continued. "Seriously though, have you got something going at work?" he persisted. "The last time I was at the embassy there were some pretty fine-looking women."

Charlie sipped the last of his beer and thought of Karen Fraser, and the sharp feeling of disappointment at meeting her handsome, wealthy husband. Perhaps he had been thinking there was a glimmer of hope there for him when he first met her. "No, nothing like that."

"Okay, so we've got to get you out."

"I don't know." Charlie preferred not to mention his last outing, which gave him the impression that he might be doomed to singledom in Tokyo. "Japanese women seem kind of ... aloof."

"So much to learn, so little time," Redford said with a mock frown. "I told you, it's all a facade. It's like everything else in this place — there's the exterior and then there's the reality below — the two are completely unrelated. Polar opposites, you might say. I guarantee you, once you've spent the night with a Japanese woman, you'll understand."

Charlie nodded. "I know you mentioned the facade thing," he said as an image of Chikako Kobayashi popped into his head. Actually, it was more than an image, because he had smelled her perfume as they had stood close together on the crowded subway car. He had to make an effort to break away from the memory and return to reality. "It just seems like it's hard to break through."

"That's what sake's for."

Charlie laughed, but Redford seemed dead serious. "I mean it. You just need the right environment, that's all. You leave it to me. But first things first, let's pay a visit to the mysterious Ms. Kimura."

"You think that's a good idea?"

"Why not? Besides, she doesn't know what I look like, so I can go in and check it out while you wait downstairs, if you like."

They paid the bill and then headed out into the street, which had become more crowded in the hour or so since they had entered the restaurant.

After a short ride on the Metro from Shinjuku, they emerged from Roppongi Station and Redford lit up. Charlie rarely craved cigarettes anymore but, with a couple of beers aboard, the smell of a freshly lit Marlboro stirred a longing that he had trouble quelling.

They zigzagged through a maze of connecting streets, and the farther they got from the Metro station, the narrower the streets became. Young women dressed in what looked like cartoon costumes offered flyers to passersby. Charlie soon recognized the street he had followed Kimura to and, though the guy who had thrust the flyer for Kimura's establishment into his hand the other night wasn't there when they arrived at the address, someone else was doing the same job. Redford had a quick exchange with him in Japanese, and then was about to walk up the steps when he abruptly turned around and yanked Charlie by the arm, pulling him back onto the street, away from the building.

"What's wrong?"

"Just keep moving," Redford said tersely, as Charlie caught a glimpse of two older Japanese men emerging from the building, both in the standard charcoal suits and white shirts. Both had sombre ties, loosened at the collar. The man on the right's dark hair was streaked with grey. Redford didn't speak again until they had rounded the corner and he had assured himself that they were alone again.

"That was Yasuo Kato," he finally said as they came to the end of the quiet lane, joined up with a more populated street, and headed back in the direction they had come from. "He's one of the senior execs at Nippon Kasuga."

"The guy with the grey streaks in his hair?"

"No, the other one. I've met him before, on the building management board."

Charlie nodded. "So bumping into him outside a strip club would be awkward, then?"

Redford smiled. "Now you're getting it. In the shame culture, it's not about whether you've done something, it's whether you get caught."

"Preserving the facade?"

"Precisely. Here." Redford stopped at a designated smoking area with a little screen and an oversized ashtray. "I'll have a smoke while he clears out, then we can head back."

"I have to say," Charlie said as Redford lit up. "I don't really understand the whole shame culture thing. I mean, if everyone knows that everyone does stuff like go to strip clubs, then what's the big deal?"

Redford laughed as he exhaled a blue cloud of tobacco smoke. "You're not the only one who doesn't understand it. I've been here for thirty years and I still don't have it all figured out. It can seem really fucked up sometimes, but there actually is a system." He paused to take another drag of the cigarette before continuing. "Let's say I did bump into Mr. Kato back there. He would have been nothing but polite and charming. The problem would be if we bump into each other a week from now, at a business meeting."

Charlie shrugged. "You wouldn't just give each other a knowing wink and move on?"

"No!" Redford said, almost choking on the smoke as he was midway through another inhale. "That's just it. There's no knowing wink here, just repressed shame."

"So he avoids you instead."

"Exactly, and that's bad for business."

"I guess I get it."

Redford took a few last puffs before tossing the rest of the cigarette into the ashtray. "We should be good now, come on." They headed back toward the club and as they arrived at the familiar building, Redford pointed across the street.

"You wait there. I'll go up and check it out. If I'm not out in thirty minutes, call in the cavalry, or come up and join me for a drink or something." Redford chuckled as he headed up the steps and into the entrance. Charlie crossed the street and slid into the shadows, so as not to draw the attention of the flyer guy, who was working the other end of the street. He was only there for fifteen minutes before Redford re-emerged, lighting another cigarette as he came out of the building.

"So?" Charlie met him on the sidewalk.

"I don't know if our friend was up there," Redford began, setting off in the direction of the Metro station, "but if that is where she works, I'm pretty sure it's not as a candy-striper, and I didn't see any phones. It's definitely a cathouse — pretty pricey, too, from what I could tell. They wanted twenty thousand yen for a private dance. God knows what the full Monty goes for in there."

"Is it possible Rob doesn't know?"

Redford shrugged. "Anything's possible, I suppose."

"Do I tell him?"

"I'm not sure how you slip that into the conversation. 'Hey, Rob, did you know that when your girlfriend's not at the hospital, she's turning tricks in Roppongi?'"

Charlie frowned, thinking Redford might have a point. If Lepage did know, it would seem judgmental, and if he didn't, it would come as quite a shock, and Charlie had a feeling Lepage didn't know.

"I'll have to figure out how to bring it up without making a big deal of it," he finally said.

Redford shrugged. "I'll ask around at work, see if anyone's heard of the place. It's possible she's just a hostess, I suppose."

They made their way back to the station and split up to head off in different directions; Redford to his apartment in Omote-sando, not far from Lepage's building, and Charlie back to Akasaka. All he could think about on the way back was how incongruous Kimura and Lepage seemed as a couple. As he emerged from Gaiemmae Station and walked down Aoyama-dori toward the embassy complex, his thoughts turned to Elizabeth Farnsworth and their lunch date for the following day. He was intrigued as to what she wanted to talk about. He decided to swing by his office on the way home and pick up a draft report that he was supposed to submit to Denault first thing in the morning. He should really give it another read, he told himself. Besides, it wasn't like he was going to miss flipping through one unintelligible television show after another. He walked down the half-lit hallway to his office and found the report, then paused at the flashing red light on his phone. He was halfway to the door when he decided to go back and check the message. It was Kobayashi, to say that she had gotten back to Tokyo earlier than expected and just wanted to give him an update, asking him to call her in the morning. He would make her his first order of business.

He left the embassy building and made the short walk to his apartment with his thoughts divided between Farnsworth and Kobayashi. In some ways, as different as two people could be, but both undeniably attractive. It was a shame he wasn't meeting either of them under less formal circumstances. As he fell into a chair and stared at the cover of the draft report, he thought of Redford's comment about Japanese women, and his insistence that Charlie get out a bit. All in good time, he thought with a sigh, as he picked up the report and started reading.

CHAPTER 18

Charlie was reading an email on a change in consular policy when he saw an incoming message from the ambassador's assistant. His heart raced when he realized Westwood was asking to be briefed on the property file. Either he had read the report that Charlie had sent out first thing this morning and had questions, or he hadn't, and wanted a verbal update. He checked the clock on his computer and realized Westwood wanted to meet in fifteen minutes. Denault, who would normally be the go-between, was in Osaka for the day, so Charlie was on his own. He gathered his notes from the Miton meeting, which had gone pretty much as Charlie had expected and had focused on the broad strokes of an exchange of properties, with details to follow. He printed off a copy of the proposal, then headed upstairs for the meeting. After a brief wait in the secure zone reception area, he was waved in by the ambassador's formidable assistant. Westwood was sitting at his desk, staring at something on his computer monitor, when Charlie took tentative steps into his office.

"Charlie, come on in," Westwood said, coming out from behind his desk and motioning to the leather sofas arranged around a glass coffee table. Charlie took a seat at the end of one of the couches, while Westwood sat in a matching chair near him. Whereas Charlie sat ramrod straight, Westwood assumed a casual air, leaning back as though he were sitting in a Muskoka chair. "Thanks for agreeing to meet on short notice." Charlie nodded, though he wasn't sure he had the option of refusing the meeting. "I read your report on the property development file," Westwood continued, tapping a file folder on the table in front of him. "You obviously know how to write a report," he added, with a smile that made Charlie wonder whether he was giving him a compliment or a gentle dig. He soon realized it was the latter. "But I'm more interested in what you really think."

"About the property file?"

"Yes. I thought it might be good to get your *unfiltered* view. I know Louis is very keen on the idea, but I wanted to know if it's something we should be actively pursuing … objectively."

Charlie nodded again. So Westwood had called the meeting knowing full well that Denault was out of town. His suspicion that Westwood was less obsessed with the project than Denault suddenly seemed confirmed. "Well, it's a bit early to say for sure, but I think there are some challenges, mostly around the financials."

"Really?" Westwood ran a finger over his top lip. "Louis seemed to think they were prepared to throw money at us, as well as build us a new residential complex for free."

Charlie picked up the report. He had to tread very carefully here — Denault was his immediate supervisor and he wasn't out to make him look bad, but after looking at the numbers it seemed pretty obvious that the developer was low-balling the value of the Canadian property they were looking to take in exchange for the new development in a less expensive area. "Well, if you factor in the cost of construction for what we're going to want them to deliver in exchange, it's hard to see how there's going to be much left over."

"You mean if they try to screw us on the value of our property," Westwood said with an assured tone that suggested he was thinking exactly the same thing about the overall viability of the deal.

"In theory, it could still work," Charlie said, taking the high road and passing up the opportunity to make Denault look like a stooge. "But I've asked them to provide detailed financials and an appraisal next week. I'll be sure to flesh out what it is they're offering, and how they got to their numbers. I'd be happy to debrief you after."

Westwood nodded, then asked a few more questions about the report, which made it clear that he had actually read it. When they had dealt with those, Westwood flipped the file folder shut, but rather than stand and bring an end to the meeting as expected, he gave Charlie a quizzical look.

"How's the consular stuff going? You finding your feet?"

Charlie nodded. "I think so. I've had a lot of help from Karen Fraser, and Louis, of course."

Westwood smiled. "How's the guy in hospital — the one who was in a coma?"

Charlie felt there was some undercurrent in Westwood's questions, but he wasn't sure. He replied straight up, anyway. "He might be released in the next few days, depending on whether we can convince the hospital that he'll have some people checking in on him. When I say we," he added quickly, "I'm including myself and Cliff Redford, who's been helping out with the hospital administration."

Westwood smiled. "Well, if Cliff's involved, I have no doubt he'll be released, if only so the hospital won't have to deal with him any longer than they have to." Westwood laughed, seeing Charlie's reaction. "Don't get me wrong, I've known Cliff a long time, and there's no better advocate to have in your corner. He's nothing if not persuasive. But the Japanese really don't know what to do with him sometimes."

Charlie nodded. "Yes, I can see how he might present them with a challenge."

"And your other file — this unfortunate death in Roppongi. Do we know anything more about how the police are treating it?"

"They've assigned an inspector, who's shared the results of the autopsy with me. Inconclusive, I'm afraid. I think she's leaning toward foul play, but there's been no official word yet. I'm supposed to get an update later this morning."

Westwood nodded. "There's a report on its way from Ottawa on this Michael Seger," he said, his features taking on a graver expression. "I'll get it to you as soon as it comes in, of course, but I gather the gist of it is that Seger may have had some unsavoury connections back in Canada."

"Really?" Charlie said, though his instinct about Seger was at odds with the surprise in his voice.

"He had some family members that were, or possibly still are, part of organized crime in Montreal. It's possible he had nothing to do with them, of course," Westwood added, with a wave of his hand as he adjusted himself on the sofa. "Just thought you might like to know."

Charlie nodded. "Yes, that certainly is of interest. You say there's a report … coming?"

"I have a friend in the senior ranks at the RCMP. We were talking yesterday about something else and he mentioned that this report had crossed his desk and thought I'd like to know, given it's related to the death of a Canadian in Tokyo. I'll make sure you get a copy."

"Thank you."

"And remind me what this Seger fellow's connection to Robert Lepage was?"

"That's a good question." Charlie was beginning to wonder just how familiar Westwood was with the file. A minute ago, it was the guy in hospital. Now he was citing Lepage's full name and the fact that Seger and he were connected somehow. Then again, Westwood seemed the type who made it his business to know a bit about everything going on in his bailiwick. "My understanding is that they were friends. Seger had apparently been in touch from Hong Kong, where he was on a business trip, and arranged to come see Lepage. The problem is that according to Seger's passport, he hadn't been in Hong Kong for months."

Westwood frowned. "What does Lepage have to say about it?"

Charlie shrugged. "Lepage can't really confirm or deny anything, because his memory prior to his accident is still patchy."

"How unfortunate. Yet he's to be released soon, you said?"

"Well, his physical injuries are healing. And his memory is returning slowly." As Charlie spoke, it didn't sound like it added up. If he was in Westwood's shoes, he might have some doubts about the veracity of this story as well.

"Well, I'm sure you'll keep on it. I gather Seger's immediate family hasn't made a formal request for the remains?"

Charlie shook his head. "His parents are dead, and there's just one sister. I spoke with her and it was clear that they're estranged. She seemed annoyed that I had bothered to call her."

Westwood shrugged. "Families," he said, then stood, indicating the end of the meeting. "Thank you, Charlie. And make sure you get the details of what's on the table with this real estate thing, will you? The last thing I need is to be reporting back on a mega project that turns out to be dust in the wind."

"I will."

Charlie returned to his office and wondered when he might get a look at this mysterious RCMP report, and what else it might say about Mike Seger.

CHAPTER 19

Charlie sat in the front seat of the embassy van, rereading the email from Elizabeth Farnsworth cancelling their lunch meeting at the last minute. It seemed odd that she would ask for the meeting, without actually specifying a reason, and then cancel on fifteen minutes' notice. Charlie couldn't detect anything unusual in the wording of the email, which he had received just as he was arriving at the appointed restaurant. He had decided to dine alone, crammed into a corner of the crowded bistro. That was one thing he couldn't get used to in Tokyo — the close proximity. It went somewhat unnoticed if you were distracted by conversation, but sitting alone, Charlie found it oppressive to the point that he had begun to hate dining by himself. His first few weeks in Havana and Moscow were different — there was always somewhere relatively quiet to hide away. Not so in Tokyo, where every square inch had a purpose. He looked up from his BlackBerry and out the window as a van pulled up at a packed intersection, as though to illustrate his point.

He turned his mind to the upcoming meeting at the hospital, where Redford was waiting with Dr. Yamaguchi to discuss Lepage's case. Redford had been cryptic on the phone, but Charlie had a strong feeling that the news would be good and that Lepage was going to be released imminently. His smile turned to a frown as he recalled the ambassador's questions about Lepage's memory loss. It had given him the same feeling as Kobayashi's comments to the same effect. He had left her a message just before lunch and hadn't heard back yet, but he was sure she would eventually get in touch. As the van pulled up in front of the hospital, Charlie thanked the driver, hopped out, and hurried in through the entrance and over to the bank of elevators leading to the now familiar fifth floor. Redford was sitting in the reception area, fiddling with his phone.

"So?"

Redford smiled and stood, clapping him on the shoulder. "Come on, let's get it straight from the horse's mouth. Yamaguchi's waiting for us."

Charlie followed as Redford led them back to the elevator and hit the down call button. "His office is on the fourth," Redford said, seeing Charlie's puzzled expression.

"All the times I've been here, I've never been invited to his office."

"Stick with me, kid," Redford said with a laugh as they boarded the crowded elevator for the brief trip. They were at Yamaguchi's door a few minutes later, where an efficient looking woman in her fifties asked them their business in Japanese, prompting a brief exchange with Redford. They turned at the sound of Yamaguchi's voice as he emerged from his office.

"Please, come in."

"Yamaguchi-san," Redford said, with his usual thousand-watt smile. "I gather you have some good news for us."

Yamaguchi didn't respond, but led them into his office instead, where Rob Lepage sat, a single crutch leaning up against the arm of his chair.

"Hey, guys," he said, his face breaking into a smile.

They exchanged greetings, and after he and Charlie had taken seats next to Lepage, Redford spoke. "I can't stand the suspense, Doc. Are you gonna tell us what happened, or what?"

Yamaguchi nodded. "The hospital's administration board has agreed to release Mr. Lepage," he said, looking at his patient. "Effective tomorrow morning."

"Any conditions on the release?" Redford said, after an initial round of congratulations to an obviously relieved Lepage.

"He's to be reassessed in one week," Yamaguchi began, though Charlie could tell there was more to come. "And until then, he's to contact me once a day, just to check in."

"That sounds reasonable," Redford said as Charlie nodded and Lepage looked on.

"There is a … catch," Yamaguchi added. "The board was concerned about potential liability … liability that would not be covered by its insurer."

"Did you mention the offer from the insurer?" Redford said.

"What offer?" Charlie asked, bemused.

Redford shrugged. "I said I could probably arrange for some coverage on a one-off basis from an insurer I represent — it's an affiliate of a Canada-based company and they've done this sort of thing in the past, for trade shows put on by the Chamber of Commerce, that sort of thing."

Yamaguchi nodded. "I may need to discuss this further with you," he said, then turned to Charlie. "I also mentioned that the embassy had been in regular contact with Mr. Lepage, that you had opened a consular file … and that you would likely continue to be in touch with Mr. Lepage after his discharge, though I was careful not to suggest that you were taking custody of him in any official capacity."

Charlie nodded. "That's fine, and I do plan to keep in touch," he said, looking at Lepage. "And I want you to know that if there's anything you need, or if there's anything I can do to help get you back on your feet, just let me know."

"Thanks, Charlie, I appreciate that," Lepage said, a look of genuine gratitude on his face.

Yamaguchi went over a few things to keep in mind with recently discharged patients generally, as well as some more specific issues for those recovering from amnesia. When he and Redford began to discuss the details of the insurance policy, Redford looked at Charlie and Lepage.

"You don't have to stick around for this if you don't want to."

Charlie shrugged his shoulders, but Lepage was quick to get up on his feet. "I'm going to take advantage of my new mobility to go outside for a bit — it looks like a beautiful day and I've been stuck inside for a long time."

"Remember to stay on the hospital grounds," Yamaguchi said, then softened his expression, "until tomorrow."

"Don't worry. I'm not planning a prison break the day before I get out of here."

"I'll walk you out," Charlie said, thanking Yamaguchi and promising to be in touch with Redford that evening for some follow-up. He joined Lepage out in the hall and watched him hobble along the hallway toward the elevator.

"I guess your leg's still pretty sore, huh?"

"I'm just glad to be up and about," Lepage said through a grimace. "Another few days in that bed and I would have lost it."

They rode the elevator down in silence. When they were outside by the front entrance, Lepage sat on a bench and rested his crutch against the armrest. "I really appreciate you helping out," he said, squinting in the sun as he looked up at Charlie, who stood to the side of the bench.

"It's nothing. I'm just as glad to see you getting out of here."

"I guess you can close your consular file on me now." Lepage looked out at the bustle of people and traffic. "Assuming this next week goes well, of course."

"I'm sure it will." Charlie smiled.

"Is that what happens?" Lepage asked. "Does my file get … closed?"

"If you're no longer in need of assistance, then yes." He watched Lepage's expression, wondering what was behind the question. Simple curiosity, he supposed. "I guess Aiko's happy that you'll be getting out tomorrow?" he added.

"Uh-huh." Lepage continued to stare out at the traffic.

"I haven't seen her in a while," Charlie continued, wondering if there was any possible way of mentioning the fact that he had discovered that Kimura appeared to be working in the sex trade, not at a call centre.

"Me neither. I'm wondering if she got fed up with me forgetting everything about her, you know?"

"I'm sure it's a difficult situation," he said, hearing Lepage's dejected tone and feeling guilty that he seemed to know more about Kimura than her so-called boyfriend.

"You got to know her a little bit." Lepage was suddenly looking up at Charlie, who averted his eyes for a moment, before regaining Lepage's steady gaze. "What do you think?"

"About you two? Geez, I don't know, Rob."

"You can tell me, Charlie, even if it's bad."

Charlie was feeling more and more awkward at the direction of the conversation, and wondered what exactly Lepage was getting at. Was it possible he had an inkling that Kimura wasn't being entirely forthright about how she made her living?

"She seemed nice enough to me, and she's obviously very attractive."

"She is pretty hot," Lepage said with a grin that quickly faded. "How could I forget … being with her?"

Charlie patted him on the shoulder. "I'm sure it will come back, just like the rest of your memories. Or you'll just have to make some new ones." They stood in silence for a moment, then Charlie glanced at his watch. "I'd better be going. Do you want a ride out of here tomorrow?"

Lepage shook his head. "Naw, I'm good. I'll give you a call tomorrow evening, though, just to check in."

Charlie was a few feet away when he heard Lepage call out. "Thanks for everything, Charlie."

Lepage watched as Charlie disappeared around the corner, then rummaged in a pocket for the cigarette and matches Kimura had left him on her brief visit this morning. Lighting the cigarette, he took a long draw and tilted his head back as he blew out a cloud of smoke, the nicotine flooding through his veins. He liked Charlie, and appreciated what he was trying to do. But he was clearly suspicious about Kimura, and who knew what other suspicions he had — about Seger, or Lepage's own selective memory? If he began to act on those suspicions, things could become very dangerous.

Lepage smoked the cigarette for a few minutes, silently contemplating his next move, then took a last puff and tossed the smouldering butt on the ground. He popped a mint into his mouth and looked up into the late afternoon sunshine. Tomorrow, he would finally be out of this hospital — that much he knew. What would happen next was much less certain.

CHAPTER 20

Charlie saw the name displayed on his office telephone and an involuntary smile briefly lit his face. He picked it up on the second ring.

"Hello, Mr. Hillier. I just got your messa—"

"I thought you were going to call me Charlie?"

There was an awkward pause at the other end of the line. "Yes, of course. How are you, Charlie?"

"I'm good. I have some business this afternoon at the Ministry of Justice and I thought we could meet to discuss the Seger investigation. I was wondering if I could buy you a coffee."

There was another pause, this one long enough for Charlie to wonder if he was becoming too informal for Kobayashi's liking. "I also wanted to let you know that Rob Lepage was released from hospital yesterday morning," he added.

"That is good news," she said. "And yes, I can meet you, but I think it's my turn to buy the coffee."

Charlie laughed. "There's a coffee shop just outside the station. I could meet you there at three o'clock."

"Yes, I'll see you there."

Charlie hung up the phone, but a few seconds later it was ringing again. This time the caller was from the Tokyo Medical University Hospital.

"Hello, Mr. Hillier. I hope I am not disturbing you." He immediately recognized Dr. Yamaguchi's voice, as well as a difference in his usually uniform tone.

"Of course not. What can I do for you?"

"Have you had any contact with Mr. Lepage since he was released yesterday?"

Charlie considered the question and felt a ripple of unease. He hadn't heard from Lepage, but he had barely been out for twenty-four hours. "No. I'm assuming he'll check in sometime today."

Yamaguchi's pause said everything. "He was supposed to check in last night. I've already spoken to Mr. Redford, who hasn't heard from him either."

"I'm sure it's nothing to worry about. He probably didn't think the first day counted." Charlie realized it sounded a bit feeble and easy for him to say — he hadn't put either his professional reputation or whatever insurance rider Redford had cobbled together on the line. "I'll try to get in touch with him, if you like."

"I've called several times, and no reply."

"Let me see if I can track him down." Charlie glanced at his watch. He had a meeting in a couple of hours, but that gave him plenty of time to take the Metro over to Omote-sando and back. "I'll be in touch."

He pulled on his jacket and grabbed his leather portfolio on the way out the door, for appearances. Twenty minutes later, he was ascending to street level from Omote-sando Station, where he joined the stream of westbound pedestrians until he reached the walkway over the gridlocked street. Lepage's building was only a few minutes farther on, and he was jogging up the front steps when he almost collided with Elizabeth Farnsworth, who was exiting through the front door.

"Oh, hi, Elizabeth."

"Charlie?" She appeared surprised by his presence. "I'm … what are you doing here?"

"I came by to check in on Rob."

"Rob? I thought he was in hospital."

"He was released yesterday."

"Oh, I didn't know." She brushed a strand of red hair back from her forehead. Unlike the last time he had seen her, she was dressed in business attire, complete with heels that put her almost at eye level, and she smelled like expensive perfume. "Listen, I'm terribly sorry about lunch yesterday. I'm such a scatterbrain, honestly."

"It's all right." He waved a hand as she glanced at her wrist, adorned by a jewelled watch. "I'm afraid I've got to rush off. Client meeting. I do want to get together, though."

Charlie shrugged as he watched her scamper down the stairs and start waving at a taxi.

"Whatever," he muttered to himself before taking the elevator up to the sixth floor. He tried Lepage's doorbell several times, then knocked. As he waited for a response, he pulled out his phone and dialed Lepage's cell number. He heard nothing on the other side of the door and after a few minutes of standing there, he gave up and decided to swing by Mori Tower before heading back to the embassy.

Ten minutes later, he was sitting in the reception area of Cliff Redford's office admiring the artwork on the wall, when he heard Redford's booming voice down the hall.

"Charlie. What brings you by?"

"Hi, Cliff. I hope I'm not interrupting anything. I was in the neighbourhood and I thought I'd drop by."

"Is this about Rob?"

"I just went by his place and there's no sign of him there. You don't find it odd that he hasn't checked in with any of us?"

Redford frowned. "Yamaguchi called me in a panic, but I wasn't too worried about it — you've got me wondering now. You say you went by his apartment?" He waved toward the couch at the far end of the reception area and they both took a seat.

Charlie nodded. "I knocked on his door for five minutes — nothing. I also dropped by Nippon Kasuga," he added, pointing to the floor.

"And?"

"He hasn't shown up there either. They looked at me like I had three heads when I asked about him."

Redford shrugged. "Not really surprising, coming from them."

"You don't suppose he's had a setback?"

"You mean with his memory?" Redford shook his head. "Yamaguchi wouldn't have let him out if he thought that was even a possibility. I'm sure he's just enjoying being out of hospital. Maybe he's in bed with the girlfriend," he added, with a wink. Charlie tried to be upbeat, but he had a bad feeling.

"Seriously, Charlie, you're worrying too much. Let's give him to the end of today before we do anything drastic, okay?" Redford patted him on the shoulder.

"Yeah, you're probably right," Charlie said. "There was something else I wanted to bounce off you, though."

"Shoot."

"I'm meeting with the TMP inspector this afternoon. I'm hoping she has something new on Seger, but I was also going to ask her about Kimura's place of work."

Redford frowned. "You sure you want to do that? Once you get the cops involved, it's hard to get them uninvolved, you know what I mean?"

"I just find it strange that she would lie about working at a call centre. To us, and to Rob."

Redford leaned forward on the couch. "First of all, how do we know Rob isn't fully aware of her occupation? He might be just going along with her fiction for appearances. Second of all, I've told you how things work here in Japan — land of the facade — so I'm hardly surprised that Kimura's been less than upfront about her real work."

Charlie considered the counterpoint. It was true that he had no evidence that Lepage wasn't fully aware — just a feeling. Maybe his feeling was wrong. For all he knew, Lepage might have met her at her Roppongi club. He felt foolish, and somewhat of a prude.

"You're right. I shouldn't jump to conclusions, and I barely know Rob."

"Your heart's in the right place, Charlie. You just worry too much. Rob will turn up, I'm sure of it." Redford stood up and Charlie followed suit.

"Sorry to waste your time like this. And I'm sure you're right."

Redford waved off the apology. "No trouble at all. Let's talk later."

Charlie returned from the biweekly administrative meeting that he had begun to loathe and sat down at his desk. He was debating getting a coffee from the machine down the hall when his computer made its familiar beep that indicated a new message. He could tell by the format of the message that it was not a standard email, but one sent on the secure system. He logged onto his secure account and opened the message — from the RCMP in Ottawa. The subject line read *Michael Seger.* He clicked on the attachment and waited for the report to open, though his interest was tempered by the fact that Westwood had already given him the gist of the report in their briefing earlier in the week. As he began to read the report onscreen, he gradually drew himself closer to the screen, so that by the time he was at the bottom of the first page, he was leaning halfway across his desk. The content of the report went further than Westwood had suggested. Not only did Seger have a cousin and an uncle with direct links to organized crime in Montreal and Toronto, Seger himself was suspected to have worked at one point for an underboss whose name was familiar enough that Charlie had read it before in newspaper articles. Seger didn't have a criminal record, though he had been questioned in connection with a couple of crimes, including the disappearance of a man believed to have been cooperating with an organized crime task force in Montreal. The man had been missing for five years, with his file still open and unsolved. Seger was pulled in because he had been seen in the vicinity of the missing man's apartment building just before he had vanished, but he had been released for lack of evidence.

The report also detailed Seger's travels in the past two years, which included several trips to Hong Kong in the last twelve months, but none during the time period for when he had told Charlie he had been in touch with Rob Lepage. In fact, the only activity on his passport in the last six months was a trip to Beijing for a week in late June, which confirmed that he had been lying about the Hong Kong trip. The report went on to surmise that if he was directly involved in illegal activity, he had done a good job of concealing it. But his travel patterns, and the people he tended to associate with, suggested that he was likely involved in white collar crime, if anything. Online scams and securities fraud were the most likely possibilities.

Charlie finished reading the report, noting the name of the investigator, as well as the fact that it had been sent to the head of mission, copied to Denault and himself. He sat back in his chair, pondering the content of the report for a while, then glanced at his watch and realized he would have to leave soon for his appointment with Kobayashi. He stared at the screen for a moment, then composed a reply to the sender of the report, asking for a call at ten p.m. Tokyo time on a secure line to discuss some follow-up questions. The contents of the report were rattling around in his mind as he gathered his things and made for the door.

Twenty minutes later, he was waiting in the corner of the coffee shop, his eye on the door as he surveyed the rest of the patrons. Given the location, he imagined most of them were either lawyers or cops. As with everywhere in this part of the city, most of the clientele was male, and most were wearing what seemed to be the standard-issue dark suit, white shirt, and monochrome tie. He wondered what would happen if someone wore a bright red tie with polka dots — a day of strange looks, some merciless ribbing, or a reprimand from a superior? He was still musing about the uniformity of Tokyo office fashion when he saw Kobayashi walk through the door. He realized she was actually the only woman in the place, apart from the staff, and while her own jacket and pants were of charcoal grey, she wore a colourful scarf and matching hair clip that made her stand out all the more. He made eye contact and watched as her face lit up with recognition as she made her way over to where he was sitting.

"Hello, Charlie. I'm sorry I'm late."

"You're not late at all," he said, happy that she was finally using his first name. He got up and pulled out a chair for her.

"I'm very glad you called," she said. "I just got some news that I wanted to share."

Charlie settled in his seat, sensing that the meeting was about to become more productive than he had originally thought, but he could tell by her expression that he had misread the statement — the news wasn't good.

"My supervisor has confirmed that there will be no further investigation into Mr. Seger's death."

"Really? I thought they were leaning toward his death being a homicide."

"I'm afraid my supervisor doesn't feel there is enough evidence of … foul play. Accidental death is an equally possible explanation, in his opinion," she added, with an undeniable expression of distaste. Charlie pictured the discussion between Kobayashi and her superior — probably an old-school guy in his late fifties who wondered how he had gotten himself stuck with a woman investigator. He imagined Kobayashi taking the news, perhaps with a bit of restrained objection, but with little hope of swaying her boss at all. "I'm very sorry, Charlie. I know this must be disappointing news."

"I know you did your best," he said, glancing toward the counter. "Can I get you a coffee?"

She nodded and reached for her purse, which he waved off. A few minutes later, he returned with a couple of cappuccinos.

"So is that it, then? I mean, I assume there's no way to change your boss's mind?"

She took a sip of the coffee and shook her head. "Unless there is new evidence that would prove Seger's death wasn't accidental." Charlie didn't respond for a few seconds, as they eyed each other, an inquisitive look on Kobayashi's delicate features. "Do you have any new evidence?" she finally asked.

"Possibly." Charlie took a sip of the steaming froth and savoured the taste for a moment, wondering how much of the report to reveal to her. He would be more comfortable if he had gotten the author's consent before sharing it with

Kobayashi, but he felt he had an opportunity here. "What if I told you I had evidence that Seger was involved in organized crime back in Canada and possibly in Asia?"

She looked at him, her eyes narrowing slightly. "What type of organized crime?"

"The kind that has international connections. Internet scams, securities fraud, that sort of thing."

Kobayashi considered the news and leaned back in her chair as she played with the rim of her cup. "I find that very interesting. Is there any evidence that Mr. Seger was connected to Mr. Lepage?"

Charlie shook his head. "Not yet." That was one of the things he intended to flesh out with the author of the RCMP report, but he had a feeling in his gut that the answer was no. "But I have to say, it does make me wonder why Seger was so interested in Lepage's condition, and trying to get him released into his custody. They must be connected somehow, though Lepage swears he can't remember anything."

"There is one possibility," Kobayashi said. "I did some checking on Aiko Kimura. I told you she wasn't registered as a call centre operator."

"Right."

"I think she may be involved in criminal activity." She paused for a moment, then reached back to her purse that hung on the back of her chair and pulled out a buff folder, which she set on the table between them. She flipped open the cover and turned it to face him. Charlie looked down at a grainy photo of Kimura, smoking a cigarette and talking to a man whose back was to the camera. "That's her, don't you think?"

Charlie looked at the picture up close and there was no mistaking Kimura, even if the quality of the image was less than perfect. He nodded. "That's her all right. Where did you get this?"

"I talked to a colleague on our organized crime squad. He recognized her from one of his active cases — the investigation of a brothel in Roppongi."

Charlie pulled out the brochure from Kimura's club and gave it to Kobayashi. "I don't suppose it's this place?"

Kobayashi took the brochure and flipped to a page in the folder and compared the names. "Yes it is. Where did you get this?"

Charlie paused as his mind searched for a suitable lie. But as he sat there, watching Kobayashi's curious expression, he decided to level with her.

"I followed Kimura ... or whatever her real name is, from the hospital a few nights ago."

Kobayashi's eyebrows shot up. "Charlie, that was very ... unwise."

He ignored the warning and went on the offensive, instead. "How is it you have all this information on Kimura anyway, given that you've decided there's nothing worthy of a formal investigation?" He regretted the retort immediately. But if Kobayashi was stung by it, it didn't show.

"You have to be very careful," she said. "If she is who I suspect she is, Kimura has some very dangerous associates, according to my colleague."

"You think they might have had something to do with Seger's death?"

She gave a subtle sigh. "I'm more interested in her connection to Mr. Lepage."

"You don't think it's a coincidence, do you? I mean, within days of meeting Kimura at the hospital, Seger turns up dead." Kobayashi said nothing, so Charlie took another look at the photo of Kimura. "Do you mind?" He picked it up for a closer look, revealing another photo beneath it. He glanced at the second photo and did a double take.

"Who's that?" He pointed to one of two men in the second photo. He was facing the camera this time, and with the better quality of the second print his features were unmistakable.

Kobayashi followed his index finger to the picture, then looked quickly around the room before leaning forward across the table and gently taking the photo from his hand, putting it back in the folder, and closing it. "Not here," she said quietly, not looking at him for a moment, then breaking into a smile. "You should smile," she added, with an affected enthusiasm. "I think we're being watched."

Charlie played along with a casual grin. "You're going to tell me though, right?" He kept the fake smile plastered to his face.

Kobayashi made a show of putting the file folder back in her purse and checking her watch.

"You remember the temple in Asakusa?"

He nodded.

"I'll meet you there at eight tonight. I have to leave you now. Look as though everything is normal."

He nodded and tried to look casual as he watched her go. When he realized that she hadn't even offered to split the tab for the coffee, he knew something was seriously wrong.

CHAPTER 21

Charlie was only back in his office for a few minutes, trying to figure out what had happened at his meeting with Kobayashi, when his phone rang. He saw the call was from reception.

"There's a Ms. Elizabeth Farnsworth down here asking to meet with you."

"I'll be right down." His curiosity piqued, he set the receiver back on its cradle and made his way downstairs. Passing through the secure door, he could see Farnsworth beyond the glass, seated on the long and twisting leather couch in the spacious lobby of the embassy. He could tell from her posture that she was nervous.

"Hi, Elizabeth."

"Hello, Charlie. I'm sorry to just drop in on you like this, but I really must apologize for the other day. You must think me a complete nutter."

"Not at all."

"Do you have five minutes? I can explain myself."

"Of course." He led her into the multipurpose room, rather than going through the security to get her into the operational part of the embassy. The large room was empty, and he led her to a table and chairs at the far end.

"What's on your mind?" he asked, as they both settled in their seats. She took a deep breath before starting out.

"I haven't been completely honest with you," she began, averting his eyes.

"What do you mean?"

She sighed. "About my relationship with Rob."

Charlie allowed the silence that followed to continue for a few seconds. But he had a pretty good idea where this was going and he couldn't resist prompting her to see if he was right. "You said you and Rob had a fling and then remained friends."

She gave an awkward smile. "It was a bit more than a fling, actually. I'm afraid I rather fell for him, and the feeling was mutual, or so I thought."

"Aiko Kimura," Charlie said, prompting a frown from Farnsworth.

"Precisely. I did go to see Rob at the hospital, but she was already there. She's come out of nowhere, and I have to say, it was all a bit of a shock. I've never had my heart broken before, Charlie."

He nodded. One look at Farnsworth was all he needed to conclude she was telling the truth about that, though he couldn't help imagining that she had broken more than one heart in her time. "So you were embarrassed at being strung along — if that's what happened — and you were a little off with the details of your relationship with Rob. That's understandable."

"Except that something's wrong."

"Wrong, how?"

"I don't know who this Kimura woman is, but I don't believe her and Charlie really are together. Oh, I know," she added, with a wave of her hand and a grim chuckle, "that's what every jilted woman's supposed to say — *It can't be so.*

He loves me…. That's why I've kept my mouth shut until now, for fear of becoming a cliché that I've always loathed."

"So, what's different now?"

"Rob came to see me last night. He seemed … odd."

"Odd in what way?"

"If I didn't know him better, I would have said afraid, but Rob's not afraid of anything. He's completely fearless."

"So why would he be afraid now?"

She looked at him, hesitated, then seemed to make up her mind about something. "I think he's in trouble. He was asking me about the night before the accident … if he had said anything out of the ordinary, or left anything with me, for safekeeping."

Charlie watched her as she spoke, deciding that she was telling the truth. "And had he?"

She shrugged her shoulders. "No, I don't even know what he could mean. I just know it has something to do with that Kimura woman."

"Did he say that?"

"He didn't have to."

"But you talked about Kimura. How did he explain her to you?"

"He can't," she said, with dramatic wave of both hands. "But then he doesn't have to, does he? He's got the perfect excuse — amnesia."

Charlie frowned. "You say that as if you don't believe him."

Another shrug and a little pout. "I'm not sure what to believe. His memory loss seems a bit … selective, shall we say. He swears he remembers everything about us and nothing about Kimura. I know that's a lie to appease me — I'm not completely naive."

Charlie frowned. "Where did he say he was going, after he talked to you?"

"Going?" She looked perplexed. He had decided not to mention the fact that Lepage was officially AWOL since the previous night.

"Did he have any plans?"

She shook her head, then looked at Charlie for a long moment. "Do you think he's in danger?"

He deflected the question. "Is there anything else you can tell me about the time before Rob's accident? Anything out of the ordinary?" She shook her head again, but he could tell by the way that she averted his eyes that she was holding something back. "Anything at all, Elizabeth — it could be important."

"It's just ..." she began.

"What?"

"Call it woman's intuition — I really am becoming quite a cliché after all."

"What did your intuition tell you about Rob, before his accident?"

She paused, fidgeting with her hands, then she looked up at him, fixing him with those deep green eyes, tinged with red. "That he was getting ready to leave me."

Charlie got off the subway car at Ueno Station and joined the flow of passengers headed up to street level. Unlike the last time he was there, it was dark, but he had no problem spotting the familiar arch with the giant red lantern hanging from the middle. The pedestrian street that lay beyond was much less crowded than when he had last been there, due to the fact that most of the stalls were closed. As he made his way toward the temple, he could see the flashes of cameras as tourists took photos on the steps leading up to the shrine.

He was nearing the bottom step when he spotted Kobayashi off to the side, waving him over.

"Come with me." She led him around to the right of the main steps and into the nearest side street. At first he thought they were headed to the same restaurant where they had lunched, but after about five hundred feet, she gestured to a small building and led him inside. Adjusting to the dim light, Charlie made out what was either a tiny restaurant or a small bar. Kobayashi led the way to the rear, and after a brief exchange in Japanese with what looked to be the owner or a waiter, she removed her shoes and slid her legs effortlessly under the low table, waiting for him to do the same. He kicked off his shoes and, after considerable effort and with a lot less grace, he had managed to squeeze his large frame into position on the opposite side of the table. His knees were already screaming but he gritted his teeth as Kobayashi smiled indulgently.

"You are quite a bit bigger than the average Japanese man," she said. "I apologize if it is not very comfortable."

He gave a dismissive wave and ignored the stabbing pain in his ankle as he adjusted himself to alleviate a similar pain in his knee. "I'm still trying to get used to sitting on the floor. I guess it takes some practice."

"I am very sorry for this morning," she began, causing him to debate whether to cut in and pre-empt any further apologies, but she soon got to the point. "I was concerned about sharing too much information with you there."

He nodded. "No problem. I thought that might have had something to do with it. We were talking about the man in the photo," he said, waiting for her to retrieve the same buff file folder from her purse that she had shown him this morning. She was reaching for it when the waiter appeared.

"Would you like some sake? Or perhaps something to eat?" Kobayashi asked.

"Sake's fine."

She placed the order and then reached into her purse once they were alone again. She pulled out the second photo and set it on the table between them. "Are you sure you recognize this man?" she said, tapping her finger on the photo of the man standing next to Kimura. Charlie looked closely again, to be sure, but there was no doubt in his mind that it was the same man he had seen outside Kimura's club with the Nippon Kasuga executive that Cliff Redford had been so keen to avoid.

"Yes, I'm sure. Who is he?"

"His name is Hiroki Miyamoto. He is a senior member of the Inagawa-kai." She let the fact sink in, until it became clear that Charlie had no idea what she was talking about. "It's the largest Tokyo-based organized crime group."

"You mean yakuza?"

She nodded. "Yamaguchi-gumi is larger. They are based in Kobe, though they have been moving into some parts of Tokyo in recent years."

"So the yakuza's for real then," he added, though saying the words made him sound hopelessly naive, even to his own ears. He could only imagine what Kobayashi was thinking.

"The Inagawa-kai are involved in many different types of criminal activity here. Protection, gambling, drugs … prostitution."

Charlie considered the last one and any possibility that Kimura's misrepresentation of her work could have a legitimate explanation evaporated. "You said he's senior. How senior?"

"My colleague in the 3rd Division — organized crime — is much more familiar with the hierarchy, which is quite complicated, but Miyamoto is one of a handful at the very top."

"So, what's he doing hanging out with the guy from Nippon Kasuga?"

Kobayashi paused as their waiter delivered a tray with a large pot of steaming sake and two little earthenware bowls, then disappeared with a bow.

"I don't know," she said, pouring the sake into the bowls. "I mentioned Nippon Kasuga to my colleague, and he was not aware of any connection to organized crime. It may not mean anything."

"Or it may mean they're mobbed up," he said, tapping his bowl off hers. "Cheers."

"Mobbed up?" she said, after taking a sip of the clear liquid.

"Connected … to the yakuza."

She nodded. "Yes, that is another possibility. That's why you must be careful."

He nodded, taking another sip of the sake. He couldn't say he had really acquired a taste for it yet, but it felt warm as it made its way down his throat and into his stomach, making him feel a pleasant numbness that suited the dim light of the bar perfectly. Kobayashi was watching him with her inquisitive look.

"What?"

"I want you to promise me that you'll let me look into Kimura," she said. "That you won't take any unnecessary risks."

He spread his palms in a gesture of submission. "But I thought there wasn't an investigation?"

"That doesn't mean I can't follow up on some matters." She put her cup down. "On my own time, of course." He had to admire her resolve. She was probably taking a significant risk by disobeying a superior. But he had the feeling she could handle herself just fine. "Do you promise?"

"I won't try to follow Kimura again. I promise," he said as she eyed him and tried to assess whether he was telling the truth. He had no intention of following Kimura again — he didn't need to. That didn't mean he didn't intend to dig a little into the potential connection with Nippon Kasuga. "Tell me something," he said, if only to change the subject. "Is it true about members of the Yakuza cutting off their fingers?"

Kobayashi's face broke into a smile — a real one, so full and bright that it lit up her whole face. "You have seen too many movies, Charlie."

"So it's a myth?"

"No, the practice — it's called *yubitsume* — is an old tradition. It was an offering to the *oyabun* … the boss, to atone for a mistake." She held her left little finger between the index and thumb of her right hand. "It would start with a piece of this finger. A second time might cost the whole finger."

Charlie frowned. "Why the left pinkie?"

"It goes back to samurai times. The left hand held the sword, and the grip would be weakened by the loss of the little finger. If the person was unfortunate enough, he might lose the third finger as well, making his grip so weak that he would have to rely on the group for protection. It was a form of submission."

"And what's the equivalent now?" he asked.

She shrugged and let out a snuff of disdain. "Money, probably. There's no honour today. And as for marking themselves, they use *irezumi* … tattoos, though most of them are concealed by clothing." She took another sip of sake. "Yakuza members have had to become experts at camouflage — many of them wear suits and look like any other Japanese businessmen."

"Because they're involved in white-collar crime now."

She nodded. "Exactly, though they still have their traditional activities as well."

They finished the sake, trading theories on how Kimura and Lepage had come to be together, or whether they were together at all. When the waiter returned and offered more, Kobayashi shook her head.

"I should go. I will see what else I can find out tomorrow and we can meet again."

Charlie nodded. He planned on doing some research of his own. It was Friday tomorrow and his day was pretty clear. "Maybe we can touch base … I mean, maybe I can call you tomorrow afternoon?"

"Yes, that would be fine. Do you have plans for the weekend?" she added, as they settled the bill by splitting it evenly. The question was innocent enough, but it sounded intimate, somehow, coming from her. She busied herself with her purse and he sensed that maybe she was thinking the same thing.

"Nothing major. I was going to check out the fish market on Saturday."

"Make sure you go early. It will be very busy."

They walked back out to the alley and Kobayashi accompanied him to the end, directing him back to the main pedestrian street leading away from the temple and toward Ueno Station.

"I'm going this way," she said, pointing in the opposite direction.

"Thanks for meeting me. I guess we'll talk tomorrow?"

She smiled and bowed, reminding him to do the same, then they went their separate ways. Whether it was the sake in his belly or the lingering scent of her perfume in his nostrils, Charlie felt a warm glow as he headed back to the Metro. But he only got to enjoy it for a few minutes before it was interrupted by the shrill ring of his phone.

"Hello?"

"Charlie, it's Rob."

He stopped in his tracks at the sound of Lepage's voice. "Rob? Where … how are you?"

"I'm fine. Listen, I'm sorry I didn't call yesterday. I've just been getting used to being out of hospital, you know, and it sort of slipped my mind." Lepage gave a little laugh in the pause that followed. "Sorry, bad turn of phrase."

"Have you talked to Dr. Yamaguchi or Cliff? They're both worried sick."

"I just got off the phone with the doc, and Cliff's my next call, believe me."

"I dropped by your place this morning."

"I must have been out ... getting groceries. The cupboards were pretty bare, you know what I mean?"

From what Charlie had seen of Lepage's apartment, he didn't eat in much, so the idea of him filling the fridge and cupboards with groceries seemed odd, but he listened to Lepage's voice for any hint of deception or duress, and detected none. He sounded like his usual laid-back self. Maybe Redford had been right not to worry. "I'm just about to hop on the Metro now. I could drop by your place — we could go for a drink or a coffee or something, if you like."

"I'm really beat tonight. I'm just gonna crash," Lepage said.

Charlie checked his watch and noted it was barely past nine, but decided not to press. He supposed Lepage's energy levels were a little out of whack after lying in a hospital bed for a couple of weeks. "How about lunch tomorrow?"

"Love to," Lepage replied airily, "but I've got some follow-up tests with Yamaguchi at eleven and it could be a while. Maybe Sunday?"

Charlie made a mental note to talk to Yamaguchi. "Sure, sounds good. So, how are you doing?"

"I feel good. Well, as good as can be expected, I guess. I'm still trying to figure out what I'm going to do long-term, you know?"

"Have you been to the office?"

"Naw, I was going to give myself the weekend to think and then go see them on Monday."

Again, Charlie was listening hard, wishing he could see Lepage's face. Something told him he was holding back. "Probably a good idea. How about Aiko?"

There was a pause and a small sigh on the line as Charlie waited for a response. "I think we're done. I can't say I blame her."

"I'm sorry to hear that," Charlie lied. This time, he was glad he wasn't facing Lepage when he said the words. "How's the memory?"

"I think it's improving. I don't know if it's being back in my apartment, or out on the street that's doing it, but I'm definitely starting to remember more and more from before the accident."

"That's a good sign."

"I guess Yamaguchi will be the judge of that. I should probably get a hold of Cliff now."

"Yeah, do that. And give me a call tomorrow so we can set up lunch on Sunday. I look forward to it."

Charlie ended the call and stared at the phone. Was Lepage lying? Charlie didn't think so, and he liked to think he could read people pretty well. But Lepage was definitely not telling him everything. He should have pushed for a meeting tomorrow night, he thought, as he slid his phone into his pocket and resumed his walk toward Ueno Station. Still, Lepage had made contact and seemed to be in good shape. As he reached the station and descended to platform level, Charlie told himself to take his cue from Redford and stop worrying.

CHAPTER 22

The warm breeze cooled the sweat on his forehead as he sat up on his towel and looked out over the glittering Caribbean. He watched as her head broke the surface, then followed her progress into shallower water. Her shoulders emerged next, covered in long, black hair that she flung back with both hands as her torso surfaced from the gentle surf, droplets of water glistening in the late afternoon sun as she headed up the beach toward him. As she approached, the delicate features of her face sharpened into focus — the ivory skin, jet-black hair in contrast to the flash of white teeth as she smiled at him. He stood to shake the sand out of her towel, but she discarded it when he offered it to her and pressed her slender body, still cool from the ocean, into his, staring up at him with a sensual look in those deep eyes.

Charlie awoke to his bed shaking. Sitting up abruptly and looking around, it took him a moment to realize that he was in Tokyo, not Havana. The digital display on his clock radio wobbled, and the water in the glass on his bedside table threatened to breach the rim. Terror filled his heart as he sat there, frozen on the bed as the world threatened to collapse around him. And then it was over. He took a moment to collect himself, to ensure he wasn't still dreaming, then ran to the window and looked outside. It was a bright, sunny morning. He watched a gardener pruning a shrub, going about his business as if nothing had happened. Perhaps he *had* imagined it.

Charlie was still getting his bearings when his phone went off. Recognizing the number, he hit the answer button and heard Cliff Redford's gruff baritone.

"Hope I'm not calling too early."

"No." Charlie noticed the time on the bedside clock and realized he had slept in. It was almost eight thirty.

"I'm heading into a long meeting, but I wanted to know if you're free for lunch today."

Charlie did a quick mental inventory of the day ahead. "Um, yeah, I think I'm free."

"I've got a meeting in Asakusa this afternoon, so I thought we'd do the City Club. Twelve thirty work for you?"

"Sure. Anything particular on your mind?"

"Just catching up. You talked to Rob yesterday?"

Charlie rubbed his eyes. "He said he was going to call you after we spoke. I assume he did?"

"Yeah, yeah. It's all good, but I wanted to run something by you. Listen, I'd better be going. We'll talk at lunch."

"Okay … wait, Cliff?"

"Yeah?"

"Was there an … earthquake … just before you called?"

"You felt it, huh?" Redford was laughing. "Just a baby. A knee-trembler."

"So it wasn't, like … a *big* one. No damage or anything?"

"We get them all the time. I'd say that was a four point O. Nothing to worry about, believe me."

"Right, see you at lunch."

Charlie hung up and tossed the phone on the bed. He was still rattled by the quake, despite having been fully briefed on the fact that they occurred regularly in Japan, and on emergency procedures in the event of a big one, like the one that triggered the tsunami in 2011 and took out the Fukushima nuclear plant. But he was also pre-occupied by the vivid dream, particularly Kobayashi's prominence, in Havana of all places. He shrugged it off and headed to the shower.

Charlie arrived a few minutes late to the club located in the basement of the Canadian embassy building, which featured a large dining area, as well as screened rooms for more private meals at traditional Japanese tables. Charlie was relieved, for his knees' sake, to see Redford sitting at a conventional table at the rear of the main area when he arrived.

"Hi, Cliff."

"Four point nine." Redford plucked his phone off the table and pointed at the screen. It took Charlie a second to figure out his meaning as he took a seat and glanced at the little screen. "This morning's quake," Redford added.

"I knew it felt like more than a four. Should we be finding a doorway to huddle under?"

"Actually, aftershocks are pretty common." Redford's expression remained grave just long enough for Charlie to realize his leg was being pulled.

"Very funny."

"You get used to them after a while," Redford said. "To the point that something like this morning doesn't even register."

Charlie smiled. "Yes, I noticed no one else seemed par-ticularly bothered by it, but I have to say I found it a little … unsettling."

Redford gave a commanding wave. "A couple of months in Tokyo and you won't notice them, either."

They chatted for a while, and after the waitress had taken their order, Redford turned his attention to his phone, looking up after a few seconds and fixing Charlie with a broad grin.

"What?" Charlie took a sip of his water as Redford continued to smirk.

"This is perfect," Redford began. "A board of trade–type dinner next week, and it just occurred to me that it might be a good opportunity for you to meet some of the expat crowd. It's a mix of locals and expats — mostly Yanks and Brits, but some Aussies and Kiwis sprinkled in for good measure. There's usually the odd Canadian there as well."

"Why do I feel like there's something you're not telling me?"

Redford scowled. "Now don't be like that. You said you needed to get out and meet some people — have a little fun," he said as the server returned with his gin and tonic. Redford then pulled out a gold lighter and a pack of cigarettes, shaking one out. "You mind?"

Charlie shook his head.

"I think *you* said I needed to get out and have some fun, actually."

"Hmm." Redford exhaled a thick cloud of aromatic smoke above the table — an act that would lead to a public flogging in Canada.

"What's with the smoking thing in Japan?" Charlie asked. "I see No Smoking signs all over the sidewalks, and no one seems to smoke outside, yet the coffee shops and restaurants are full of smokers. I don't get it."

Redford laughed. "Let's just say the tobacco lobby here is strong. I figure the diehards like me have got a few more years to puff in peace before the health nuts take over. Until then, I intend to enjoy it." He took another long drag of the cigarette and chased it with a sip of the fragrant coffee.

"So, you talked to Rob last night?" Charlie asked.

"I told you not to get all worked up about him. He was just making up for being bedridden for a week. Although," Redford said with his trademark grin, "he might have been right back in the sheets with the lovely Ms. Kimura."

"He says they're on the outs." Charlie hoped it was true.

"Too bad."

"He sounded okay to you?"

Redford shrugged. "How's he supposed to sound?"

Charlie smiled and took a sip of his water. Maybe Redford was right. Maybe he should worry less about Lepage and more about his own situation. And why shouldn't he go to the dinner next week? What the hell was his problem? A fleeting and incongruous image of Kobayashi on a Cuban beach passed before his eyes. He reminded himself that was a just a dream.

"Charlie?"

He looked up and realized he had been having an internal debate with himself while Redford smoked his cigarette.

"I was just thinking you're probably right, that maybe I'm making a mountain out of a molehill with Lepage."

"Good. Now, let's get onto more important stuff," Redford said, crushing the last of his cigarette in the ashtray and rubbing his hands together. "Like all the unattached women who'll be at this dinner."

Charlie couldn't help but laugh, seeing how much Redford was enjoying his role as matchmaker. He had no intention of going to the dinner, but he didn't have to heart to ruin Redford's plan. "I'll think about it, okay?"

It was almost six by the time Charlie made it to the hospital, due to an impromptu consular team meeting called by Louis Denault, the purpose of which wasn't entirely clear, though Charlie had the sense that part of Denault's intention was to keep tabs on him. He had mentioned the RCMP report on Seger twice, and a few of his comments suggested that he knew Westwood had met with Charlie in his absence, something Denault was sure to not easily forgive or forget.

Maybe I'm overthinking it, Charlie had considered. He had shared his concerns with Karen Fraser after the meeting and learned from her that Denault had been called back to Ottawa for meetings on HR reform, and that the meeting likely had more to do with that than anything else. She seemed more worried about the Department's ever more aggressive trend toward shrinking the Foreign Service.

Charlie put all that out of his mind as he rode the elevator up to the fourth floor and made his way to Yamaguchi's office. He thought he might have missed the neurologist after he arrived outside his office and saw Yamaguchi's assistant's empty chair. He was instinctively glancing at his watch when he spotted Yamaguchi rounding the corner, his eyes focused on the document he was holding in front of him as he walked. He looked up and saw Charlie standing there and his face lit up with his usual smile.

"Charlie. How are you?"

"I thought I might have missed you."

Yamaguchi gave him a puzzled look, as though to suggest the improbability of any self-respecting Japanese professional — let alone a neurologist — missing a scheduled meeting. "Come," he said, leading the way into his office, flicking on the lights and gesturing to one of the chairs opposite his spotless desk. He flipped the cover back on the report he was reading and dropped the folder on his desk, then sat in his chair.

"I heard Rob came by for some tests today?"

Yamaguchi nodded. "I told him he had to check in more regularly," he added, with his lips slightly pursed.

"I said the same. Cliff was the only one who wasn't worried."

Yamaguchi laughed at that. "Ah, Redford-san. Worry is not something that comes to him naturally."

"So, how was he? Rob, I mean."

Yamaguchi stripped off his glasses and set them gently on top of the file folder, which sat squarely in the middle of his desk blotter. "His test results show improvement, all within the normal range."

Charlie smiled. "Well, that's good news."

"Yes." Yamaguchi's slow and unconvincing nod suggested something else was on his mind.

"What is it?"

"When you spoke to Mr. Lepage yesterday, how did he seem to be adapting to life outside the hospital?"

Charlie shrugged his shoulders. "Fine, I guess. Why do you ask?"

"Some of his responses to the questionnaire were ... inconsistent with his test results."

Charlie frowned. "What do you mean, inconsistent?"

Yamaguchi seemed almost reluctant to say more, preferring to look at Charlie for a moment before continuing. "Retrograde amnesia recovery patterns are not always ... precise, but there are general principles."

"And you don't think he's following the pattern?"

Yamaguchi opened the file folder on his desk and flipped to the back of the pile of documents inside, plucking out a sheet of paper. "I did a full set of tests when he first came out of the coma, which included a questionnaire designed to assess what he could remember from before the accident." He paused and tapped the top page in the folder. "I compared his responses then to his answers to yesterday's assessment."

"And?"

"Some are consistent, some are not." Charlie tried to get his head around what Yamaguchi was saying, and wished he would cut to the chase. His frustration must have been apparent. "What I mean," Yamaguchi continued, "Is that Mr. Lepage's responses yesterday suggest reduced recall over a time period that seemed to be unaffected based on the initial assessment."

"You mean he's saying he can no longer remember things that he originally could?"

Yamaguchi nodded. "Precisely."

"I take it that's not normal?"

"The neurological test results all indicate recovery, not regression," Yamaguchi replied, frowning. "and as I said at the beginning, it is generally inconsistent with usual recovery patterns for retrograde amnesia."

They both sat in silence for a moment as Charlie digested the information. He leaned forward in his chair. "So what could explain this inconsistency?"

Yamaguchi shrugged. "I have no explanation."

"But there must be possibilities."

"I suppose he could have mistakenly reported his recollections in the first assessment, but that seems unlikely, given that his answers were quite specific."

There was a pregnant pause as Yamaguchi visibly held back, waiting for Charlie to prompt him to spit out the words.

"Or?"

"Or he is not accurately reporting now."

"You mean he's lying, or faking an ongoing memory loss that no longer exists?"

Yamaguchi was clearly uncomfortable with the directness of Charlie's choice of words and waved a warning hand.

"I don't like to suggest that a patient is lying. He has been through a very traumatic experience and we are dealing with the brain, after all. There is always an exception to every rule."

"Of course," Charlie said, though he was sure Yamaguchi didn't believe his own words. In his indirect way — the Japanese way — the doctor had told him all he needed to know. He had to remember the cultural discomfort with confrontation and directness. "So where do we go from here — with his treatment, I mean?"

"His medical condition is excellent, and as I said, from a neurological perspective, he appears to be on his way to making a full recovery. I'll give him a final assessment in a few days, after which he can be unconditionally released."

"Well, that's good," Charlie said, to conceal his internal turmoil. He felt like he had to get out of the confined office. "Thanks for your time today, and let me know if there's anything I can do," he added, getting up to leave. Yamaguchi walked around his desk and followed him to the door.

"Will you see him this evening?" he asked.

"I wasn't planning on it. He's supposed to check in by phone."

Yamaguchi frowned. "Perhaps you should visit him, if you can."

"Perhaps I should." Charlie nodded and gave a bow before stepping into the hallway.

He rode the elevator down to the ground floor in silence, his mind spinning with all the possible reasons why Lepage would lie to his neurologist about his recovery. Could he know more about his girlfriend's involvement with organized crime than he was letting on? And what about Mike Seger? Had Lepage known him well? Did he know why his supposed childhood friend had ended up dead in a Roppongi alley? Yamaguchi was definitely suspicious, and so was Charlie. What did he really know about Rob Lepage? Had he been lying to them both all along?

Charlie checked his watch as he stepped onto the sidewalk and pulled up the collar of his jacket against the cool night air. Walking toward the Metro station, he pulled out his phone and dialed Lepage's number, letting it ring a dozen times with no answer and no service to leave a message with. He put the phone away and pulled out his wallet, searching for a Metro ticket and pausing as he caught sight of a plain, white plastic card — the key to Lepage's apartment that Charlie hadn't gotten around to returning. He stood there on the sidewalk for a moment, staring at the card as the crowd flowed around him toward the station. Then he made up his mind and set off.

CHAPTER 23

Charlie got off the elevator on the sixth floor and looked both ways before setting off in the direction of Lepage's apartment. He was half expecting Elizabeth Farnsworth to poke her head out from further down the hall as he reached Lepage's door and rang the bell. He waited a few seconds, then rapped lightly and waited until he felt certain Lepage wasn't there. Sliding the key into the lock, it occurred to him that he was technically breaking the law from this point on. At least he would be in Canada, and he assumed the Japanese authorities equally frowned on unauthorized entry.

Once inside, he shut the door and leaned his back against it, surveying the dimly lit apartment. It seemed a little more lived-in than the last time he had been there, and for a moment he had a horrible thought that perhaps Lepage was sleeping, or in bed with Kimura, and hadn't heard the door. He considered calling out Lepage's name, but realized he had no plausible explanation for how he came to be inside the man's apartment. He decided to stop worrying and get on with it, so he could get out again as soon as possible.

He went straight to the master bedroom, being the farthest point in the apartment, and after confirming that it was indeed empty, he did a quick search of the dresser, night table, and closet, finding nothing of interest. He did a quick scan of the ensuite and medicine cabinet, before moving on to the next room, where Lepage had set up his study, and where Charlie had found the novelty pen on his last visit. He resisted the temptation to turn on the lights and sat at the chair in front of the desk, where Lepage's monitor displayed a snowy mountain scene that looked like the Rockies. He didn't even try to search the computer, focusing instead on the files on the little desktop rack, which hadn't been there the last time around. A quick search revealed that they were nothing more than his discharge papers and some correspondence from an insurance company about Lepage's wrecked Nissan. He put the files back and slid open the top drawer of the desk, freezing at what he saw. Sitting on top of a bright-yellow legal pad was a handgun. He sat staring at it for a moment, plucking a tissue from the box on the desktop and using it to move the gun aside as he looked through the rest of the drawer, finding nothing. He gently put the gun back in its place and slid the drawer shut again.

What's a banker doing with a gun?

Charlie tried to think of plausible reasons that were consistent with innocence but had a hard time. He opened the second drawer and recognized most of the same stuff he had seen before. Some immigration papers, tax forms, and the like. Nothing that shed any light on anything, least of all why Lepage suddenly needed a gun. One file folder looked new, and Charlie plucked it out, finding only a blank yellow legal pad inside. He was about to toss it back in, but decided to flip through the first dozen pages or so, stopping on the fifth page. Written across the middle of the page in pencil was a simple diagram of four circles in a row, connected by dotted lines. The first one contained the initials "AK"; the second, "MVA"; the third, "MS"; and the fourth circle was drawn around a hashtag symbol. He stared at the diagram for a moment, trying to make sense of it, then pulled out his BlackBerry, lined up the page, and took a couple of photos. When he was satisfied that he had captured all of the scribbled text and the diagram, he put his phone back in his pocket and the notes back in the folder, sliding the drawer shut.

On his way back to the entrance, he did a quick scan of the kitchen — the fridge barely had any more food in it than the last time he had seen it — and the living room, which offered no further clues. He decided it was time to leave and quickly made his way out into the hall toward the elevator, with the sensation that someone was watching him from down the hall. He turned around once to confirm that it was nothing more than a feeling and continued on to the elevator. He was thinking about the gun in the desk drawer when the elevator dinged. Two seconds later, the doors slid open and Lepage was standing there.

"Charlie?"

"Oh, hi, Rob." Charlie tried not look as he felt — caught like a rat in a trap. "I just dropped by, hoping I'd catch you home."

"Oh yeah?" Lepage stepped out of the elevator and into the hall. He was eying Charlie with what looked distinctly like suspicion. "Well, here I am."

"I just wanted to see how you were doing."

"I'm doing pretty good. How are you doing?" There was an awkward pause as the two men stood face to face in the hallway, then Lepage slapped him on the shoulder. "What's the matter? You look like you need a drink. Come on." He led the way toward his apartment and Charlie followed, his mind racing to find an excuse to leave and coming up empty. "So, what did you want to see me about?"

"I talked to Dr. Yamaguchi," Charlie said as they arrived at Lepage's door and he slid the key card in. Charlie's heart leapt into his throat as Lepage swung the door open. Had he left a light on, or some other clue that he had just been there? Lepage's expression remained neutral as they entered the apartment.

"He told you my tests were normal, then?"

"Yeah, but he thought I should try to see you. Make sure you're adjusting okay, see if you need anything."

Lepage led the way into the kitchen and hit the wall switch, bathing the ultra-modern kitchen in halogen light. "That's very … thoughtful of you." He gestured to the marble-topped table. Charlie hated lying and was grateful that Lepage's back was to him as he searched in the fridge, unable to see the guilt on Charlie's face. By the time Lepage came over to the table with a couple of beers though, he had managed to compose himself.

"Here you go." Lepage opened the first beer and handed it over. "Cheers." They both took a sip. "Ah, that's good. I never really knew Japanese beer existed until I came here, and it turns out they're pretty good at it."

"Couldn't agree with you more." Charlie smiled.

"So what did Yamaguchi have to say?"

"He said you passed your neurological tests with flying colours."

"He say anything else?"

Charlie sipped his beer, considering his response. "He mentioned you were still having some trouble with your memory from before the accident."

"To be expected, I guess." Lepage watched Charlie's reaction.

"Have you seen Aiko?" Charlie thought it might be a good change of subject, but it came out wrong, and Lepage seemed surprised.

"I told you, man. We're done."

"I'm sorry to hear that. Look," he said, gathering himself. "I hope you don't think I'm poking my nose where it doesn't belong, I just want to make sure you're doing okay."

Lepage ran his finger around the top of the bottle and looked at him. "I'm sure you've only got my best interests at heart, Charlie, but you don't have to worry. I'm doing just fine. Speaking of my memory," he continued after a slight pause. "Do you still have that postcard — the one you brought to me in the hospital?"

"Um, yeah. I'm sure I have it back at the office."

"I was thinking it might help me, you know ... trigger some memories or something. If you don't mind giving it back?"

"Of course. I'll find it over the weekend and get it to you."

"Thanks."

The two sat in silence for a moment, each sipping their beer.

"That reminds me," Lepage said suddenly. "Don't you still have a key to this place? I don't think I ever got it back from you."

Charlie slowly swallowed the mouthful of beer before nodding. "Yeah, I think you're right. It must be back at the office, as well. I'll drop it over with the postcard."

"Great."

"I could check here first." Lepage started to get up, gesturing to the hallway and his study beyond. "Make sure it's not in my desk drawer or somewhere like that." Charlie tried not to display any sign of the panic inside him as Lepage gave a little laugh. "You know, my memory isn't so great."

Charlie waved a hand. "I'm pretty sure I still have it."

Lepage paused, then nodded and relaxed in his chair.

"I should be going and leave you in peace." Charlie checked his watch.

"You just got here," Lepage protested, but Charlie was already up and headed to the door. "Well, thanks for dropping by," he said as they stood together at the door.

"No problem."

"Oh, and Charlie," Lepage added, his hand on the half-open door, blocking Charlie's exit.

"Yeah?"

"Don't forget to have a look for that key. I'd hate to think it was lost and someone could just come in here … whenever they wanted."

Charlie averted his gaze and nodded, pushing his way out into the hall. "I'll get it to you tomorrow, for sure."

"Good night, Charlie."

CHAPTER 24

Charlie sat at his dining room table — big enough to seat eight but which had only needed to handle him so far — with a half-empty beer next to his laptop as he scanned the search results on the yakuza's activities in Japan. Not surprisingly, there was a lot of online information about the various organizations that fell into the collective category. They liked to call themselves *ninkyō dantai*, which loosely translated as "chivalrous organizations," but there was no question about their real nature, given their main business lines were the same as organized crime groups everywhere, from the U.S. to Russia: protection, gambling, prostitution, and drugs. They were apparently involved in the illegal weapons trade in Asia, as well.

But the segment he was focused on now dealt with their growing involvement in white collar crime. He was surprised to learn that one of the yakuza groups, the Yamaguchi-gumi — he remembered Kobayashi mentioning that it was the largest group, and pausing at the incongruity of the name being shared with Lepage's very proper neurologist — were thought to have been the largest equity investor in the country in the early nineties, when the real estate bubble burst. The fallout had been bad for everyone, the yakuza included.

While the authorities had seemed prepared to turn a largely blind eye to their activities before, the public backlash from the knowledge that the yakuza had a lot to do with the bad debt bloating the marketplace meant they were scrambling for cover in the midnineties, as the authorities cracked down. Charlie was just finishing the article when the phone rang and he glanced at the computer clock, which read nine forty-five p.m. He didn't recognize the number displayed on his phone as he hit the receive button.

"Charlie Hillier."

"Charlie, I must apologize for calling you so late."

Charlie smiled at the sound of Kobayashi's voice, and the familiar refrain of yet another apology. Would she ever stop?

"It's fine. I was just doing some reading," he said, suddenly aware of how sad that sounded; a single man in his forties sitting home alone on a Friday night in a bustling city like Tokyo.

"I learned some information that I think you will be interested to hear," she continued, snapping him back to reality. Something in her tone suggested a guardedness that he found slightly unfamiliar.

"About the case?"

She ignored the redundancy of the question and continued in the same hesitant tone. "I'd rather discuss it with you ... in person," she said, adding quickly: "You mentioned wanting to visit the Tsukiji Market, and I thought if we met there in the morning, we could discuss the case and I could also show you the best parts of the market ... if you would like."

"The fish market? Yeah, that sounds great."

"It is quite busy, but as long as we're not too late ..."

"Early's fine with me. Name a time and a place."

"Nine o'clock, at the Tsukijishijō Station entrance."

"I'll be there."

"I'll leave you to your reading then," she said, her tone back to normal. "Good night, Charlie."

"Good night."

He ended the call and stared at the phone. Was she just being nice to a hapless foreigner, or was the nervousness in the air every time they met indicative of more than just his own attraction to her? Don't overthink it, he told himself. He was meeting her in a quasi-social setting that she had arranged — something that could only be described as shockingly forward in this society. He clicked the search engine window shut and downed the beer. He was still thinking about the tone in her voice when she had suggested the meeting when his phone went off again. For a split second he thought it might be her, calling to cancel the whole thing, but the area code of the incoming call was 613 — Ottawa. He hit the receive button and put the phone on speaker, setting it down on the table as a male voice on a distant sounding line echoed through the speaker.

"Is this Charlie Hillier?"

"Yes, it is."

"This is Sergeant Bill Dixon, with the RCMP."

"Oh, hi. I was hoping to get in touch with you, to discuss your report."

"I realize it's late there, but can you get to a secure line now?"

"Give me your number and I'll call you back in ten minutes," he said, then took down the number, hung up the phone, and hurried over to the embassy to make the call.

"Thanks for getting back to me," Charlie said when Dixon answered.

"No worries. Any progress in the investigation into Seger's death?"

"Not really, in part because the Japanese aren't sure whether to launch a homicide investigation. I was hoping I could use your report to try to convince them."

There was a slight pause on the other end of the line before Dixon spoke again. "I'd have to check, but it's probably okay. I'm pretty sure we have a reciprocal agreement with Japan for this kind of stuff. I'll confirm and get back to you. Why are they so reluctant to consider to it a homicide?"

"Seger was found in a part of town where foreigners are often victims of scams — the kind of thing where the victim wakes up in a cab back to his hotel with his wallet missing, you know? They're not saying that a crime wasn't involved, but they think that the death might have been accidental. It's still a wrongful death, but I guess they treat it differently. Then there's the fact that he's a foreigner, which complicates things."

"Understood."

"I think if they felt Seger was mixed up in organized crime back in Canada," Charlie continued, "that might be worth some further digging here, and that's the other thing I wanted to ask you. The report kind of hints that he might have been involved, but doesn't really say it in so many words, and I was interested in your thoughts."

Dixon gave a little laugh at the other end of the line. "If you're asking for my opinion off the record, Seger was dirty, for sure. The only reason I couldn't say so is he'd done such a good job of covering his tracks. No criminal record, no direct link ever made between him and illegal activity, but it's just beneath the surface, believe me." Dixon paused before continuing. "A guy like that, with his sort of pedigree, his family connections to known OC associates, it'd be a one in a million for him not to be involved somehow.

Then there's his travel pattern over the past few years. In the Caymans a couple of times the year before last, then in and out of Hong Kong regularly, more so in the past eighteen months. Then you look at his line of work."

"You mean banking?"

"I guess you'd call it that."

Charlie wasn't sure what he was getting at, and needed to cut through the double-talk. "What do you mean?"

There was a short sigh on the other end of the line. "We're in the middle of a big investigation into online securities fraud, and I'm pretty sure we're gonna find he was involved somehow. It's an international thing, covering North America, Eastern Europe, and Asia."

"And his travel patterns fit with him being involved."

"That and the work he was doing, the people he was meeting ... it all fits. If he hadn't ended up dead, he probably would have landed in jail in the next couple of years — although he was a slippery fuck, I'll give him that."

"Not slippery enough, I guess."

"They say crime doesn't pay," Dixon said with a laugh. "There's something else, that's not in the report. I just found out yesterday that there might be a connection between Seger and one of the Canadian companies allegedly involved in the securities fraud."

"Oh yeah?"

"I'm still sifting through it, but it seems that Seger was employed by a firm called APP, which had a contract with the one we've been looking at, based in Montreal."

"What's the name of that one?" Charlie asked.

"Advantage Securities," he said, going on to explain that the connection was still being investigated. But Charlie had stopped listening after hearing the name — a name he was sure he had seen on Rob Lepage's immigration forms. He tried to stay focused on Dixon's comments on his report over the next ten minutes, but rather than Mike Seger, all he could think of was the increasingly disturbing connections being made to Rob Lepage. It occurred to him that Seger had told him Lepage worked for a company based in Toronto, not Montreal. Then there was the fact that Lepage's first words when he came out of his coma had been French.

"Well, thanks for getting back to me with this," Charlie said after Dixon had wrapped up. "It's been very ... enlightening."

"I'll shoot you an email tomorrow to confirm that you can share the report. Like I said, it shouldn't be a problem, but I want to run it by my boss, to be sure."

"Always a good idea. Thanks."

Charlie hung up the phone and sat in the quiet of the room for a few moments before riding the elevator back to the fourth floor, getting off into the dimness of the after-hours lighting, walking past one empty office after another until he reached his own. He flicked on his desk lamp, preferring it to the harsh light of the overhead fluorescent, and slid the top drawer of his desk open. He plucked out the postcard he had offered as an *aide-mémoire* to Lepage. In his frustrated phase — just after coming out of the coma — Lepage had rejected it, but now he suddenly wanted it back.

Charlie reached into his front pocket and retrieved the key card for Lepage's apartment, which had been burning a hole in his pants as he had sat there in Lepage's kitchen after almost being caught breaking into the place. He closed his eyes and replayed Lepage's words and his facial expression when they had parted ways by his front door. He had guessed something funny was going on, but had he known Charlie was in his apartment just seconds before he had stepped off the elevator? It occurred to him that he might have left something out of place in his hasty search, though he thought he had been careful. Then again, the presence of the gun had freaked him out, to the point that he might have been less cautious than he thought. And maybe Lepage had left a piece of string in the door or something.... *This is getting ridiculous*, he told himself, tossing the card onto the desk. If Lepage had figured it out, there was nothing he could do about it now. He should be more focused on possible reasons why Lepage would have a gun in his desk drawer. For protection, most probably. But from whom? He frowned as he realized the obvious flaw in that explanation, namely that if he got the gun for protection, why hadn't he been carrying it when he was out? What if he got the gun for offensive, rather than defensive, purposes?

Charlie got up and glanced at the clock. It was past ten, and he felt exhausted. He put the key card back in his pocket and was about to do the same with the postcard, when he flipped it over and examined it under the lamplight to confirm that there really was nothing written on it. A blank postcard featuring a picture of a snow-capped Mount Fuji. Why was it suddenly of interest to Lepage, when it had obviously triggered nothing whatsoever when he first laid eyes on it in the hospital? He leaned the postcard against the base of his monitor, flicked off the lamp, and left his office. He would have to return the key card tomorrow, but he was going to hang on to the postcard for a little while longer.

CHAPTER 25

Charlie had no doubt about whether he had gotten off at the
right stop when the smell of saltwater and fish overwhelmed
him as he came up out of Tsukijishijō Station. It wasn't yet
nine on Saturday morning and already the station was busy.
As he arrived at street level, he noticed the sky had cleared
and the sun was shining. He found his way to the southern
exit and was barely there a minute when he saw Kobayashi
coming up the steps. She was wearing capris and a light
jacket over a striped shirt, with her hair tied back in a ponytail. He did a double-take at this new casual, sporty version
of the normally formal Kobayashi. She gave him a tentative
smile, apparently recognizing his appraising eye.

"You look so … different," he said with a broad smile. "It
really suits you."

"Thank you." She glanced at her shoes. "You look very
nice also," she said, making him feel better about the outfit
he had managed to cobble together from the remnants of
his clean clothes. He was going to have to do some laundry
soon. "Shall I show you around?"

He gave her an enthusiastic nod. "Lead the way."

They walked out of the station and joined a stream of
pedestrians walking down the crowded street. Charlie had

read that the sprawling market occupied over fifty acres, and as they approached the entrance, Charlie saw that it was laid out like an enormous outdoor warehouse, with little loaders buzzing from stall to stall, depositing containers of fresh seafood. The air was filled with the sound of vendors shouting out their wares, competing with the beeping of reversing loaders. As they passed the last little side street on the way to the main entrance, Charlie noticed a crowd gathered outside the window of a tiny store. From the expectant look on everyone's face, they were clearly waiting for something momentous.

"What's going on over there?"

Kobayashi followed his gaze and nodded. "*Maguro* … tuna," she said, pushing her way politely but with an effective determination through the edge of the crowd, getting as close as a few rows back. She said something in Japanese to an elderly woman with a string bag on her arm, then turned to Charlie.

"They're about to carve a tuna," she said, just as two men in blue smocks emerged from the store carrying a massive, silvery, finned creature that looked more like a shark than any tuna Charlie had ever seen.

"It's massive," he remarked, as the crowd oohed and awed to the delight of one of the smock-clad men.

"Probably fifty kilos," Kobayashi said as the first man deposited his end on the raised carving table and began shouting out to the crowd, waving a large knife that looked like a machete in overhead arcs like a samurai preparing for battle. With a fluid motion, he began to slice at the head of the massive fish, his partner grabbing the handle at the other end of what Charlie realized was a saw. A few seconds later they were through, and the first man raised the head up high and displayed it theatrically, to shouts of great approval from the crowd. Setting the head at the end of the large table, they went to work on the fins and the tail, then the main carver sliced a thin wedge of flesh from the side of the tuna and held it up. The crowd went wild, arms extending to get the first piece, which went to the old woman with the string bag. Charlie and Kobayashi stood and watched as the two men continued to carve up the massive fish, then she motioned toward the market.

"I prefer to get my tuna at another stall. Less crowded," she said, and it was Charlie's turn to gently push his way back out to the main street, with Kobayashi following close behind as the crowd closed in around them. Entering the covered part of the market, Charlie was overwhelmed by the sights and sounds around him, and he followed Kobayashi as she led him from stall to stall, pointing out the vast array of fish and seafood, from the mundane to the most exotic, not to mention expensive.

"Is that right?" he said, pointing at a sign over a particularly nasty-looking fish with a dizzying number of zeros after the yen sign.

"Blowfish," she said with a nod. "Very expensive. Not my favourite, personally."

A few stalls farther on, an old man in a stained smock hurried out from behind a table with bins of various seafood arranged on beds of crushed ice. They chattered in Japanese as they enthusiastically bowed. She introduced Charlie, who bowed and did his best not to mangle a standard greeting too badly. The old man seemed pleased with his effort, and responded in kind, bowing again several times as he gestured to the table and resumed his rapid-fire chatter with Kobayashi.

"He has the best tuna in the market," she said, translating for the old man, whose toothless face beamed at the compliment. He waved her over excitedly and put several thinly-sliced pieces into a little container and covered it with ice before sealing it.

"Look at those crabs," Charlie remarked. They were larger than any he'd seen before. Before Kobayashi could translate, the old man was loading up a bag of the plumpest ones. "I guess I'm getting some," he said, eliciting a little grin from Kobayashi. "As long as it's not the same price as the blowfish."

"His prices are the best in the market." Kobayashi gave him a reassuring nod, as the old man handed him his crabs and then followed Kobayashi to the other end of the table, where they chatted for a few minutes as he prepared two more small bags of what looked like crayfish and possibly salmon, but Charlie wasn't sure. When he was done, the vendor did the tally and Charlie tried to understand but failed. "How much did he say?"

"It's very reasonable," she said, reaching into her purse, but Charlie was first off the draw, handing the old man a ten thousand yen note. He grinned and took the note, turning to his cash box to produce six thousand yen in change by the time Kobayashi had her purse out and realized what was going on.

"No, Charlie. I can't let you …"

"It's done," he said, taking the bills and bowing. "*Arigatou gozaimasu.*"

The old man bowed and gave him a broad grin, then muttered something to Kobayashi, who responded with an admonishing frown.

"What did he say?" Charlie asked, as they made their way on to the next row of stalls.

"He says silly things sometimes." She turned away in embarrassment. "Would you like to get a coffee?" she asked, as they made their way back toward the market entrance.

"Thought you'd never ask."

They found a coffee shop on the main street leading away from the market, halfway back to the Metro station, and Kobayashi ordered cappuccinos. She insisted on paying and he decided not to fight, finding them a table by the window instead. Outside the sun was still bright and warmed the inside of the crowded café.

"I did some research last night," he said, after they had settled in their seats and had begun to sip their coffee.

"What kind of research?"

He described what he had learned about the yakuza, from their roots that went all the way back to samurai days, to their role in the bubble of the early nineties, and their current incarnation. She listened intently, sipping her coffee and nodding from time to time.

"And why were you doing this research?" she asked when he was done.

"I was thinking of that photo, and the possible connection between Nippon Kasuga and the yakuza guy."

"Hmm." She gave him her usual inscrutable look.

"What?"

"I did some research, as well," she said, after a brief pause. "I spoke to my colleague in organized crime, about whether he had heard of Nippon Kasuga."

"And?"

She shook her head. "They're not known to have connections to illegal activity, but he mentioned that their name came up in a bid-rigging investigation."

Charlie's ears perked up at the news. He had noticed that this type of scam was one of the yakuza's bread and butter business lines. It was usually related to construction projects, though.

"What sort of government contracts would be awarded to a securities firm?" he asked.

"Their alleged involvement was ... indirect. And anyway, it looks like they may not have done anything wrong."

"Could they be involved in securities fraud with the yakuza?"

She drank the last of her coffee and set the little cup back on the saucer in the delicate and precise manner that he had noticed in all of her movements. "Yakuza organizations are involved in securities fraud," she began. "But things have changed since the nineties. There are frequent investigations into banking irregularities now. Companies that break the rules are de-listed all the time."

Charlie nodded. What she wasn't saying was that her precrash predecessors had been all too willing to turn a blind eye to the yakuza saturating the market with bad debt. The staggering losses had changed all that, and forced the authorities to start enforcing the rules. He understood her reluctance to divulge this to an outsider, respected it, even. She had her pride.

"What are you thinking?" she asked, surprising him — with the probing question, but also with the look in her eyes, which had become interrogative.

Charlie shrugged. "I was just trying to imagine what the connection to Nippon Kasuga is."

She kept her eyes on him for a moment and then, just like that, her features reverted to the soft and delicate version; a demure smile teased the corners of her mouth, then faded as quickly as it had appeared. "It is possible that they are not involved willingly."

"What do you mean?"

"Have you heard of *sōkaiya*, Charlie?"

He shook his head. For all he knew it was one of the exotic species of seafood that they had seen on display at the market.

"The word in English is ..." She paused for a moment, looking out the window for a second until he saw the flash of recognition in her eyes and she turned back to him. "*Extortion*."

"Do you mean corporate extortion?"

She nodded. "It begins legitimately. Individuals linked to yakuza gradually buy up stock, become involved in a corporation. At first, no one knows. Then they attend a shareholder meeting and make themselves known."

"And tell the directors to start following their instructions, or else?"

"Something like that, yes."

Charlie nodded. "And I guess not too many people say no to the yakuza."

Kobayashi said nothing for a moment, running her finger around the rim of her cup. "How much do you know about Mr. Lepage's activities back in Canada?"

Charlie shrugged, hoping his internal debate about whether to share the details of the RCMP report with her remained hidden behind a casual facade. Dixon had not emailed a confirmation to proceed, though he thought that likely had more to do with the fact that it was Saturday morning and Dixon hopefully having a life outside work. It would probably come in on Monday morning. "Not much, I'm afraid," he lied, deciding to withhold Dixon's discovery that the company Lepage worked for might be linked to white collar fraud. He hated lying at the best of times, but it felt especially wrong right now. He looked down at his cup and stirred the foam at the bottom. When he looked up, he was expecting to be caught in those piercing eyes, but Kobayashi was smiling.

"You like him, don't you?" she said.

"Who, Rob? Sure, he seems like a stand-up guy."

"What is stand-up?" she asked, cocking her head to one side.

"It means decent ... good."

"Ah." She nodded.

They chatted about the case for another ten minutes when she suddenly changed the topic.

"So, how do you like Tokyo?"

"I like it just fine." He leaned back in his chair. "I'm starting to get more familiar with the Metro stations, and the crowds."

"Is it so different in Canada? You have big cities there as well, no?"

"Big is a relative term, and I spent most of my time in Ottawa recently. I'm from the East Coast originally, where the cities are much smaller. A lot more open space."

"You miss it, I can see."

He shrugged, wondering whether that was true. He didn't miss Ottawa, particularly the memories it evoked, and though he did have a soft spot for St. John's, he'd been away so long that he felt like he'd lost the connection. In fact, it occurred to him that he didn't have any real connection to anyone or anything that he could think of. He could have said that was the price you paid for going from one foreign posting to the next, but he had only been in the rotational stream for a few years. The way he had spent the previous fifteen were what bothered him now.

"I didn't mean to ... pry," she said, and he realized his face must have betrayed his thoughts. He smiled and shook his head, noticing the containers of seafood sitting on ice in their bags at the end of the table.

"I was just thinking about what I'm going to do with all those crabs."

"You have to eat them, Charlie." Her face lit with her smile. "And while they're fresh."

He pointed to Kobayashi's bag of tuna. "What about you. How do you eat the tuna?"

"Sushi," she said, as though it went without saying. "Please take some and try for yourself."

"I wouldn't know what to do with it." He waved a hand as she reached for the bag.

"It's very easy to make. I could show you."

He looked at her and couldn't resist trying. "How about now? I have a pretty well-stocked kitchen, even if I don't know how to use half of the stuff," he added. She looked down momentarily and her eyes had changed when she looked back up. He had made a gross miscalculation and crossed the line. He went into damage control right away. "I'm sure you have better things to do on your day off," he said with a nonchalance he didn't feel. "Besides, I have a family recipe for crab au gratin that never fails."

"I have an ... engagement with my parents this afternoon."

"Of course," he said quickly, wishing he had kept his big trap shut.

"But what about this evening?" she said. Charlie hesitated for a moment, not sure if he had heard her correctly, then she added: "I can show you how to make sushi and you can show me how to make crab oh ..."

"Au gratin," he said, finally able to unfreeze the blank expression on his face. "That sounds great. I live on the embassy compound, so I could meet you at the front entrance to the Aoyama-itchōme Station ... around seven?"

"Seven is good." She handed him the bag of tuna. "I look forward to it."

CHAPTER 26

Charlie stood at the Aoyoma-dori entrance to the Aoyama-itchōme Station — the nearest to the Canadian embassy — and looked for Kobayashi among the ever-present swell of people emerging from the station onto the street. There had been a noticeable drop in temperature when the sun had gone down, and Charlie could feel the damp chill seeping in through his raincoat. He didn't really have a medium-weight coat that would be suitable for a Tokyo winter, and the heavy one he had used to survive Ottawa and Moscow seemed over the top here, though he noticed many of the passing crowd were dressed in parkas and puffy coats worthy of the Yukon Quest, despite the temperature still being well above zero.

He was thinking where he might find something without spending a month's salary — from what he had seen so far in store windows, clothing wasn't cheap in Tokyo — when he spotted Kobayashi coming up the stairs. She had switched her capris to black pants tucked into low-heeled boots and substituted a peacoat for her windbreaker. He saw recognition in her eyes and also noticed, as she came closer, that she was wearing makeup. It wasn't much, just a subtle highlighting of her eyes and lips, but the effect was significant. He wondered whether the occasion called for a two-cheek peck but decided to stick with the bow. When in Rome …

"Hello, Charlie," she said, after reciprocating the bow then rubbing her arms and giving a noticeable shiver.

"It's really cooled off, hasn't it?"

She nodded, then smiled. "You must think me foolish for believing this is cold, with you being from Canada."

He shrugged as they set off down Aoyama-dori. "Actually, I was just thinking I need a warmer jacket." He pulled at the collar of his raincoat. They chatted as they walked the short distance to the embassy compound, where they stopped briefly at the front gate to sign Kobayashi in as a visitor before proceeding to the complex of staff apartments behind the main embassy building.

"It's very quiet," she remarked as they made their way up the stairs and Charlie got out his key.

"It usually is. Saturday night, so most people are probably out." He opened the door and showed her in.

"It's very … big," she said, surveying what to Charlie had seemed a somewhat compact single apartment by Canadian standards.

"Really?" He took her coat and gave her a quick tour of the living room, dining room, and kitchen. "There's a bedroom and a guestroom that I use as a study," he added, then felt suddenly awkward for some reason, as though Kobayashi might find such a waste of space for one person reprehensible. But if she was offended, she gave no indication.

"Would you like a glass of wine? Or I've got some sake."

"Wine would be very nice, thank you."

Charlie busied himself with uncorking the wine and pouring it into the glasses that he had carefully washed and polished an hour ago. When he turned around to hand her a glass, she accepted it with one hand and held out a gift-wrapped box with the other.

"Oh, you didn't have to ... thank you." He accepted the rectangular box, beautifully wrapped in green paper and silver ribbon.

"Please, open it." She seemed to sense his hesitation.

He obliged, setting his glass down on the counter and carefully undoing the wrapper. Inside the box were six sets of chopsticks, the handles decorated with the same intricate carving beneath a colourful lacquered finish. There were six matching, curved oblong discs at one end of the box that looked a bit like pebbles rounded by ocean waves. He recognized them as the stands for the chopsticks to rest on when they were not in use.

"They're beautiful."

"I thought you should learn on a good set," she said with a smile.

"Now I feel bad." He set the box down on the kitchen table. "First you supply the tuna, now this?"

"But you forget that you're the host, Charlie."

"In that case, thank you, and welcome." He raised his glass. "And cheers."

They drank their wine and chatted for a while, then Kobayashi got down to business, pulling the tuna out of the fridge and some seaweed wraps out of her purse. Charlie focused on the rice and paid attention as she described her family's method of preparing sushi that had been handed down for generations. He had prepared the crab in advance, so it was only a matter of putting it in the oven, and before he knew it, the meal was ready and they moved into the dining room, where the table was already set. Charlie had never considered himself much of a sushi fan, but whether it was Kobayashi's recipe, her preparation, or the atmosphere, he found himself enjoying the meal immensely. They had also switched to sake for the meal, and he poured the last of the first bottle into their cups as they finished up the sushi. Eventually, the conversation turned to business. It was Kobayashi who brought it up — Charlie being quite content to continue discussing Japanese culture and where to eat in Tokyo all night long.

"Do you have any more thoughts about your Mr. Lepage?" she asked. Both her tone and body language were consistent with a casual inquiry, but Charlie felt immediately on edge. Whereas Kobayashi had been pumping her sources for any information on a possible link between Lepage and Nippon Kasuga, he had been sitting on the RCMP report. Dixon still hadn't emailed, but as he sat there, inches from her across the table, with a glass of wine and half a bottle of sake warming his insides, he knew he had made up his mind.

"Actually, I did learn something interesting myself." He drank the last of the liquid in his cup as he took the plunge. "It turns out that Lepage's employer back in Canada might have been involved in some shady dealings."

Kobayashi's face remained impassive but she leaned forward ever so slightly at the news. "What kind of dealings?"

"Fraud of various kinds. Stock fraud, insider trading, online scams. But much like Nippon Kasuga here, there's no hard evidence to incriminate the firm, just indirect evidence. They've never been officially charged and I'm not even sure if they're under surveillance."

"That is interesting." She tipped back her own cup. He reached over to the side table and took another bottle from his thinly stocked bar and opened it. He hesitated before filling her cup. "Would you like me to warm it ... or chill it?"

She shook her head. "Room temperature is fine. But maybe I've had too much already."

He waved off her protest and continued pouring. "It's not like you're driving anywhere."

"It really is very good sake," she said, making him glad he had followed Redford's recommendation, there being a dizzying array of different brands available. It was a bit like buying vodka in Moscow, where the prices and qualities varied so much from one brand to the next.

"So you don't think Mr. Lepage or Nippon Kasuga were involved in anything illegal?" There was a hint of challenge in her voice, just below the calm surface.

"I didn't say that. I'm just having a hard time imagining Rob was knowingly involved in something illegal. I mean, you said yourself this practice of *sōkaiya* — or corporate extortion — is pretty common. Maybe Nippon Kasuga was involved and he didn't know."

She nodded, apparently turning something over in her mind before continuing. He was half expecting her to switch into interrogation mode, but the smile on her face and the way her shoulders relaxed suggested just the opposite.

"You like to see the good in people, don't you, Charlie?"

"I like to think I know people — deep down, you know?" He shrugged, adding: "I'm not always right, but I'm not always wrong either, and I'd prefer to err on the side of good." She was nodding, but he wondered if she thought him a fool. "Maybe that makes me naive."

She frowned at the word, and shook her head vigorously, before placing her slender hand on his. "I don't think so. I think to see good, makes you good."

He smiled at her simple eloquence, then looked down at the delicate bone structure of her hand, enjoying the way her cool touch sent a shock wave up his arm and down his back. He decided to throw the last of any caution to the wind.

"I learned something else about Mike Seger," he said, watching as she remained impassive. "He was a consultant for a company that did some business with Lepage's company."

"So, it is possible that they worked together?"

He nodded. "Although Seger never mentioned that — only that he and Rob knew each other growing up."

"But you said you had doubts about whether that was true," she pressed. "And there was nothing on Lepage's email to confirm that Seger had been in touch with him on a personal level ... and we know now that Seger did not come to Tokyo from Hong Kong, as he said he did." Charlie had to admit that, objectively, it was much more likely that they were connected on a professional level rather than a personal one. It didn't help that Lepage's missing memory left him unable to confirm whether he and Seger had been friends at some point. "And you say Lepage can't remember Seger as a friend," she added, as though reading his mind.

"So he says, yeah." He sipped his sake as Kobayashi processed the change in his tone.

"You think maybe he can remember more than he is telling you?"

He sighed. "I want to believe him, but I really don't know anymore." He didn't want to get into the doubts he was having about whether some or all of Lepage's ongoing memory loss was genuine, or Yamaguchi's concerns about the apparent inconsistency between what his testing revealed and what Lepage was describing.

"You are troubled, I can tell." She put her hand on his again. "You want to believe in the good in him, but you are finding it difficult."

He smiled and looked at her across the table. He could smell her subtle perfume from where he sat, and the feeling of her hand, which had remained on his, was intoxicating.

"Would you like some dessert?"

She didn't reply, just continued to look at him with those deep eyes, until she slowly began to lean forward. He found himself doing the same thing, almost automatically, until their lips met halfway across the table. They kissed for what seemed like a long time, then she pulled back. He was wondering what cultural divides he had inappropriately crossed until he remembered that she had initiated the kiss.

"I don't want dessert," she said. "Perhaps you would show me your bedroom, though."

Charlie had to process her words for a moment, if only to confirm what he thought he had heard, but though they were phrased as a question, she seemed not to expect an answer. Rather, she stood and slowly walked around to his side of the table, holding out her hand. He rose and took it, leading her down the hall, pausing as he entered the master bedroom and spotted the jumble of clothes on the corner of the bed. He swept it to the floor and when he turned back around, Kobayashi was slowly, deliberately, unbuttoning her blouse. When she was done, she took one of his hands and placed it on the delicate lace of her bra, her other hand tugging at his belt as their bodies pressed close and their lips crushed together. He heard his own pulse in his ears as his hand pressed into the soft flesh of her breasts and the other slid up her thigh. Their lips came apart and he felt her hot breath on his neck as he tore off his shirt. She freed him from his pants, then pulled him to the bed, where she crawled on top of him. In the soft light of the room, he could just make out those mysterious eyes through the dark hair that fell forward over her face, before she tilted her neck back and began to rock slowly, intensifying the motion until they were both swept away on waves of pleasure.

They lay in the dark on his bed, the only light the display on his clock radio. He was on his back, her head on his chest and one leg draped over his, her hand running up and down his side very slowly.

"I hope I didn't shock you," she said quietly. The truth was, he had been surprised by her agreeing to dinner, but dumbstruck by what had happened afterward. Then again, Redford had told him as much, and he seemed to have a habit of being right.

"No," he said. "I just had this idea that … I don't know."

She let out a little laugh. "You thought a Japanese woman would never … initiate, is that it?" She raised herself up on an elbow and smiled at him. "It is a very common impression, I think, but not always correct."

"I guess not," he said with a grin.

"*Sake-wa honshin-wo arawasu*," she said, prompting a puzzled look from Charlie.

"What does that mean?"

"Sake reveals the true heart."

They shared a laugh. "You really are a bit of an enigma, aren't you?"

She cocked her head to the side in the way she always did when she was searching for a meaning. "What is an enigma?"

"Well, you sort of have two sides — this beautiful, sensuous woman on the one hand, and a successful, intelligent, take-no-prisoners investigator on the other."

"Take no prisoners?"

"I mean you're very competent and confident — and I mean both as a compliment."

She smiled and laid her head back on his chest. "Unfortunately, I'm also … unexpected."

It was his turn to look puzzled. "You said that before. What do you mean by *unexpected*?"

"I mean I am not honouring my parents with a career they approve of .... or with a husband and children. Thankfully, my brothers will ensure my family will continue ..."

They lay in silence as he wondered what to say, wishing he understood Japanese culture better. She lifted her head and glanced over toward the bedside table, then set her chin gently on his chest, with a little sigh. "I have to go soon. The Metro stops running at midnight."

He looked over at the clock and saw it was almost eleven. "I'll go with you."

She laughed. "I'm a police inspector, Charlie, and I've been riding the Tokyo Metro all my life. You don't have ..."

He put his finger across her lips. "I insist."

She smiled up at him, then pulled herself up to kiss him. "That's very ... gentlemanly."

"Chivalry isn't dead yet," he said as they sat up and collected their clothes from the floor. She disappeared into the bathroom for a few minutes while he buttoned his shirt, then they were ready to go. Charlie felt a bit like he was doing a perp walk as they left the building and crossed the common area leading to the main entrance, but they didn't encounter anyone other than the guard, who smiled and bowed as they headed out onto Aoyama-dori.

"You won't have time to catch the last train back," she said, glancing at her watch as they reached the entrance to the Metro station.

He shrugged. "I'll probably make it, and I can always get a cab."

She turned to him and put her hand on his chest. "I must insist." She stood on tiptoes and craned her neck to kiss him.

He savoured the taste of her lips for a brief moment and held her close. She stepped back.

"Thank you for a wonderful evening, Charlie."

"Thanks for the chopsticks," he said as she laughed and started toward the stairs. "Can I call you tomorrow?"

She nodded and waved. "Good night."

He felt light as air as he turned and headed back toward the embassy, oblivious to the night's chill, or to the sight of Aiko Kimura slipping from the shadows and hurrying down the stairs to the Metro station after Kobayashi.

CHAPTER 27

Rob Lepage browsed kimonos of every colour, size, and fabric hanging on display in the basement floor of the Oriental Bazaar on Omote-sando Avenue. Glancing around the crowded store, he could see why she had picked it — the clientele was mostly Westerners. In fact, the staff seemed to be the only Japanese people in the place, a distinct difference from anywhere else in Tokyo, where his fair hair and skin, not to mention his height, sometimes made him feel like some sort of alien.

"Find anything you like?"

He turned with a start to see Kimura standing at his side. "Where did you spring from?"

"I watched you come in," she said. She was dressed casually, her long hair mostly hidden under a peaked hat.

"I came alone, if that's what you're wondering."

She smiled. "I know you're not that stupid." She moved off toward a display of T-shirts featuring everything from slogans in Japanese to pictures of samurais and swords in different colours.

"So, what's up?" he asked quietly. To anyone watching they looked like a couple out for a leisurely shop.

"Your friend at the embassy is becoming … troublesome."

"Hillier? He's not my friend; I'm just his consular case."

"He's been working with the police, asking questions he shouldn't be asking." Lepage felt a stab of alarm. It must have shown on his face, because Kimura picked up on it immediately. "What?" Her voice was almost a hiss.

He shook his head. "It's probably nothing, but he was at my apartment the other day. He may have been inside ..."

"Could he have found something?"

Lepage shook his head. "No way. I've scoured the place from top to bottom, plus he doesn't even know what he's looking for."

She gave a little grunt. "Neither do you, apparently."

"I told you, it's just a matter of time. My memory's coming back."

"Hmm." Kimura moved on to a display of lacquered boxes in varying shapes and sizes. She picked one up and examined it. They were all mass-produced, probably in China, but they were the sort of kitsch tourists couldn't get enough of.

"You don't believe me?" He picked up a smaller box next to the one she had selected.

"I spoke to your doctor yesterday. He said your test results were normal."

"So?"

"So why can't you remember where you put it?"

"I told you, I can remember some things but others are still a blank. Yes, my test results were normal, but that doesn't mean shit, and Yamaguchi would tell you the same thing if you bothered to ask. Amnesia is not an exact science." He paused and set the box back on the table and turned to look her in the eyes. "I'm not holding out on you."

She smiled, but her eyes retained the same chill. "That's good, because that would be very unwise."

"So, what's Hillier been asking the police?" he asked, as they kept moving toward a display of fans.

"He's been getting very cozy with that bitch Kobayashi, and she's been asking about Nippon Kasuga, whether they have any yakuza connections."

"But what would lead them to Nippon Kasuga?"

She shrugged. "I don't know, all I know is that Kobayashi has been sniffing around the organized crime unit for details."

"And you know this how?"

She stopped and gave him a condescending look, as though parent to child, and he realized the naïveté of his question. "Because you have people on the task force, obviously. So what do you want to do?"

"I think it's time something unfortunate happened to Mr. Hillier, before he stumbles onto something he really shouldn't," she said, picking up a fan and spreading it out to reveal the image of a cherry tree in full bloom.

"Won't that just make Kobayashi more suspicious?"

Kimura shrugged. "She's on her own — there is no official investigation. But perhaps she should have an accident as well."

Lepage nodded. "Do what you have to. In the meantime, I'll keep looking. Sooner or later, it's going to come back to me."

"You better hope so." Kimura set the fan down and headed off toward the stairs.

Lepage waited a few minutes before following Kimura upstairs and out onto Omote-sando Avenue. He glanced up and down the sidewalk, at the late morning crowd of Sunday strollers into which she had immersed herself. He started walking south, past the high-end stores where the price tags in Japanese yen looked even more astronomical than they actually were, then pulled his phone out of his pocket and dialed. Lepage was about to end the call when he heard a voice at the other end.

"Hi, Charlie. I didn't interrupt anything, did I?"

"I was just getting out of the shower when I heard the phone. What's up?"

"I was wondering if you had any plans for lunch." Lepage stepped out of the moving crowd in the brief pause that followed. "My treat," he added. "As a thank-you for all the work you put in on my case, visiting me in hospital … everything."

"That's my job. You don't have to …"

"No, I want to," Lepage persisted. "It occurred to me that I never really thanked you. Come on, lunch is the least I can do."

"Um, sure. Where did you want to meet?"

Lepage looked up the street. "There's a sushi place on Omote-sando. Just up from Meiji-jingūmae Station. You like sushi?"

"Yeah, of course," Charlie replied, taking down the coordinates.

"Noon okay?" Lepage asked. "They get pretty jammed up after that."

"That works. I'll see you there."

Lepage ended the call and put the phone back in his pocket, the smile he had worn a few seconds before now replaced with a grimace. He liked Charlie, but he had to remind himself that this was business, and serious business at that. Sometimes people put themselves in the wrong place at the wrong time. There was nothing he could do about that.

Charlie arrived at the restaurant at ten past and had to fight his way through the lineup outside just to make it to the hostess. He had begun an attempt to explain that he was meeting someone inside when Lepage appeared at his side, thanking the hostess in Japanese as he pulled Charlie with him toward a little table at the back of the main dining room.

"You weren't kidding when you said it gets busy," Charlie said as he took a seat.

"I haven't been here in a while, but it's always good." Lepage pointed to a pair of beers on the table, the cold liquid creating beads of condensation on the outside of the glasses. "I took the liberty of ordering a drink. Wasn't sure if you liked sake or not."

"Beer's good." Charlie followed Lepage's lead and picked up the glass. They tapped them together and drank.

"To you, Charlie. You were a lifesaver. I don't know what I would have done without a fellow Canuck in my corner."

"My pleasure. Here's to your continued good health."

"So, how are you liking Tokyo, anyway?" Lepage asked. "You've been here — is it a month yet?"

"Not far off." Charlie nodded. "I have to say, it was a bit of an adjustment at first, but it's really starting to grow on me."

"You used to the crowds yet?"

"Yeah, they take a bit of getting used to, for sure." He moved his chair in as the table next to them filled with a half-dozen people, as if to underscore the point. He and Lepage shared a laugh.

"How about you? How are you feeling?"

Lepage took another sip of beer. "Pretty good. Still a bit frustrated by the gaps, you know, but it's coming. And Yamaguchi is staking his reputation on me recovering fully, so it must be so."

"I'm sure you will. Are you going to go back to work?"

"I'm not really sure what I'm going to do," Lepage said, after a waitress had taken their orders. "In a way, this whole thing has made me re-examine my priorities a little. I was thinking I might try my hand at something a little different. Maybe take some time off, do some travelling."

Charlie smiled. "Sometimes a clean slate is a good thing."

"You sound like you know what you're talking about, Charlie."

Charlie shrugged and took a sip of beer. "All I know is if you have the chance to take some time for yourself, you should do it. Who knows what's around the corner."

"That's exactly what I was thinking."

The conversation moved on to Lepage's plans for the future, then to their respective impressions of Tokyo as their food arrived and they ate it leisurely. Eventually, Lepage shifted the conversation to Mike Seger.

"Is there anything new on what happened to him?"

Charlie shrugged, then shook his head. "I'm afraid not. The police are treating it as a scam gone wrong, so I'm not sure we'll ever find out."

"Really?" Lepage seemed genuinely surprised. "And you can't, you know, pressure them since he was a Canadian?"

"I've tried, believe me. We're doing all we can." Saying the words, Charlie realized how hollow they must sound. Of course, he failed to mention the fact that Kobayashi seemed to be carrying on a pretty thorough investigation despite the fact that, officially, none existed.

"It's too bad, because that detective seemed pretty sharp. I got the feeling that if she was on the case, it wouldn't be long before we had some answers."

Charlie nodded. "Yeah, she's very bright."

"Not to mention beautiful." Lepage gave a little whistle. "Must be tough for her in this culture. I mean, in that line of work and when you add in her sex appeal.... She must have to deal with a lot of shit at the office."

"Yeah, I guess." Charlie pretended to focus on picking up the last few grains of rice with his chopsticks.

"No disrespect," Lepage added, and Charlie wondered whether he sensed his discomfort at the subject. Lepage glanced at his watch. "Well, I should probably get going and let you get on with your day." He glanced around until he spotted the waitress and made the sign for the cheque.

"Thanks for lunch. It was great," Charlie said, reaching into his pocket until Lepage spotted the move and waved him off.

"No way — this is on me. You can get the next one."

Charlie nodded, but pulled out his wallet anyway. "That reminds me," he said, in response to Lepage's puzzled look. "Here's your room key."

"Oh, right," Lepage said, accepting the plastic key card and putting it in his pocket. He settled the bill with the waiter, and as they were about to get up, he tapped his fingers on the table. "Say, do you have that postcard?"

Charlie was expecting the question, so his disappointed expression came off as genuine. "I couldn't find it. I looked everywhere, but it must have gone into recycling or something." He looked at Lepage, and there was a moment of hesitation as the two men held each other's gaze, then Lepage shrugged.

"That's too bad. I was hoping to see if it might help me fill in some of the remaining gaps, but it's not a big deal."

"I'm really sorry," Charlie said as the awkwardness passed and they got up from the table, making their way to the door. "I'll have another look."

They paused outside on the front step and shook hands.

"Don't bother," Lepage said with a little smile. "I have a feeling you won't find it. Stay well, Charlie."

"You, too."

Charlie watched as Lepage headed off in the direction of his apartment. He glanced up at the sky, which had darkened in the hour since he had gone into the restaurant. The grey clouds seemed threatening, and as he considered whether they were getting ready to unleash a torrent of rain, the wind whipped up and sent leaves scattering down the sidewalk and the wide boulevard of Omote-sando. Charlie zipped up his coat and headed for the Metro station. He felt unsettled, but not by the weather. It was the look in Lepage's eyes — there was something he was holding back. Suddenly the good-natured offer of lunch seemed like just a pretext, but for what? To get his apartment key back, for one. But there was more. And what was so special about that damned postcard? More than anything else, he was beginning to suspect that his fundamental assessment of Lepage was off, and in Charlie's experience, that was never a good sign.

CHAPTER 28

Lepage had been turning it over in his mind since leaving the restaurant, and by the time he was back at his apartment building he was convinced that Charlie was holding out on him. It was the postcard … it had to be. Maybe he hadn't pieced it all together yet, but it was only a matter of time. As he rode the elevator up, Lepage thought of Kimura's plans for the consular officer. Would she act today, or tomorrow? Locking his front door behind him, he sat at the kitchen table, pulled out his cellphone, and dialed her number.

"What is it?" Her clipped tone said everything.

"You need to hold off on what we discussed yesterday."

There was a pause on the other end of the line. "We should meet if you have something to say." He heard a rustle on the line and then silence for a few seconds before she came back on the line. "Why hold off?"

Lepage's pulse quickened as he detected something in her voice that suggested it may already be too late. For all he knew, Hillier had just been pushed in front of a train at Omote-sando Station.

"He knows something," he said, wishing he had thought the conversation through before calling.

"Are you saying he has what we're looking for?"

"No," he added quickly, realizing he may be putting himself at risk. "I just need a day, maybe two. If I'm right, I can find out what we need and then you can go ahead. But if he gets spooked, there's no telling what will happen."

Kimura was silent for a moment, assessing the information with her usual detached calculation. "You have twenty-four hours, no more. And don't call this number again."

The line went dead before he could respond. He slammed the phone down on the table and grabbed his head in his hands, willing himself to focus, to concentrate, to *remember* ... but it was pointless. He took Charlie's card out of his pocket and stared at it. He had to find out what the consular officer knew, and fast, or they were both dead men.

Charlie was almost at the end of the gradual ascent as he made his way east on Omote-sando and wondered whether he should just keep walking. It was probably only thirty minutes back to the embassy compound and he could probably use the exercise. He scanned the clouds overhead and while they still looked a little grey for his liking, they hadn't opened up yet, and he thought they might hold off until he got home. He passed a convenience store and was considering picking up a cheap umbrella, just in case, when his phone went off. He pulled it from his pocket and saw that the number was blocked. He stepped to the side of the moving crowd on the sidewalk.

"Charlie Hillier."

"Charlie, how are you?"

He felt an involuntary smile at the sound of Kobayashi's voice. "Chikako?" He imagined her looking embarrassed at his use of her first name, but she conveyed no such discomfort on the phone. In fact, she seemed all business.

"I was hoping we could meet today."

"Where are you?"

"Kasumigaseki," she said, referring to the headquarters of the Tokyo Metropolitan Police.

"Do you want me to meet you there?"

"Perhaps not." This time, he picked up on a trace of discomfort in her voice, but whether it was due to the sensitive nature of the information she wanted to share, or the fact that they had slept together the night before, he wasn't sure, and he didn't really care.

"I'm near Omote-sando." He checked his watch. "I could meet you at the embassy in about fifteen minutes."

"I'll see you there."

Fifteen minutes later, he was standing at the edge of the park adjacent to the Canadian embassy. He had glanced down at his BlackBerry for a split second when he heard his name. The sound of Louis Denault's voice, unlike Kobayashi's, didn't elicit a smile. Just the opposite, but he tried to manufacture one just the same.

"Hi, Louis." He tucked the phone into his pocket and glanced over Denault's shoulder, thinking how uncomfortable it would be if Kobayashi arrived at this particular moment. Then again, they were consenting adults, and it was none of Denault's goddamn business if he …

"Everything okay, Charlie? You seem a bit perturbed."

"What?" Charlie tried another smile, realizing his face must have conveyed some of what he was thinking. "No, I just … I didn't sleep very well last night."

"You're not still dealing with jet lag, surely?"

"I guess not."

Denault's expression softened a bit. "It can take a surprising amount of time to adjust to the time change. You'll get used to it eventually, I promise."

Charlie nodded, wondering how to avoid a drawn-out encounter, but he needn't have bothered. Denault was pointing to his watch. "I hate to rush off, but I'm late already."

"Don't let me keep you."

"Have a nice day."

"You, too, Louis," he said, watching Denault hurry off east across the front of the park. He had all but disappeared from view by the time Charlie turned back and saw Kobayashi approaching from the other direction. They exchanged a strangely formal greeting and then headed to the front gate, past security, and on to Charlie's apartment.

"Can I get you a coffee, or some tea?" he asked as they stood in the living room.

"No, thank you." He could tell from her posture that she was as nervous as he was, and he wondered if she had planned the meeting to tell him what a bad idea last night was, as opposed to giving him information related to Seger or Lepage. He was tempted to pre-empt her with an apology of his own but he held his tongue as they took a seat at opposite ends of the sofa.

"So, what's up?"

"I was reviewing the file on Mr. Lepage's accident and I noticed there was no mechanical report," she began.

"You were reviewing the case file on a Sunday morning?" Charlie couldn't help thinking that he had spent most of the morning lounging in bed.

"I had to deal with another matter and … anyway, I spoke to the mechanic who inspected Lepage's vehicle and he said he found evidence that the brakes had been tampered with."

Charlie was silent as the information sank in. "Someone disabled his brakes?" he finally asked, almost as a question to himself.

"It was not a conclusive finding," Kobayashi continued, "but he says he indicated the possibility on his report."

Charlie frowned. "I thought you said there wasn't a report?"

"He prepared a report. It just didn't make it into the file."

There was another silence as they both considered the possibilities. "Are you saying what I think you're saying?" he finally said.

"I think we have to consider the possibility that Mr. Lepage's accident was not an accident at all," she said, side-stepping his real question. "Which leads us to ask why someone would want Lepage dead."

Charlie stood and paced across the living room floor as his mind processed emerging possibilities. "It's starting to look like Rob may not be the clean-cut banker I thought he was. Maybe he was mixed up in something shady." He noticed her expression and substituted a less colloquial term. "Illegal. It's got to involve Kimura ... I knew from the moment I first saw her that she was bad news." He shook his head and sat back down next to Kobayashi. "But if someone was prepared to cut his brakes a couple of weeks ago to get rid of Lepage, why hasn't anything else happened since? Rob's been out of the hospital long enough that if anyone wanted to finish the job, they could ..." He stopped as he recalled the gun he had found in the top of Lepage's drawer. Its presence made sense if Lepage was thinking the very same thing — that someone was coming for him, whether he knew his car had been tampered with or not.

"What is it?" Kobayashi asked.

"Nothing, I just ..." Charlie muttered, buying time as he weighed whether to tell Kobayashi all he knew. She wore a puzzled, almost hurt look as she waited for him to say more; perhaps realizing he had been holding out on her. "I went to Lepage's apartment the other day and I found a gun."

"You entered his apartment without his permission?" Her eyes had widened noticeably.

"He gave me a key, when he was in hospital." He shook his head. "I hadn't given it back yet so I went to see him and he wasn't there," he felt the need to add, although it wasn't entirely accurate. "Then I bumped into him in the hallway when I was leaving."

"Did he know you were in his apartment?" There was a new urgency in Kobayashi's question.

"I don't think so … I don't know, he was acting weird, like at lunch today."

"You met him today?"

"He wanted to take me to lunch, to thank me for everything I had done." Charlie watched her reaction as he spoke and felt immediately foolish. "God, I'm such an idiot," he said, slapping his head.

Kobayashi shook her head and put a hand on his arm. "No, you're not. But you have to be careful. It may be dangerous for you."

"For me? Why?"

"Because Lepage is likely in danger himself, and his actions as a result may be … unpredictable."

Charlie nodded. As usual, she had seen through the veil that had fooled him so easily.

"What did you talk about at lunch?" she continued.

"Apart from chit-chat, there wasn't much," he said, with a shrug. "He seemed surprised that there wasn't going to be a formal investigation into Seger."

"Surprised or relieved?"

"I didn't really sense relief from him." Charlie tried to recall his exact expression on learning the news. "The only time I noticed him acting strangely is when I gave him back his apartment key, but not the postcard."

"What postcard?"

"It was one of the few things I collected from his apartment, right after he came out of the coma — you know, to try to help his memory along. I brought it to the hospital and showed it to him, but it didn't seem to trigger anything. He got sort of frustrated and told me he didn't want it."

Kobayashi frowned. "But he obviously remembers it now."

"He asked whether I had it. I told him I couldn't find it."

"But you do have it?"

He stood and went into the kitchen, returning with the postcard of Mount Fuji that he had been keeping on his fridge. "It's just a blank postcard," he said, handing it to her. She turned it over and examined both sides, paying particular attention to the postmark in the top left hand corner on the back. Other than Lepage's address, there was nothing on either side of the card.

"It's a Roppongi postmark." She set the card down on the coffee table and took out her phone. "Do you mind if I take a photo?"

"Be my guest." He watched as she took one picture, then turned the card over to take another of the back. The process reminded him of the legal pad he had found on his second trip to Lepage's apartment. "You made me think of something," he said, taking out his own phone and pulling up the picture of the diagram and showing it to her.

"What's this?"

"I found it in a drawer of Lepage's desk."

Kobayashi looked at him for a moment. "The first time, or the second?" she asked, and he realized he had already confessed to breaking and entering to a Japanese police officer.

"The second," he said, thinking that was the least of his worries right now. Kobayashi picked up the phone to get a better view. "*AK* must be Aiko Kimura," she said.

Charlie nodded. "And *MVA* must be his accident." He paused as Kobayashi looked on with a puzzled expression. "Short for motor vehicle accident, at least I assume that's what he meant."

"Ah." She nodded her agreement. "And *MS* is Mike Seger. But what is the significance of the number sign?"

He looked at the diagram again. "I was thinking it was a hashtag, but you're right, it could also be a reference to a number." He shrugged. "I really don't know." She puzzled over the diagram for a while, then picked up the postcard again and examined the postmark. "This was mailed the day before the accident."

Charlie pointed to the handwritten address on the postcard. "And I'm not sure, but that looks like Rob's handwriting. I saw some of his notes in the files in his desk drawer."

"So he sent it to himself." Kobayashi was frowning again. "But why?"

Charlie shook his head. "I wish I knew."

"We need to find out." Kobayashi seemed to be making the statement aloud to herself, then looked up at him suddenly. "You should be very careful with Lepage. Don't agree to any more meetings with him," she added. Her tone approached admonishment.

"I can take care of myself, you know."

She looked at him for a moment, then moved closer to him on the couch and put her arm on his.

"If he's involved with the yakuza, whether he knows it himself or not, he is in grave danger, as is anyone close to him. I know how they operate, and I don't want you to end up …"

"Like Seger?"

She leaned in and kissed him. "I just don't want you getting hurt," she said, pulling back and looking him in the eyes. In the soft light of the living room, she looked more alluring than ever.

"I'll be more careful," he said, leaning in to return her kiss.

CHAPTER 29

Charlie returned from the cafeteria with a cup of steaming coffee and took a seat at his desk. He had spent most of the morning trying to clear his inbox, but it was almost mid-morning and he had barely scratched the surface. He sipped the coffee and looked out at the bright sunshine, which concealed what was a surprisingly cool morning outside. It had been downright frosty when he had accompanied Kobayashi back to the Metro station around eleven the previous night. He smiled at the thought of her. On the surface, she was everything he imagined a Japanese woman to be — demure, self-effacing, and always apologizing for something — which made what lay beneath the facade even harder to reconcile. Kobayashi was more passionate and uninhibited than anyone else he had been with.

For all his bullshit, it seemed that Cliff Redford really did have a handle on Japanese culture. It stood to reason, Charlie supposed, since Redford had been here for almost thirty years and was married to a Japanese woman. He wondered what Kobayashi really thought of their relationship, and it occurred to him that perhaps it was just a physical outlet for her. He imagined the energy she would have to expend each day, maintaining the facade — putting up with the shit from her male co-workers, trying to appease her parents, who'd rather she taught preschool or worked as a secretary than in the male-dominated, dangerous, and — as she had put it — unexpected career she had chosen. Whatever her motive, he was glad that fate had crossed their paths.

"Daydreaming?"

He looked up with a start to see Karen Fraser standing at his door.

"I was just thinking about that memo from HR."

"Really?" She took a seat in one of his chairs. "You looked like you were thinking far more pleasant thoughts than that. I read that thing and it just made me wonder how much longer I'll have a job with the department."

He smiled. "They'll always hang on to the good ones, Karen. You don't need to worry."

"Well said." She raised her coffee cup in a mock toast. "So, how was your weekend?"

He thought he detected a playful tinge to the question and he fought back a smile as Fraser sat there, looking innocent. "It was great, Karen, how was yours?" he said with mock severity. She held up for a split second, then laughed out loud.

"All right, I guess I'm busted. And it's none of my business," she added, waving a hand. "I just couldn't help noticing …" Charlie nodded. He had wondered whether he had seen someone near the entrance to Fraser's building when he was walking Kobayashi out the night before, but he thought they had slipped by unnoticed. Apparently not. "It really is none of my business, Charlie."

He smiled. "I suppose this is the downside of living in the same complex as your co-workers."

"Yes, we're one big, happy, nosy family."

He let the silence grow for a moment, as Fraser sipped at her coffee, before speaking. "She's just someone I met — a friend."

"Friends are good." Fraser looked up from her cup. "I think it's great. You seemed kind of, I don't know, lonely when you got here. You seem a lot happier now."

Charlie considered the statement, and realized it was accurate. Despite his unease at whatever was going on with Lepage, he *was* a lot happier. On the other hand, maybe it wasn't such a good idea to be so obviously smitten by someone he was supposed to be interacting with on a purely professional basis. He suddenly wondered whether there was actually anything wrong with what they were doing. They were consenting adults, after all, and there was no Seger investigation, at least officially. He was considering whether to say more when his phone rang. He held up a finger to Fraser and answered the call from reception.

"Charlie Hillier. Oh really? Okay, tell him I'll be right down."

"It's right *up*, actually," Fraser said as she stood to go, reminding him that they were a floor below the reception level.

"Thanks for straightening that out."

"You're obviously distracted by more pressing matters," she said with a wink.

"That's Cliff." He motioned to the ceiling. "I'll catch up with you later, though."

"I want details, Charlie." Fraser was pointing a severe finger at him. "Details."

He laughed and headed off down the hall to the elevator. A few minutes later, he walked through the secure door and saw Redford sitting on the reception couch, fiddling with his phone.

"Hey, Cliff, what's up?"

"Charlie, my man. How are you?"

"You want to come through?" He gestured to where he had just come from, but Redford waved him off.

"Naw, let's not bother with all the security crap," Redford said as Charlie took a seat next to him. "I was passing through and thought I'd drop in. You talk to Rob lately?" he asked, putting his phone away.

"I had lunch with him yesterday."

"Yeah? How was he?"

"He seemed fine, I guess." Charlie wasn't planning on sharing his unease over the lunch meeting, or what Kobayashi and he had been discussing, if for no other reason than to avoid dragging Redford into something that could end up being unpleasant, or dangerous. He should have known that was easier said than done with Redford, who always seemed to be one step ahead.

"I talked to him yesterday, too," he said. "He seemed a little off to me," Redford added. He seemed to be monitoring Charlie's reaction for a sign that he was holding out on him.

"How so?"

"Nothing I could put my finger on. He just seemed a bit agitated. He was asking about the Seger investigation, for one thing."

Charlie frowned. "There isn't one, officially."

"That's what I told him," Redford said, pausing before adding: "And unofficially?"

"Chikako is doing a bit of digging, off the books."

"Chikako, is it?" Redford grinned and Charlie immediately regretted the misstep. "Glad to see you're making inroads there — cross-border co-operation and integration and all that good stuff."

Charlie laughed it off, then Redford's expression became more serious.

"I've been doing a bit of digging of my own, and I found out some interesting stuff about Nippon Kasuga." Charlie waited for it, ready to put on a surprised expression at the news of something Kobayashi had already told him days ago, and feeling guilty for keeping Redford out of the picture.

He hadn't mentioned that the man they had seen with the Nippon Kasuga executive outside Kimura's club was a high-ranking member of the Inagawa-kai. "They might be involved in a massive insider trading investigation in Hong Kong," Redford continued.

"Hong Kong?"

Redford waved a hand as if to explain. "One of my client banks has an office there, and they got subpoenaed in connection with this sting." He waved his hand again. "They had nothing to do with it and we dealt with the subpoena, but in going through the supporting documents, it looks like an affiliate of Nippon Kasuga based in Hong Kong was involved." Charlie shrugged, unsure of the ramifications of this information. He also wondered if it was the same investigation the RCMP guy, Dixon, had mentioned. "This sting was based in Hong Kong," Redford continued. "But it was really targeting an international scam, set up by a series of organized crime outfits from Asia, with the possible involvement of the Russian mafia."

"That doesn't sound good." Charlie recoiled at the mention of the Russian connection, his own interaction with that world in Moscow still fresh enough in his mind to make him distinctly uncomfortable. He considered the news, and Kobayashi's explanation of the practice of *sōkaiya*, where the yakuza bought up shares of a company and then started sending their operatives to shareholder meetings to influence corporate decisions. Taken to its ultimate limit, it would mean the corporate target would become a shell or a puppet, with the yakuza pulling the strings.

"It got me thinking," Redford pressed on as Charlie's mind whirred. "Seger spent a lot of time in Hong Kong, didn't he? What if he was the yakuza's rep on-site, reporting back to his masters here? Or he could have been working for

Nippon Kasuga directly." He paused and shook his head. "Memory loss or not, it always seemed odd to me that Rob didn't remember someone who was supposed to have been a childhood friend."

Charlie was still processing the information, and trying to fit it with what he already knew. It occurred to him that if the insider trading scam had international connections, Seger might just as easily have been working for a Canadian organized crime outfit — as well as, or instead of, a Hong Kong one. He made a mental note to call Dixon, and find out if he was aware of the Hong Kong sting.

"You in there, Charlie?"

He looked at Redford and it occurred to him that he really knew as little about Lepage as Charlie did, but he seemed to have a better handle on Nippon Kasuga.

"Answer me something, Cliff. Do you think Rob could be involved in something illegal?"

Redford paused to consider the question. "At first, I would have thought no way, but I'm starting to wonder. And Nippon Kasuga's starting to look less like the choir-boys I thought they were a week ago." He shook his head. "I really don't know."

Charlie returned to the embassy from a meeting at the Japanese Ministry of Foreign Affairs around two in the afternoon and got off the elevator on the third floor. He debated diving straight into the half-dozen matters that he hoped to get done before the end of the day, but opted to fortify himself with a coffee first. He was feeling tired, though he had slept like a baby last night, after returning from the Metro station to see Kobayashi off. He was preoccupied with a search of the bottom of his pockets for some change as he passed Denault's office and heard his name.

He looked up to see him at his desk, waving Charlie in.

"There you are." Denault stepped around his desk and gestured for him to have a seat, then pulled the door shut behind him.

"What's up, Louis?" he said, looking in puzzlement at the closed door.

"You'll forgive me for asking, Charlie, but I feel I have no choice. Is there anything you want to tell me?"

Charlie stared at him for a moment. "About?"

Denault shrugged and played with a cuff link. "About the Lepage file, perhaps, or your … interaction with the Tokyo Metropolitan Police?" Denault's tone was innocent but the slight grin teasing the edges of his mouth told Charlie exactly where the conversation was going. He thought back to his earlier conversation with Fraser and though he was sure she wouldn't have said anything, it was obvious that Denault could just as easily have seen Charlie and Kobayashi either entering or leaving his apartment the night before. Was it possible that Denault had met Kobayashi before and recognized her? He felt his cheeks grow hot with an embarrassment that quickly morphed into anger and indignation, until he realized that he might actually be on dangerous ground here.

He held his tongue as he realized he might actually be on dangerous ground here. *Was* it appropriate for him to be on intimate terms with Kobayashi?

"I just want to be sure we're on the same page, Charlie," Denault said, taking a different tack, though Charlie was sure the conciliatory tone misrepresented how Denault would react if he spilled the beans.

"And what page is that?"

"There's no need to get defensive. I did warn you about staying within the parameters of …"

"Just what are you trying to say?" Charlie interrupted, letting his anger get the better of him. Suddenly something occurred to him, and he decided to play a hunch. "Has someone made a complaint against me?" Denault was shaking his head but it didn't seem like a genuine denial, so Charlie persisted. "Was it Lepage?"

Denault's reaction was one of genuine surprise, accompanied by one of his usual derisive snorts. "Lepage was just here, as a matter of fact, to let me know what a good job you've been doing on his file." There was an awkward pause. "You look surprised."

"Lepage was here today?"

"He even brought you a token of his appreciation," Denault added, with a hint of sarcasm that Charlie ignored.

"Where is it?"

"In your office," Denault said, surprised by the urgency in Charlie's response, even more so as Charlie swung the door open and headed off down the hall. "Wait a minute," Denault called out, following him out into the hall and down to his office. Charlie was standing in his doorway, looking at the little box sitting in the middle of his desk blotter.

"*He* put this here?"

"Well, I was standing right here," Denault said, as though suddenly realizing a weakness in his position, as Charlie hurried into his office and began scanning his desk. He froze, staring at the corner of his desk nearest the window.

"Was he in here by himself?"

"Of course not." Denault gave an exaggerated huff. "I'm quite familiar with the protocol for escorting visitors in the operational zone. I wrote them, after all."

"Funny," Charlie said, looking directly at Denault, whose smug smile was starting to show signs of cracking. "I don't remember the part about allowing visitors into consular staff offices when they're not there."

"I told you, I was standing right where I am now. You make it sound like your office has been ransacked, or I allowed him to rummage through your files, which is nonsense."

"So what exactly did he say — before you let him in here, that is?" Charlie enjoyed putting the screws to Denault, who was starting to fidget.

"I already told you. He was full of praise."

"So what is it you wanted to talk to me about, then?"

"It's not important," Denault huffed, then beat a hasty retreat to the doorway. "Just remember your actions are a reflection on all of us," he added weakly, before disappearing back into the hall. Charlie watched him go, then gave a disgusted laugh and returned his attention to the corner of his desk.

"Everything okay?"

He looked up to see Fraser at the door, a look of concern on her face.

He shrugged. "Just Louis being Louis," he muttered, taking a seat behind his desk.

"If this was about … what we were talking about earlier today, I didn't breathe a word to …"

"It's not about that, and I know you wouldn't …" He saw her features relax as relief set in. "Did you see Rob Lepage here earlier?"

She nodded. "I saw Denault standing outside your office talking to someone, and I knew you were across town, so I went to investigate."

"And?"

"Lepage was dropping that off," she said, pointing to the brightly wrapped parcel still sitting on his desk.

"And you and Denault were out in the hall. Did Denault talk to you while Lepage was in here?"

She shrugged. "He reminded me that the amendment to the HR report was overdue."

"While Lepage was in here?"

"Yes, typical Louis. What's wrong? Is something missing?"

He shook his head. "No, nothing's missing," he lied, staring back at his desk, where he had put the postcard of Mount Fuji this morning, thinking it would be safer in his office than his apartment. Ironic, since it wasn't there anymore.

CHAPTER 30

Charlie sat at his desk, staring at the little box of chocolates on his blotter. Had they really been just a pretext for Lepage to get access to his office? He took the top off and surveyed the dozen assorted chocolates, wondering if they were poisoned or whether the box concealed a microphone or GPS tracker. Maybe inside one of the chocolates …

You're being ridiculous …

He sighed and looked out the window at the darkening sky. On a logical level it made no sense. Lepage couldn't have known the postcard was in Charlie's office, and in any event, the damn thing was blank, so he still failed to see its importance. But he couldn't ignore the fact that its disappearance coincided with Lepage's presence in his office. He thought about Kobayashi's warning about desperate people doing unpredictable things and tried to imagine what it was that Lepage was becoming desperate about, and what he might do next.

"I'm out of here."

He looked up to see Fraser standing in his doorway.

"Okay, have a good one."

"You heading back or sticking around?"

"I've got a couple of things to finish up here," he said.

"You're not still thinking about Denault, are you? He can be a bit of a douche sometimes, but he's harmless."

He smiled. "Naw, I'm fine."

"All right, I'll see you tomorrow."

He watched her leave, her image lingering in his mind for a moment, reminding him of someone else. He reached for his phone and dialed, getting an answering service. He scrolled though his contacts and found an alternate number — a cell — and tried that. A familiar voice answered on the third ring.

"Hi, Elizabeth, it's Charlie Hillier calling."

"Oh, hello, Charlie. What can I do for you?"

"I was wondering if you were free for a quick drink. There's something I wanted to ask you."

"This about Rob?"

"Kind of, yeah."

There was a pause before she spoke again, and Charlie had the sense that she was inventing an excuse.

"I'm still at the office, and I've got a function to go to later," she said, "but I've got to stop by my apartment first. If you want to meet me there in half an hour, we could have a quick chat."

"That's perfect. I'll see you there."

"Is everything … okay with Rob?"

"What do you mean?"

"It's just that … never mind. I'll tell you when you get here."

Charlie stared at the phone for a while after the call had ended, wondering what it was Farnsworth was getting at. It occurred to him that she might have accepted the meeting because there was something about Rob that she wanted to discuss with him, as opposed to the other way around. Perhaps he should have asked her to elaborate, but he would find out soon enough. He wrapped up a couple of emails and then left his office, giving himself twenty minutes to get over to Omote-sando Hills. It was almost dark outside — a combination of storm clouds and the ever-shortening fall days — by the time he walked out onto Aoyama-dori and headed west toward the nearest Metro station.

The man standing at the western end of the park next to the embassy fell into the stream of westbound pedestrians as soon as Charlie passed by. He stayed a good fifty feet behind and gathered his coat around him, his hand feeling instinctively inside the fabric for the gun in the inside pocket.

He kept his distance as Charlie made his way down to the Metro and stepped onto a westbound train. Boarding at the far end of the same car and concealing himself in the crush of passengers, the other man knew exactly where they were headed as soon as he saw Charlie head toward the subway doors at Omote-sando Station. He moved quickly through to the next car and got to the far end as the doors opened, then rushed out into the crowd headed for the exit, knowing he would reach the escalator up to street level first. He kept walking up the left side of the escalator and broke into a run as soon as he reached the street. When Charlie Hillier eventually reached his destination, he would be ready for him.

CHAPTER 31

Charlie arrived at the entrance to the Omote-sando Hills apartment building and rang Elizabeth Farnsworth's buzzer.

"It's me, Charlie."

"Come on up," the tinny voice replied, followed by an electronic buzz that indicated that the front door lock was temporarily disengaged. Charlie swung it open and stepped through into the empty lobby, crossing the tiled floor to the elevators on the far side. He pressed the call button and checked his watch. He was a few minutes late, but it didn't matter — he knew Farnsworth was there.

He looked up at the sound of a muted chime and then the doors slid open, revealing an empty car. He stepped inside and hit the button for the sixth floor, going over in his head what he was going to ask Farnsworth and how much he was going to reveal about Lepage in the process. He had to strike a balance between enough information to encourage her to understand the seriousness of the situation, but not enough to alarm her to the point that she clammed up. It occurred to him for the first time that she might be involved herself. He thought of Kobayashi and her warning not to go it alone. Too late now, he thought, as the chime sounded again and the doors slid open on the sixth floor.

He had only taken a couple of steps down the hall, which seemed dimmer than usual, when he felt something cold and hard being pressed against the base of his skull that felt very much like the barrel of a gun.

"Keep moving," said a gruff voice from behind him, as a hand grabbed the collar of his coat and propelled him forward.

"What's going on?" he heard himself say, out of instinct.

"Quiet," the voice behind him hissed as they passed a little alcove to the right, with a utility room at the back, its door ajar. "This way."

Charlie felt himself being pushed into the door, which gave way as he entered the darkened room, tripped over something and fell to the floor, his arms protecting his head as he felt the concrete beneath him. He was sitting up again when he heard the sound of the door click shut and then a fluorescent light came on, temporarily blinding him. A dark form in front of the door slowly took shape behind a gun, the perfect circle of the barrel's end pointed at his chest. The man wielding it took a step forward and threw back the hoodie that had concealed his face.

"What the hell?" Charlie started to get up. "Rob?"

"Stay down," Lepage ordered, kicking him in the shoulder and keeping him on the floor.

"What the ... what are you doing?"

"I could ask you the same thing, Charlie. Why are you here?"

"I came to see you," he said, though not until after a brief hesitation that hadn't escaped Lepage's notice.

"Bullshit."

"Look Rob, I'm here to help." He tried a different tack. "I know you're in trouble ..."

"You don't know shit, Charlie."

"So enlighten me."

"And you can stop fucking around and playing the innocent. You told me you lost that postcard, so I know you found something."

"What is it you think I found, Rob? It's a blank postcard that you mailed to yourself. So maybe you should start —"

"You don't seem to understand." Lepage took a step closer, shortening the distance between the end of the gun and Charlie's head. "I'm not who you think I am, and if you don't tell me whatever you know, you're not going to be leaving this room."

Charlie put up a defensive hand. "So, maybe you're not the clean-cut securities trader that I thought you were. But you're not a killer, Rob."

"Oh no?"

"Look, I know you're in trouble. I know Kimura's connected to the yakuza," he added, thinking he detected slight surprise in Lepage's expression. "And that they want something from you. But shooting me isn't going to help."

"You're wrong about that. It might buy me some time." Lepage still had the gun trained on him.

"I'm not the only one that knows there's something funny going on," Charlie continued. "With you, with Seger's murder."

"Bullshit," Lepage shot back. "You told me yourself the Tokyo Police aren't even investigating that."

"Well, they are."

"I know you're pretty cozy with that cop, but I think you're lying."

"I can help you, Rob. Maybe Kobayashi can, too. Just put the gun away, will you?" He started to get up again, his hand held out as he slowly rose.

"Don't think I won't do it, Charlie."

"I didn't come here to see you." Charlie kept his hand up. "You're right about that. I came to see if I could get to the bottom of whatever's going on. I'll figure it out sooner or later, and it will be sooner if we work together. I can protect you."

Lepage laughed, but took a step back in response to Charlie's slow advance. "You can't do shit, and you know it. These people can do whatever they want. They're *everywhere*."

"And yet we're both still here, which means they think one of us has something they want really badly."

"You don't know who you're dealing with …"

"I think I do, and I think you're better off with my help than without it. Now put the gun down and let's figure this thing out."

Lepage was shaking his head as Charlie took another step forward. "Stay where you are, damn it."

"Rob, I'm your only friend here and you know it. When you were lying in that hospital bed, I'm the only one that came to see you, looked out for you — other than Kimura, and we both know she doesn't give a shit about you." He took another step forward, his hand was inches from the gun now. "In fact, did you know your brakes had been tampered with?" Lepage's eyes widened slightly at the news, and Charlie saw the chance to press on. "I know you've been lying to me and Yamaguchi about your memory loss, and maybe you still don't remember some things before the accident, but whatever you were then, you're not a killer now. Put down the gun."

Lepage stared at him for a moment, then raised the gun slightly, as Charlie's heart quickened.

"What the fuck am I going to do?" he finally said, dropping the gun to his side and slumping into the chair by the door.

CHAPTER 32

"What is it they want? What's the big secret?" Charlie was sitting at Lepage's kitchen table, and whatever he had planned before, it was clear that Lepage had made up his mind to take his chances with Charlie now, though he still appeared to be struggling with the prospect of a confession. He sighed and put his head in his hands.

"It's an account number."

"An account ... like a bank account?"

Lepage nodded.

"So why don't you just give it to them, be done with it?"

He gave an irritated laugh. "It's not that simple, Charlie. I couldn't give it to them even if I wanted to."

"Why not?"

"Because I can't ... I can't fucking remember it."

"You mean because of the memory loss. I thought you were faking that."

He shook his head. "Not about that. Some stuff I faked, yeah. But I still have gaps, *real* gaps."

"So, tell me about this account."

"This is so fucked up." Lepage shook his head, then looked across the table. "You should just leave, get out while you can. You have no idea what you're getting yourself into."

But Charlie was having none of that. "I'm already involved, Rob, and I'm not going to just walk out the door, so you'd better start telling me the truth." He paused, then leaned forward across the table. "Start at the beginning. What really brought you to Tokyo?"

Lepage let out a breath of air that was part laugh, part sigh. "I was working in Montreal, for a brokerage firm. I was making good money and everything was going well."

"This is when you were with Advantage Securities?"

"How'd you know that?"

"We'll get to that. Go on."

Lepage's puzzled frown remained in place for a few seconds before he continued. "Anyway, that's when I first met Seger. He was on some kind of consulting contract with Advantage, at least that's what I was led to believe."

Charlie nodded, and chose not to add that he knew Seger's employer, APP, as well.

"Did you know Seger before ... I mean, before you worked with him in Montreal?"

Lepage shook his head. "That stuff about us growing up together was bullshit. He made that up — I guess he thought it would get him in to see me in the hospital."

"Did you recognize him when he visited you?"

"Not at first. I really didn't know who he was, until we started talking and he told me I had some really important information locked away in my head."

"Did he threaten you?"

"Not in so many words, but he said a lot of people were counting on me getting my memory back ... soon." Lepage looked down at his hands. "He talked about what we'd done in Montreal, places we'd had dinner, going to a Habs game — that sort of thing. When he left the hospital that night, I lay in bed and it started to come back to me. It was just, like, an outline first, but then things sharpened into focus. And then I knew ..."

Charlie looked at him in the silence that followed. "You knew what?"

"I knew that I wasn't who I thought I was." He looked up and Charlie could see he was struggling with the words. "I knew I was ... bad."

Charlie considered it for a moment, the thought of coming out of a coma with a bunch of strangers around you telling you what your life was, and then coming to the realization that they were wrong — that you were actually a criminal. It had obviously made quite an impression.

"That remains to be seen." Charlie patted him on the arm and coaxed him on. "Let's go back to Montreal. You were doing legitimate work until Seger came along?"

"As far as I knew, yeah. I was working on this program on the side, a sort of trading algorithm. I guess I was naive — I mentioned it to someone at work and the next day Seger turns up. I could tell within five minutes of meeting him that he wasn't interested in my sales, or the clients I'd landed. It was the algorithm that interested him. He said he knew a company in Hong Kong that was looking for just that kind of product, and if we could give it to them, they'd be willing to pay a fortune."

"So, how'd you end up in Tokyo?"

Lepage frowned. "After a couple of weeks, I'd given him the nuts and bolts of the program. How it worked. Mike said he wanted to run it by his people in Hong Kong first, so he went off and did that. A couple of weeks later, he's back and he tells me we're on. Next thing I know, my boss is telling me I'm going to Tokyo."

"Did your boss know what was going on?"

Lepage shook his head. "I don't think so. Actually, he

was kind of pissed. It was like he didn't have a choice. Like someone over his head had made the call."

"So you come to Tokyo," Charlie prompted.

Lepage nodded. "I come here, and I start putting together the program at Nippon Kasuga. Then I meet Aiko, and pretty soon she's asking me to make some tweaks to the algorithm. And that's when I knew for sure."

"Knew what?"

Lepage looked at him with raised eyebrows. "Come on, Charlie, how hard are you going to make this? I knew what I was doing was illegal."

"Why, what did Kimura ask you to do?"

"The algorithm I designed in Canada was based on publicly available data about the contributors — completely legal. She wanted to adjust it to mine for more sensitive information."

"The kind that's illegal to collect?"

Lepage nodded. "Plus, I learned later that the plan was to only report about 75 percent of the profits. The other 25 perent was going into an offshore account in Nippon Kasuga's name."

"So Nippon Kasuga knew about the skimming?" Charlie asked, still unclear as to who knew what.

"They knew all right, though it wasn't as though they had any choice."

"You mean because it was the yakuza pulling the strings." Lepage didn't respond, but his silence was as clear an answer as anything he could have said. "Did *you* know they were behind it?" Charlie asked.

Lepage shrugged. "I knew Aiko wasn't hooked up with the Salvation Army, if you know what I mean. A guy came by her place one night when I was there — to make a point."

"You mean to threaten you?"

"It was more subtle than that. He didn't have to say a word. I knew the minute he walked through the door what he was, and what I was into."

"And you never considered going to the police?"

Lepage laughed. "These people have pretty good connections with the police, from what I'm told. For all I know, Kobayashi's working for them." Charlie's eyebrows shot up. "I'm just saying."

They sat in silence for a while, Lepage recovering from the act of unburdening himself, Charlie trying to process the information into a scenario that made sense to him.

"But you say the work you were doing in Montreal was legal?" he finally asked.

Another shrug from Lepage. "As far as I knew, yeah. I was too busy making money to ask questions. When the Tokyo thing came up, I should have known something was wrong. They threw a big bonus at me, set me up here with this place." He looked around them, and Charlie figured the apartment was probably worth ten thousand dollars a month. "And the car, and a base salary that would make your head spin." Lepage paused and thought for a moment. "You said you think someone messed with the car?"

Charlie nodded. "Kobayashi said the brakes could have been tampered with."

"Why is this the first time I'm hearing about it?"

"She doesn't know why it didn't make it into the police report, but I think it's obvious."

Lepage's eyes flashed. "You see? They're everywhere. I'm telling you, Charlie, this isn't Canada. Things work differently here."

"If you're going to try to convince me Kobayashi is yakuza, then forget it." Charlie shook his head. "I'll never believe it."

"What about her boss?"

Charlie was caught off guard by the remark, which rang disturbingly true in light of the apparent suppression of the mechanical assessment of Lepage's car, not to mention the decision not to investigate Seger's murder. He considered Lepage's warning about Kobayashi for an uncomfortable moment. If she had been paid to get close to Charlie.... He dismissed the thought as quickly as it appeared. Some things he just knew in his heart, like the certainty that Lepage wouldn't have shot him in cold blood twenty minutes ago.

"So you were drawn into something you didn't understand," he finally said, after they had both sat in silence for a while. "You wouldn't be the first. Maybe there's still a way out for you."

"Come on, Charlie, I'm fucked and we both know it. I took the money, and I'd still be taking it if I hadn't forgotten where it is."

"So you lost the account number ..."

"The second account," Lepage corrected. "The one with all the skim in it. I set it up without telling anyone, as an extra layer of security."

"And what kind of money are we talking about?"

Lepage shrugged. "The last time I checked it — at least that I can remember — it was almost five million."

"Dollars?" Charlie's eyes widened.

Lepage nodded. "Which is why Kimura and her people are not going to just let it go. I'm pretty sure they're starting to think I'm holding out on them."

"Why do you say that?"

Lepage sighed. "Let's just say I'm on a short leash. If I haven't given them the coordinates to the money in the next couple of days, I think I'm done." He paused and looked down at his hands. "You have even less time."

"*Me?*"

He nodded. "They wanted to take you out a couple of days ago, but I stalled them."

Charlie's initial alarm switched to incomprehension. "But why do they want to get rid of me?"

"They think you know something, and they're concerned that you're egging Kobayashi on, or vice versa."

"Is she in danger, too?" Charlie's alarm took priority.

"Like I said," Lepage replied, with a sigh, "they have people everywhere. No one's safe, not even Kobayashi."

Another silence descended over the kitchen, then Charlie pulled his phone out of his pocket.

"Who are you calling?" Lepage asked.

"I have to warn her, Rob, and it's not negotiable," he added. He saw resistance in Lepage's eyes, but it quickly faded and he said nothing as Charlie put the phone to his ear.

"Voicemail. Shit!" He left a message and then put the phone on the kitchen table.

"What are we going to do, Charlie?"

"We're going to start with why I came here this evening in the first place."

Lepage looked puzzled. "What do you mean?"

"Does Elizabeth know about any of this?"

"Elizabeth? Why were you coming to see her?"

"Does she know?"

Lepage gave another sigh. "She's not going to be able to help us locate the account number, if that's what you mean."

"I meant does she know you're involved in something illegal. And we don't have time to beat around the bush here, Rob. You need to start telling me everything if I'm going to have any chance of helping you."

He shook his head. "She doesn't know, but I think she does suspect something. One of the reasons I cut things off with her — romantically — was that I didn't want to drag her into anything."

Charlie nodded. "You see, Rob," he said, getting up and patting him on the shoulder, "you are a good person deep down. Come on, let's go."

They were almost at Lepage's front door when Charlie's phone rang. He breathed a sigh of relief at seeing Kobayashi's number.

"I need you to meet me at Rob's apartment in half an hour." He looked at Lepage as he listened to her response. "I'll explain everything when you get here. Just be careful and don't tell anyone where you're going."

CHAPTER 33

Elizabeth Farnsworth opened the door and stood back to let Charlie in.

"I was beginning to wonder if you'd gotten lost on your way ..." She trailed off when Lepage came into view, standing next to Charlie.

"I bumped into Rob, and we decided it would be best if we both had a word with you, if that's all right."

"I'm sorry to bother you, Elizabeth," Lepage said, as they made their way inside and she shut the door behind them, "but it looks like I've gotten myself into a bit of a jam."

She stood there for a moment, then nodded. "I was afraid of that." She touched his arm, then set off for the kitchen, waving for them to follow. "Come in and tell me all about it, and we'll see if there's anything I can do to help."

"We're looking for an account number," Charlie began, when they were all seated around the table. "An offshore account number, or anything that might lead us to it."

"You've lost an account number ...?"

"Forgot it, actually," Lepage interjected. "I've still got some gaps in my memory, from the accident. I can remember where I put my running shoes, but not the number of an offshore account that's turned out to be pretty important."

Farnsworth nodded slowly. "I assume it involves the people like the gentleman we ran into that night?" she asked Lepage, who nodded and turned to Charlie.

"We were at dinner," Lepage gestured to Farnsworth, "and one of Kimura's associates stopped by our table for a friendly hello. He was yakuza, for sure."

"Now you tell me." Farnsworth paled a little.

"I didn't know for sure at the time, but I … I guess I did, but I didn't want to admit it to myself — that I was getting in over my head." Charlie watched the two as they assessed each other, feeling somewhat like a marriage counsellor.

"Is that why you ended things?" she asked.

Lepage was looking down at his hands. "I didn't want you getting hurt. We shouldn't even be here now," he said, starting to get up.

"You're not going anywhere." Farnsworth put an authoritative hand on his forearm. "And here I thought I'd been thrown over for that little tart, Kako."

Lepage laughed. "It's Aiko, and believe me, it was only ever business with her. I liked to think of her as my own personal praying mantis."

Charlie frowned at the use of the past tense. "Except that she's still out there, along with all of her friends."

Farnsworth looked to Charlie, then Lepage. "So, what can I do to help?"

"Did I say anything before the accident," Lepage asked her, "or give you anything for safekeeping? We're looking for anything that might have been a clue to that damn account number."

She frowned as she searched her memory, then shook her head. "No, and we haven't really seen much of each other since you gave me the cold shoulder," she added, obviously enjoying Lepage's discomfort at the barb. They spent a few minutes asking her to recount every interaction with Lepage in the weeks before the accident, particularly anything out of the ordinary that he might have said or done, but it was clear that it was pointless. Charlie glanced at his watch, aware that Kobayashi would be arriving soon, and eager not to involve Farnsworth further if there was nothing she could do to help anyway. He exchanged a look with Lepage and they both stood.

"Wait," Farnsworth said. "Aren't you going to tell me what this is all about?"

Charlie looked at Lepage, who sighed, then put his hand on Farnsworth's shoulder. "The less you know, the better it is for you. Bottom line is I screwed up and did something I shouldn't have done. To be honest, the smartest thing you could do now is forget you ever knew me."

"Well, that sounds a trifle harsh," she said as they reached the door and Lepage turned to face her. All joviality was gone from his expression. "I mean it, Elizabeth. You do not want to end up on the wrong side of these people, believe me. If you do think of something, it's probably better you get in touch with Charlie. And be careful. Don't open the door to strangers or walk around alone at night until all of this blows over."

"And when's that likely to be?"

He paused at the door. "I wish I knew. I really am sorry, you know … for everything."

She smiled and surprised him by leaning forward and giving him a peck on the cheek, adding before she shut the door. "And you two be careful as well."

Charlie nudged him in the arm as they headed back to Lepage's apartment. "I think she forgives you."

Kobayashi, Charlie, and Lepage sat in the rear corner of a dimly lit bar across the street from Lepage's apartment, a silence descending over the table following Charlie's brief explanation of Lepage's dilemma.

"I don't blame you if you don't want to help," Lepage finally said, looking down. "I made my own bed, and now I have to lie in it."

Charlie looked to Kobayashi. "It means he ..."

"I know." She gave him an indulgent smile, then turned to Lepage. "Kimura has threatened you?"

Lepage nodded, then gave a little gulp. "Actually, she wants to get rid of Charlie, and ... she also mentioned you. She thinks you're both becoming dangerous."

Kobayashi turned to Charlie with a look that said *I told you so.*

"I was thinking." Charlie ignored the rebuke. "I might be able to talk to the RCMP liaison guy about making a deal. Obviously, they'd want co-operation from you, Rob — information about what you were doing and who's involved."

Lepage shrugged. "I've got nothing to lose at this point, but why would the RCMP want anything to do with it?"

"Because there's already an international fraud investigation that includes the Montreal company you worked for. I don't know what they have on the Tokyo end of things, but I'm thinking you could be a very valuable source of information to them." He turned to Kobayashi. "I assume this is linked in some way to the investigation you said your organized crime unit was conducting, that identified Nippon Kasuga as being on the fringe of something illegal."

"They're more than on the fringe," Lepage said.

Kobayashi nodded. "I can find out more." She noticed the odd expressions on their faces, and the awkward silence that followed her comment.

"Kimura said she had a source somewhere in the Tokyo Metropolitan Police — someone feeding her information," Lepage said. "That's how she knows you're digging into the yakuza angle, and why she sees you as a threat."

"You don't trust me?"

Lepage shook his head and Charlie jumped in. "Rob's not talking about you, but we need to be careful from here on in about who knows what information we're accessing."

Another silence enveloped them, then Kobayashi slowly nodded. "I understand. But there is a way that we could use this source to our advantage."

Charlie looked at her and suddenly understood. "You mean disinformation?"

"That's a good idea." Lepage was nodding his agreement.

"We can start by telling Kimura that you've found a clue to this mysterious account," Kobayashi continued. "Something that keeps her interested, and ensures that she doesn't act against Charlie."

"Or you," Charlie said with a frown. "I live on a secure compound. You don't."

Kobayashi shrugged, then Lepage cut in. "I've already tried to buy time with her, and she gave me until tonight. I don't know what else to tell her to get us another day."

"Tell her you want to meet tomorrow night," Kobayashi said. "That you'll have what she needs by then. Be vague."

Lepage frowned. "I don't know if she'll buy it, but I guess we don't have much choice."

"I'll float the idea of the deal with the RCMP tonight," Charlie said. "If we need someone at HQ to sign off, we'll have to have it by tomorrow night."

Kobayashi nodded. "And I'll spread the word around tomorrow that I've abandoned my inquiries into Seger and you," she said, gesturing to Lepage. "Hopefully that will get back to Kimura and buy us some time. In the meantime, we all need to be careful." The three of them sat in silent acknowledgment of the pact, then Lepage broke the silence with a question.

"Where's the meeting tomorrow night?"

"The Sensō-ji Temple in Asakusa," Kobayashi replied. "It's public."

"We get in touch tomorrow if anything changes, otherwise we meet under the lantern gate at six." Charlie turned to Lepage. "Tell Kimura you want to meet on the front steps of the temple at seven."

CHAPTER 34

Charlie sat at his desk reading an email, vaguely aware that he was reading the same paragraph for the third time. It was impossible to think of anything else but Lepage, and whether or not there was any appetite for the deal Charlie had proposed to the resident RCMP liaison officer, Ted Hudson, the night before. He had only met Hudson a couple of times, and he could tell from the surprise on the young Mountie's face when Charlie had knocked on his apartment door the previous evening that he would have an uphill battle.

But after laying everything out, Charlie had been pleasantly surprised by Hudson's apparent openness to the possibility of at least considering some sort of deal for Lepage. Hudson was aware of the ongoing fraud investigation — it was one of his active files — and also of the fact that the various international law enforcement entities involved in it were becoming frustrated with the inability to close the loop on the main players. Maybe the possibility of breaking the case wide open had appealed to him, but whether Hudson's motives were rooted in sheer ambition or something more altruistic, Charlie didn't much care, as long as he went for it.

Hudson had been careful not to offer immunity and had warned that whatever happened, Lepage was likely to have to pay some price for what had definitely been active participation in criminal activity. They had parted company at about eleven, with Hudson promising to get in touch with his superiors in Ottawa to see if there was something that could be done. He was also going to contact the white collar crime expert, Dixon, to make sure he had all the current information.

Charlie turned his attention back to his monitor and stared at the same email he had been trying to focus on for the last fifteen minutes when he looked up and saw Hudson standing in his doorway with a smile on his face.

"I think we're on."

"What's the deal?" Charlie waved him in and closed the door behind them.

"If your guy can connect the dots between Montreal and Tokyo on this thing, we can work something out. It's not going to be immunity, but his co-operation will be taken into account when it comes time for a plea bargain."

"He's risking a lot for us," Charlie said.

"He's also made a lot of money by participating in global fraud." Hudson's tone was even but firm. "But, like I said, his co-operation will be taken into account. You're gonna have to trust me on that."

Charlie hesitated only for a moment before nodding his agreement. "So, what do we do?"

"There's something else," Hudson said, and Charlie's ears perked up. "Dixon told me that one of the Montreal-based guys that the OC task force there is monitoring just arrived in Tokyo this morning."

Charlie frowned. "Who is he?"

"We think he's connected to Seger. His passport's been flagged, but he's got no official restrictions on his travel."

If Hudson was trying to reassure him, it wasn't working. "And what do we think he's doing here?"

Now it was Hudson's turn to frown. "We really don't know. We don't think he's an enforcer, but we can't be sure. Best we keep him in mind when we're making our plans, that's all."

Great, Charlie thought. Now it wasn't just Kimura and her yakuza pals that they had to worry about. But something wasn't adding up. "Isn't that … *unusual*?"

"What?"

"His coming here. I mean, if they're all working together, wouldn't the local yakuza look after any loose ends?"

Hudson was nodding in a way that made Charlie think he had already come to the same conclusion. "Unless they don't think they're cleaning it up quick enough. There's a lot of money at stake, and your guy's been out of the coma long enough that they should have their account information by now."

"If their interests are diverging, we might be able to use that," Charlie said, eliciting a slight nod from Hudson.

"Maybe."

"It also means thing are going to come to a head … and very soon," Charlie mused. He wondered what progress Kobayashi had made at her end, and whether they would be able to get everything in place by this evening's meeting. It seemed hopelessly close. "We're running out of time," he said, more to himself than for Hudson's benefit.

"One other thing." Hudson pointed a finger at him. "These people are dangerous, so we have to be careful. That means I have to coordinate and approve any interaction between Lepage and any of his former associates." He paused and looked at Charlie. "We're clear on that?"

Charlie nodded. "Sure."

"Same goes for your dealings with the Tokyo Metropolitan Police. What's your next planned contact with Inspector Kobayashi?"

"We're supposed to touch base today, but nothing firm."

Hudson nodded. "Okay, let's set up a meeting ASAP."

"I'll call …" He stopped as he glanced at his computer in response to the sound of an incoming message. "That's her now," he said, clicking the message open. "She wants to meet in about an hour."

"Where?"

"A coffee shop just down the hill on Aoyama-dori."

Hudson nodded. "That works. Go ahead and confirm."

Charlie sent a quick reply, as Hudson stood to leave.

"I'll meet you out front in forty-five minutes."

Charlie watched him leave, then noticed he had an administrative meeting in half an hour. He would have to skip it, which he knew would put Denault on the warpath, but that was the least of his worries.

Charlie and Hudson sat on one side of the table by the window, eyes on the street.

"There she is."

"Her?" Hudson followed Charlie's glance and watched Kobayashi's approach to the coffee shop. Once inside, she spotted Charlie and headed toward their table.

"Not what you were expecting?" Charlie concealed a smile as he sipped his coffee.

"Uh, I guess not."

"Don't let her appearance fool you. She's all cop."

They stood as she arrived at the table, and Charlie took care of the introductions.

"Ted has been working with some of your colleagues on the international investigation."

Kobayashi looked at Hudson. "It must be the 7th Division — Superintendent Yoyogi's unit?"

"That's right. You know him?"

She nodded. "I know his work, and I have friends in the 7th division." She looked at Charlie. "Financial crimes."

Charlie began to break down the situation, including the need to connect the Montreal and Tokyo elements of the operation in order to establish a cross-border fraud that would unlock the powers and penalties available to bring down the ring and prosecute the members to the fullest extent, as well as to secure some leniency for Lepage.

"We've also heard that someone we think is involved in the operation has just arrived in Tokyo from Montreal," Charlie added. "We think he's connected to Seger."

Kobayashi frowned. "Do you know the purpose of his visit?"

Charlie and Hudson both shook their heads. "We were wondering about that ourselves, and thinking it might be evidence of a rift between Montreal and Tokyo," Hudson said. "Whatever really happened to Seger, Montreal can't have been impressed, especially since no one here has been able to extract the account information from Lepage. Maybe they think Tokyo's being too lenient."

Kobayashi frowned. "He's in Tokyo now?"

"Arrived this morning. Your colleagues have eyes on him, and so far he hasn't left his hotel."

"Shouldn't we get Lepage somewhere safe right away, just in case?" Charlie looked to Hudson, then Kobayashi.

Hudson shrugged. "We can protect him at the embassy."

Kobayashi waved a hand. "But we run the risk that someone following him will find out he's co-operating with us." They sat in silence for a while before she continued. "We must continue as normal for now, at least until the meeting this evening."

Hudson leaned forward and put his arms on the table. "On that note, we'd better figure out how we're going to run this meeting."

CHAPTER 35

Charlie was barely in his chair, having just returned from the meeting with Kobayashi, when Denault appeared at his door.

"Do you mind telling me what the hell you think you're doing?"

Charlie sighed. "I know I missed the administrative meeting, but I ..."

"I'm not talking about that," Denault snapped, and Charlie felt a sense of foreboding. "I'm talking about this so-called investigation, or whatever it is you've cooked up with Hudson."

"I ran everything by him, and the RCMP's on board. Just ask Hudson yourself."

"Well, I'm not on board, and neither is the ambassador."

Charlie was feeling more and more insecure, as it occurred to him that both he and Hudson ultimately reported to the same guy — the head of mission. Charlie could be forgiven for leaving Denault out of the equation, but not advising Westwood was a serious oversight and could jeopardize the whole deal, not to mention landing him in big trouble.

"I was going to — "

Denault held up a hand. "You can save it, Charlie. Come on," he added, motioning to the hallway.

"Where are we going?"

"You can explain it all to the ambassador yourself. He's waiting."

Charlie ignored Denault's little smirk and considered his other options, which he quickly realized were non-existent. He took a deep breath and steeled himself for what was no doubt going to be a very uncomfortable meeting.

They rode the elevator up in silence and for once they didn't have to wait outside Westwood's office, his assistant waved them straight in. Charlie noticed an unfamiliar expression on her face as he walked past her, and felt like a condemned man headed up the steps to the gallows. Westwood was standing by his desk when they walked in.

"What on earth is going on, Charlie?" he said, before they had even reached the sitting area. The normally unflappable Westwood seemed agitated, which Charlie took as another bad sign of what was to come.

"I can explain," he began, putting his hands up in a calming gesture.

"How you converted a consular file into some sort of sting with the RCMP, without letting me know? Is that it?" Westwood said, staying where he was as Charlie and Denault awaited permission to advance. The ambassador shook his head and waved them to take a seat as he joined them. Instead of his usual, relaxed posture, leaning back on the sofa with one leg dangling across the other, Westwood was hunched forward, as though waiting either for information or to pounce across and throttle Charlie.

"I should have briefed you, or Louis," Charlie began, gesturing to Denault, who sniffed derisively next to him. "It's just that everything is happening so fast."

"Should I remind you that you're a consular officer in your first month of a posting. You're in no position to start setting up clandestine operations. If you'd come to me, I could have told you so."

"I only approached Hudson last night, as a result of a discussion I had with Rob Lepage. I didn't really have a chance to think through the right procedural steps," Charlie said. "I'm sure Ted didn't either."

"In case you're thinking of throwing Hudson under the bus, I've already talked to him," Denault jumped in, with an eagerness that Charlie found particularly annoying, not to mention ominous as he realized for the first time that Hudson's absence from the current meeting might have been Denault's doing. "He assumed, quite reasonably, that you had already received at least an informal approval from the HOM to proceed."

Charlie wasn't convinced that Hudson was all that concerned about anything other than headquarters sign off, but he wouldn't score any points here by mentioning that, and he had no intention of trying to blame Hudson anyway. Charlie was the one who had stepped in a big pile of shit, and it was up to him to get himself out of it. He thought he saw a slight frown of disapproval on Westwood's face at Denault's statement, and seized on the opportunity.

"It was poor judgment on my part, I admit." He spoke directly to Westwood. "But there is an opportunity to do some real good here. Lepage could be the key to taking down an international fraud network that's scammed millions from unsuspecting investors around the globe."

"That doesn't excuse running roughshod over our internal procedures," Denault countered in a raised voice, as though he was running the meeting. He seemed to realize he had overstepped as he spoke the words. Westwood looked at him with slightly narrowed eyes in the silence that followed, then turned back at Charlie.

"Tell me more about Lepage."

Charlie proceeded to lay out the details, as Denault sat, quietly seething, next to him. When he got to Lepage's decision to co-operate, Westwood held up a hand.

"And you're sure his willingness to co-operate is genuine?"

Charlie nodded. "I don't blame you for being skeptical. I asked myself the same thing, but I really don't think he's trying to string me along."

"Because he's in danger himself?" Westwood asked, to which Denault starting nodding vigorously.

"I'd say he's desperate to save his own skin."

"I disagree," Charlie said, prompting a furrowed brow from the ambassador and a look of sheer contempt from Denault. "I really think this coma shook him up, and changed his perspective."

"You can't be serious," Denault scoffed.

"I would say he was willfully blind before, or maybe worse. But now I do think part of it is him realizing that what he's involved in is wrong." Charlie paused. "I know it sounds corny, and maybe a bit naive, but I believe it."

"Well, say you're right, and we decide to proceed, what's the next move?" Westwood was sitting back on the sofa now, the interrogation phase of the meeting apparently over with. Charlie relaxed a little while Denault moved closer to the edge of his seat, not liking the direction the conversation was heading but having no way to control its course.

"We're supposed to meet Kimura this evening," Charlie said.

"Who's *we*?" Denault wasn't moving on so easily.

"Me and Lepage. Inspector Kobayashi will be there, behind the scenes — Hudson, too, of course."

Westwood shook his head. "I can't have you directly involved with the yakuza, Charlie. You're a consular officer, not a cop, and you're my responsibility."

"But —"

"No buts, Charlie. It's a non-starter." Westwood shook his head. "You can go along provided you're safely out of the firing line. I've asked Hudson to flesh out the coordination with the Tokyo Police," he added, sending a shock wave of fear down Charlie's back.

"But they're already in the loop. Kobayashi's going to be at the advance meeting at Lepage's apartment tonight."

"It seems that your friend Kobayashi suffers from the same inability to understand chain of command as you, Charlie," Denault said with sufficient glee to warrant a frown from Westwood that quickly shut him up. Charlie still had to marshal all of his self-control to stop himself from slugging his immediate superior.

"As I said," Westwood continued, "Hudson is working with the Tokyo Police to determine the makeup of the team that will attend tonight's meeting."

Hearing the words, two thoughts occurred to Charlie. The first was that the meeting was a go, and that regardless of his procedural lapses, Westwood wasn't going to pull the plug on the whole thing. The second was the distinct possibility that a broader discussion with the Tokyo Police might alert Kimura and her associates that the meeting was a trap. He had to hope that wasn't the case, especially for Lepage's sake. He felt ill as he imagined trying to explain to Lepage how, in less than twenty-four hours, the tight little plan he and Kobayashi had hatched had been taken out of their hands. Would Lepage trust Hudson and whoever Kobayashi's replacement might be?

"There really isn't any alternative, Charlie," Westwood added. "You can understand that, surely?"

He nodded but chose to say nothing, following Westwood's lead as he stood and made his way to the door.

"I know things happened fast." Westwood put his hand on Charlie's shoulder. "And I can understand why you might not have thought through all of the procedural angles to this thing. No harm, no foul."

"Thank you, sir."

"Besides," he added, "you're still a key player in all of this. Lepage trusts you. You need to be our liaison now, make sure he's on board with Hudson."

"I'll do my best."

"I know you will." They shook hands and Charlie started for the door. Westwood called out after him. "And Charlie?"

"Yes, sir."

"Regular updates, all right?"

Charlie smiled, despite feeling nothing but unease. "Of course."

CHAPTER 36

Charlie felt anxious as he got off the subway at Omote-sando Station and glanced at his BlackBerry. He was relieved to see no new messages since he had slipped out of the office twenty minutes ago, and he reminded himself he wasn't doing anything wrong, at least technically. He had decided to come to Lepage's apartment early, to give him a heads up on the new arrangement with Hudson. The RCMP liaison might be pissed that he had gone alone, but as long as Lepage was onside, everything would be fine. He had tried to contact Kobayashi with no success and wondered whether she had been sandbagged by her superiors in the same way he had. He hoped that she wouldn't face any disciplinary fallout for helping him.

The afternoon light was fading as he took the steps up to the top of the pedestrian overpass that crossed the Omote-sando Avenue and joined the constant flow of commuters going from the station toward the glitzy shops and high-end residential buildings on the other side. A few minutes later, at the door to Lepage's building, he buzzed up and waited impatiently for a few seconds before repeating the process. He glanced at his watch and confirmed that he was more than ninety minutes ahead of the appointed meeting time, but something about the silence from above made him nervous. He scanned the board, found Farnsworth's name, and tried her apartment. He was on his third attempt when he sensed someone at his side, turned, and saw Farnsworth standing there. Like the first time he had met her, she was clad in form-fitting running pants and a bright top. She removed her ear buds and pointed to the panel.

"I'm not there," she said with a smile as she caught her breath.

"I came to see Rob, but he's not answering."

"You want to come up and try knocking on his door?" She took her key card out of her jacket pocket and swiped it on the keypad. He nodded and followed her inside and across the lobby to the elevators. "How are things going, anyway?" Farnsworth asked, wrapping the cord of her headphones around her hand as they waited for the elevator.

"We're making progress, I think."

Whether it was the shrug that accompanied the words, or his tone, he apparently wasn't very convincing. "That doesn't sound good," she said as the doors slid open and they stepped inside. "I've been racking my brain since yesterday, but I haven't been able to think of anything that might help."

"Hopefully, we'll have it all figured out soon," he said, prompting another quizzical expression from Farnsworth.

"Are you sure everything's okay?"

"It's fine, really. It's under control."

They rode the rest of the way in an awkward silence, and then got out on the sixth floor. When they got to Lepage's door, Charlie went to knock on it and saw immediately that it was ajar. His senses went on high alert and he stepped back.

"That's odd," Farnsworth said, looking on.

"Maybe you should go back to your place," he suggested, but she put her hands on her hips in a stance that suggested she wasn't going anywhere, so he pushed the door open slowly, then stepped inside. They both stood in the entrance in silence for a moment, before Farnsworth spoke.

"Oh Christ." She put her hand over her mouth. Charlie was too busy surveying the disarray to speak, the scene all the more drastic in light of Lepage's normally spotless apartment. Now, it looked as though a tornado had ripped through the place, overturning furniture, spilling the contents of shelves onto the floor. The kitchen cabinets and drawers were all opened. After a quick survey of the bedrooms at the back confirmed that there was no one there, Charlie and Farnsworth found themselves standing in the kitchen, staring at each other.

"What the hell happened here?" Farnsworth's face was ashen.

Charlie was about to respond when he heard the unmistakable creak of the front door opening, then clicking shut again. Farnsworth backed up into a corner of the kitchen and Charlie followed, grabbing a large cutting knife from the counter as he did, putting his finger to his lips as they inched forward together from the corner and tried to get a peek out into the entranceway.

"Charlie?"

Charlie and Farnsworth exchanged surprised looks at the female voice, then Charlie stepped out of the kitchen to confirm it was indeed Kobayashi's.

"What are you doing here?"

"I hoped to find you here ..." She stopped when she spotted the knife in his hand, then Farnsworth emerging from the kitchen behind him.

"This is Rob's friend, Elizabeth Farnsworth," he said, putting the knife on the counter. "She lives down the hall. This is Inspector Kobayashi, with the Tokyo Police."

The two women exchanged a hasty greeting.

"What happened here?" Kobayashi was surveying the chaos around them.

Charlie shook his head. "We just got here a few minutes ago.... Listen, we have to talk."

Kobayashi seemed to know what he was about to say. "You're off the case. So am I."

Charlie ignored the look of confusion on Farnsworth's face and pressed on. "I think I might know who's responsible for this."

Kobayashi shook her head. "If you're thinking it's Seger's associate from Montreal ..." She paused. "The TMP task force was aware of his arrival as well. No doubt they were informed by your colleagues at the embassy. In any event, we've had him under surveillance for the past several hours. He's been at his hotel all afternoon."

"So who, then? And where's Rob?"

Kobayashi shrugged. "It must be Kimura, or her superiors."

"So tonight's meeting at the temple —"

"Is a waste of time," Kobayashi said, cutting him off in a rare display of impatience, or anger.

Charlie struggled to understand the ramifications. The destruction around him suggested that Lepage had been taken in a violent struggle, by people who had grown tired of waiting for him to produce what they wanted so badly. It suddenly occurred to him that it might already be too late. "My God, you don't suppose ..." Kobayashi said nothing in the silence that followed. "What are we going to do?"

Kobayashi was frowning, deep in thought. "We have to get to Kimura while there's still a chance. Give her something that will make her think twice about killing Mr. Lepage."

"We've tried that," Charlie said with a sigh. "We've got nothing to bluff with, just a page of scribbled notes and an unsigned postcard of Mount Fuji. His computer's gone, too," he added, gesturing to the study, which had housed Lepage's computer, until whoever had broken in had snatched it.

"What's all this about a postcard of Mount Fuji?"

Charlie turned to look at Farnsworth, who had been listening in silence to the whole exchange. He had almost forgotten she was there. "Nothing. Rob sent a postcard to himself before the accident, but even he couldn't remember why. One of his ongoing memory gaps."

Farnsworth looked at Kobayashi, then back at Charlie. He could tell by her face that there was something on her mind.

"What is it?"

"*I* got a postcard of Mount Fuji. I thought it was just sent in error. It was blank, and I didn't —"

"Do you still have it?"

"I-I threw it in my recycling pile," she said as Charlie breathed in with a hiss.

"Shit!"

"No, I mean I still have it." Farnsworth was waving her hands. "I have a pile of paper recycling that I only get around to dumping every month or so. It's in my apartment," she said, motioning to the door. They followed her down the hall, closing Lepage's apartment door behind them and entering Farnsworth's apartment. She emerged from her home office a few seconds later bearing the postcard. She handed it to Charlie as Kobayashi looked on.

"It's identical," he said, flipping it over as Kobayashi leaned in and examined the postmark.

"It's got the same postmark. The date is the same as well," she added.

"Do you have the other one?" Farnsworth asked.

Charlie's felt an immediate sense of despair at the thought that Lepage had taken it from his office. Then he saw Kobayashi pull out her phone.

"I have pictures." She brought up the two photos she had taken in Charlie's apartment and zoomed in on the stamp. "The dates are the same."

"And from the same post office?" Charlie was straining to see over her shoulder.

"Yes."

"But why would he send me a blank postcard, and send himself the same thing?" Farnsworth said as Charlie turned the postcard over and examined both sides in detail, looking for any difference from the one Lepage had sent himself.

"Can you zoom in on these numbers?" He pointed to a row of numbers in small font in the bottom right corner of the back of the postcard. As she did, he noticed there was a neat black line under the last ten digits, and it was difficult to tell whether it had been added by hand or sold that way.

"Here." Kobayashi handed him her phone and he made out the numbers in the picture. There were also twelve, but they were different, and there was no underlining.

Farnsworth leaned in for a look.

"Are those numbers handwritten?"

"I can't really tell. Here." He handed her the phone and she enlarged the image as much as she could without distorting the numbers. "I think they are," she said, excitedly.

"What are we looking at?" Charlie sensed that Farnsworth had a theory, and he was eager to hear it.

"I think these are country, bank, and branch codes." She pointed to the underlined numbers on the postcard she had received. "I never even noticed they were there, much less paid any attention … they're so small."

"You mean, for a bank account? Do you know where?"

Farnsworth was nodding as she returned her attention to the pictures of the other postcard. "Cayman Islands. I don't know which branch, but I think it's Global Bank."

"You are in banking?" Kobayashi asked, eliciting another nod.

"I deal with them all the time, that's why I'm pretty sure but … wait a minute." Farnsworth put the phone down on the table and raced off to her study, returning a few seconds later with a printed email. Charlie could see a series of numbers in the text of the email.

"Yes, there it is. This is from a different branch — the last four digits, but the first six designate Grand Cayman and Global."

Charlie followed her finger to the ten digits that followed. "And is this the account number?"

She nodded. "Ten digits, just like on your photo."

Charlie looked back and forth between the photo and the postcard, then back at the email. As he looked at the bottom of the page, his eyebrows shot up. "I've seen that logo before," he said, pointing to the words *Global Bank* over the image of a spinning globe topped by a set of laurels. "In Rob's desk … I saw some correspondence when I was looking for something to jog his memory. I'm sure of it." He was looking at Kobayashi now, who was watching him intently. "So he sends two postcards on the same day — one to himself, and one to Elizabeth which, when read together, contain the account information."

Farnsworth looked suspicious. "Why would he do that?"

"He did not want all of the information in one place?" Kobayashi said, eliciting a nod from Charlie.

"Because he knew, even before the accident, that something was wrong, and that account number was crucial."

"Except he forgot not only the number but the fact that he mailed this to me?" Farnsworth's skepticism was obvious. Charlie shrugged. "I honestly don't know, but if you're telling me that these numbers could represent an offshore account, then that seems like an awfully big coincidence. Either that, or it really is the account number everyone's been looking for."

"Well there's no need to speculate." Farnsworth grabbed a pen, scribbled the numbers onto a pad, and opened her laptop.

"What are you doing?" Charlie watched as she opened a new email.

"I'm going to find out if it's Rob's account."

Charlie looked at Kobayashi, who returned the same inquisitive look as his own. "Anyone can just email the bank and find out who has an account?"

"No, but I'm not anyone." Farnsworth looked up at him with a grin, as she typed an email at lightning speed and then hit the send button with an emphatic click.

Charlie looked at his watch. "How long do you think it will take to confirm?"

"Not long," Farnsworth said with a shrug, then pointed at the computer. "This gal's not exactly a nine to fiver, if you know what I mean. If she has access to the information, she'll get back to me soon."

Charlie turned to Kobayashi, and whatever excitement he had felt evaporated with one look at the strained expression on her delicate features.

"I do not think the meeting tonight will proceed," she said, gesturing toward Lepage's apartment. "Someone has decided to accelerate the process."

Charlie nodded but said nothing, unsure how to voice his fear that the reason they had snatched Lepage might have been that they had learned of the larger involvement, on both the embassy and the Tokyo Police side, in the meeting. He should have known that she could read his mind.

"I fear that someone on my side has compromised the meeting. I am very asha—"

He waved his hand. "We don't know that for sure, but I agree that the more people are involved, the greater chance that the yakuza is going to find out what we're planning." He frowned, trying to think of his next step, when Farnsworth's computer gave a little ping that indicated an incoming email. Charlie and Kobayashi looked on in silence as Farnsworth clicked the message open.

"She confirmed Lepage is the account holder," she said, in an animated voice. "She wouldn't say much more, but it must be a significant account."

"Why do you say that?" Kobayashi asked.

"Because she refers to him as an *NKA*," Farnsworth said. "*No questions asked* — I think we've got our answer."

Charlie heard footsteps out in the hall and looked with alarm toward Kobayashi. Seeing their fear, Farnsworth went to the door and looked through the peephole.

"It's just my neighbour, coming home for the day."

"Well, Lepage's place is going to be full of people before long," he said, taking the scrap of paper with the account number written on it and putting it in his pocket with the postcard, as Farnsworth looked on.

"You should delete that email, and leave the apartment. Maybe stay with a friend, or in a hotel."

"I'm not going to tell anyone if that's what you —"

"That's not what's worrying me," he said. "You have knowledge that people are willing to kill for, so you don't want to take any chances."

Farnsworth turned to the laptop and deleted the email. "I'll go to a friend's for the night. I'll just throw some things in an overnight bag."

"Are you going to stay and wait for your colleagues?" Kobayashi asked as Farnsworth disappeared down the hall.

"If I don't manage to convince Kimura that I have something worth trading for Lepage, I have a feeling he's not going to make it through the night. You stay," he said. "If you could tell them that you haven't seen me ..."

Kobayashi's eyes narrowed. "I will not allow you to go to Kimura alone. You don't know how things work here."

He met her stare and then smiled. "I was hoping you'd say that. Come on. We've got to get out of here."

She followed him to the door as Farnsworth re-emerged with a leather tote bag.

"Is there a way out the back?" Charlie asked her as they stepped out into the hall. She nodded and pointed to the end opposite from the elevators.

"There's a service entrance at the back. I'll show you."

CHAPTER 37

Kobayashi said something in Japanese and the cab pulled over to let them out in Shibuya. Charlie followed as she led them onto a side street and then into a small, dimly lit bar, where they took a seat in the corner.

"So how do we get in touch with Kimura?" Charlie said as they settled in their seats.

Kobayashi was shaking her head. "I think we need to go above Kimura. We need to talk to Miyamoto."

Charlie remembered the name, belonging to the man he and Redford had seen with a Nippon Kasuga executive outside Kimura's club. "Okay, so how do we meet him?"

"Meeting him will be the easy part," Kobayashi said. A waiter came to their table and she ordered sake. "Convincing him to release Lepage will be more difficult."

"I give him the account number," Charlie said, with a shrug. "That's what he's after. Obviously, I insist on getting Rob back first."

She frowned. "If he knows you have the account information, you will be in a very dangerous position. He may well kill you, as well as Lepage. He has to have a reason not to."

Touché, Charlie thought. He wasn't keen to be subjected to whatever means the yakuza had at their disposal to make him divulge the account information. He imagined himself in a Yokahama warehouse having his fingers snipped off, one by one. "We have to make it worth his while," he said. "A sweetener."

Kobayashi nodded. "Miyamoto is driven by greed, so we must use that against him, but how?" They sat in silence for a moment, then she cocked her head and smiled.

"What?"

"Perhaps instead of a sweetener, as you say, we offer him a ... good reason not to kill you, or Lepage."

"You have something concrete in mind?" he asked, as she leaned forward over the table and lowered her voice.

"Miyamoto is a senior member of the Inagawa-kai," she said. "They are the largest Tokyo-based gang, but there have been a lot of changes in recent months, with the Yamaguchi-gumi becoming more and more active in Tokyo."

"And you said they're not based in Tokyo."

Kobayashi shook her head. "No, Kobe, but they are much bigger than the Inagawa-kai and they have been expanding, trying to establish themselves outside Japan. The sort of operation that Lepage was involved in is exactly what they are trying to pursue more actively."

"I take it Miyamoto's gang is not that receptive to the Yamaguchi-gumi trying to set up shop on their turf."

She was shaking her head again. "There was a similar attempt to expand into Tokyo a few years ago, and there was much violence. Then it was quiet for a while, but they seem to have renewed their efforts. We have begun to see incidents between the rival gangs in the past few months. Some of my colleagues in the gangs unit thought that Seger's death might have been related to that struggle. There have been other deaths that are not so easily explained. Both sides are said to be gathering funds and preparing for a war."

They went quiet while the waiter delivered their sake and poured it into little earthenware cups. Charlie leaned forward over the table after he had left. "So that's how to play him. Miyamoto has to think that I'm capable not only of refusing to tell him where the five million is, but also of giving it to the Yamaguchi-gumi if he doesn't give me Lepage. It would be a double loss for him." He was still thinking it through as he sipped the warm sake. Kobayashi was frowning again.

"There is another problem," she said.

He knew what she meant — what had been left out of the discussion so far. He nodded. "Even if we get Lepage back, the price will be to hand over millions of stolen money to one criminal gang or another. By the time the authorities catch up, they'll have cleaned out the account and gotten away."

"Your embassy will be very angry with you, no?"

"I don't imagine the Tokyo Police will be too happy with you either, if you go along with some half-baked scheme that gets Lepage back but screws up the fraud investigation."

"Half-baked?"

He smiled. "Unsanctioned."

"Ah." She drank some of her sake. They sat in silence for a while, then she looked at him. "You believe your friend is worth saving, even if the consequences for you are … grave?"

Charlie considered the question and put his cup down on the table. "Whatever he was before, I think he wants to do the right thing now, and I gave him my word I would try to help him." He frowned. "On the other hand, a lot of people have done a lot of hard work to get the fraud investigation to where it is now. I don't really want to undermine that either, but we both know that we can't involve the whole team in our plans, not without risking another leak."

She smiled. "You must choose, Charlie. Whatever your choice, I will make it with you."

He watched for a moment as she put her hand on his, then a flicker of a smile appeared on his face and he looked up at her. "Maybe we don't have to choose, after all."

CHAPTER 38

Charlie followed Kobayashi's directions to a side street in Shinjuku and spotted the bar he was looking for, its doorway bookended by two large-framed men in dark suits. He was beginning to wish he had taken Kobayashi up on her offer to accompany him to the meeting, but he knew she had other things to do and, having been the one to drag her into this mess, the least he could do was pull his own weight. Besides, he was confident that greed — in this case, the possibility that Charlie had the means to access the considerable funds in the mysterious offshore account — would prevail over all other motives, at least in the short term. It was solid logic, and it had seemed even more so when Kobayashi had given a reluctant nod to his reasoning an hour ago, but he couldn't help a sinking feeling as he approached the bar and felt the cold stare of the two men at the door. To think that just a couple of months ago he was safely tucked away in a basement cubicle in the Pearson Building writing policy papers no one would ever read. Now, here he was on the threshold of Tokyo's shadowy underworld.

What the fuck are you doing, Charlie?

A terse command in Japanese from the larger of the doormen brought him out of his uncomfortable reverie and he took a deep breath, remembering why he was here — Rob Lepage.

"I'm here to see Mr. Miyamoto," he said as the first man scrutinized him, then looked to his partner, who barked something at Charlie which he interpreted loosely as *get lost*. He stood his ground and added calmly: "Please tell him Charlie Hillier is here to meet him, regarding Rob Lepage." The nearest man took a step toward him, but Charlie had seen a flash in the other man's eyes at the mention of Lepage's name, and he put his arm on his colleague to restrain him, then gave an order and disappeared inside the bar as his partner watched Charlie with a mixture of disdain and curiosity.

A minute later, the other man emerged and waved him inside. Charlie followed him into a dimly lit bar with throbbing music reverberating through the smoke-filled room, its tables occupied mostly by men in dark suits. Women in revealing tops and tight-fitting skirts shuttled between the tables with drinks. Charlie found himself under a series of watchful stares as he followed the doorman to the rear of the club with a corner booth in a semi-circle around a glass table. A man in his fifties sat alone at the table, and Charlie recognized his sharp features and grey-streaked hair immediately. A tall man with a scar on his left cheek seemed to be standing guard next to the booth. He stepped forward at their approach, exchanging a quick word with the doorman before ordering him away and motioning for Charlie to sit.

"Welcome, Mr. Hillier," the seated man said. Charlie bowed and took a seat while Scarface looked on.

"Mr. Miyamoto."

"I am surprised to see you here," Miyamoto said, sipping his drink. "There are some parts of Tokyo that are dangerous for *gaijin*."

"I'm here about Rob Lepage."

Miyamoto smiled. "I don't know what you mean."

"As I'm sure you know, there was supposed to be a meeting tonight with Ms. Kimura and Mr. Lepage, but it seems that things have changed." Miyamoto said nothing, just eyed Charlie in silence until he continued. "So I came directly to you to propose an alternate arrangement."

"And what arrangement is that?" Miyamoto's manner was offhand, but Charlie sensed that it concealed an underlying interest.

"Things have gotten complicated, with so many people involved from all sides," Charlie said. "I'd like to simplify them. For you, and for me. I know why you're holding Rob and I know what you want from him. I'm prepared to give it to you."

Miyamoto smiled again, showing small, white teeth. "I think perhaps you are mistaken Mr. Hillier, about many things."

Charlie shook his head. "I have the account number you're looking for, and I'm prepared to give it to you, but only in exchange for Lepage." Miyamoto's smile vanished and he took on a different expression, one that made Charlie see how he had risen to the position he had. It was sheer menace. Charlie tried his best to ignore it and continue with his pitch. "Tonight at midnight, the temple at Asakusa. You bring Lepage and I'll bring the account information."

"What makes you think you're in a position to demand anything of me?" Miyamoto finally said.

"Because I know how much you want access to that account. Besides, I'm not involved in all of this — I'm an outsider, on the fringes, and killing me will only cause you problems in the long run." He paused as Miyamoto listened in silence. "Bad for business," Charlie added, managing a smile.

Miyamoto sat back in his seat, as though reclining with a book — perfectly comfortable and in control. "It's an interesting proposal, Mr. Hillier," he said. "I cannot accept it of course, as I have no idea of Mr. Lepage's whereabouts." Charlie searched his face for some unspoken message, but saw nothing, then Miyamoto threw him an inquisitive look. "Where's your girlfriend, Mr. Hillier? I'm surprised that she would let you put yourself in this most dangerous position."

Charlie was quick with another affected smile, to display a confidence he definitely lacked. "She's watching my back."

Miyamoto let out a little laugh, but Charlie thought he detected a slight recoil, and there was definitely a quick glance to the scarred man, but he couldn't see any response.

"Well, Mr. Hillier, I am grateful that you would think of me for your proposal, but I must refuse. And if you will forgive me, I have other business to attend to."

Charlie stood and gave a quick bow. "I appreciate your time."

"Be careful, Mr. Hillier. Shinjuku can be dangerous."

"Thanks for the warning," he said. With that, he was on his way back to the front door, under the same succession of watchful gazes. He stepped out into the street and drew a deep breath of cool night air as he walked away from the club, back toward the main street nearby, wary of anything in his peripheral vision. He had barely gained the other side of the street when he turned to see the man with the scar approaching. He tensed for a confrontation, but the other man stopped a few feet away and spread his hands in a gesture of peace.

"Midnight at Asakusa," he said, before turning back toward the club, as Charlie breathed again and hurried toward the safety of the crowds on the main street just a few feet beyond.

CHAPTER 39

Charlie descended the stairs into Shinjuku Station, dropped a few hundred yen into the machine and waited for his ticket. His pulse was still racing from the encounter with Miyamoto, and the walk to the station in the cold evening air had done nothing to staunch the sheen of sweat on his forehead. He grabbed up the ticket and made his way to the turnstiles, scanning the overhead signs for the Marunouchi Line as he slid his ticket into the reader. He hurried to the escalator and joined the mass of humanity headed down to platform level, where his train was waiting. Installing himself in a corner near the door, he looked at the map and confirmed he had five stops to go. He didn't bother with his phone — there was no reception in the Metro, and he was glad for a few minutes to catch his breath. The meeting with Miyamoto had gone as well as could be expected. All he could do now was hope that he showed up at Asakusa.

Taro Furuno stood at the opposite end of the car, content to join the studious avoidance by everyone else of direct eye contact with the foreigner at the far end of the crowded car.

But while he might appear to be focused on the doors of the subway car, Furuno had the *gaijin* square in his sights. The man was either stupid or endowed with balls of steel, Furuno thought, to venture onto the Inagawa-kai's turf and start making demands. As the car braked, Furuno twisted himself away from an adjacent passenger, who had pressed up against the side where his razor-sharp knife lay concealed in its sheath. He scowled at the elderly man, who averted his eyes after he took in Furuno's stature and icy eyes. Furuno kept his own eyes on the doors as they opened and closed — the foreigner staying put in his corner, oblivious to the fact that he was being watched.

Furuno suppressed a smile at the shock the *gaijin* would get when he found himself confronted with the Inagawa-kai's most feared enforcer. The hapless bureaucrat would give up his secret quickly enough, or take it to his grave.

CHAPTER 40

Charlie started moving toward the doors as the automated female voice announced Akasaka-mitsuke Station as the next stop. Emerging from the station, he pulled out his phone and headed north, crossing Aoyama-dori and pausing at the end of the crosswalk to check the message from Kobayashi: You have a tail. I'm right behind. Proceed to rendezvous. Don't look back.

He slid his phone back into his jacket pocket and set off over the bridge, fighting the urge to glance back over his shoulder. He had to trust that Kobayashi could close the gap in time if need be. Arriving at the familiar entrance — he had stayed at the New Otani Hotel until his apartment was ready, and was familiar enough with the attached shopping mall on the concourse level — he made his way to the escalator leading to the Garden Tower. As he reached the top, he glanced at the mirrored glass and caught a glimpse of a tall man stepping onto the escalator at the bottom. He didn't dare risk eye contact, so he couldn't be sure, but he thought he recognized the man from the Metro. As he walked down the carpeted hallway leading to the hotel, Charlie realized he had seen no sign of Kobayashi below, but then she wouldn't be so close as to give herself away.

He pulled out his phone and was comforted to see she had texted again: Remain calm. I'm right behind you.

He breathed a sigh of relief and continued along the hallway of the massive hotel, passing by a row of closed shops on the right whose windows displayed the sort of designer menswear, luggage, and jewellery that he could only afford in another life. The muted clink of china and glassware from the restaurant to the left competed with the soft classical background music as patrons dined overlooking manicured gardens beyond massive windows.

At the end of the restaurant, Charlie took a hard left, down a ramp that led to a door to the outside, and a set of steps down into the garden. Apart from a solitary smoker standing by an ashtray, the open part of the garden was empty. Charlie continued toward the red bridge leading over a large pond, its red spans adorned by strips of light that reflected in the water below. He had strolled the gardens a couple of times during the day, and while the gravel paths were lit by floodlights every few feet, the serene calm of the daytime experience was replaced with a rather eerie feel now. Arriving at the bridge, he paused by a wooden bench and texted Kobayashi, then carried on, with a casualness that was in stark contrast to the anxiety he felt as he approached the darker part of the gardens beyond the bridge.

At the far end, he paused again and checked his phone. Nothing. He kept walking and took the path to the left, veering away from the little restaurant that lay off to the right. He was almost at the secluded rendezvous point that Kobayashi had selected when he glanced to his left and saw the outline of someone descending the stairs from the hotel. Even from this distance, and in the dim light, there was no mistaking the man he had seen at the bottom of the escalator and on the subway. He checked his phone again — still nothing from Kobayashi.

Something's wrong.

His instinct was to head back to the safety of the better-lit area closer to the hotel. The only problem was that the man following him lay on the direct path — or did he? Looking up from his phone, Charlie saw no sign of the man who, only seconds before, had been headed toward the red bridge. He set off down the path back to the bridge, reassured as each step drew him closer to the relative security of the bridge, yet troubled by Kobayashi's absence.

He was twenty feet from the bridge when a blur to the right of his field of vision alerted him — too late — to the presence of the man from the hotel escalator. Charlie froze as the other man blocked his path, his initial shock transforming into terror as he noticed a glint in the dim light from the long steel blade extending from the man's right hand. The dark eyes staring back at him were only slightly less terrifying, and when they glanced up the path Charlie had just come down, he obeyed automatically, slowly retracing his steps as the Japanese man followed a few feet behind.

"What do you want?" Charlie heard himself ask, as they approached the darkest part of the garden trail.

"Stop."

"Who … who are you?"

"I am Furuno." The self-assured tone made it clear that Charlie should recognize the name, though it meant nothing to him.

"What do …?"

"Silence."

Charlie turned and faced him, taking in the tall man's menacing glare. He was obviously one of Miyamoto's men, and while drawing him out had been part of the plan, Kobayashi's absence was not.

"Where is it?" Furuno's tone was brusque, and alerted Charlie to the fact that he had very little time. His eyes darted around and confirmed the obvious — that there was no one within earshot or sight. If he was going to get out of this alive, he was going to have to do something himself.

"Where's what?" he said, taking a subtle step back and assessing his situation. He was facing a man who looked very comfortable with the knife in his hand, which was Charlie's main concern. There was nothing around him that he could use to fend off an attack, unless he was planning on using a bonsai tree.

"You will tell me now, or you will not leave here alive," the man said, raising the knife to emphasize his point.

"I will give Miyamoto what he wants at midnight, not before," Charlie said, stalling as he racked his brain for a way out, and taking another step back. He was taking a mental inventory of his pockets when it occurred to him that the thick leather of his belt might hold up to a slash of the knife. He had bought it at a market in Havana and the iron buckle, although not overly large, might actually do some damage if he managed to swing it hard enough. Noticing that the other man had chosen not to close the gap between them, Charlie unclasped the buckle and quickly slid the belt off, as the man looked on, bemused. His eyes narrowed as Charlie took a few practice swings, the swish of the buckle cutting through the cool night air.

"Do not be foolish." Furuno took a step forward, his right arm extended, the knife blade glinting in the dim light of the path. Charlie stepped back and swung the buckle again, though it seemed a pathetic gesture in response to a six-inch blade in the hand of someone who looked like he knew how to use it. As Charlie took a second step back, he realized that the khakis he had bought a couple of years ago when he was a size larger at the waist were beginning to slip. He tugged them up as the man continued to advance.

"You need to back up," Charlie warned as Furuno did the opposite and assumed a crouched position that looked like the first stage of an attack. It suddenly occurred to him that as desolate as their surroundings seemed, they were still in the New Otani private gardens, and he had seen hotel security guards at various other locations — surely someone was patrolling the gardens.

"Help!" he yelled, prompting a flash in the man's eyes that was immediately followed by a frontal assault. Charlie grabbed both ends of the belt and managed to block the other man's stabbing motion.

"Over here!" he yelled again as Furuno regrouped and lunged a second time. This time, the knife thrust was to the opposite side, and Charlie got just enough of it with the belt to deflect it into the side of his jacket, slicing a hole in the fabric just above his ribs.

"Silence," the man hissed as Charlie stared at his side, wide-eyed.

His pants had begun to slip again, but that was the least of his worries as Furuno came at him a third time. Realizing he was at the edge of the trail, he took a step forward, a move that seemed to surprise Furuno, and Charlie's decision to go on the offensive with the belt was looking like the right one, as the little iron buckle whipped through the air toward his opponent's face.

Unfortunately, its arc was interrupted as Charlie's momentum took him forward over a tree root — a stumble he would have recovered from easily, had it not been for his khakis slipping down to almost mid-thigh, cinching his legs together and compounding his stumble. Suddenly, Furuno, who had instinctively thrust his knife hand high to fend off the iron buckle, found all of Charlie's off-balance weight bearing down on him at chest level.

As Charlie's shoulder hit Furuno in the chest, he dropped the belt and flailed for the knife that was somewhere in the melee as their bodies twisted and fell to the ground. Charlie felt the air leave his chest as he landed on top of Furuno, who was on his side on the gravel path.

Still unaware of where the knife was, Charlie grabbed his attacker in a bear hug to pin the other man's arms at his side. He squeezed with all of his might and was surprised to hear an odd gurgling sound from Furuno, whose face was half in the gravel. His strength running out, Charlie let go and scrambled back on his hands to a safe distance, then stood.

He continued to stare at Furuno, who lay motionless on the path, and then slowly approached, noticing a dark stain by the prone man's mouth that he realized was blood. As he came closer, looking for the knife, he caught sight of the black handle sticking out of the base of the other man's neck and gasped in shock.

He was about to step forward for a closer inspection when he heard footsteps on the path from the direction of the bridge and spun around in time to see Kobayashi, followed by a man in a leather jacket.

"Charlie, what —" Kobayashi's breathless inquiry was interrupted as she spotted the motionless man on the ground. "What ... happened?"

"I ... I don't really know. He attacked me." He pointed at the dead man, as Kobayashi's companion knelt down to get a look at the face, prompting a puzzled look from Charlie.

"He's with us," Kobayashi said, gesturing to the man crouched over the body. "We were delayed before we got to the hotel —"

"*Nanda ittai!*"

"What'd he say?" Charlie looked on as Kobayashi and the other man had an exchange in Japanese, before he looked at Charlie for a moment, shook his head, and gave him a wide berth before disappearing down the path, headed away from the bridge. "Are you going to tell me what the hell's going on?"

Kobayashi knelt and searched the dead man's pockets, coming out with a phone. "Come," she said, gesturing to him as she grabbed the man's legs. Charlie took his arms and they walked him over to the darkest part of the path and swung him into the bushes. "We must leave here — quickly," she said, pulling a stunned Charlie by the arm, leading him in the same direction the other man had gone. When they were back on the street a few minutes later, she began to talk.

"The man with me was a member of the Yamaguchi-gumi."

Charlie knew the name well. "Miyamoto's rivals? But why?"

"I needed to bring him to prove that Miyamoto is desperate."

"I still don't understa—"

"The man you … the dead man, back there," she continued. "His name is Taro Furuno. He is one of Miyamoto's top assassins. I don't believe he was sent to kill you, though," she said, "just get the account information, but his presence is more than enough proof."

Charlie's head was swimming as they approached the Metro station. "Proof of what?"

Kobayashi's response was interrupted by an unfamiliar ring tone that they both realized was coming from the phone she had retrieved from Furuno's jacket. They exchanged glances, then Kobayashi put the phone to her ear as they approached the pedestrian crossing at Aoyama-dori. Charlie

waited, watching Kobayashi's expression for some sign of
what was going on, still confused by the events of the past
twenty minutes. As Kobayashi continued to talk, he looked
down at his wrist and saw a speck of dried blood.

You just took another man's life …

He was still reeling when Kobayashi put the phone in her
pocket and walked over to him. "Are you all right, Charlie?"

"I just want to know what the hell's going on."

"I'm sorry, Charlie. The men who held me up earlier —
I'm pretty sure they were sent by the 7th division."

"They were Tokyo Police?"

Kobayashi nodded. "I'll deal with them later. That was
Miyamoto. He was … surprised to hear about Furuno. But
he'll be at the meeting."

Charlie frowned. "But if I understand what you're saying,
some of your colleagues in the 7th division know all about
the meeting at —"

"I just changed the meeting to Shibuya, and it's at eleven,
not midnight." Kobayashi smiled.

Charlie looked at his watch. "But that's in less than thirty
minutes."

She nodded. "Exactly. Not enough time for them to move
whoever they had waiting for us into place at Shibuya, at
least not without our noticing."

He looked at her, his mind still whirring at all of the
recent developments. "Our?"

"Come. I'll explain on the way." She grabbed him
by the hand and pulled him toward the entrance to
Akasaka-mitsuke Station.

CHAPTER 41

Charlie and Kobayashi stood outside the entrance to Shibuya Station, scanning the crowd for any sign of Lepage, Miyamoto, or Kimura. It was nowhere near as crowded as the last time Charlie had visited the crossing, but there were still thousands of people crossing to and fro, many emerging from the last subway trains of the evening. Charlie watched as the crowd near the crosswalks swelled while the cars whizzed through the intersection. Then the lights changed and the crowd was released, like lemmings over a cliff, to cross the street for a few seconds and disperse, until the lights changed again and the process repeated itself.

"Do you think he'll really show?" Charlie checked his watch for the third time in the past few minutes, growing more and more anxious with each minute that ticked away. It was almost five past, and no sign yet.

"Be patient, Charlie. He has every reason to come."

Charlie sighed and resisted the temptation to glance at his BlackBerry. He was actually afraid to look, guessing that there were likely a series of dire warnings from Denault, Hudson, maybe even the ambassador himself, of what would happen to him if he didn't check in immediately. If he wasn't already fired, that is. He tried to push all that aside for the moment, preferring to fall back on the rationale that circumstances gave him little or no choice than to act as he had. *Tell that to Denault*, he thought.

"There." Kobayashi gestured toward the east side of the crossing.

"Where?" Charlie followed her finger but couldn't see anything until he spotted Lepage, his tall, blond profile standing out in the sea of dark hair. "Let's go."

He took a deep breath as they walked toward Lepage, who was accompanied on one side by Miyamoto and his scar-faced guard, and Kimura on the other.

"I see you have decided not to come alone." Miyamoto gave a disapproving look to Kobayashi.

"Are you all right?" Charlie asked Lepage, ignoring Miyamoto's remark. Lepage nodded silently, looking sheepish. Maybe it was the strain of the past few days catching up with him, or something else — Charlie wasn't sure. He noticed Miyamoto's guard was carrying a thin laptop.

"How do I know that half of the Tokyo Metropolitan Police force is not part of this crowd?" Miyamoto asked.

"The same way you knew tonight's meeting at the shrine was a bust," Charlie countered. "You probably know more about their activities than we do," he added, sensing Kobayashi cringing slightly, but remaining stoically silent next to him.

Miyamoto seemed to concede the point and move on. "You have the account number?"

"Come here, Rob," Charlie said. Lepage looked to Miyamoto, who hesitated a moment, then nodded.

"You sure you know what you're doing?" Lepage whispered to Charlie as the scar-faced man opened the laptop and handed it to Charlie. The Global Bank page was already up and waiting for a code.

"Don't worry," Charlie said quietly, as he entered the digits representing the various codes and the account number, then hit the return key. Everyone stood in silence, oblivious to the people passing by as the worry circle spun in the middle of the screen, then a large green check mark appeared on the page and the account information came up. Miyamoto took the laptop and scanned the screen.

"It seems your activities have been very profitable, Mr. Lepage," he said with a grin, which vanished as quickly as it had appeared when he returned the laptop. "Now, the transfer."

"Transfer?" Charlie said.

"We're not going to let you just walk away without being sure that the funds are under our control," Miyamoto said, prompting an exchange of looks between Charlie and Kobayashi.

They had little choice at this point, and after a rushed exchange of whispers, Charlie turned to Miyamoto. "Fine," he said.

Lepage took the laptop and started a series of keystrokes that ended a few seconds later. He passed it back to the scarred man, who entered the destination account number. There was another breathless moment as they all watched for the confirmation screen, which appeared to be taking longer this time. After thirty seconds, the tension was unbearable.

"Is there a problem?" Charlie asked, but before anyone could respond, the confirmation screen was up.

"Are we good?" Lepage looked to Charlie, then Miyamoto, who was looking at Kimura as the other man folded up the laptop.

"One last thing," Charlie said. He saw a slight hesitation in Miyamoto's eyes, and an expression that for the first time didn't convey utter confidence that what was about to happen hadn't been anticipated and planned for — the cardinal sin. Charlie pressed on. "In case you were thinking of not honouring your side of the bargain and letting us out of here," he said as Miyamoto's eyes narrowed further. "We're not exactly alone here."

Miyamoto glared at Charlie for a moment before his smile returned, but it was forced.

"You have no police to help you here." He shot Kobayashi another look of disdain.

"I didn't say anything about police. You asked me where my friend was earlier." Charlie gestured to Kobayashi. "And I told you she was watching my back. I wasn't lying — it turns out she managed to negotiate protection from your competition. I don't know what she offered in exchange but she's apparently very persuasive."

"What are you talking about?" Kimura spoke for the first time, eliciting a terse order from Miyamoto to be silent.

Kobayashi met Miyamoto's stare and moved her head in the direction of the opposite sidewalk, where two men stood watching. Unlike the rest of the crowd, they were stationary. Even from a hundred feet, there was no mistaking their menace. He followed her gesture to another pair in front of the Metro station, then a third by another crosswalk. Miyamoto's eyes burned like embers, but he retained his pasted-on smile. He seemed to be making a great effort to avoid eye contact with either Kimura or his scar-faced bodyguard and had the body language of a cornered rat, which Charlie knew meant danger. Miyamoto continued to look at Kobayashi and seemed to be considering something, then he shrugged his shoulders.

"I have what I came for, Mr. Hillier. You are free to go," he said, gesturing to the scar-faced man and turning on his heel, leaving Kimura standing there, looking shocked. She stood motionless on the sidewalk, watching as Kobayashi hailed a cab and the three of them got in. As soon as they were away from the intersection, Lepage spoke.

"What the fuck just happened? Why did they let us go?" he asked Charlie, who had pulled out his BlackBerry to make a call. He turned to Kobayashi.

"It's a long story," she said.

Hudson answered and Charlie spoke into his phone. "Did you get it?" The inside of the cab was silent for a few seconds, then Charlie turned from the front seat, looked at Kobayashi and smiled. "Yes, we've got him. We're headed to the embassy right now. We'll be there in ten."

"Is somebody going to tell me what happened back there?" Lepage was looking at Charlie, whose face broke into a broad smile as he tucked his phone in his pocket and leaned back in his seat.

"Let's just say we did something … unexpected," he said, glancing over at Kobayashi. It wasn't exactly a smile that appeared on her face, but there was an unmistakable twinkle in her eyes as Lepage looked on with confusion.

EPILOGUE

Charlie had the same eerie feeling of calm that he had first felt as he followed the wide path through the old-growth forest leading to the Meiji Shrine. The only difference this time was that he wasn't walking it alone.

"When do you leave?" Kobayashi's voice sounded different here in the muffled stillness of the park.

"Tonight," he replied, with a finality that could have been interpreted as acceptance, as opposed to the helplessness he felt. They walked along in silence, over the bridge and around the corner, until the massive gates to the temple came into view ahead.

"There is no hope of a … a pardon?" Kobayashi finally said.

Charlie shook his head. "It's a question of liability, really. As long as I'm here, there's always a risk that I'll be targeted, as payback. Plus, I'm pretty sure they'll be glad to be rid of me. I seem to have a habit of causing trouble wherever I go."

"It would be difficult to argue with the positive results you have achieved in this case."

Charlie smiled. It was true that the end result of his activities was to close the loop on an international fraud investigation, even if he hadn't exactly followed protocol. One thing he had been sure to do was to tell Hudson that the funds in the offshore account were likely to be transferred, and that following the transaction would be key to connecting the illicit money to the ringleaders of the scam — in this case an account controlled by Miyamoto.

"Lucky for me, Miyamoto didn't have time to set up an account that was far enough from him to avoid implicating himself, otherwise the results may not have been so favourable, and things could have gone very badly for me. You, too," he added, turning to look at Kobayashi, who had faced her own share of criticism from her superiors in the aftermath. But she had protected herself by uncovering communications between Aiko Kimura and two members of the 7th Division, who were bearing the brunt of her superiors' anger, at least for the time being.

"It seems we both survived," she said.

Charlie frowned. "I'm not so sure. I've had three postings, all of which have been terminated early due to ... well, maybe I'm just not cut out for consular work."

"I don't believe that," she said as they passed under the massive gate and approached the outlying complex of buildings that lay before the main temple. She led them over to a little stall where an old woman was selling small paper scrolls. Charlie recognized them as the papers affixed to the large racks that he had noticed on his first trip here. Each scroll had a handwritten wish or prayer. The old woman smiled at Kobayashi, and the two had a brief exchange in Japanese which resulted in the purchase of two scrolls for a few hundred yen.

"I always make a wish when I come here." Kobayashi handed him a scroll and made her way over to one of the tables near the racks, where pencils were supplied. Charlie followed her over and picked up one of the pencils, scribbling on his scroll and watching as she completed her own inscription and walked over to the rack, securing her paper among the thousands of others. He did the same and then stepped back.

"There," she said, giving a little bow.

"I guess we're not supposed to ask what the other wished for."

Kobayashi smiled. "I think you know, Charlie."

He nodded, and they moved on toward the temple. "There's something I've been meaning to ask you."

"Please do."

"How *did* you convince the Yamaguchi-gumi to provide protection for us? I mean, I know the official answer — you convinced them that allowing Lepage and I to go would result in significant damage, financial and otherwise, to their main rival. But I have the feeling there was more to it."

"Why do you think that?" she asked, as they entered the courtyard of the main temple.

"It just seemed ... too easy, I suppose."

There was a hint of a grin on Kobayashi's face as she looked at him. "The desire to undo one's enemy is powerful, Charlie."

He had the sense that she was leaving something out, but decided not to press. Whatever she had done, it had worked, and he was ever grateful. He only hoped she hadn't done something that would come back to haunt her.

"And you aren't concerned about any reprisals?"

She paused as they reached the steps to the main temple, then turned to him and shook her head. "To kill a woman, even an inspector, would be ... dishonourable."

"You're prepared to stake your life on it?"

"Yes," she said with a conviction that told him she really did, and that gave him some comfort. They were silent for a few minutes as they strolled through the temple and took in its sights and sounds and the smell of incense. Back out in the main courtyard, they sat on a bench and enjoyed the early afternoon sunshine. It was almost one o'clock, and

Charlie was going from the embassy to the airport at three. This last meeting with Kobayashi had been an indulgence by Westwood, and Charlie was grateful not only for the act of kindness, but for the hope it gave him that, maybe, the worst of his sins had been forgiven. As he sat there on the bench, though, he was overcome by another thought — that these would be the last moments he would spend with Kobayashi. He would not be returning to Japan, and it was unlikely that she would be travelling to Canada — or anywhere else he might be — anytime soon.

"What will happen to Rob?" she asked, breaking his sombre reverie.

"He'll be all right." Charlie was happy for the chance to think of something more positive. Lepage had been flown out on a U.S. military transport plane the day after the Shibuya exchange and was already back in Canada. He would be a star witness in the inter-jurisdictional fraud sting and after he had served his purpose there, he would have a brief sentence in a minimum security facility, after which he would be free to start his life over again. Charlie thought of his last words before leaving the embassy — a heartfelt thanks. They discussed Lepage's possibilities for the future for a while, then Kobayashi turned to look at him.

"What about you, Charlie. What will you do?"

Charlie paused to take in the beauty of her face — the small, delicate features, bright eyes, porcelain skin, and the floral smell of her perfume, and all he felt was … loss. "I really don't know. Maybe it's time I went home for a while."

"Back to Ottawa?"

Charlie shrugged. "I'm not sure that's home for me anymore."

They sat in silence for another moment, then he glanced at his watch. "I should really be going."

"I'm very sorry to see you go, Charlie," she said. She was not the type to display emotion openly, but he could see that she was struggling in her own way. "But I'm very glad that I met you."

They kissed for a long moment, then separated and stood, starting the journey back to the main gate.

"You asked me what I wished for," she said as they passed the racks of paper scrolls and she put her arm through his. "I wished that you will find happiness, wherever you go."

As they made their way back to the path, Charlie had a brief fantasy of skipping the ride to the airport and running away with Kobayashi, somewhere no one would find them. But as the path came to an end and they left the tranquility of the park behind them and the bustle of Tokyo reappeared before their eyes, he knew that wasn't real. He didn't know where he was headed next, but he was glad of where he had been.

ACKNOWLEDGEMENTS

Thanks to the great team at Dundurn, including Kirk Howard, Beth Bruder, Margaret Bryant, Michelle Melski, Laura Boyle, Jenny McWha, Rachel Spence, and particularly my editor, Allison Hirst. Thanks also to Dr. Greg Brown for your advice on all things medical and to Wilf Wakely and Yoshiyasu Yamaguchi for sharing your insights on Japanese culture.

Book Credits

Acquiring Editor: Allison Hirst
Project Editor: Jenny McWha
Proofreader: Rachel Spence

Cover and Interior Designer: Laura Boyle

Publicist: Michelle Melski

Dundurn

Publisher: J. Kirk Howard
Vice-President: Carl A. Brand
Editorial Director: Kathryn Lane
Sales Manager: Synora Van Drine
Publicity Manager: Michelle Melski

Editorial: Allison Hirst, Dominic Farrell, Jenny McWha,
Rachel Spence, Elena Radic
Design and Production: Laura Boyle
Marketing and Publicity: Kendra Martin, Kathryn Bassett, Elham Ali

🔲 dundurn.com   📷 dundurnpress
🐦 @dundurnpress   📌 dundurnpress
📘 dundurnpress   ✉ info@dundurn.com

FIND US ON NETGALLEY & GOODREADS TOO!

🏛 DUNDURN